Amanda James has written since  asked her parents for a typewrite imagined her words would ever dream of becoming a writer can first short story published.

Originally from Sheffield, Amanda now lives in Cornwall and is inspired every day by the wild and beautiful coastline. She can usually be found playing on the beach with her family, or walking the cliff paths planning her next book.

 twitter.com/amandajames61
 facebook.com/MandyJamesAuthorPage

Also by Amanda James

WISH UPON A CORNISH MOON

AMANDA JAMES

One More Chapter
a division of HarperCollins*Publishers* Ltd
1 London Bridge Street
London SE1 9GF
www.harpercollins.co.uk
HarperCollins*Publishers*
Macken House, 39/40 Mayor Street Upper,
Dublin 1, D01 C9W8, Ireland

This paperback edition 2023
1
First published in Great Britain in ebook format
by HarperCollins*Publishers* 2023

A catalogue record of this book is available from the British Library

ISBN: 978-0-00-860576-6

Printed and bound in the UK using 100% Renewable Electricity
by CPI Group (UK) Ltd

To all those who have ever wished upon a Cornish moon.

Prologue

1899

The scene is set. The ocean powers in to shore, the moonlight rides the waves casting chips of silver before it like ethereal confetti – a celebration of the night, the moment, and the wonder of nature. On a dark headland above the sand, a lone figure stands uncertain. A girl, no more than sixteen. A night breeze is sent to lift her silken tresses with gentle fingers and whisper encouragement. The cove holds its breath. Waiting…

———

Mary swallows her nerves and picks her way around the last few rocks at the end of the cliff path, clambering down onto the moonlit beach. In the heavens, a thousand diamond-bright stars dance attendance, as a huge June moon rolls centre stage above the whispering ocean, commanding a gasp of awe from her audience of one. The beauty of it all is overwhelming, and Mary catches her breath, swept away by the majesty of the scene. A few moments later she exhales, and pulls the object wrapped in her old cloth bag tighter to her chest. Magic Cove. This spit of sand is certainly living up to its name tonight. The moon's path shimmers across the waves and along the beach, bathing Mary in its silver light – an ethereal finger directing her action.

Gooseflesh runs along her skin and a shiver of excitement prickles the hairs on the back of her neck as she feels the enchantment at work in the 'grace of the moon, the power of the ocean and the magic of nature'. Could the old wives' tales really be true? Her mother believes them, and lots of the older women of the village knew of someone who had found their true love because of nights like this, and on this very beach. There are those who say that it's all just a myth though, and such ancient ideas have no place in modern times. It is almost the twentieth century after all. Besides, Mary's mother had told her she had to believe in what she was about to do with all her heart, or nothing would come of it. But did she? Did she really? She holds her breath and then releases it. Only one way to find out.

Three more steps along the beach and Mary stops. The sheer madness of what she's about to do almost makes her laugh out loud. She keeps quiet though, just in case others are about in the shadows. Mary glances to the left and right and strains her ears for any sound on the still air – but there are none, save the shush of the waves. Right-ho, time to do the deed. Then a voice of doubt nips at her enthusiasm. *Who*

2

would be out on a little beach at past midnight anyway, apart from silly girls like me? The shadows on the moon's face toss a frown at that thought, so Mary sets her shoulders back and walks closer to the water's edge.

Her boots and stockings removed, Mary hitches up her skirts and tucks them under her belt and pulls from her cloth bag a heavy glass bottle. Cradling its smooth curves in her two hands, Mary holds it aloft and watches the moonlight add a sprinkling of stars along the glass neck. She heaves a sigh. Inside is a simple scroll of paper carrying all her hopes and dreams for the future. With such a heavy responsibility, the bottle ought to weigh much more than it does. A shot of adrenaline fuels Mary's next action, and her heart thuds in her chest, echoing her footfall on the wet sand as she strides into the ocean.

The cool swirl of water around Mary's ankles brings her up with a start and an image of her good friend Derowen Gunwalloe surfaces in her mind. Last week, Derowen had scoffed at Mary when she'd shared the idea of sending a message in a bottle from Magic Cove to find her true love, like so many other women had done before her. When Mary had stated that her own mother had revealed that her grandmother had found her grandfather in this way, Derowen had snorted and said that it would have just been a coincidence, or made up to entertain gullible simpletons. Folk tales and myths were completely nonsensical, and only a foolish dunderhead would entertain them seriously. Derowen was the cleverest girl in the village, so she should know. Derowen would be running her own ironmonger's shop very soon once her granddad retired, and everyone knew you had to be clever with figures for that kind of thing. Mary kicks her foot against the surf. Hmm. Her friend definitely knew what she was talking about. What would she say if she found out that Mary had sent a message in a bottle? Would she still want to be friends? Or would she tell others what a foolish dunderhead Mary had been?

A glance at the moon sends more doubt into Mary's resolve, because half of its face is now obscured by a fan of black cloud. That might well be a sign that she should forget the whole notion. Maybe it's time for the moon's curtain call, and an end to the show. Her mother had said she had to believe her dreams would come true, and she does, but Mary isn't sure that she believes *enough*. What if she sends the bottle off tonight with hope in her heart, only to have it dashed on the rocks along with the bottle? Could she cope with the disappointment of it? Could she live with the shame of having tried and failed? If nothing comes of it, then there must be something wrong with her. Other girls had claimed their true love over the years, but maybe Mary doesn't have the gumption or the belief to win her heart's desire?

Mary's mother had sent a bottle, but nothing had come of that, so Mary knew it didn't always work. Her mother had simply said, 'So be it,' but she still believed that the magic was real. 'There are things afoot in this world that we can't always explain, mark my words, Mary, my girl,' she'd explained. But then her mother was one to let things lie and let fate take a hand. Mary wants more certainty in life. Mary wants to be clever and successful like Derowen too, and she knows that hard work and determination will be more likely to get her these things than fanciful notions of wishing on June moons and sending messages in bottles.

From her coat pocket, she pulls a scrap of paper with the words her mother had written down for her to say, just before she tossed the bottle into the water. By the dimming light of the half-moon, she reads:

> *I give my words to the grace of the moon, the power of the ocean, and the magic of nature. Please grant me the things I truly deserve.*

Say them or not? Go or stay? A new sense of doubt swells in her belly and becomes so large and heavy that any hope is crushed and consumed by it. Mary shakes her head. No. This is a fool's errand, and before she can change her mind, she scrunches up the paper and tosses the words into the ocean. Then she wraps the bottle up again and makes her way quickly back up the beach.

Chapter One

CORNWALL

1938

Lamorna was never entirely sure when Grandma Mary was spinning one of her yarns. Yarn spinning was her speciality, and Lamorna, even at the age of fifteen, still had to concentrate very hard on Grandma's demeanour and expression to catch any tell-tale signs. Today, for instance, as Lamorna helped Grandma Mary fold the freshly laundered towels in her homely farmhouse kitchen, a twinkle of humour in the older woman's lively hazel eyes tussled with her serious face and furrowed brow. Was the twinkle a clue that Lamorna had just been spun a yarn? She thought so, but as usual, she couldn't be absolutely certain. Grandma Mary shrugged off her granddaughter's scrutiny with a derisory sniff, leaned her ample bottom against the kitchen sink, and hitched up her bosom with folded arms.

'I can see you don't believe me, girl, but I'm telling you that there's magic in the moon and that big sea out there.'

Grandma Mary cleared her throat and winked. 'Dreams come true for them as take those old tales to heart –' Lamorna received a finger-jab across the kitchen '– and only those who do, mind. It's no good pretending to swallow the story whole and then spit it out later, like I did.' A hand flap. 'I never believed in magic when I was a girl. Well, not enough, more's the pity.' Grandma Mary gave a sigh heavy enough to sink a battleship and stared out of the window at the distant ocean.

Lamorna smoothed the last of the towels, put them on the shelf next to the open fire to air, and lifted the kettle from the stove. 'I'm not saying I don't believe you, Grandma Mary, all the locals know about the old tale, but it does seem a bit of a tall story, all this wishing for the ocean to send a sweetheart at the full moon in June.' She ran water into the kettle. 'Shall I make some tea?'

Mary nodded, sniffed again and drew a chair up to the big, scrubbed pine table. 'All I know is that if I had done what my mother had told me, I could be happy and living the high life now in my old age. But no. I went there all ready to go through with it, but threw in the towel at the last minute. Now here I am trying to make this farm pay, with just you and them turnip-heads Jory and Fred to help me.'

Lamorna took the cups from the cupboard and shook her head. 'I'm not sure I understand.'

Mary puffed air through her lips and the furrow between her eyes grew deeper than the ploughed fields surrounding the house. 'Haven't you been listening, girl?' She puffed again, shoved her hand through her auburn and grey curls, and scooped up some toast crumbs in a damp cloth. 'Lord above. I do wonder how you young things survive nowadays. Your heads are full of them silly romantic pictures from that Hollywood, and them music radio programmes too. All that jiving and butterjigging. No wonder you can't follow a simple conversation.'

Lamorna hid a smile and poured boiling water onto tea leaves in the big brown teapot. 'It's jitterbugging, Grandma Mary.'

'Pah! I don't care what it's called, it's unladylike, new-fangled and it'll addle your brain.' Another finger-jab. 'I'll tell you this for nothing. If I'd have sent a message in a bottle off under that full moon in June, when I was your age, I would have found a true love to look after me. It would have saved me all this toil.' Mary screwed up her face and glared at the backs of her hands. 'Look at them,' she implored Lamorna. 'Them's the hands of a worker. All red, gnarled and rough, not the hands of a lady. So much for wanting to be clever like Derowen.'

'Who?'

'Never mind.'

Lamorna brought the tea tray over to the table and set it down. Grandma Mary was certainly telling the truth now. There was no twinkle in her eyes, only sadness, bitterness and regret. With a heavy heart she said, 'But you had Granddad. Weren't you happy together?'

Mary pulled her chin back and raised her eyebrows. 'Happy, she says? How could I be happy with a man who thought more of the damned cows and chickens than he did of his own wife?' Her face softened and she nodded to herself as though she'd been asked a question nobody else could hear. 'Your granddad worked hard on this farm; I'll give him that. And when we were courting, he wasn't too bad, but most of the time he was a sour-faced, tight-lipped miserable old so-and-so. Some days I'd have to talk to myself to stop myself going mad, as all I got was a grunt now and then from him. The only time I saw him anything like happy was when your dad and Aunty Zelah were born.' Mary raised her eyes to the rafters and blinked away tears. 'All he cared about was this bleddy place and passing it down the line to your dad. Waste of time *that* was.' She glanced back at Lamorna and wiped her eyes with the corner of her red, flour-smudged apron. 'He never once said he loved me.'

Lamorna looked away from the despair contorting her grandma's face. She couldn't bear to watch because it was too raw, real … overwhelming. Such displays of emotion were rare in her family, especially in her grandma's case. The fact that her dad had preferred fishing to farming didn't help matters either. Lamorna knew it had been a bone of contention between him and his mother after Grandad Jack had died. Staring at her tea cup, she said quietly, 'I didn't know you were so unhappy with him, Grandma Mary.'

'Why should you? He died when you were five – dropped dead in the field of heart failure. You can't remember that much about him, I expect.' Grandma Mary sipped her tea and stared at the whitewashed stone wall, but the faraway look in her eye told Lamorna she was walking in the past, revisiting old ghosts.

Lamorna thought about Granddad Jack. She did

remember him actually, but only in disjointed, unconnected sections, as if the whole had been divided into smaller pieces and jumbled up. Some memories were clear, but most of the colours were beginning to fade around the edges like the iridescent wings of a butterfly she'd once seen, pinned inside a glass case. Granddad Jack was a quiet man, methodical in movement and aim. True, his mouth was a thin, flat line, unused to the warmth of a smile, but he had always been kind to her. A memory of them both in the barn, her helping him rub down a new-born calf with straw, came to mind, and inside her head, she heard him telling her she was a natural with animals. Angry on his behalf, before she could stop herself, she snapped, 'If he was so miserable, why did you marry him, then?'

Grandma Mary's eyes glittered and her cheeks flared red as if she'd been slapped. 'How dare you talk to me like that, young lady.'

Immediately Lamorna regretted her words. She didn't want to upset her grandma more than she was already. 'I'm sorry, Grandma Mary. I was trying to understand, that's all.'

Mary shook her head sadly and sipped her tea. 'As I said, he wasn't too bad at first when I met him at the village dance. My parents said he was a good choice because he came from a decent farming family and went to church. I thought he was just shy. The thing was, I wanted to be swept off my feet, fall in love proper, like the heroines do in them Bronte and Austen novels.' She paused to drink more tea and Lamorna had to bite her tongue. It was only a few minutes ago that Grandma Mary had been rubbishing the 'silly romantic' Hollywood films! 'Anyway, by the time I

11

decided he wasn't for me...' her grandma stopped again and cleared her throat '... I, er...'

Lamorna could tell her grandma was wrestling with the best way to continue. The two high spots of colour were back in her cheeks and she couldn't look Lamorna in the eye. 'You don't have to tell me, Grandma. Let's just change the subject and—'

'It was too late. I had to marry him because I fell pregnant.' The sentence was delivered like bullets from a firing squad. Grandma Mary looked about as shocked as Lamorna felt. Perhaps she'd not meant to let it out, and was thinking better of it, but after a few seconds the heavy atmosphere between them lightened and evaporated like a cloud on a hot day. 'It was all my friend Jennifer Tregony's fault. She brought some brown ales to the summer picnic, we were celebrating because me and her had just turned seventeen, and let's say I wasn't used to a drink. Neither was your granddad, come to that.' Grandma Mary was back to her brusque matter-of -act tone. 'It was a warm summer night and we took the long walk back through the fields hand in hand ... and well, the rest, as they say, is all water under the bleddy bridge. Your father was the result. I was tempted to give him "brown ale" as a middle name but didn't think it would go down well. We got married quicker than you can say pudding club.'

Lamorna found herself laughing, partly because of her grandma's silly jokes, but mainly to hide her embarrassment. She'd never heard her grandma talk so openly about personal things, and she'd never realised pregnancy had forced her grandparents into marriage. But then why would she? Her dad would have kept it hush-hush, as he certainly wouldn't have wanted it bandied about. Back in those days it would have been a scandal if Grandma's secret had got out round Porthtowan Village. Lamorna knew that sex before marriage was still a huge sin these days too, though she had heard rumours that one of her friends' sisters had been 'free and easy' with a boy, as she'd put it, and *she* was only sixteen. Lamorna, a year younger, hadn't even had a boyfriend. Though lots had asked, none of them had interested her.

Grandma Mary was watching the wall again, lost in thought, and Lamorna's heart went out to her. All those years married to the wrong man and simply making the best of things ... it was so sad. Lamorna knew she would never live like that, and would be absolutely sure that she loved a boy before marrying him – she'd read the same books as her grandma after all. To cheer her up she asked, 'Do you honestly think that if you had sent the message in a bottle from Chapel Porth, or Magic Cove as you call it, you would have met your true love? Because if you do, I might try it. It's June in a few weeks and what do I have to lose?'

'I do honestly think that! Everything felt right that night I went to the cove, but I fought against it. Thought I knew best and it was all poppycock ... and truth honestly be told, most of all I was worried I'd fail. Silly ninny that I was. But there was proper magic at work there sure enough, I just wasn't brave enough to take it.' Grandma Mary's face fell as she stared over Lamorna's shoulder at a distant memory. Then her expression lit up as a huge smile stretched her lips. 'Anyway, it's your time now. Send a bottle, or you could just go down to the cove and ask that old moon sailing over the water to send *you* a message. Works both ways. I heard tell of a woman from here who found a man from Ireland when she picked up his bottle.

'You have nothing to lose, Lamorna my girl. Your aunty Zelah thought it was all nonsense like I used to, so she never tried. Luckily, she met her husband Peter, who is a lovely man, but I don't know...' she stopped talking and stared intently into her granddaughter's hazel eyes, so like her own '...something is telling me that big Atlantic Ocean out there –' she nodded through the window '– will bring you a sweetheart. A true love.' Lamorna swallowed hard as her grandma squeezed her hand. 'You have far to go, my girl. Far to go, and far away. But through it all, I know happiness will be your friend.'

Lamorna smiled, but the idea of going far away made her stomach turn. She had always been a home-loving girl, and despite what her favourite teacher, Miss Hawker, had said about Lamorna being clever enough to be a teacher like herself, after leaving school, she'd been mostly content to work on her grandma's farm, a ten-minute walk along the coast path from her own home. Surely there was plenty of time ahead for going far? Lamorna was already worried sick about this Hitler fellow 'rampaging around Europe', as her dad put it. He said the prime minister was useless, and all this appeasement rubbish would give Hitler the green light to do whatever he bleddy well pleased. But what if there was another war? Unthinkable after the horror of 1914–18. Her dad had fought, and wouldn't talk about what he'd seen, but she'd overheard others remembering it in the pub beer garden once. All Lamorna wanted was to stay put in her little village and pretend none of this Hitler nonsense was happening. 'Sounds very exciting, Grandma ... but maybe I am a little young to be wondering about sweethearts and the future for now.'

'Too young? I met your granddad when I wasn't much older than you. And an 'andsome young maid like you? They will be queuing up to take your hand.' Grandma Mary gently pinched Lamorna's cheek. 'Big hazel eyes, rosebud mouth, and all them dark spiral curls. Why, you could give that film star Kay Francis a run for her money.'

Lamorna flushed and looked at the table. 'Thought you didn't hold with those Hollywood films, Grandma?'

She received a bark of laughter as an answer. 'Right, sitting round chattering isn't going to get those cows milked. Off you go.' Mary scraped her chair across the flagstone floor as she got up from the table. 'And when you see those two potato-brains Fred and Jory, tell them to buck their ideas up. I swear they spend more time smoking and chewing on straw than they do working these days.'

Chapter Two

The more Lamorna thought of the conversation she had with Grandma Mary last week, about the message in a bottle, the more she thought it was a silly idea. Never mind what the local legend said, what kind of a feeble-minded ninny walks along the cliff path to the next cove, in the dead of night, to ask the full moon and the ocean to send her a true love? And on a practical level, what kind of a bottle would the feeble-minded ninny need? It would have to be very well sealed and robust, because the tides and huge waves of the Atlantic take no prisoners. If Lamorna were honest, even if there was some ancient magic in the cove, and the elements as her grandma and some of the older local women believed, it was far more likely that the bottle would be smashed to smithereens on the rocks after five minutes than that it would find its way any distance into the hands of a true love.

'Lamorna!' her mum shouted up from the kitchen. 'Can

you come downstairs and keep an eye on your sister, while I get the dinner on?'

The book Lamorna had selected for a quiet read on her bed was snapped shut, followed by a huff. She yelled back, 'Yeah, coming!'

It would be nice if just once she could have a Sunday afternoon to herself without being roped in to look after Morwenna. Lamorna's dad and her elder brother, David, never get asked, do they? No. No of course not, because they're men. And looking after children and cooking were women's jobs. When she'd once asked her mum why that was, she'd been told that's just the way things were, and she should think herself lucky she had a roof over her head and food on the table. Didn't she appreciate that her dad worked very hard day in and day out on the fishing boats for them all?

Lamorna put the book on her bedside table and straightened her yellow and white polka-dot Sunday dress. She really was grateful, but she'd seen Kay Francis, whom Grandma Mary said she looked like, in a film where she was the boss of a magazine and hired a male secretary. It was called *Man Wanted*, if memory served. On the way back from the picture house, Lamorna had mentioned to her friend Betty how great the film was and that she was surprised that women could be bosses of men. Betty had pointed out it was only a film, and anyway things in America were very different to England. True, but as Lamorna made her way down the rickety, twisted staircase of the fisherman's cottage, she acknowledged that she'd seen pictures of women in the newspapers driving posh cars, drinking champagne and smoking cigarettes, and that wasn't in America… It wasn't in Cornwall either, but still.

'Perhaps you could take Wen out to the beach for an hour?' Lamorna's mum said, closing the oven door with her foot as she tied her floral pinny and pushed her dark wavy hair out of her eyes. 'She loves building sand castles, as you know, and some fresh air will make her sleep tonight.'

Lamorna nodded while thinking her mum looked like she could do with some sleep herself. Poor Mum was always on the go with keeping the house nice, cooking, working part-time at the bakery and running around after them all. Lamorna did what she could to help after a hard day's work on the farm, but her mum wasn't getting any younger. Having their Morwenna at the age of thirty-eight, three years ago, had taken its toll. There would be no late babies for Lamorna. Women of today could make something of themselves, if the films were to be believed. Maybe she could even be a teacher one day, like Miss Hawker had said. So why was she considering slinging a message in a bottle at the sea, instead of trying to do just that?

'Mum, do you know that old wives' tale about sending a message in a bottle from Chapel Porth Cove to find a sweetheart?'

'Yeah, what of it?' her mum asked distractedly, wiping her hands on a tea-towel.

'Do you believe it?'

'No! I tried it the summer I turned seventeen and nothing happened.' She blew a damp curl from her forehead from the corner of her mouth. 'Went looking for an answer nearly every day for three months, then gave up. Met your dad the next week,' she adds with a smile. 'Why? Are you going to try?' Her mum's eyes danced with a merriment and she folded her arms over her apron.

'No. Just wondered. Gran reckons I should, but I think it's all a bit daft.'

'I think it's a lot daft, never mind a bit.' She furrows her brows and flaps the tea-towel at Lamorna. 'Now, can you take your sister out please, and give me a bit of perishing peace?'

'Morwenna, no. Come back this way!' Lamorna couldn't take her eye off her sister for five minutes, it seemed. The idea of a little read under the warm afternoon sun as the ocean shushed in her ears, stretched out on the old beach blanket while Wenna played in the sand, was just that. An idea. Wearily, Lamorna set her book down for the tenth time and hurried across the beach to where Wenna had gone in pursuit of a seagull, her little legs pumping like a traction engine, the two pink ribbons tying her fair hair in bunches fluttering in the breeze like rose petals.

The seagull flew off with a surprised squawk as Wenna snuck up behind, cocking its head at something in a rockpool. Wenna laughed as Lamorna arrived, and pointed at the gull, who was now balanced on top of a huge barnacle-encrusted rock, glaring down at them from its sharp yellow eyes. 'Nearly got it, Morna!'

'You must have heard me shouting at you, Morwenna!

You need to mind me and not run off after seagulls, otherwise I'll tell Mother and she'll smack your legs.'

The little girl's big blue eyes filled with tears and her bottom lip wobbled. 'Sorry, Morna.' She lifted her arms to be picked up.

Under the warm summer sunshine, looking at the woeful little face staring up at her, Lamorna's icy resolve melted. She couldn't cope with tears. Wenna was only little after all. And if you couldn't run after seagulls when you were three, when could you? This wouldn't have happened if Lamorna wasn't resentful of the fact that she had to look after her sister, instead of doing as she pleased on her only day off. She picked up Wenna and carried her back along the beach. What was wrong with her lately? If she were honest, she thought it all started with Grandma Mary's message in a bottle nonsense. It had unsettled her, made her dissatisfied with her lot. Yes, if it worked, it might start an exciting chapter in her life, but what would happen if nothing came of it? She'd be stuck in her boring existence working on the farm and helping her mum around the house until the cows came home. Literally. Lamorna had had enough of cows. The smell of them, the back-breaking work of milking them, and mucking out the stalls when they were inside the cowshed. It never used to bother her until she'd listened to Grandma's old tales about magic and having a better life. Grandma Mary certainly had wanted more, it seemed. But then today her mum had said it was all nonsense too. What a dilemma!

Setting Wenna down next to the red and white checked

blanket, she picked up the bucket and spade. 'Here, dig me some nice holes and I'll help with the castle.'

Wenna's smile was like the sun coming out on a cloudy day. 'Big castle?'

'I'll try my best.'

They set to work. Wenna's frown of concentration and pursed rosebud lips as she dug the blue metal spade into the damp sand brought a smile to Lamorna's face. Oh, to be a child again. Carefree, no jobs to do or future to puzzle over. After making ten perfect sand castles, Lamorna dusted her hands and sat back on the rug to watch the Atlantic rollers gallop into shore, led by a flurry of white horses. To the left of the beach, the horses smashed themselves into a jagged dark rock and magically turned into a myriad sparkling water droplets. Lamorna released a long breath and felt all her tension ebb away on the tide. She adored this beach, the sun on her face, the cry of the gulls in her ears, the kiss of the salt wind on her lips. How anyone could live in a city or big town was beyond her. This ocean was in her blood, the ancient ebb and flow of the tide as much a part of her as was her calm, steady heartbeat. On days like this it was easy to imagine the magic of nature at work here. And then once again her thoughts began to turn over like milk in a churner.

Wenna stopped digging and pouted at her sister. She obviously wasn't best pleased with Lamorna's laziness. She pushed her damp fringe from her forehead and sighed. 'More castles?'

'Slave driver.' Lamorna giggled and picked up the bucket once more. 'Now, my dear. What do you think I

22

should do about this message in a bottle, then? Do you think the old tales are true? Yes, or no?'

Wenna hurled a spadeful of yellow sand up into an impressive arc across the blue sky. 'Yes.' She didn't look at her sister, just knelt on the sand and dug the spade in again. She was wearing her concentrating face again, complete with furrowed brow.

Lamorna smiled and scooped up some more sand in the bucket. 'You do? All right. Should I send a message, or wait for one?'

'Yes.'

'Which is it – wait, or send?'

'Send.'

'At the full moon next week?'

'Moon.'

'Next week?'

'Night time beach.' More sand arcs.

Lamorna stopped scooping sand. Until now, Wenna had just repeated words, not paying much attention to anything but digging the hole, so how did she know to say 'night time beach'? Lamorna hadn't said anything about night time. She supposed Wenna could have associated moon with night time, but beach?

'Yes, night time beach.' Lamorna knelt on the sand and tipped the bucket over and tapped the end of it with a rock. Maybe Wenna's comment was because of the magic at work on the beach already. Perhaps Wenna was drawn to the place just as Lamorna had always been. The huge blue expanse of ocean over there had always filled her with

23

inexplicable yearnings. Far away, and far to go, hadn't her grandma said?

'Yes. Night time.'

'Will I get my true love?'

'What?' Wenna asked over her shoulder, as her spade deposited sticky wet sand in Lamorna's hair.

'Careful!' Lamorna brushed it out and gently lifted the bucket to reveal another perfect castle.

'Twoo lev.'

Lamorna found herself chuckling. 'Yes, true love. Will I find one?'

Wenna sighed and jumped in the hole, which now came up to her ankles. 'Yes.' She yawned. 'Home now?'

'You tired?'

'Tired.'

Lamorna picked up the bucket and spade and took her sister's hand. 'Come on then. I bet Mum has nearly got tea ready. You hungry?'

'Hungry.'

As they walked up the path from the beach, Lamorna decided that Wenna had just parroted everything she'd heard. There was no mystery to it, no good omen, no magic … just Lamorna being fanciful. There was no rush to make a decision about the bottle either. She would sleep on it a few nights and then maybe even toss a coin on the subject. Mind you, just in case the coin told her to do it, she had better find a strong bottle.

Through the bedroom window, Lamorna watched the silver moon rise higher in the dark velvet sky, pinned with stars. Beyond the fields, it poured an endless flow of diamond chips across the Atlantic's horizon and bathed the brow of the hill above the beach in its day-bright shimmer. If Lamorna was the kind of girl to be taken in by tales of magic and flights of fancy, tonight would be the perfect setting. The thick, heavy ginger beer bottle that Lamorna had found at the back of the pantry with just a sticky residue left inside, had been washed, dried inside thoroughly, and hidden in her bedroom for three days. Paper and a fountain pen waited on the night stand; the pen warm from her indecision. Lamorna had picked it up and put it down countless times over the last hour, and now a silver coin balanced on the crook of her thumb and first finger like a miniature full moon.

Lamorna looked at the coin, back at the moon, took a deep breath and whispered, 'Heads I do it, tails I don't.' She flicked the circle of metal, watching it turn over before landing beside her on the bed. It winked under the moonlight, the head of King George clear to see. Excitement fluttered in her chest like a captive bird, and she blew out a long breath. It looked very much like she was the kind of girl to be taken in by tales of magic and flights of fancy, then. Now for the message. Lamorna had planned the message in her head for ages, but now it was time to actually write it, there was something stopping her. It was probably a mixture of nerves and feeling like a ninny. But the coin had led the way and she must follow. Picking up the pen she wrote:

June 1938

    My name is Lamorna Williams. I am fifteen years old, and live with my parents and elder brother and younger sister in Porthtowan, Cornwall, England. I have long, curly brown hair and hazel eyes, and though I am not what you might call a genius, my teacher Miss Hawker said I'm a clever one, and that I could be a teacher like her, if I tried hard. I ended up on my grandma's farm instead though, as it was expected of me. My parents said the likes of us don't become teachers. I am happy to help my family, but I sometimes wonder if I could make something of myself.

Lamorna stopped and read it back. She decided that she needed to come to the point of the whole thing, as she was rambling on a bit.

The thing is, Grandma Mary told me there is magic in the June moon and in the ocean and nature. She told me there have been many marriages through the ages because of messages like this one, sent to sea by girls looking for a sweetheart on summer nights, when the moon is watchful. It's a bit of a local legend.

She paused again and bit the end of her pen. *That sounds good, especially the watchful bit!* Lamorna smiled; she had always been good at writing at school, or 'composition' as it was called.

It might all be nonsense of course, but what have I got to lose? I hope my bottle finds its way into the right hands. My address is

*below, so you can write to me. By the way, I don't really like
ginger beer, it was the only strong bottle I could find.*

 Yours truly,

 Lamorna Williams.

Miss Lamorna Williams,
 Skylark Cottage,
 Tywarnhale Lane,
 Porthtowan,
 Cornwall,
 England

The clock on the chest of drawers said 11.30. Grandma
Mary hadn't said that the bottle had to be launched at
midnight, but doing so appealed to Lamorna's sense of
adventure. She rolled up the message and slid it into the
bottle, screwing the top on as hard as she could. Then, for
good measure, she glued some fabric and wrapped it tight
with string around the join. Lamorna put the bottle into a
cloth bag and set foot on the top stair, hoping that the old
wood wouldn't creak and give her away. The last thing she
needed was having to explain her actions to her mum.
Placing her stockinged feet on the edges only, she sneaked
her way downstairs and into the kitchen – luckily the stairs
kept her secret. Quickly putting on her work boots, she
grabbed her woollen jacket and slipped from the house like
a shadow.

Unfortunately, because of the moonshine, there were no
shadows to hide in as she hurried through the garden and
down the lane. As she passed two of the neighbouring

cottages, Lamorna worried that any light sleepers might be watching her progress from behind curtains, like hunters tracking a deer. Her quick mind offered a good explanation in case she was questioned afterwards. She'd just been off to collect some seaweed to ease her grandma's lumbago, and it was always best to gather it at this time of year. Whether they would swallow that particular old wives' tale was up to them.

Once she was on the cliff path, Lamorna's heart kept time with her footsteps as they thumped along the sandy trail. Her little pocket-watch showed her it was nearly midnight, so she upped her pace until in the near distance she could see the tall brick chimney of the old Wheal Coates tin mine, pointing at the moon like a dark finger. Lamorna stopped to get her breath, and spared a thought for all those poor men, women and children that had toiled in the mine far under the sea in the last century, and then she turned and ran the last few yards down the steep incline to Chapel Porth Cove.

As she stood on the floodlit shoreline, watching the moon shine a glittering path from the heaven directly to her feet across the calm navy ocean, she could understand why the old ones had named this place Magic Cove. The waves gave a gentle sigh as they broke on the sand and sucked in a breath as they retreated, while a playful breeze lifted Lamorna's curls and whispered in her ears. In the magic of the moment, she imagined setting foot upon the silver path and walking across the ocean and up into the sky to join the moon and stars. Such a perfect night for an unusual activity. Gooseflesh ran along her skin and a shiver of excitement prickled the hairs on the back of her neck as she felt the enchantment at work in the 'grace of the moon, the power of the ocean and the magic of nature'.

Lamorna smiled as she thought of the words that she had memorised. Grandma Mary had dictated them to her and said that every girl who'd found a husband would have uttered the very same to the heavens, on June nights like this. Before she tossed the bottle into the waves, Lamorna held it up to the moon, watched the glint of moonbeams dance along its curved edges. Feeling not remotely like a ninny, she said in a strong commanding voice,

'I give my words to the grace of the moon, the power of the ocean, and the magic of nature. Please grant me the things I truly deserve.'

Lamorna bowed her head to the ocean to show respect, and then tossed the bottle up and out as far as she could. It landed with a faint splash, and for a moment she could see nothing but the ever-changing waves. Fearful it had somehow hit a submerged rock, Lamorna kicked off her boots, tucked her dress into her drawers, and paddled out up to her knees scanning every ripple and splash … but there was no sign. 'Please,' she whispered and took a breath, holding it in anticipation for a few moments … but no. No, it had gone. Thoroughly deflated, her eyes wet, Lamorna was just about to turn back and go home, when there … bobbing along the silver path, was the dark shape of her little bottle, pulled on the tide towards the moon.

Lamorna's heart swelled with hope as she smiled and raised a hand. 'Godspeed, little bottle. Godspeed.'

Chapter Three

GLOUCESTER, MASSACHUSETTS

1940

H arry Marshall watched the silver-grey skyline meld with the rise and fall of the ocean as he clasped his hands together, braced his feet on the boat's deck and stretched his arms high over his head to ease his tired muscles. Boy, his back was complaining after three hours hauling nets and lobster pots without a break, and he glanced across the deck at his younger brother John with a frown. That guy might as well have stayed home rather than come on this fishing boat today. After they'd dropped anchor to collect the lobster pots, John had hauled a few over the side, grabbed the biggest lobsters and thrown the pots back, but afterwards, he'd just sat on his butt. Even though he was the oldest brother and put in charge by Pop, Harry shouldn't have to be on John's back directing him the whole time. They'd both been working the boats long enough that they could probably do each task with their eyes closed. Trouble was, right now, John looked like that was exactly what he was going to do, but minus the tasks.

'Hey, John. No time for sleeping on the job, we need to get the net in.' Harry, none too gently, touched John's thigh with the toe of his boot.

John's eyes flickered open. 'Hey, that hurt. And I'm not sleeping, I'm inspecting the insides of my eyelids.'

'Ha ha, very funny. You should be on Broadway.' John grinned and closed his eyes again. Harry saw red. 'Hey, get up and help me winch the net in, or I'll tell Pop what a deadweight you are lately!'

John's sea-green eyes shot open and he held up his hands. 'Okay, don't get your pants in a bunch!'

He dragged himself up and yawned long and loud before manning the winch, and then they both hauled in the net. As their vessel was only a little family-owned boat, the net was small so it didn't take long to heave the catch onto the deck. It was an abundant catch, nevertheless, and Harry counted a number of sea bass, pollock, cod, haddock and a fat bluefin tuna. Pop would be pleased – this was the third good haul of the day. 'You get them in the ice troughs, I'll check the net,' John said as he tossed a few sea bass along the deck towards Harry.

Harry shook his head and walked up deck. Not so fast, lazy boy. 'No, you do the fish, I'll check the net. You've had an easy ride today, my man.' What a surprise. John was ignoring him again, crouched to his haunches, staring into the writhing bodies of the fish, as if he'd lost something. Jeez. 'John, for Pete's sake...'

'I could have sworn I saw something just then that weren't no fish.'

'What kind of thing?'

'Beats me. Thought it was something shiny.'

'Fish scales are shiny.'

'Yeah, but the sun came out from behind a cloud, and this thing caught the light. Real shiny, like.'

'John, just get on with sorting the fish for chrissakes, and I'll check the nets.' Harry had had a bellyful of John today.

'Okay, don't flip your wig!' John turned with a scowl, strode past Harry, and shovelled a few fish down deck to the ice troughs.

Harry stretched up his hands to check the first part of the net as it swung back and forth on the boom, when from the corner of his eye he saw something glinting amongst the remaining fish on deck. Curious, he left the net and made towards it ... and as he did so, all the hairs on the back of his neck stood to attention and his heart stepped up a pace. What the hell was that about? And what the hell had he found? Peering closer he saw, half obscured by a drape of seaweed ... a bottle ... a bottle with a little scroll of paper inside... About to reach out and pick it up, he heard John's rubber boots thundering up the deck behind him.

'That's what I saw! Leave it alone, I wanna... OW!'

Harry snapped his head round to see John on his butt in a puddle of seawater. 'You okay?'

John got to his knees and rubbed his butt. 'Tripped over that goddamn tuna.'

Harry grinned. 'You'll live.' He turned back to the bottle and scooped it up. Holding it to the light, he saw it said

'Ginger Beer' in raised letters along its flank, and he could just make out some writing under the curve of the scrolled paper inside. 'Well, would you look at that? A message in a bottle,' he whispered to himself. But John heard him.

'That's mine. I saw it first – give it to me.'

'No. You didn't *see* it, exactly. Just said you thought you saw something shiny.' Harry felt a bit of a heel, as John had in all honesty probably seen it, but Harry felt drawn to this bottle. Inexplicably and overwhelmingly. This bottle was meant for him. He realised immediately how crazy that thought sounded, even in the confines of his own head, but his gut insisted. He couldn't shake it.

'Goddamn it, Harry! No fair!'

'Ah, put a sock in it, John.' Harry tucked the bottle into the big pocket inside his waterproof coat and fastened it tight. 'It's mine and it's staying mine. Now let's finish up here and head for home.'

John glowered at him but, knowing he was beat, stalked off to the ice trough muttering some choice expletives, while dragging the tuna behind.

As soon as he could that evening, Harry made his excuses to his family and hurried up the stairs to his bedroom. John had been bellyaching to Pop about the bottle, but Harry had made light of it, said it was just an old bottle and nothing of real interest, then he'd changed the subject and John had stomped off into town to see his girlfriend. Now alone in his room, Harry turned on his bedside lamp and took the bottle out of his wardrobe where he'd put it upon returning home. He had an idea that John might have tried to sneak a peek if Harry had left it in his coat. Weighing the smooth glass in his hands, a tickle of excitement began in his chest and once again the hairs on his neck prickled, followed by those on his forearms. As the cosy amber glow of his lamp caressed the curves of the glass, the bottle seemed full of mystery and promise.

Cross-legged on his bed, he used a wrench to help free the top of the bottle. It had been sealed well and the ocean's current had pitted and welded it too, so it took some time to work loose. As he did so, he wondered what the message would say and who it was from. It didn't look like a particularly rare bottle, but he had to admit, he'd not seen ginger beer in a bottle quite like this before. Perhaps it had come from outside the USA. Taking a pair of tweezers, he carefully removed the scroll of paper and gently unrolled it. His eyes grew round as he read:

June 1938

My name is Lamorna Williams. I'm fifteen years old, and live with my parents and elder brother and younger sister in Porthtowan, Cornwall, England. I have long, curly brown hair and hazel eyes, and though I am not what you might call a genius, my teacher Miss Hawker said I'm a clever one, and that I could be a teacher like her, if I tried hard...

The bottle came all the way from England and took two years to get here. Wow! 'Lamorna.' He spoke the name softly ... sounds almost poetic. *Long brown curls and hazel eyes, bet she's a beaut.* She was fifteen when she wrote the letter … so might be seventeen now. Three years younger than himself. Harry quickly devoured the rest of the letter and smiled at her last few lines…

> *By the way, I don't really like ginger beer, it was the only strong bottle I could find.*

Lamorna Williams seemed like the kind of gal he'd like to shoot the breeze with. She sounded like she'd got her head screwed on right – wanted to make something of herself. He traced the address with his fingertip – Skylark Cottage. Pretty name. Like something out of a fairy tale. He laughed out loud. In fact, the whole thing was like something out of a dang fairy tale!

Harry scrubbed at his short blond hair with his knuckles and caught his reflection in the glass of the wardrobe. He looked real wacky. Like a kid at Christmas. His blue eyes twinkling with excitement and with a smile so wide, it fairly made his face ache. He switched off the lamp and lay back on his bed thinking about the words he'd write to Lamorna. Because write he would. There was no doubt of that. Harry had never been good with words, so he needed to make sure what he said made a good impression. He needed the right words. But how would he begin? That was the conundrum.

Heaving a sigh, he turned on his side as the round face of the moon sailed out from behind a cloud and shone a beam of silver through his bedroom window.

Harry got up from his bed and gazed across the harbour

to the wide Atlantic beyond. The moon rode higher on a canopy of stars, its mercury path drawing his eye further towards the ocean's ink-black horizon. Placing the palm of his hand on the pane, he tried to picture Lamorna on the other side of that ocean. He knew England was ahead of America in terms of time, but not how far, so he imagined Lamorna sleeping in Skylark Cottage, the same moon shining through her window, highlighting the contours of her pretty face, her curly brown hair fanning loose on the pillow.

Suddenly, the words that had hitherto eluded him found a place in his head and heart. Harry knew what he had to write and he needed to write them now. Pulling a sheet of paper from an old school notebook in his drawer, he took up his pen, smiled at the moon, and began to write.

Chapter Four

CORNWALL

December 1941

L amorna sat on the edge of her bed and took her secret letters out of her lockup box. Though her eyelids felt like lead, her routine was to re-read her latest letter before going to sleep. She sighed. Sleep was in short supply since she'd become a trainer of the Land Girls, sent here from all over the country. Because of Lamorna's experience, she'd been teaching weeding, ploughing, dairy work, and, to those confident enough, tractor operation She smiled to herself as she thought of the fun she'd had today. The girls were all jolly, so she enjoyed her work and 'doing her bit', even though she was exhausted most nights and was asleep as soon as her head met the pillow.

Settling back against her pillow now, she plucked a letter from an envelope and thought about the person who wrote it. Harry Marshall, her blue-eyed American boy. Lamorna's heart swelled with love and longing as she untucked the flap of another smaller envelope and looked at a photo of Harry sitting on a deserted beach, the wind in his curls, a nonchalant smile curving the edges of his wide, full mouth. The photo was black and white, but she knew his hair was sandy-blond, and his eyes were blue, because of his letters. If only she could see that cheeky twinkle in real life. One day she would. He promised they would meet, in his last letter. It might be sooner rather than later, because Lamorna's dad said that the recent attack by the Japanese on Pearl Harbor had really changed the course of the war. He thought that England would be better off with the 'Yanks' properly on its side.

Gazing into Harry's eyes, she could hardly believe it had been nearly a year since she had received his first letter. The time had flown past, what with all the Land Army work, and the organisation that took out of her day. Lamorna had hardly time to draw breath, but she was glad, because if time went fast, it wouldn't be long before they beat that evil tyrant Hitler, and the world could go back to how it was. That thought pulled her up short. It wouldn't ever go back to how it was, would it? There had been too many lives lost, others wounded or missing, too many families left grieving and hoping the dreaded telegram would never be delivered. Was she selfish thinking of herself – her own happiness – while so many she knew would never be happy again? Perhaps. She traced her fingernail along the contours of Harry's face. *But if you don't have hope for the future, you might as well give up now, hadn't you?*

As she unfolded the two pieces of paper to read the letter before she dropped off, Lamorna whispered a thank you to Grandma Mary for suggesting she sent a message in that bottle three years ago. Two years later, Harry had written from Gloucester, Massachusetts, and her world had rocked on its axis. On that moonlit night in June 1938, when her fifteen-year-old self had bade the bottle Godspeed, in her heart of hearts she hadn't really believed anything would come of it. But it had. It had brought her the love of Harry in seven letters. Lamorna would forever believe in the grace of the moon, the power of the ocean, and the magic of nature. The old tales were true about Magic Cove, no matter how silly it all seemed. Grandma Mary certainly knew a thing or two.

With a contented sigh, she held the sheet of paper nearer to the lamp and read:

My darling Lamorna,

I miss you more each day, and dream of the time when we will be together. I have saved nearly $50 and hopefully by this time next year, I will have enough for the ship over. If this dang war is over of course! I have been working day and night on the fishing boats to get the cash, but that's no hardship if it means I can see you.

Sometimes, I sit on the beach and look across the Atlantic and imagine you at the other side of it looking back. We should make a time and date for us both to do that, look at our photographs and send our love over 3000 miles across the waves. I often think of how lucky we were that your little bottle was scooped up into my fishing net. My brother nearly got to it first, but he slipped on a tuna fish and I grabbed it! Ha ha!

Thank you for your last letter. I have read it about a hundred

41

times as it makes me feel closer to you. I can almost picture you on the farm organising everyone to their chores. Your little sister Wenna is a real doozy, and sounds as stubborn as a mule for a six-year-old. I bet your mom is happy for you to take charge of her and make her do her chores. I wish I could have seen her whooping as she jumped out the hay loft behind the gals working in the paddock. They must have died a death!

My mom and pop know all about you now, and I showed them your photo. Pop is tickled that your dad is a fisherman too like him, me, and one of my two brothers. I bet your dad is itching to get back to it after the war. My younger sister Martha was impressed by your hair and is trying to roll hers just like it. Though I would never hurt her feelings, she is way off the mark. Her curls stick up so high, it's as though she's jammed her fingers in an electrical outlet!

Tomorrow's Sunday, so we are off to church and then even though it's December, we are having a walk along the shore. I will be looking across and whispering sweet nothings on the breeze, in the hope it will carry them to your ears. Can we arrange to look out across the ocean, say, the 25th, 10am my time, three p.m. your time? Christmas is a special day, and if I know you're looking for me, we will be together in spirit, if not in the flesh. Oh, that sounds a bit forward. It wasn't meant to!

Anyways, Lamorna, I have to go now as my pops is calling me for the boat. Write back soon and tell me all your news. You made me laugh in your last letter when you told me about the girl who fell in a pile of horse dung! These city girls have a lot to learn from you. But after the war, I know you will get to be a teacher like you want, one of these days. Then lots more will learn from you too!

All my love, your Harry xxx

Lamorna folded the letter and brought it to her lips, inhaling the trace of ink and, if she wasn't mistaken, a hint of sandalwood cologne. How sophisticated Harry was. None of the boys she knew wore cologne. He believed in her too. Her secret hope of making something of herself didn't seem silly to him at all. The war had put a stop to her dreams, but it wouldn't last for ever, would it? She put the letter back in the box, tried to clear her mind and settle to sleep, but her thoughts drifted to war. Harry had written this letter a couple of months ago – it had taken an age to get here. Because of the war, they were lucky their letters were reaching each other at all though. Suddenly a thought punched her in the gut and her eyes shot open. Why hadn't she realised before! Now the Americans were in the war, Harry would be called up – or drafted, as they said – wouldn't he? He wouldn't be able to write because he'd be in God knows where. And what if...? No. No, she wouldn't allow herself to think of her darling Harry being injured or... Forcing her imagination to present a picture of her and Harry strolling along a beach hand in hand, she snapped off the lamp and closed her eyes.

Christmas Day brought with it a new scarf and gloves, a breakfast of mackerel, and a chill wind whipping around the ankles, as Lamorna and her family stepped through the door of Grandma Mary's old farmhouse. Christmas

Day without Grandma Mary was unthinkable. She ensured the day was filled with warmth, love, light, turkey, party games and laughter. Laughter was the dominant thread running through her Christmas memories, as was the smell of cinnamon, mincemeat and old Christmas decorations, each one holding a special memory of its own.

After hugging her grandma, and slipping off her thick red wool coat, a warm glow spread through her chest, and she was enveloped by the remembrance of Christmases past. She looked at the huge pine tree in the corner by the fire. On the very top was a bedraggled angel in a faded blue gown that her auntie Zelah had made when she was six, and her dad's yellowing tin foil stars clung onto the lower branches, though many were now falling apart. In the middle of the tree was a teddy bear Lamorna had knitted in orange wool, from unravelling an old scarf, and stuffed with straw from the barn. A knot of emotion swelled in her throat as she remembered her Grandad Jack on the last Christmas he was alive, telling her it was the best teddy bear he'd ever seen. She didn't have many memories of him, but the ones she had were precious.

Tears weren't allowed on Christmas Day, so she blotted them with the sleeve of her cardigan and walked over to the tree, stroking her fingers over the new colourful paper chains threaded in and out of its branches that Grandma Mary must have made. New tinsel too, if she wasn't mistaken, hung like sparkly icicles, and a bright robin and big round snowman bauble jostled next to old familiar ones, chipped paint and all. She was lucky to have found new tinsel with the rations and shortages, but Grandma Mary was a magician.

'Oh, I like that robin, Lamorna,' Wenna said, reaching out to touch it, tinsel and fire reflected in her big blue eyes.

'Don't let Grandma Mary catch you, it's brand new and if you drop it, she'd go spare.'

'How about this one?' Wenna poked a finger at an old Father Christmas on a little sleigh, the red paint of his coat flaking and his beard made from what looked like cotton wool, grey and sparse.

'I think that's okay. I remember playing with it when I was your age, and younger. That's probably why it looks like that.'

'That used to be mine when I was a kid,' their dad said, coming up alongside, a nostalgic smile on his face. 'My dad got it for my first Christmas.'

'And this was for my first Christmas,' Auntie Zelah said, gently stroking a tin reindeer, its dark antlers faded to a dirty rust. Lamorna's eleven-year-old twin cousins Jennifer and Mark ran over and pretended to be reindeer, snorting and capering around the tree. Wenna gave chase, until a few moments later they all fell on the floor, helpless with laughter.

'Hey, you young 'uns, stop that now. We don't want the tree on top of you!' Grandma Mary said, coming over with a twinkle in her eye and her rolling pin held aloft like a baton. 'Oi, I said stop it!' she cried, and gave them all a gentle poke in the belly with it. This made them laugh even more, and in the end, Auntie Zelah and Lamorna's mum had to intervene before the tree really did go over.

Lamorna folded her arms and leaned her hip against the big farmhouse table laid to lunch with golden crackers, cranberry jam and Grandma Mary's best china, and watched the chaos, a big smile on her face. Though there was a strange feeling in the pit of her chest as she realised that, unlike her cousins, her time for pretending to be a reindeer and rolling on the floor helpless with laughter had long passed. It didn't seem that long ago that she and her brother Tony had played like that, but it was. Those days seemed like another life now Lamorna was eighteen and Tony was twenty-one and engaged to be married. Maybe if everything worked out with Harry, and the war ended, she would be too.

A mix of melancholy and happiness settled in her heart as she watched Grandma Mary, her mother and Auntie Zelah bring the chicken – no turkey as there 'is a war on' – and big dishes of vegetables to the table. Grandma Mary had on her red Christmas apron depicting a laughing snowman, her hair escaping from its tight bun and wisping around her face, pink from the efforts of the day, as the result of the rolling pin activity. Lamorna's dad, brother and Uncle Ronald were trying out a tot of whisky or two by the fire, their deep laughter rich and warm. How many more Christmases would they share together here in this house? Where would they be in a few years' time – or even next year? How much longer would Grandma Mary be able to put on such a wonderful show? Where would they all be if bloody Hitler won?

Startled from her contemplation by Wenna slipping her

hand in hers, she looked down and asked, 'Having fun, Wenna?'

'Yes. I love Christmas. It's so jolly when we're all together. It makes you forget about the war and everything, doesn't it?' Wenna looked up at her sister, a smile lighting her face.

Lamorna chided herself. Wenna lived in the here and now, enjoyed life minute to minute like all children do. Lamorna needed to pull herself together and do the same, put all her worries behind her, if for just one day. 'It does, maid. We are very lucky to be here together when thousands are apart. Good job farming and railway work are reserved, otherwise there would be no dad, brother and uncle here.' Wenna nodded and skipped off to the kitchen. Lamorna gazed after her and took in the whole lovely scene, each happy face, capturing the image in her mind, and tucked it away in her memory drawer for safe keeping.

———

At last, Lamorna had managed to slip away from the family as the sherry and full bellies led to the men dozing, and the women chatting quietly by the fire, while the children played with their Christmas toys. Most had been handmade, as the war had caused so many shortages, but the simple toys were made with love and appreciated all the more for it. Without telling them where she was going, because she didn't want company, Lamorna tiptoed out to the hall, shrugged on her coat and quietly closed the farmhouse door behind her.

The path to Chapel Porth Beach was deserted as she hurried along, wrapping her new red scarf twice round her neck as an icy blast from the Atlantic pulled her hair and nipped her cheeks, seemingly determined to turn her back. There was no chance of that, because it was almost three p.m. and her darling Harry would be waiting for her on another beach, right at this moment, all those miles away. The fine yellow sand dragged at her heavy boots as she jumped down onto it from the path, a whoop of excitement in her throat. Not a soul was to be seen, just as she'd expected and wanted, because if there had been people, they would have wanted to stop and chat and the whole thing would be ruined. Checking the curve of the headland to her right and left, she took off her boots and socks, tucked her dress into her bloomers, let out a yell, and ran like a hare to the shoreline, her heart beating in her chest like a seagull's wings.

Frothy waves broke over Lamorna's toes and, laughing, she took a sharp breath in and did a little dance, kicking the water into high white arcs against the ice-blue sky. This is what it was like to feel truly alive, she thought. To feel your heart thumping, your senses electric with anticipation, lungs full of salt air, skin tingling and hope swelling in your chest. The tide sucked away and then flowed back fast and eager to meet her like an old friend. A few backward steps took her out of its reach, and she lifted her arms to the side like a bird in flight and looked at the far horizon, blue and steadfast like Harry's gaze in his precious photo.

'I'm here, Harry. Here and sending every ounce of love to you, my darling. One day soon we will meet at last. Our hearts will beat as one and –' Lamorna paused, looked once more behind and to her right and left to check she was still alone '– and our lips will join in an eternal kiss.' The wind picked up again and the ocean roared as if in hearty approval of her words.

Wrapping her arms tightly around herself she imagined that Harry was sending her a warm hug across the miles. Closing her eyes, she pictured him right there in her arms, his warm breath on her cheek, his… Her eyes snapped open as a shiver ran up both arms and down her back as the salt wind whispered in her ears, and through it, a strong voice with an American drawl murmured, 'Merry Christmas, dear Lamorna. My heart is with you today and always.'

A giddy lightness filled her head and heart that she felt she might float above the ocean, to his side. She hadn't imagined his voice, it wasn't just the wind, he was calling to her right now at this very moment, from his beach to hers. He was sending his love across the great expanse of blue, and she could hear her name and his echoing through each breaking wave on the shore.

Lamorna spread her arms wide, as if to reach across the miles. 'I can hear you! Happy Christmas, Harry.' Lamorna wasn't surprised to find her voice breaking and tears pushing for release. 'I know you can hear me … and feel my love all those miles away. Goodbye for now, sweetheart, and I will write soon.'

She raised her hand in farewell, and a sob caught in her throat as once again unbidden thoughts of what might happen to Harry, now the Americans were in the war, muscled in on her happiness like playground bullies.

Determined to beat them, she took a deep breath and turned for home, only to see Grandma Mary picking her way around the boulders at the head of the beach.

'There you are!' she called, as Lamorna hurried up the beach towards her.

'What's wrong, Grandma Mary? Has something happened?'

'No. Nothing. I was worried about you when I saw you sneak out and go off like a firework down the lane. I climbed the ladder in the barn and saw you from the hayloft heading for the beach, so I threw a coat on and followed you.'

Lamorna's heart sank. Now she'd have to explain why she'd been talking to the ocean, her dress in her bloomers, with her arms out to the sides like a proper old silly ninny. 'Umm...'

'You been crying?' Grandma Mary tied her head scarf under her chin and peered into Lamorna's face with those miss-nothing hazel eyes.

'Umm...'

'You have, I can tell.'

'Umm...'

'Will you stop saying umm? Don't tell me that lovely Harry has given you the brush-off?'

Lamorna smiled and slipped her arm through her grandma's. She was so pleased she'd chosen to confide in her. At first, Lamorna thought she wouldn't tell a soul about her secret love, because she worried that if she did, it would all go wrong. But in the end, she'd had to tell Grandma Mary, because she was bursting to tell someone, and she kept asking if Lamorna had heard anything from her message in a bottle. 'No, Grandma, quite the opposite, actually. Let's go over to those boulders and sit down a minute and I'll tell you.'

After Lamorna had told her story, her grandma's worried expression gave way to a huge smile. 'That's the dearest, sweetest thing I ever heard. True loves sending their hearts across the ocean on Christmas Day.' She chuckled. 'At first when I saw you stood there with your bloomers on show, arms wide, talking to yourself, I thought you'd gone soft in the head, my girl.'

Lamorna laughed too and they both looked out to the horizon lost in thought, Lamorna wondering if Harry was still there, or had gone home for his Christmas dinner. 'I do feel a bit soft in the head, truth be told. My heart aches with happiness and longing for him, but I worry that it will all be for nothing.' She covered her mouth to stop a sob escaping.

'There, there, lamb.' Grandma Mary slipped an arm around her. 'Why would it all be for nothing?'

'Because of this bloody war!' She glanced at her grandma. 'Sorry for swearing, but I'm so scared that he will be sent into danger and get killed.'

Grandma Mary's forehead creased into a frown and she took both her granddaughter's hands in hers. 'Don't you worry about bloody swearing, this war is enough to try the patience of a saint, and I'm not one of those!' She gave a little laugh. 'Now, listen to me. Your Harry might have to go into danger like thousands of others, but I'll tell you this for nothing, he won't get killed. You *will* meet him one day and be very happy.'

'Why are you so sure?'

'There's magic at work here today. I felt it in me old bones as I came down here and saw you. I didn't really think you'd gone soft in the head at all. You looked ... otherworldly, if you will? Can't explain it, my love. But I feel it inside. He'll be safe, that man of yours.'

Those words sent Lamorna's soul soaring up into the cold blue sky, and she swore the winter sun shone a little brighter. There was certainly magic here. 'I hope that's true...' Another worry that had been nagging at her like a paper cut in salt water came to the surface, escaping before she could stop it. 'What will happen if we do get married though? We live an ocean apart, but we'll have to pick one side or the other to live. If I go with him to America, I wouldn't see my family anymore... I don't know what I'd do without Mum, Dad, Tony and our Wenna, even though she is a little monster at times. And you ... Grandma Mary. What would I do without you?' Lamorna found she could hold back her tide of emotion no longer, and leaned sobbing into her grandma's shoulder, the familiar comforting smell of baking and lavender making her cry all the more.

Grandma Mary held her tight until there were no tears left to fall, and then in a voice full of emotion she said, 'Your family might be able to visit once the war's over, and things get back to normal. I knew a woman in the next village who went to see her grandchildren on one of those big liner ships. There's always a way.' She cupped Lamorna's face between her gnarled rough hands and cleared her throat. 'The main thing is to just follow your heart, my love. You belong with Harry, and you *will* be happy. As I said, I know it in here.' She thumped her chest, her eyes shining with love and tears. 'Just like I knew you'd find your true love with that message in a bottle.'

'You really think so?'

'I do.' Grandma Mary stood and dusted sand from her good coat, saying wistfully, 'Just wish I'd have acted on my instincts back when I was a kid. My whole life could have been so different. But you know what they say. If wishes were horses, beggars would ride. Now let's get back home before they send out the Home Guard to search for us.'

Arm in arm they made their way back to the path, Lamorna treasuring every precious moment of their walk, and she vowed to treasure every future moment they would spend together. Because if what her grandma said was true, she knew there couldn't be too many of them left.

Chapter Five

CORNWALL

October 1943

Lamorna wanted her mum to shut up. Why couldn't she understand that the only man for her was Harry? Trying to tune out her mum's constant nattering about Tom Keller, she concentrated on shelling peas at the kitchen table, occasionally glancing out at the rain-soaked garden. The slate grey sky reflected her mood. Sullen and stormy.

'I mean, you haven't heard a peep out of him for months, have you?'

Oh for Pete's sake! Lamorna threw a pea-pod on the table in frustration. 'Letters go astray, or can't get through, ships carrying them get sunk… There's a war on, haven't you heard?'

Her mum whirled round from the sink, a wet potato in one hand, a peeler in the other, which she jabbed through the air at Lamorna like a weapon. 'Don't you give me any of your cheek, young lady,' she replied, her eyes flashing. 'You might be nearly twenty, but I'm still your mother and deserve respect!'

Lamorna folded her arms and stared straight back at her mum, unwilling to be the one to look away first. Her mum put the potato and peeler back in the sink and brushed a curl of muddy potato peeling from her yellow and pink floral apron. Then she lifted her head and stared again at her daughter, defiant, waiting. Lamorna took a deep breath. Might as well get this over with. 'Sorry, Mum.'

Her face softened with a heartfelt sigh and she dried her hands on a tea-towel. 'Look, love, I only want the best for you. For all we know, by now this Harry might be...'

'No. Don't say it.'

Her mum raised her hands and let them fall. 'Well, he might well be. Lots of soldiers go missing or worse every day, and as much as I'd like your Harry to still be alive somewhere ... if he was, you'd think he would have written before now.'

Her mum tucked a stray hair back into the roll over her forehead, which had many more grey hairs than it used to, Lamorna noted. She realised that she only wanted the best for her daughter, but why wouldn't she listen? And why had she told her mum about Harry at all? Because she needed her approval, she supposed. Setting her jaw, she said quietly, 'As I mentioned, letters go missing too, every day.'

'But you're just wasting chances, mooning after someone and something that might never be.'

'I love Harry.'

'But you've not actually met him, so how do you know?'

'I just do. The magic of the cove brought us together, and I found out all about what he's like and his life from his letters.' Lamorna shrugs. 'It's meant to be.'

'You won't really know though until you meet. If you ever do...' Her mum raises an eyebrow. 'The thing is, you could learn to love Tom. He's from a decent family and proper handsome. And he thinks the world of you, always coming over before he goes home after he's finished in the fields. The lad's here from early and home late, but he always tries to see you for a few minutes every day.' She twisted her mouth to the side and sniffed. 'You hardly give him a second glance, more's the pity.'

Trying to keep her temper, Lamorna picked up a pea-pod and squeezed the peas out into a saucepan. 'That's because I love Harry,' she replies, through gritted teeth.

'Oh, for goodness' sake, girl! How can you love someone you haven't even met?' Her mum scraped a kitchen chair across the tiles and plonked herself on it.

'For goodness' sake, Mum. I've already said. It's the magic at work ... and I feel like we have met through our letters and photos. Grandma Mary—'

'Grandma Mary has a lot to answer for! Silly woman should never have encouraged you in the first place. Damned stupid idea sending messages in bottles all the way to America. I should know. What's wrong with a good Cornishman, hmm?'

How dare she talk about Grandma Mary like that? Lamorna's temper wouldn't be kept anymore, and out of her mouth came, 'Grandma Mary believed in true love and the magic of nature. She was a wonderful woman, and don't you dare speak ill of her!' Lamorna scraped her own chair back and marched to the kitchen door, her heart thumping in her chest. 'Harry is the one for me, whether you like it or not, so just stop going on about bloody Tom Keller!' Lamorna saw her own shock at what she'd just said reflected in her mum's face. She'd never spoken to her like that before. But so what! Hell, she'd deserved it. Lamorna stomped out of the door and slammed it behind her.

On the shoreline, Lamorna at last stopped for breath, inhaling deeply the salt air and fixed her eyes on the gunmetal grey horizon. The waves hurled themselves at the rocks, the crash of their impact drowning out the seagulls. Lamorna wished she was a crashing wave, drowning out the moaning and constant complaining of her mother. Tying her orange and black headscarf more tightly around her hair, she stomped off to sit on her usual boulder at the head of the beach. A woman and a young boy were walking towards the cliff path to her right, but apart from them, she was alone.

As was her wont when she came here, her thoughts went immediately to Harry and also to the last time she was here with her grandma. Christmas Day 1941, almost two years ago. Six months later, her beloved grandma had been coming down the stairs with a bundle of laundry, tripped on a sheet, fallen and hit her head. Lamorna had been utterly devastated, as had they all. Later, her dad had reminded them that despite the awful shock her death had caused, she'd always said she didn't want a lingering end. Lamorna wanted to say that Grandma Mary had only meant that when she was a very old woman, and she'd only been sixty-eight, for goodness' sake. She hadn't said it, of course, because if it comforted her dad to think that, then all well and good.

Things had not been all well and good at all since then for Lamorna. Everything had been all unwell and bad. Around that same time Harry's letters had stopped and they'd sold the old cottage and moved into the farmhouse as her dad at last fulfilled his own father's wishes and took over the farm. Living there meant she'd felt closer to Grandma Mary, but she worried that if Harry did write, the letters would go to the cottage and might be missed. Lamorna's mum had told her not to be silly, because the Jacksons, who'd bought the cottage, would have told her. Even though she knew it to be true, she popped down there every week, just to be sure.

In a rockpool by her feet, a crab peeped out from behind some brown and green seaweed and retreated when the shadow of a seagull's wings passed overhead. Lamorna felt like the crab. Hoping that the future will be bright, but then finding dark shadows threatening it all too often. The dreams of making something of herself and finding love with Harry had turned out to be just that, hadn't they? Dreams. Reality is war and all its savagery. And in Lamorna's little world, it's being nagged at by her mother to settle for someone like Tom Keller. She thought of her mother badmouthing her grandma again. How rude, when she left her and Dad the bloody farmhouse in the will. A big part of Lamorna knew she ought to not be so hard on her mum, because war had changed everyone. Everyone seemed to live on their nerves more than they used to, and that brought out their less charitable side. It was only to be expected.

The crab peeped out again and scuttled across the pool to grab a few little shrimps. Lamorna found herself smiling. If Grandma Mary were here, she would tell her to wait for Harry, not set her cap at any man who showed interest. She'd also tell her to grab her opportunities when she could, just like the crab. An idea that had been buzzing around in the back of her head for a while flew to the front, and wouldn't be swatted. Lots of American soldiers had come into England and some to Cornwall over the last year or so – she'd even seen some around the village now and then. In the last few weeks, her best friend Gladys said there had been a load of them turn up at the Truro camp.

As she sat there gazing at the ocean, the idea evolved into a plan. She could go to Truro, try and speak to one of the officers in charge, and see if they could help her find out what had happened to Harry. Lamorna's heart fluttered as she thought of doing such a bold thing. They might think she was a silly goose, turning up like that with an impossible request, and send her on her way with a flea in her ear. But what choice did she have? She could send a letter to his parents, but that would take so long, and their reply might not get through anyway. No. She had to be like the crab, come out of the seaweed and grab a shrimp. Take the opportunity to ask the US Army. They might not be able to help, but then again, they might. Then she'd know once and for all about her Harry, wouldn't she? She would go tomorrow with Gladys on her day off.

————————

Gladys looked like she was ready for a dinner-dance, not a bus ride to Truro, when Lamorna met her at the bus-stop the next morning. A clingy yellow and red polka-dot dress, black jacket with shiny silver buttons, a matching wide-brimmed hat and wearing more make-up than Carmen Miranda. Next to her, even though she'd made a bit of an effort with her smart sage green dress and brown belted mackintosh, Lamorna felt positively matronly.

'Blimey, you look glamorous, Gladys,' she said with a smile, nearly suffocating on the cloud of strong perfume as she kissed her friend's cheek.

Gladys pouted her crimson lips, and with her dark eyes twinkling with mischief said, 'We're going to a US Army base, Lamorna. Goodness knows who we might meet! Might be a Clark Gable look-alike who will fall instantly in love with me and whisk me off to Hollywood with him.'

Lamorna had to laugh. 'Hollywood? There's a war on, Glad. That's why they're over here.'

Her eyebrows shot up into her hat. 'O ye of little faith. The war won't always be on, will it?' Slipping her arm through Lamorna's, she waved her hand at the approaching bus. 'Now, come along. Put your best smile on and get ready to dazzle 'em.'

An hour later, outside the camp, Gladys didn't look so confident. A Jeep full of soldiers had just driven through the gates, and a couple of them had given them wolf whistles and lascivious looks as they'd gone past. Suddenly she seemed less like Carmen Miranda and more like Little Red Riding Hood.

'Not sure this was such a good idea,' Lamorna muttered, fishing her gloves out of her bag and pulling them on. 'I feel a bit uncomfortable and out of my depth, going up to those gates.' She nodded at the big iron gates and the two armed soldiers standing next to them.

Gladys shook herself and put her shoulders back. 'It will be fine. We just walk up to those GIs and ask to speak to the one in charge.'

Oh God … was that really the best approach? Lamorna was just about to voice her opinion when Gladys set off at double-quick march towards the soldiers. 'Erm, Glad? Gladys…' she called, but all Lamorna received was a dismissive wave back over her shoulder.

At their approach, the GIs stopped chatting to each other and looked at them both with a mixture of surprise and keen interest. 'Good morning, pretty ladies,' one of them drawled and gave Gladys a cheeky wink. He wasn't a dead ringer for Clark Gable, but tall, dark and handsome nonetheless.

To Lamorna's embarrassment, Gladys batted her eyelashes and giggled. 'Good morning. We'd like to speak to the one in charge of you.'

'Nobody's in charge of me, babe. I'm in charge of myself.' His eyes twinkling with mischief, he nudged the other soldier, who was about as tall, with fair hair. 'You heard this kid, Larry?'

'I did, Dwight. Maybe she wants to speak to the officer in charge of the camp,' he said with a warm smile at them both. He had none of the swagger of his comrade and Lamorna hoped he might be able to help.

'You think? Hmm.' Lamorna could tell that Dwight was only pretending to puzzle over this, exaggerating his frown and stroking his chin. 'That so, little lady?' He directed that to Gladys, who was still batting her eyelashes, oblivious to his play-acting. Lamorna wanted the ground to open up and swallow her.

'Yes, that's right.' Gladys nodded at Lamorna, and then pouted her lips at Dwight before she continued. 'My friend here has been writing to her sweetheart, who's American and in the army like you, but she's not heard from him for a very long time. We were wondering if you could find out anything about him, please?'

Dwight turns his lively brown eyes to Lamorna. 'Hmm, that so? Your friend have a tongue in her head?'

Lamorna's cheeks flared under his scrutiny and she wanted to say something to wipe the teasing smile off his face, but instead, she took a deep breath and replied, 'Yes, I do, thank you. His name is Harry Marshall, he's twenty-two and from Gloucester, Massachusetts –' Lamorna took a gulp of air, her throat feeling desert-dry with nerves '– oh, and he's in the infantry.'

Larry's kind green eyes found hers. 'Okay. What division?'

'Division?' Her voice sounded squeaky – weak.

'Yeah, gal. What infantry division?' Dwight folded his arms and shook his head at her as if she were a prize ninny.

Damn and blast. She did know, but it had completely gone out of her head. 'Er … I can't remember.'

Gladys looked sidelong at her and flashed her eyes. 'Never mind. Could you find him by looking up his name?'

Dwight sniggered. 'Not the sort of thing we have time for, honey.' He puffed out his chest and bragged, 'We're on guard duty and later we'll be training, in case the Nazis decide to show their ugly mugs across here. Gotta protect folks like you, because France isn't so far away, you know?'

Lamorna rolled her eyes. Did he think they were so stupid they didn't know where France was? 'That's why we wanted to see your superior,' she blurted. 'They would have more idea of how to find out about Harry than you.'

Dwight had clocked her eye-roll and his handsome face grew stern. He looked as if he was going to dismiss them, until Gladys put her hand on his arm and gave him her winning smile. 'I'm thankful we have soldiers like you to protect us from the Jerrys. Lamorna and me, well, we'd be very grateful if you could help us out.'

Larry said to Lamorna, 'That's a pretty name. Fits you perfectly.'

Lamorna looked away, pink-faced. 'Thank you.'

'Hey, what say we take your name and address and if we find anything out, we can let ya know?' Dwight took a notebook and pencil from his top pocket. 'Can't say when it'll be 'cos as I said, we're busy with the war an' all.'

Gladys smiled and put her hand back on his arm. 'That would be very kind, wouldn't it, Lamorna?'

To the floor she replied, 'Yes. Thank you.'

After he'd written down Gladys's name and address, he slid the notebook into his pocket and winked at Gladys. 'And I know you'd love to come to a dance we got going on here soon, wouldn't you?'

Lamorna's heart sank and the little bit of hope she had tucked away in her heart floated off on the wind. It was obvious that Dwight had as much intention of helping her find Harry as he did of flying to the moon. He was only interested in getting them to go to the dance, or Gladys at least.

'Ooh, a dance here. That sounds wonderful, doesn't it, Lamorna?' Gladys clapped her hands like an excited child. Oh dear. Lamorna gave a non-committal nod.

'Hear tell a big star is coming to rally the troops soon, too.' He lowered his voice to a conspiratorial whisper and leaned in close. 'Rumoured to be Bob Hope or someone like that. They already had Glenn Miller up at the Burtonwood Airbase.'

Both of Gladys' hands flew to her mouth and her eyes grew round. 'Oh my goodness!' A shrill giggle escaped her and Lamorna felt like asking if she'd wet herself with excitement. 'Imagine that, Lamorna!'

'Yes, I actually can, the way you're carrying on.' Lamorna smirked.

Frowning, Gladys asked, 'Eh?'

'Never mind. I think we should probably be going now.' Lamorna slipped her arm through her friend's. 'Thanks for your help, gentlemen.' She smiled at Larry and turned to go, but Gladys stayed rooted to the spot.

'But … but what about the dance?'

Dwight sighed and tapped his top pocket. 'I have your name and address; I'll swing by soon with an invitation. How would that be, honey?'

Gladys beamed at him. 'That would be, as you Americans say, swell!'

Dwight gave a hearty laugh. 'It would be swell, all right.' He took her hand and kissed the back of it. 'I'll see you soon, Gladys, honey bun.'

'Will you be coming, Lamorna?' Larry asked, his expression hopeful. 'I know you have a sweetheart, but these dances are lots of fun.'

Lamorna smiled. 'I'm not sure I feel in the mood for dancing at the moment, Larry. But thanks for asking.'

They took their leave, and Lamorna guided Gladys back down the path, trying to be happy for her friend as she erupted like a volcano about how excited for the dance she was, and how wonderful Dwight was. They clicked straightaway, didn't she think? And wouldn't it be marvellous if they could have a double wedding. Her and Dwight. Lamorna and Harry?

'I think you might be jumping the gun a tiny bit, Glad. You've only just met him.' *And there's not a chance he's at all serious about you, or finding Harry, sadly.*

'Yes, but as I said. We clicked. They say you know when you meet the man of your dreams.' Gladys put both hands over her heart. 'It was love at first sight,' she whispered.

Lamorna couldn't stand it. She was worried that her friend would get herself into trouble, she was so gullible, and naïve. Lamorna was hardly the most worldly wise, but she had a good dollop of cynicism and a sensible head on her shoulders to keep her safe. As they walked to their favourite tea shop to have a cuppa before returning home, Lamorna decided she would try and gently persuade Gladys not to go to the dance, but deep down she knew it was a waste of time. Her friend had too many stars in her eyes, and was completely dazzled by Dwight and his smooth talking. The sensible thing would be to go to the dance with her, to keep an eye out, but Lamorna didn't have it in her to even pretend she would be enjoying it. Without knowing if Harry was dead or alive, even though she'd be just dancing, it would feel like a betrayal.

After seeing Gladys back home, Lamorna set off down the lane to her own house, but halfway there, something made her head towards the old cottage where they used to live. It had been nearly a week since she'd popped in to ask Mrs Jackson if there had been a letter for her. Pinning a sliver of hope back in her heart, she hurried up the path and knocked on the door. Mrs Jackson, a stout middle-aged lady, came to the door, flour on her apron and in her red hair.

Mrs Jackson watched Lamorna's eyes go to her hairline and she dabbed a tea towel at her curls. 'I've got flour in my hair, haven't I? My Bob's always telling me about it. What I do, you see, is when I get hot when I'm baking, I shove my hair from my face and…' She laughs. 'Well, you can see the evidence.'

'Never mind, Mrs Jackson, it'll come out. I was wondering…'

'If there was a letter yet? I'm sorry, dear, there hasn't been. I would have come up to the farm with it if there had.' Mrs Jackson's eyes twinkled with amusement, which under the circumstances, Lamorna found to be most unusual, not to say unkind.

'Oh. Well, not to worry. I'll check back soon,' Lamorna said, a little stiffly and made as if to leave.

'But I'll tell you what did come to the door, no more than five minutes before you did. Or I should say who.' The twinkle in her eyes had become mischievous and her lips stretched into a beaming smile.

'Who?' Lamorna wasn't in the mood for silly games.

'I was about to wash my hands and run up to the farm when you knocked. Just to make sure he turned up at the right place, you know? Don't want him getting lost after all, do we?'

'Who?' Lamorna asked again, beginning to sound like a barn owl.

'Your American sweetheart, this Harry chap you've been pining over. And I can see why. Proper handsome he is! Why, if I was thirty years younger and not married to my Bob…'

Lamorna watched Mrs Jackson's mouth moving but couldn't take in her words. She felt like she was in a trance or a dream; her heart was galloping in her chest and her legs felt all trembly, like they did when she stood on the edge of a cliff looking down at the great ocean waves crashing against the rocks far below.

'Harry?' she heard herself say. 'Harry's here?'

'That's what I've been telling you. Run on to the farm, you'll catch him up in no time.' Mrs Jackson clapped her hands in front of Lamorna's face. 'Wake up, maid. Be after him!'

Lamorna set off like a greyhound down the path and along the lane, her footsteps unsure and wobbly like the rest of her. *Harry is here? Harry is here? Harry is here?* The question was on repeat, echoing her thundering heartbeat. A few minutes later, a little way off up the sandy path flanked by Cornish hedges, she saw a tall figure in uniform striding ahead. An American uniform. Dare she allow the sliver of hope to grow into a mountain? She knew she wouldn't cope if it turned out not to be him. Then she came to a halt. What if he didn't like her? All her mum's comments about Lamorna not having met him, so how could she possibly know if they loved each other, whirled like a tornado in her head. What if the reality didn't live up to the dream her heart had built over the past few years? Nerves sent butterflies flitting around her tummy as she blotted her clammy palms on her coat.

Then Grandma Mary's words from Christmas Day 1941 echoed clear in her mind and Lamorna set off walking down the lane again. She'd told Lamorna that she and Harry belonged together, and that she just knew it inside, somehow. Lamorna just knew too. But what if Harry didn't? What if she didn't live up to his expectations? And anyway, the man in in the uniform a little way ahead might not even be him. Lamorna shook herself and braced her shoulders. Only one way to find out. Stopping, she cupped her hands around her mouth and yelled through them, 'Harry!'

The figure halted and whirled round, raising a hand to shield his eyes against the sunlight. He tentatively raised the other in a wave. *Oh my God.* Lamorna rested her hand on a stone wall for support. Oh my God. Her question had been answered. Yes. Harry is here! 'Harry! It's me, Lamorna!!'

They both set off at a run, swiftly closing the gap as they hurtled towards each other until they were only a few feet apart. There they stood, in a Cornish lane, birds singing in the hedgerows, face to face, just staring, taking in every inch of each other. Harry took off his hat, and smoothed his short fair hair, his eyes bluer than she had ever thought possible, crinkled at the edges as a broad smile found his lips. 'Lamorna...' His voice caught and she saw his Adam's apple bob. 'Gee, I'm so nervous.' He gave a little laugh. 'Lamorna. It's really you, my love.'

She nodded as tears of happiness streamed down her cheeks, eventually managing, 'Yes ... yes, it is. This must be a miracle. Oh Harry, thank God you're here.'

Harry stepped forward, looked deep into her eyes, and gently wiped away her tears with his thumb. All her fears were forgotten in this one perfect moment. There was no doubt about it – they were meant for each other. Then he took her in his arms, and she was lost in the warmth of his kiss and the strength of his love. Lost, and never wanting to be found.

Chapter Six

CORNWALL

May 1944

Lamorna had been floating on a cloud for the past seven months. Seven months of being Harry's 'gal' as he called her. Seven months of walking hand-in-hand across windswept beaches and coast paths, sharing kisses, private jokes, their life-stories, and, most of all, their love. Now as she sat on a fence looking across a green field that rolled to the ocean, she wrapped her arms around her torso, in eager anticipation of doing the same to Harry's in a few minutes. This field high above the village had become their meeting spot. It was mainly deserted and a sandy trail led through a little wood, which joined up later with the coastal path. She and Harry spent many happy hours here, and sometimes went back to the farmhouse for tea with the family. Lamorna smiled when she remembered how her mum had wanted her to forget about Harry and show interest in Tom Keller instead. Thank God she'd stuck to her guns. Her mum was coming round to Harry now too, thank goodness. How could she not, when he was charm itself? However, she felt her cheeks grow hot when she thought about what sometimes happened in the little wood. Her mum would certainly not approve.

Over the brow of the hill came Harry, and her heart swelled with happiness. Her man. Tall and smart in his uniform, his hat sat at a jaunty angle, and he was whistling the popular tune 'Don't Sit Under the Apple Tree', which blew before him on the wind. Lamorna couldn't believe her luck that he was stationed here. Actually, she believed it was more than luck or coincidence. She knew that there were thousands of GIs stationed all over the UK now, from Scotland to Cornwall and all the parts in between. But she reckoned the reason he was in Cornwall, and not Scotland, was once again because of their special magic at work.

Harry raised a hand and smiled, his white teeth like pearls in his suntanned face. Lamorna's mum had commented that Americans seem to have brighter smiles and whiter teeth than the English. She didn't know about that, but it was true of Harry. He seemed bigger and brighter in every way because he had a larger-than-life presence. When she was with him, she laughed more, felt prettier, and had more gumption about her. He made her feel like she was the most important person in his life. Lamorna sometimes couldn't believe her luck to have found him. She had to pinch herself when she thought about being his gal – his one and only, as he often told her.

Harry closed the gap between them and swung her round in his arms. 'How's my beautiful gal today, hmm?'

Lamorna was unable to answer as his lips found hers and he kissed her soundly. After he released her, it took a moment for her senses to return from the heights of passion where he'd sent them. She took a breath. 'I'm much better for seeing you, Harry. It seems like a year, not five days, since I saw you.'

Harry gently pinched her cheek and gave her a wide grin. 'Same here, sweetheart. So let's make the most of the time we have.' He took her hand and they set off down the sandy path to the little wood.

Under the dappled sunlight filtering through the multitude of green foliage, Harry drew Lamorna to him and leaned his back against an ancient oak tree. The gentle kisses he dropped on her cheek, mouth, and down her neck became more urgent, hot with passion, and she felt her body respond in kind. Every time she was with him like this, her skin was alive with electricity as an exquisite ache of desire started in her stomach and moved between her legs. At first, feelings like that had made her ashamed, but when she'd confessed to Gladys, she'd replied that it was okay as long as you loved the man. And boy did she love Harry. They had never gone all the way, Harry was too much of a gentleman, but the feel of his excitement against her thighs, and his fingers on her breasts and most intimate parts, made her wish he wasn't. 'Oh, Harry,' she moaned into his collar, as his hands cupped her bottom and pulled her firmly against him.

'Yes, my darling?' he whispered into her ear, with breath still minty from his discarded gum.

'I...' She didn't know how to say it, but she wanted him

to know there were no restrictions. She wanted him. She needed him to love her totally and utterly.

He stopped kissing her neck and looked intently into her eyes. His were the colour of the stunning sky peeping through the leaves. 'Do you love me?'

'You know I do. More than anything.'

Harry gave her a long, slow, beautiful smile and held her at arm's length. 'Well, I'm mighty glad to hear that, because I have a question for you.' He put his hand into his trouser pocket and looked suddenly unsure, nervous even.

Lamorna watched his Adam's apple bob and he blinked a few times before looking at the ground between them. 'What is it, Harry?' Then she gasped as he dropped to one knee and looked up at her, love shining from his face.

'Lamorna … will you do the honour of becoming my wife, when this miserable war is over?' Her hand flew to her mouth, and she couldn't take her eyes off a gold ring with a little pearl in the centre, gripped between his thumb and forefinger. 'I know it doesn't look like much, because it isn't. It's the only one I could afford and I promise, if you say yes, I will get you a new one when—'

There was a big lump of emotion in the way of Lamorna's reply, but she held her hand up to stop him continuing. Then she took a huge breath and gulped back the tears. 'Oh, Harry. Yes. Yes, of course I will be your wife!'

Harry's whoop of joy scared a few crows from the trees and they flew off, squawking fit to deafen them. 'You will? I can't tell you how happy that makes me! I've been so nervous!' Harry laughed and slipped the ring on her finger.

'It fits!' Lamorna giggled, holding her left hand up to the

dappled sunspots. 'It is so pretty.' The idea that she was going to wake up from a wonderful dream wouldn't leave her alone and she was about to ask Harry to pinch her, when he pulled her to him again in a bone-crushing hug and danced her around the woodland floor.

'I'm the luckiest guy alive!' he said and kissed her so long and hard that she thought she would faint.

When they came up for air, Lamorna said, 'No, I'm the luckiest gal!' Her heart thundered in her chest, and she had to grab hold of his arm to halt the whirlwind of giddiness in her head. Just wait until she told her family and Gladys! Then Harry's expression grew solemn, and his gaze steadfast. Lamorna felt as though his soul was reaching inside her, finding her deepest and darkest worries and turning on all the lights. They were bound together in spirt, and when he kissed her again, she wanted the same for their bodies. Once more, as she felt his excitement growing, she boldly reached for him, and a little shiver of pleasure ran through her as she heard his responding moan.

Harry's hands roamed frantically over her body but then stopped abruptly and he took a step back. 'I'm gonna lose my head if we keep on,' he said, taking his hat out of his pocket and jamming it back on his head, as if to keep it in place.

'Would that be so bad?' Lamorna could hardly believe how forward she was being, but she didn't care.

'I want us to wait.' Harry threw his hands up and squawked like the crows. 'What am I saying? That's not true. I couldn't think of anything I'd like to do more right now … but my folks brought me up to believe that we should wait until our wedding night, in our marriage bed. That's the Christian faith.' He took her hand and kissed the back of it.

Despite her disappointment, she knew he was right. She'd been brought up the same, and now they were betrothed, it would be worth waiting for. If only they knew how long the bloody war would last. Thoughts of war brought storm clouds rolling in over their sunny day and she pulled Harry close, resting her head against his chest. He smelled of gum, cigarettes, Lifebuoy soap, and the subtle 'manly' smell as she described it to herself. Lamorna loved him so much, she couldn't bear the thought of anything happening to him. 'I hate this bloody war!' she cried, as a sob escaped.

'Hey, hey!' Harry lifted her chin with a finger. 'Look at me, baby. It will be over soon; you'll see. And then we'll be married and be happy. We have the rest of our lives together.' Lamorna found the beginnings of a smile as she tried to push away the dark clouds. The smile wobbled and faltered when they pushed back stronger, and she couldn't meet his eyes. 'Hey, cookie. You listening to me? Hmm?'

Lamorna took a breath, fixed her gaze on her fiancé's concerned face and swallowed her tears. She needed to keep strong for them both and hope for the best. 'Yes, I'm listening,' she managed, in a small voice.

'Good. Everything's gonna be all right, okay?'

She nodded and found a proper smile. 'Okay,' she replied, and kissed him.

Lamorna was so excited she could hardly breathe. Today she and Harry were going down to Chapel Porth Beach, otherwise known as Magic Cove, to have a picnic. They'd visited the magical place, where Lamorna sent the little bottle bobbing across the waves nearly six years ago, before, of course, but never with a picnic. On the surface of things, having a picnic hardly seemed the most exciting thing in the world, but to them it really was. It felt normal. Nothing had felt normal since this damned war had started, so any chance to do an everyday thing together like a normal young couple who were in love felt incredible. As she packed the last of the food into Grandma Mary's old wicker picnic basket, Lamorna realised this would only be a brief interlude in the hell that had become their lives for the past five years, but if brief interludes were all they had, then they'd jolly well make the most of them.

A warm breeze ruffled salt fingers through Lamorna's curls as she waited for Harry at the top of the path leading to the cove. Even though Wenna had told her she looked like Rita Hayworth in her new one-piece flower-patterned swimsuit, she felt a little self-conscious when she thought about having to reveal herself in it to Harry later. Lamorna had never been the most confident about her figure, thinking her bottom was a little too round. Heaving a sigh, she adjusted the straps of the suit and smoothed the skirt of her red summer dress she wore over it. Then she saw Harry hurrying down the road towards her, a huge grin lighting up his handsome features, and all her worries were snatched away on the breeze.

'Hey there, doll. You look good enough to eat.' Harry

kissed her soundly on the lips and Lamorna pulled away giggling. Kissing in public like that was not something she was used to.

'You're not so bad yourself. And I have lots of things in this basket that are good enough to eat, too.' Lamorna smiled and took his hand. 'Come on, let's find a picnic spot.'

Once on the beach, Harry whistled. 'Wow, this place is awesome. I swear it gets more beautiful each time we come.'

'That's because of the magic.'

'Yup, I guess it is.' Harry pushed his floppy blond hair from his eyes and pocketed his hat. 'The day I found your bottle, I looked out across the ocean in the evening and tried to picture you.' He stroked his fingers across her cheek, his ocean-blue eyes holding hers in an intense gaze. 'In the days afterwards, I tried to picture this beach too. Both you and it are a thousand times more beautiful than I could ever imagine. Can't believe I'm really here standing on this exact spot with you next to me. I have to pinch myself every day.'

Lamorna boldly returned his gaze and joy rushed into her heart, lifting her higher than the wheeling gulls above their heads. The way he was looking at her was so impassioned, it was as if he could look inside her soul, see her yearning, know her every thought, hope and dream. Almost as if they were becoming one person. 'I love you so much, Harry,' she whispered, holding him close.

'I know. I can feel it coming off you in waves ... never felt like this before.'

'Me neither.' She looked up at him. 'I can't wait for the day the war ends and we can be married. The yearning is like a proper ache in my chest.' Lamorna placed her hand over her heart.

'Can I have a feel?' Harry had mischief twinkling in his eyes and she pushed him away.

'Certainly not.' She dropped her voice. 'Well, not here, anyway.'

Harry laughed and spun her round. 'Lamorna Williams, you shameless hussy,' he whispered in her ear.

Giggling she said, 'Put me down, you big lug. Now let's have a picnic before the lemonade gets too warm.' She hurried over to a spot near some rocks that provided a bit of shade and shelter from the breeze and shook out the old red and white beach blanket.

Harry flopped down on it and stripped off his jacket and shirt. 'How about a swim after? We said we would.'

Lamorna cast her eyes swiftly over his tanned muscular chest and biceps. *My goodness, Harry is certainly a dreamboat.* Then he unzipped his trousers to reveal a pair of close-fitting black swimming trunks. Lamorna looked away with a face as red as her dress. Her tummy did a somersault and landed somewhere in her chest. She felt even more nervous stripping off in front of him now. 'Erm, I'm not sure. The water looks a bit cold.' Lamorna nodded at the calm and sleepy ocean, wishing it had seven-foot waves crashing to shore, like it often had.

'Nah. It's perfect swimming weather and the sun's been warming it up for a good few days. Besides, I can't wait to see you in your swimsuit.' He knelt by her side and ran his finger under the strap of her dress, taking a peek inside. 'Looks a pretty colour.'

Watching a slow lazy smile curve his lips, and the yearning in his eyes, Lamorna suddenly grew bold. She stood up and undid the buttons of her dress. 'Okay, let's do it now if we're gonna do it. The picnic can wait.' Letting the dress fall to the sand she held her breath, until she saw the look of appreciation in his eyes.

'Wow! You look knockout, honey!'

Releasing her breath in a relived whoosh, she replied, 'Thank you. Right, I'll race you. Last one in the sea is a smelly sea urchin!' Lamorna's chuckle of excitement carried on the air, as she set off running towards the ocean and into the gentle waves shushing over the wet sand. The sound of Harry's laughter and pounding footsteps behind her spurred her on and despite the initial chill as the water swirled over her knees and thighs, she kept going, until Harry's strong arms enfolded her from behind, halting her progress.

'So I'm a smelly sea-urchin, huh?' he growled in her ear, and a shiver ran down her neck.

'Yes, you are!' Lamorna giggled and tried to break free without success.

'Take that back, or you're going in the water!'

'No. I won't take it back!' Lamorna yelled, gasping as a playful wave broke across her chest. 'And if you chuck me in, you're coming with me.' She hooked her leg over his knee, making him lose balance slightly in the shifting sand beneath their feet.

'Oh, I don't think so, missy!' Harry laughed and grabbed her shoulders as if to push her in.

Quick as a flash, she shifted her weight and pushed back

against his chest, holding her nose as they both went under the waves backwards, with a huge splash.

'You crazy?!' Harry blurted when they both surfaced again, gasping for air.

'Yes!' Lamorna laughed. 'Crazy in love with my fiancé.'

As Harry scooped her up and kissed her passionately, it seemed to Lamorna that the gulls cheered overhead and the tide pulled the waves around them in a joyful embrace. This time she didn't care that there were other people on the beach who might be watching. This was their beach. Their magic cove. Their time. Whatever the future brought them, the magic that had thrown them together was alive and coursing through their veins like lifeblood. Right here, right now … that was all that mattered.

Chapter Seven

CORNWALL

July 1944

'It's been four weeks since D-Day, Glad, and there's been no word. I can't eat, sleep, and hardly breathe for fretting about Harry.' Lamorna's stomach turned over for the umpteenth time as her imagination offered possible scenarios about what might have happened to her beloved fiancé. None of them good.

Gladys tossed her hair and sighed. 'You're such a worrier, Lamorna. I've not heard from Dwight either, but they'll be back. We have to believe it.'

Lamorna thought that not hearing from Dwight, who saw Gladys when he could be bothered, and not hearing from Harry, her fiancé who spent every second of his leave with her, who held her in his arms, kissed her until her lips were sore and whispered his undying love in her ear, were hardly the same thing. 'Hmm. But you know as well as I do that the Americans lost a lot of men. I overheard some soldiers talking about it the first week after.'

She got a withering glance from her friend as she helped Lamorna heave a hay bale onto the tractor. 'Never mind "hmm" and listening to gossip. They will both come back across the Channel as soon as they're allowed. Heavens, maid, they can't just storm the damned beach at Normandy, fight the Nazis off and then say, "Right, I'm off back to Cornwall for me tea," now, can they?' Gladys' eyes twinkled full of merriment as she stuck her hands on her hips and cocked her head to one side.

Lamorna realised Gladys could never understand what real love was like with Dwight, in the same way she could with Harry, that's why she found it all a big joke. Then she smiled, despite the situation. 'You've got hay in your hair.'

'What if I have?' Gladys plucked out the offending strand and waved it at Lamorna. 'You jealous?'

'No. I have my own here.' Lamorna laughed, sticking a few in her own hair. As they worked, she decided there was wisdom in believing everything would be okay, just as Gladys did. No use in worrying until there was something to worry about, her mum always said. But then again, the news broadcasts as well as those soldiers in the shop the other day, had said there had been lots of lives lost, despite it being a successful operation and getting Hitler on the run. 'I wonder if they knew they were going on the sixth of June?' she mused, staring out over the fields towards the ocean. 'I saw my Harry on the fourth, and he never said.'

Gladys signalled to the girl on the tractor to move off, and brushed her trousers clean of hay seeds. When the rumble of the engine had died down, she said, 'I do wonder about you sometimes, Lamorna. It would have been top secret, wouldn't it? Those lads would have only known at the last minute, and not a second before, to stop any news of the invasion getting out and back to the Jerries'

Indignant, Lamorna folded her arms and frowned at Gladys. 'It was hardly top secret, when locals have been talking about hidden landing craft up the River Fal, the Helford and God knows where else for weeks.'

'Yes. We all knew that's why the Yanks were here, but nobody would have known exactly what day they were going, would they?' She chewed thoughtfully on a stalk of hay. 'Nobody but the higher ups would have.'

Lamorna realised she was being silly and that Gladys was right, but she wished poor Harry had been more prepared. At least then they could have said a proper goodbye, instead of just 'see you in a few days'. It was a comfort to know they had said they loved each other, as they always did upon parting, though. The familiar tickling of tears started up and she swallowed hard to banish them. They refused to be banished though, and so she turned away and walked down the field to get away from Gladys and the other girls. Their laughter and idle chatter about day-to-day things grated on her nerves.

The hayfield, fence, farm buildings and blue of the ocean blurred into one as the tears fell, her imagination presenting various images of Harry, wounded on Omaha Beach ... all alone, bleeding and left for dead. Perhaps he was in a field hospital though, recovering and soon able to write? Or what if he was indeed mortally wounded? Did he think of her at the last moment? Would she actually know if he hadn't made it? They were united. As one. Her heart told her she would know if he were gone, because how could it keep on beating if his couldn't? A hand on her shoulder gave her a start and she turned to see Gladys behind her, a concerned expression on her pretty face.

'Come on, Morna. Buck up. It will all be right as rain.' She slipped her arm through Lamorna's. 'It's time to down tools. Let's go into Truro for a nice pastry if they have any, and a cuppa. We can even go to the camp again and see if there's been any news.'

Lamorna sniffed and dabbed a hanky under her eyes. 'We went last week and the week before. You know as well as I do that they aren't supposed to give information to anyone who isn't family.'

'Yes. But I think that tall fellow with the kind smile on the gate is often there on Wednesday. He's worth a try. He knew my Dwight too – saw 'em together in the pub more than once. Think he was called Bobby.'

Lamorna sighed. What harm would it do? At least it would take her mind off Harry being missing, or worse, for a while. Mum would be asking her to help in the kitchen too if she went home, and she needed a break. It was about time that little madam Wenna did a bit more around the place as well, now she was almost nine years old, instead of swanning off to the beach with her friends. Lamorna would sneak in and out without her mum knowing, otherwise she'd be put to work again. 'All right.' She smiled. 'I'll run home, get changed and meet you at the bus stop.'

The bustle and high spirits which surrounded Truro camp before D-Day had been absent since, and though soldiers still went in and out, on foot and in trucks, there seemed a quiet stillness about it now, and Lamorna felt that it wasn't just because there were far fewer men stationed there. It was as if the mourning and melancholy felt in the hearts of mothers, wives, and family of the fallen had found a home here. She shook herself. Her imagination needed reining in at the best of times, and this was certainly not one of those. Gladys, by her side and dressed to the nines as ever, grabbed her arm.

'Ooh, we're in luck. It's the tall Bobby one with a kind smile I mentioned earlier.'

'Let's hope he can tell us something,' Lamorna replied, not really thinking he would, but Gladys was hoping for the best, so she should too.

As they walked towards the soldier, he looked across at them and smiled, and a shiver ran down Lamorna's spine. While his smile was indeed kind, it was shaped by a dose of melancholy and sadness. Gladys, oblivious, put her hand on his arm and gave him her best dazzling smile. 'Hello again, I remember seeing you with my Dwight in the pub a few times. How are you? Bobby, isn't it?'

The soldier nodded and cleared his throat. He was nervous, and Lamorna tried to rein her imagination back again, but it was champing at the bit. 'Yeah, I'm Bobby. I remember you, honey ... you and Dwight were walking out.'

Lamorna noted the past tense 'were' but said nothing.

'Yes. I was wondering if you had heard any news of him, or of Lamorna here's Harry. Harry Marshall.'

He cleared his throat again. 'I'm not supposed to tell people news who aren't family, Ma'am.'

Gladys giggled. 'Ma'am. I do love that. But no need to be so formal, call me Gladys.'

'You do have news, then?' Lamorna interrupted.

'I'm afraid I can't say, Lamorna.' Bobby's face struggled between a frown and a smile and his cheeks reddened.

'I know you know something.' Gladys poked him cheekily on the arm and fluttered her eyelashes.

Oh for goodness sake. This is not the time or place for flirting. Lamorna grabbed Gladys's arm and made as if to leave. 'Thank you, Bobby. We don't want to get you in trouble, goodbye.'

Gladys shook her arm free. 'Hold up a minute.' She glared at Lamorna, revealing a glimpse of panic behind her eyes for a second. Perhaps she'd tuned into Bobby's nervousness and melancholy too. 'If you know something, please let us know. I promise nobody will hear it came from you.' Gladys draws her finger twice over her chest and holds Bobby's gaze. 'Cross my heart.'

Bobby looked around quickly and then stooped his shoulders and dipped his head towards them. 'Okay. Now this is not gonna be easy listening, honey,' he said to Gladys, and set his mouth into a grim line. Lamorna slipped her arm through Gladys's and felt a tremor run through her. 'I don't know about your Harry,' he directed at Lamorna, then switched his gaze back to Gladys. 'But I'm so sorry to have to tell you … that Dwight sadly didn't make it.'

Trembling, Gladys slumped against Lamorna, a low moan escaping as she shook her head. 'N … no. Noooo. He's coming back, you must have made a mistake,' she said to the floor, clutching her chest.

Bobby gave Lamorna a beseeching glance and stepped back. 'I'm so sorry, Gladys, there's no mistake.' He tossed a nervous glance behind through the camp gates and shook his head. 'I think you'd better take your friend home now, Ma'am.'

Lamorna nodded and slipped her arm around Gladys, who was sobbing and mumbling that there had been a mistake, and there must be hundreds of Dwights in the army. 'Come on, Glad. Let's get you home and I'll make you some hot sweet tea for the shock.'

'Tea? I don't want bloody tea! I want my Dwight!' She leaned against the wall and covered her face with her hands, tears escaping between her fingers.

———

Eventually, she allowed Lamorna to lead her down the hill and back to the bus stop. By the time the bus came, she was silent and pale-faced, apart from a few faded streaks of mascara. Lamorna noted she looked so young without her make-up, vulnerable and desperately sad. Lamorna's efforts to comfort her on the journey gained no response, and once she'd been delivered into her mother's care, Gladys never looked back as the door closed behind her.

The rainclouds that had threatened all day decided to shed a few tears too, as Lamorna trudged back up the lane to the farm. Poor Gladys. Underneath all her bravado, brash confidence, and devil-may-care attitude, it was clear from her reaction that she had loved Dwight very much. How utterly tragic that she'll never see his face again, never be held in his arms. Shame poked Lamorna's conscience when she thought of the high and mighty comparison she'd made in the field earlier, between her relationship with Harry and that of Gladys and Dwight. Imagining that Gladys couldn't know what real love was like. She made a promise never to judge anyone else in future, because how could she know what others really felt? The only thing she could be sure of was how she felt about Harry. Her darling American guy. Raindrops mingled with Lamorna's tears, and she sent a prayer heavenward, asking that she might be spared the same fate as Gladys, as she walked through the gate and up the path.

Wenna looked up from her book as she sat at the kitchen table, and her face became a mask of concern once she saw Lamorna. 'What's wrong, Morna?' She stood up and hurried over. 'You've been crying.'

The feel of Wenna's hand in hers and the concern in her eyes started Lamorna's tears again and she allowed herself to be led over to the comfy chair by the fireplace. She slumped down into it, her legs refusing to support her any longer. 'Why is life so bloody cruel?' she asked the cracked flagstone at her feet, trying to stem a torrent of tears with a hankie.

'What's happened?' Wenna asked, patting her big

sister's back. When no response was forthcoming, she added, 'I'll get you some hot sweet tea.'

Lamorna was tempted to repeat Gladys's reply from earlier today when Lamorna had mentioned tea to her, but that would hurt Wenna. The poor girl was trying her best to help. 'Thank you,' she managed with a sigh.

'I've put three sugars in. Best not tell Mum, or she'll start moaning about rationing again.' Wenna tried a little laugh as she handed Lamorna a cup of tea, and then grew serious as she sat opposite on the old three-legged milking stool. 'Is it bad news about your Harry?' Lamorna took a sip of the tea and pulled a face. Heck, that was sweet. She took a few more sips and felt a rush of energy reviving her spirits a little. 'No, it's Dwight.' Lamorna told her sister what had happened and then a huge sigh escaped her. 'I suppose I'm crying for poor Dwight, for Glad ... and for me and Harry too. What if Harry didn't make it either?' She felt her throat closing over again so took more tea.

'He will be all right,' Wenna said, without much conviction. 'Best thing to do is hope for the best, put your faith in God and just keep going.'

Lamorna looked up from her cup, and her heart squeezed at her little sister's earnest expression. A nine-year-old shouldn't have to live through so much misery and anguish. Never knowing from one day to the next what would happen and worrying about an uncertain future. Thank goodness they didn't live in a big city, where so many lives had been lost in the horrific bombings during the Blitz. 'That's all any of us can do, eh, maid?' Lamorna took Wenna's hand. 'Thanks for being so kind and looking after me.'

Wenna blushed. 'You used to look after me enough times when I was little. I loved the days we spent on the beach...' Wenna looked away to hide the upwelling of tears in her big blue eyes. 'You'll be gone across the sea though, if Harry's all right and you get married... I'll never see you again.'

This was something that had been buzzing round and round in Lamorna's head for the past few years like a swarm of angry bees. The thought of leaving her parents, brother and sister thousands of miles away had become like a physical weight in her chest. But what was the alternative? A wife must follow their husband, she supposed. That was how things worked. And her family wouldn't come with her, would they? Desperate to cheer her sister up she said, 'Maybe you could come and stay for a while, when you're a little older?'

This seemed to do the trick, as her sister turned a beaming face towards her. However, Wenna's sunny expression lasted only moments before dark clouds rolled in. 'But when would that be? Years, I'll bet,' she snapped, folding her arms across her chest. If looks could have killed, Lamorna would be dead. Wenna stamped her foot. 'It wouldn't be the same as living here anyway. You'll forget all about me. I'm just a silly child after all!'

'Hey, where has this come from? You're not a silly child.' Lamorna went to take Wenna's hands in hers, but she flapped them away.

'You said it to Mum once. I was coming downstairs and I

heard you. You were moaning that you had to take care of me for her one afternoon.'

Had she? Lamorna couldn't remember, but it wouldn't be hard to imagine. She had definitely resented having to be a babysitter a few years ago. But then when she'd spent time with her sister, normally on the beach, it had been fun overall. 'If I said that, I'm sorry. It must have been years back and I was just being a silly goose. I love having you as my sister, honest.' Lamorna hoped her earnest and heartfelt words were accepted. Poor maid had obviously been harbouring the hurtful things Lamorna had said all this time.

Wenna shook her head. 'As I told you just before, I loved being on the beach with you, but the truth was, I knew you didn't really want me. I was just a pain in the neck. Seems everybody thinks so. You're always the favourite with Mum and Dad. Even over our Tony. Grandma Mary liked you best too.'

Lamorna's mouth dropped open in shock. 'That's not true, Wenna,' she said, once again trying to take her sister's hands in hers without success. 'Our parents love us all the same.'

'No, they don't. I overheard Mum tell Aunty Zelah when she'd had a sherry or two last Christmas that she had been too old to have me.' Wenna frowned. 'Something about she should have kept her legs closed that night, but I don't know what that had to do with it.' She shrugged. 'Anyway, that's what I heard … that Mum never wanted me.'

Oh no! Poor little mite. Mum never could hold her

drink. Now what? Taking a deep breath, she tried to steer this floundering little ship into calmer waters. 'Mum loves you.' Lamorna gave Wenna an encouraging smile. 'I overheard her saying to our dad the other day what an angel you are, when you'd brought the washing in without being asked.'

Wenna brightened. 'Did she?'

Well, not quite. What Mum had actually said was at last the little minx was pulling her weight round the place, but Lamorna thought 'angel' was a better choice of word under the circumstances. 'Yes. So I think what she said at Christmas was just the sherry talking. Perhaps Mum's worried about getting old and not being able to do things as she used to.' Lamorna stood up and smoothed her hair. 'Right. Do you want to help me finish making that skirt I've been working on? You have nimble fingers and make lovely neat stitches.'

Wenna heaved a big 'put upon' sigh in a show of pretence, but her act couldn't cover the obvious pride in her eyes. 'All right … I'm not doing anything, so I suppose I could give you a hand.'

———

Three long weeks had dragged by since they discovered Dwight was gone, and there was still no sign of Harry. After work one day, Lamorna decided she couldn't face going straight home and getting on with helping Mum make tea, or bringing the washing in like always. Her mind was too full of 'what if's and unwelcome images, so she needed to clear her head. If only Grandma Mary were alive. She'd be just the person to share her woes with. Alongside a sharp pang of grief, an idea of how to almost make that happen came to her, and so Lamorna hurried across the fields back to the farmhouse and sneaked in the side door. Mum was in the garden chatting to one of their neighbours, so once she'd changed her boots and washed her face, Lamorna escaped again.

The hedgerows and coast path were alive with a show of late summer colour, and Lamorna was able to harvest a beautiful bouquet of pink thrift, white and yellow ox-eye daisies, and red valerian, along her route to the little chapel on the hill. The old stone building faced the ocean, resolute and strong, despite having a salt wind and storms hurled at its doors for hundreds of years. Lamorna liked to think that the hopes, fears, happiness and tears of those who had worshipped here were collected in its walls and always remembered. So many people over the years had sought sanctuary here, or celebrated a wedding or a birth. She placed the palm of her hand on the sun-warmed Cornish stone and closed her eyes. Even though it was just a man-made structure, it felt like a living, breathing entity.

Lamorna smiled, feeling the calm and peace of the place permeating every inch of her, and for the first time in weeks she was able to relax a little. Her shoulders came down from somewhere around her ears, and she released a long, slow breath. Around the corner behind the chapel was a small, well-kept graveyard where the late afternoon sunlight covered the ancient headstones in a soft ochre blanket. Under an ancient oak tree, a newer headstone nestled in the dappled emerald and gold light filtering through the leaves. Lamorna made her way towards it and knelt, placing her wildflower bouquet gently down upon the grave.

Mary Williams 1873 – 1942
Beloved Mother, Wife, and Grandmother
Gone, but never forgotten. Always in our hearts.

Lamorna smiled through her tears and traced her finger across the word 'Grandmother'. Once she'd regained some composure she said, 'Hello, Grandma Mary. I know it's been a few months since I popped up here, but I have been as busy as ever with the Land Army. That bloody Hitler fellow as you called him is still causing merry hell, but D-Day has sent him running from France. There's hope that this will be the beginning of the end for the evil monsters.'

Lamorna brushed a few dried leaves from around the headstone. 'Poor Dwight, Gladys's fellow, didn't make it … and my Harry went to France too … but he…' She stopped, unable to get her words past the lump in her throat for a few moments. 'He didn't come back and nobody seems to know where he is.' She looked up through the leaves at the clouds drifting across the bright blue sky. 'Oh, Grandma Mary … I don't know what I'll do if he…' A sob choked off her remaining words and she was helpless to do anything other than allow her tears to flow unchecked, rocking gently back and forth, her arms wrapped tightly around herself.

As if in answer, the wind soughed in the trees, and a sense of calm filled her heart with hope. Gooseflesh ran the length of her forearms and she felt a smile lift the corners of her mouth. Was this Grandma Mary's way of telling her everything would be well? That her beloved Harry wasn't dead? 'Please let it be true, Grandma Mary,' Lamorna whispered, kissing the palm of her hand and pressing it to the headstone. 'I love you and miss you every day. And thank you for listening.'

Lamorna stayed in quiet contemplation a while, until the nip of a chill wind at her cheeks made her realise the weather was turning. Above her head the sky had swapped blue for grey and a flurry of raindrops spattered the ground. Saying her goodbyes to Grandma Mary, she brushed earth from her knees, and set off for home.

'Oh, there you are!' her mum said, as soon as she set foot in the farmhouse kitchen. 'I realised you sneaked in and out while I was chatting to Hettie earlier, because your mucky work boots were in the hall.'

Lamorna noted her mum's stance. Folded arms, narrowed eyes, pursed lips. She couldn't be doing with a grilling right now, not after the uplifting experience she'd just had with her gran. Sticking out her chin she said, 'Yeah, I hurried in and out and then went to see Grandma Mary. I've not been up to see her for a while. It helped to talk to her about Harry and poor Dwight.'

Her mum's expression softened and she heaved a sigh. 'Yes, I know it's a worry for you. And my heart goes out to poor Glad… How many more will this damned war take, eh?' Lamorna frowned as her mum pulled a brown envelope out of her apron pocket and held it out to her with a shaking hand. 'This came for you this morning, but I couldn't give it to you when you got in, because you went straight out again.'

Lamorna's stomach clenched, then plummeted, and her heart raced like the clappers. *Oh God. Please no. Not Harry. Please God not Harry.* The small part of her mind that was able to think logically told her she wouldn't have got a letter informing her of Harry's death, because she wasn't next of kin, or family. But all she could see in her blurred vision, despite the feeling of calm she'd had at the chapel, was Harry on some blood-soaked beach, pale, alone, lifeless. She gripped the edge of the table and lowered her shaking body onto a chair. 'Oh, Mum … do you think it's bad news?'

Pensive, her mum pressed her lips together and then an encouraging smile lifted her expression. 'I don't know, love. Let's hope not. But until you open it, we'll never know, will we? Come on, maid, be brave.' She placed the envelope on the table and poured out a mug of tea from the old brown teapot, and put a heaped teaspoon of sugar into it.

The fact that Lamorna had talked of making hot sweet tea for Gladys wasn't lost on her, neither was the reason for it, and a wave of nausea crashed through her. As if in a trance, she watched her fingers pick up the envelope and turn it over. Her name and address had been typed neatly and the stamp was marked Portsmouth. Portsmouth? Now where had she heard that mentioned recently? Then it came to her. One of the soldiers she'd overheard in the shop had said that many of the soldiers who'd been wounded in Normandy had been shipped from field hospitals there, to hospitals in England ... and Portsmouth was one of them.

She mentioned this to her mum, and then stared back at the envelope. Were they writing to tell her Harry was okay, or had Harry told them her address and name before he ... and asked them to write to her if...?

'Come on, Morna. Open it ... or do you want me to?' Her mum came and sat next to her, slipping a hand into hers.

Lamorna could only nod and pushed the envelope towards her. 'Please.' Her mum heaved a sigh as heavy as the dark clouds outside, and quickly pulled out the letter. Her eyebrows raised and her lips moved as she read, spelling out the words to herself, as she never had been a fast reader. Time stood still, the beat of Lamorna's heart keeping pace with the drumming rain on the window. She could stand it no longer. 'Mum!' she cried. 'Tell me. Is Harry alive?'

Chapter Eight

Lamorna's mum looked up from the letter, flapped it at her daughter and smiled. 'Yes, thank God. Your Harry is alive!'

Lamorna's heart rose up from her boots and a rush of joy spread though her body so fast it made her head swim. 'Oh, Mum.' She looked at the letter but didn't take it, in case by some nightmare it was an hallucination. 'I can't believe it, after Gladys losing her Dwight, I thought...'

'I know. Here, read the bloomin' letter, girl.'

Lamorna wiped her eyes with the back of her sleeve and took the letter with the words 'Portsmouth Hospital' in the top right corner.

Dear Miss Williams,

I am writing to inform you that your fiancée, Harry Marshall, is alive and recovering in our hospital. He asked me to let you know, as he knew you would be anxious about his welfare. Harry was injured in Normandy, and was in a field hospital for a while, before being shipped back here. He has a number of injuries, one to his right arm and hand, which has prevented him writing to you himself. He would be very grateful if you could visit as soon as you can. Our address is at the top of this letter.

Very best wishes,

J.P. Carstairs. Matron.

'He's alive…' Lamorna whispered, still not able to believe the evidence of her own eyes, which scanned the words over and over, as if they held some hidden clue. Then a rush of joy surged through her veins and sent her heart into overdrive. 'He's alive!' Jumping up, she grabbed her mum's hand and shook it up and down, as she did a little jig on the flagstone kitchen floor.

'Yes, I've just told you that!' Her mum laughed, pulling her hand free. 'I expect you'll be off tomorrow, will you? I can lend you some money, if your savings from Grandma Mary are a little low—'

'—Off where?'

A puzzle furrowed her mum's brow. 'Portsmouth, silly.'

'Yes, Portsmouth,' Lamorna heard herself say, a dreamlike quality to her voice. It all seemed so unreal. How would she get there? She'd never been outside the county before. And to do her first trip away all by herself was sending a few bird-sized butterflies flapping around her belly. Then a thought of Harry and his fellow soldiers running into machine-gun fire on Omaha Beach snapped her out of it. If he could face that, she was damned sure she could take a lone trip to Portsmouth.

'I'll pitch in with the Land Army work, and I'm sure your friends will too, while you're gone. You should start getting ready, instead of standing there catching flies.'

'Hmm?' Lamorna was wondering what she would find when she saw Harry again. How badly injured was her poor darling?

'You need to get your clothes sorted out, make sure you have enough clean smalls for a few days. That kind of thing. You'll have to get a lodging house too, once you're there.'

'Lodging house?'

'Yes. A room to sleep in.' Her mum shook her head and clicked her tongue. Then she got up and took her hand. 'Come along with me. Big as you are, I can see you still need your mother to look after you and get you organised.'

The sun came out of a cloud as Lamorna stepped off the train, and looked at the address of the hospital she'd scribbled on a bit of paper. It's a wonder she didn't have it stamped on her memory, the times she'd read and re-read the thing. The journey had been fine, but her stomach still kept tying and untying itself, ever since she'd left home, what with worrying about Harry, and being off on her own for the first time in her life. Drawing a breath of smoky steam and train-oil into her lungs, she set off in search of the ticket office. Her mum had said they'd know how far the hospital was, and if she'd have to get a bus or not.

The ticket office wasn't busy, thank goodness, and a kind-faced lady stood behind the counter. Lamorna cleared her throat, pushed her shoulders back and pretended to be Gladys. Unfortunately, a memory of her friend the last time she'd seen her presented a broken and grief-stricken image, so Lamorna pushed it away and decided to be herself, instead. 'Hello, I was wondering if you could tell me if the hospital is far away from here, and if I'd need a bus?'

'You would need a bus. But luckily one stops right outside here, and will take you about ten minutes or so to get there. Here, I'll write down the number and an alternative in case you miss it.'

Lamorna gave her a relieved smile. People were just as helpful in Portsmouth as they were at home. Before she could stop herself, she blurted out her reason for visiting and that she was a bit nervous, especially about finding somewhere to stay. 'I don't suppose you know of a lodging house near the hospital, do you?'

'I do as it happens. My Auntie Vi owns one. I'll write the address of that too – just say Katherine sent you.'

'Oh, thank you so much. You have been a godsend.'

Katherine smiled. 'I do my best, love. Hope your Harry is on the mend soon.'

As Lamorna walked up the driveway to the grand red-brick hospital, the buoyant mood she'd enjoyed since arriving began to deflate little by little, and as she opened the big doors, it had all but disappeared. Her mum's words came back to her as she asked for Harry at the desk. *Now, maid. Be prepared for anything. Your Harry won't be exactly the same, you know. He might not carry some awful scars, but then again, he might. You have to be ready. Because if he sees your face fall, that will wound him more than any bullet.*

Lamorna remembered her Uncle Fred, her mum's elder brother, whose face had been scarred after the Great War, but it healed after a fashion. He'd never recovered from the scars that nobody could see, though. Those scars gave him fits in his sleep and her Auntie Dot had been woken many a night by his blood-curdling screams, as he'd fought again in those blood-soaked trenches in his nightmares. Lamorna's mum had been convinced that's what led to his fatal stroke a few years ago. Her own dad had fought too, but he never talked about it.

This will not do. I need to be strong for my Harry and thinking like this is doing the opposite, she told herself, as the nurse gave her directions to the garden. The garden? Well, that was encouraging, wasn't it? If Harry was in the garden, he couldn't be as bad as she'd imagined. Not a pale wraith in a hospital gown in a bed, tucked in tight at the corners, helpless as a baby. Nevertheless, until she saw him, she wasn't going to count her chickens. *Now, maid. Be prepared for anything.*

The sun-drenched grounds were lush with verdant lawns, and a riot of late summer flowers. Lamorna's heart lifted as she saw patients in bath chairs pushed by nurses along the winding paths, patients on benches under shady trees reading books or newspapers, patients playing cards on a table set out on a paved area by the grand doors, and members of staff serving tea, or helping patients to exercise with the aid of sticks and walking frames. Which one was her Harry? Shading her eyes from the sun, she cast about for a blond head, an easy smile, a flash of those baby blues in that handsome face. *Be prepared for anything.*

Her heart knew before she did. It leapt and bounded like a greyhound itching to race, even as she squinted at a man sitting in a bath chair, under a spreading chestnut tree a little way off down the hill. His left leg was extended along a board attached to the chair, and looked to be in plaster, and his right arm was bandaged. The sunlight danced in his golden hair; he was reading so she couldn't see the blue of his eyes... Was it him? She should go nearer to be absolutely sure, but her heart was having none of it, impatiently tugging at the leash, and so were her feet. They acted together, heart and feet hurrying her forward down the hill, her mind whirling, her head giddy.

The man looked up when she was a few feet away, a flash of blue, his face a question mark. Then he smiled in that long slow sweet way of his. Yes, yes, it was Harry. Her Harry. And he bore no scars, well, not physical ones. A sob left her as she closed the gap and knelt at his feet, his face a blur now, as her tears flowed unchecked. 'Lamorna. Gee, Lamorna. It's really you...' Harry's voice trembled with wonder and he took her hand in his.

'Yes, Harry. Yes, it's me. Thank God we're together again. I have been out of my mind with worry.'

'I bet. I wasn't well enough to let you know before the other day, and I couldn't write myself because of this.' He held up his bandaged hand and arm. 'But I'm getting better now. I might even be able to walk with a stick in a few months, the doctor said.'

Lamorna found a handkerchief in her bag and dabbed at her eyes. A glance at his neck and right ear revealed that he'd not got away scar-free after all. The skin was red and bumpy as if it had been in contact with maybe a chemical, or fire. *Don't let him see you're shocked.* Ignoring his neck, she asked, 'What happened to your poor arm and leg?'

Harry sighed. 'The leg got machine-gunned and the shin and thigh bone were splintered in eight different places. The doc said it was a hell of a job to patch it up again.' She watched his Adam's apple bob and he blinked rapidly. Lamorna had to take a deep breath to stop herself collapsing in floods of tears. 'The arm and hand … and my neck and ear were burnt. A Jeep was hit and exploded nearby as we ran up the beach … the flames caught me.' He looked away across the lawn to the men shouting and laughing at the card table. 'It's not pretty, as you can see. My arm and hand are a lot worse.'

Lamorna wanted to rage, cry, curse, rail at the unfairness and brutality of the damned war, against all the tragedies, all the sadness and grief. But she couldn't, because instinct told her he needed her to be strong. 'Oh, Harry, my love,' she whispered, stroking his cheek. 'I wish I could make it all go away. You've suffered so much.'

'Yes, but I'll pull through. So many others had it worse, or didn't make it. You…' His voice caught and he shook his head, looked into the distance at some horror she couldn't share. 'You wouldn't believe the things I saw.'

Lamorna squeezed his good hand and gently kissed his lips. 'Talk to me about it if it helps.'

'No. I want to try and put it out of my mind and you

certainly don't need the burden of that knowledge, honey.' Harry looked at her and then away, speaking to the leaves whispering in the light breeze above their heads. 'I wondered about not contacting you at all. Now I'm injured and scarred, it didn't seem fair to hold you to our engagement. But I was too much of a coward to let you go without a word. My heart wouldn't let me.' When he held her eyes again, she could see them glistening. 'I promise you that if you do want to call it a day, I will certainly understand. No hard feelings and—'

His words were stopped by her finger on his lips. 'Don't you dare try to get rid of me Harry Marshall.' Lamorna swallowed down an ocean of tears. 'I'm your fiancée, I love you and one day we'll be married, just like we planned.'

Harry blew his nose and cleared his throat. 'But my scars and—'

'You are just as handsome as you ever were. And as I said, I love you. More so if that's possible, because of what you've been through. You've come back to me, Harry. Not everyone is as lucky. Poor Dwight didn't make it. Gladys is devastated. We're the lucky ones. It might not seem like it right now, but your arm and leg will heal, and the scars on your neck will fade more. You've been through hell and out the other side… I want to help you get better, Harry. I'm not going anywhere.'

Harry made a choking noise in his throat, drew her close with his good arm, and planted kisses on her cheeks, neck and a long lingering one on her lips. 'What did I do to deserve you, huh?' he whispered into her ear.

'What did I do to deserve you, you mean?' She kissed

him hard on the mouth, pouring all her longing, passion and relief into it, until she felt as if they were soaring up into the treetops.

When they came up for air, Harry grinned. 'Boy, I'm feeling better already.'

She laughed. 'Me too.'

'If you're sure you wanna be my wife, what say we get married as soon as we can? I know the US Army are giving GI brides free passage to the States. I guess I'll be shipped home soon, 'cos I'm no good to the war like this.'

Lamorna's heart sailed beyond the trees and up to the heavens. It was a shock to think she could be married so soon, and even more of a shock to think she'd be so quickly setting out for a whole new life across the Atlantic. But it didn't upset her. She wasn't scared. Her overwhelming feeling was one of joy. This must be the right thing to do. Her heart belonged to this man and he belonged in America. Therefore, they belonged there together.

She took his lovely face between her two hands and said, 'Let's do it.'

Chapter Nine

'I 'm so glad you're my chief bridesmaid. Do you hear me? I'm *glad*, Glad,' Lamorna said, tempering her tearful show of emotion with humour.

'I'm glad too.' Gladys dabbed a handkerchief at the corners of her eyes. 'But then you know my name's Glad, we've been friends for years.' A cheeky smirk completed their double act and Gladys concentrated on making sure the veil was straight over Lamorna's hair.

Lamorna could hardly believe this day had come so quickly. The past few months had flown, the lush green countryside giving way to the first russet brush strokes of autumn. Her mum had said September would be a lovely month for a wedding because it would hopefully be fine, yet without the heat of summer. Lamorna looked at her bouquet of red and white roses and thought about the day she'd told her parents about Harry's suggestion. She'd said she didn't want a fussy wedding, as it had been sprung on them very quickly, but Dad had said they had been putting a bit by for this day for a very long time.

'No daughter of mine is having less than everything she wants – shortages and rationing permitting,' he'd said, his eyes glistening.

Lamorna had never seen her dad show much emotion, and as she remembered it now, she saw her eyes fill again as they looked back at her from the full-length mirror in her bedroom. Her dark curls had been tamed into a chignon, a slick of pink lipstick enhanced her 'rosebud mouth' as Grandma Mary had described it, and a touch of mascara opened up her hazel eyes, now bright with standing tears. She dabbed them with a hanky. If she didn't stop getting emotional, the mascara would run down her cheeks. Not the look she'd been going for.

The dress was exactly what she'd been going for, however. Lamorna turned to the side and back again, loving the way the sleek 1920s style clung in all the right places. It was perfect, cream and white lace with a heart-shaped neckline, and, best of all, it had been her mum's. Her mum said they could afford the material to make a new one, if it wasn't running short like everything else, but Lamorna wouldn't hear of it. This was the dress her mum had worn on her wedding day. If it was good enough for her, it was good enough for Lamorna. If her marriage to Harry was half as happy as her parents' had been, they would be very lucky.

Gladys stopped fussing with the veil, smoothed her pale blue dress and looked at her watch. 'It's about that time, Morna.'

Heaving a sigh, Lamorna said to her reflection and Gladys behind, 'Will I do?'

'You'll more than do. I hope I look half as beautiful, if I ever get married.'

Gladys's smile looked uncertain and then turned upside down. She pretended to fuss with the veil again, but Lamorna could tell she was fighting to keep her emotions in check. Dwight must be on her mind. Guilty, because all she held in her heart was happy anticipation of the ceremony to come, she turned and placed a kiss on Gladys's cheek. 'Your day will come, my dear.'

She received one of her friend's trademark theatrically bright smiles, which swept any trace of sadness from her expression. 'Yes, of course it will. Farmer Bill has asked me to the dance next week at the village hall. He's quite a catch, so I might be joining you up the aisle before the year's out.'

'Farmer Bill?' Lamorna asked, aghast. Farmer Bill was in his fifties at the very least.

'Yes.' Gladys frowned. Then she must have caught on, because she added, 'Not old Farmer Bill, silly. His son's called Bill, too.'

Lamorna laughed. 'You mean William? Now he is a catch, very handsome.'

'Well, I call him Bill, and he seems to like it.' Gladys fluttered her eyelashes and patted her hair.

'You're a real tonic, Glad. Don't ever change.'

As they linked arms and walked to the stairs, Lamorna had to swallow hard. The big black cloud that had been hovering over her for the past few months was back, and with it an added threat of thunder. Not for the first time, she wished Harry was English, because there were so many people she'd have to leave behind. Mum, Dad, Wenna, Tony, Gladys and all the people living in the village she'd known all her life. Every time the cloud had appeared she'd thrown sunshine thoughts at it, scared it off with imaginings of making a home in America with her beloved. But it was too real now. By the end of next week, she'd be gone. Far away from her loved ones, and God knew when she'd ever see them again.

Wenna was waiting in the kitchen, a posy of wildflowers in her hand and wearing a blue dress matching Gladys's. She had an unreadable expression on her face as Lamorna walked towards her. 'How's my chief bridesmaid then? All ready?' she asked with a bright smile.

A frown and a pout were Wenna's response. 'I'm not your chief bridesmaid though, am I? I heard Gladys bragging to Hettie next door that she was chief.'

'You both are. Now, come on, let's get on the wedding tractor. Dad and Gladys are waiting.' Lamorna held on to her smile, though she could see Wenna was on the edge of one of her outbursts.

'How can we both be chief? One has to be in charge.'

'Wenna, come on. Don't spoil things, you're in charge, okay?' Lamorna said through gritted teeth and held out her hand.

Wenna ignored her sister's hand, blinked back tears and shook her head. 'I always spoil things. Mum said so the other day. That's why you're happy to leave me here while you go off to the other side of the world.'

Lamorna's heart squeezed as she saw a huge tear escape Wenna's eye and roll down her cheek. She had to swallow hard as an image of them both playing on the beach when Wenna had been a toddler surfaced in her mind. Happy days. Carefree days. Before Hitler made the whole world go to war. Lamorna took Wenna's face in her two hands and made her look at her. 'That's not true. I'm going to be so sad to leave you all. My heart's breaking over it. You have to believe that.'

Wenna wiped away her tears. 'All right. Will you take me with you, then? America looks so much more fun than here in this boring old village.'

Lamorna couldn't bear the look of hope on her sister's earnest little face. 'You've only seen Hollywood films, maid. Real life won't be so glamorous, I'll bet.'

'But everyone says it's full of adventure and opportunity. Crikey, even their anthem says it's the land of the free and the home of the brave.'

Mindful of the time, and the fact that no matter what she said next, her little sister would end up being disappointed, Lamorna offered, 'Let's see what the next few years bring, hmm? When this damned war's over and you're a bit older, you can come—'

'That won't happen! You'll just forget me,' Wenna cried, rushing past and out through the kitchen door to the waiting wedding tractor and flower-bedecked trailer.

Lamorna's heart went out to Wenna, but there was nothing she could do to change the situation. America was going to be Lamorna's new home and Wenna would have to stay behind. The bride-to-be took a deep breath and followed on, hoping that her little sister would see sense and be happy for her in the end.

Harry looked so handsome in his uniform as he turned and smiled at her, standing at the end of the aisle, leaning on a stick. His walking had improved no end and the bandage on his burnt arm wasn't wrapped as thickly as it once was. Lamorna had seen it when it had been dressed by a local nurse, and it wasn't pretty. The pink skin looked as if it had melted, and the middle and index fingers of his right hand reminded her of a lobster claw, the way the skin had fused over them. But he was getting strength back, slowly but surely, and he was hoping he'd eventually be able to handle the fishing nets when they got back home to Gloucester, Massachusetts.

In the old chapel by the sea, which their family had attended for generations, and where Grandma Mary lay under the oak tree, Lamorna's dad squeezed her hand, and then slipped into a pew beside her mum. The sound of her mum sniffing into a hanky did nothing to halt the swell of emotion tightening her throat and threatening to ruin her mascara. Then everything became a blur as she gazed into Harry's sea-blue eyes. As they said their vows, she looked at her hand in his, and felt the cool metal of the wedding ring slipping onto her finger. That was it. They were officially man and wife. Harry's lips found hers and sent her heart soaring to the rafters. Then as her family and friends looked on, smiling, the organ played them out into the crisp September afternoon.

———————

This couldn't be really happening, could it? Her parents stood on the platform, both wearing identical pale and pinched expressions, except her mum's had added tears streaming down her face. Her dad cleared his throat and pulled his wife tightly to him, and she leaned against him, trembling so much that her skirt hem jiggled against her legs. Tony, stoic as always, looked at the train, feigning interest in the sighs of steam escaping from the chimneys, the machine an image of a dragon at rest, and lastly Wenna, glowering at everything and everyone, except her big sister. Lamorna couldn't get eye contact with her at all, let alone a conversation. In the days after the wedding she had tried to get Wenna to understand why she was leaving them all behind, but though her sister had been civil, there was a new distance between them which, try as she might, Lamorna couldn't bridge. Maybe Lamorna would wake from a dream any second now and find that it wasn't time to get on the train and leave for the ship that would take her and her husband across the sea, away from Cornwall and English shores. Away from everything and everyone she had ever known.

Her stomach rolled as if they were already at sea, and an ache started up in her heart. If she had to put a name to it, she'd call it melancholy. A longing for the old days, when

Grandma Mary was alive, when everything had been simpler, where the first war was just a memory, and the present one not dreamt of. But then she wouldn't have her Harry, would she? Despair flowed through her, pulling frustration in its wake. Why couldn't she have fallen for a local man? If she had, she'd be able to stay with her family. Her parents would become grandparents, see her children grow. Spoil them with sweeties and cake ... but who knew if they would ever meet? It all became too much, and she leaned her head on Harry's lapel, sobs wracking her frame.

'Oh, Lamorna, my girl. Don't go upsetting yourself, now,' Lamorna's dad said, patting her shoulder. She could hear echoing sobs from her mum and turned into the tight embrace of both parents. Over their shoulders, through her tears, she saw Wenna brushing off Tony's hand of comfort, her face stone-hard.

Harry patted the shoulders of her parents and said, 'This is a sad time for everyone, but I promise that once we've saved up the fare, we'll bring you over to stay with us and my family. My parents can't wait to meet you.'

'I'll save our own fare, boy,' Lamorna's dad said, thickly. 'You'll be needing that money to get a house settled.'

Harry nodded. 'How about we both save, sir? We're family now. We'll all work towards the same goal.' He stuck out his left hand and her dad shook it. Both men looked too full of emotion to speak.

Lamorna stepped over to Wenna, wiping her eyes. 'I'll miss you, little sister. But I promise we'll meet again, as Vera Lynn says.' Her theatrical beaming smile obviously needed work, as Wenna just folded her arms and looked the other away. 'Honestly. It might not be for a while, but we will see each other and—' Lamorna's words died in her throat as Wenna stalked off along the platform, nose in the air.

'Little madam, she'll get a piece of my mind when we get back,' her mum said.

'She's upset, Margaret. She's only ten and losing her big sister,' her dad said.

Her mum's answer was to blow her nose and lean her head against her husband's shoulder. 'I'm losing my daughter, Albert. But we have to learn to accept it and wish her all the happiness.' She looked at Lamorna. 'Because you deserve it.' Then she patted Harry's shoulder. 'You both do.'

Tony stepped in for a hug and then shook Harry's hand. 'Look after yourselves, eh? We'll definitely meet again, little sis.'

This set Lamorna off again, and then her heart jumped in her chest when the guard blew his shrill whistle and yelled the immortal words, 'All aboard!'

Once aboard, Harry stowed their luggage and quickly pushed the train window down to wave to her parents and brother, huddled there together on the platform like abandoned puppies. Lamorna tried to smile, but it kept wobbling and sliding off her face. Valiantly, she wiped her eyes free of tears, because she wanted to remember this moment. Wanted to imprint the faces of her lovely family onto her brain – to keep this memory as clear as a framed photograph, that she could take out and look at whenever she felt homesick.

The whistle shrilled again as the dragon woke, stretched its stiff limbs and, with a series of clanks and steam exhalations, slowly chuffed off along the track. Her mum waved her hanky and smiled bravely though her tears, her dad nodded, a little smile playing over his lips, and Tony grinned and blew a kiss. Lamorna hung out of the window waving and blowing kisses, all the time hoping that Wenna would come running for one last goodbye. But hope died as she watched her little group grow tiny, and suddenly disappear from view as the track took a westward turn.

Wenna

June 1954

C ome on, Wenna. You have to let yourself go and believe in it all, or you might as well just go home. With this self-admonishment echoing around her head, Wenna picks her way across the last patch of slippery seaweed and follows a damp path around the rocks, until finally she's striding across the smooth dark sand at the water's edge. In the velvet inky black sky, suspended by a thousand stars, the June moon hangs large, round and as shiny as a new coin. A gentle wind blows a few threads of dark cloud across its face, but it's no match for the mercury moonlight.

Wenna cannot tear her gaze away from the heavens, as a frisson of excitement ignites her insides and she hugs herself in anticipation of what she's about to do. The waves wash over her bare toes, frothy as wedding lace, and she inhales a deep breath of salt air. There are a few shreds of doubt still lurking around, unwelcome as a snow in harvest, because her mum and Grandma Mary were unsuccessful in their quests. Lamorna wasn't, was she, though? No. A familiar pang of jealousy brings a few uncharitable thoughts to the fore. But then Lamorna wouldn't be, would she? Lamorna is successful at everything she does. Look at her now – a lovely husband, a home by the sea, she's teaching part-time in a school and has two beautiful children to complete the perfect picture.

Wenna's life is far from perfect. Nineteen years old, spending her days tending farm animals and driving a tractor. No excitement or adventure in *her* life, was there? No. Unless she counted the village dance every four weeks, dancing with the same few uninspiring partners, and a visit to Redruth to have her hair done once a fortnight with her friend Maggie. They even had a cup of tea and a slice of cake in the Corner House Tearooms sometimes. *Be still my beating heart.* Wenna exhales a long breath and with it tries to banish any unwelcome thoughts of self-pity. This was her chance to make a change for the better. All she has to do is believe in the old magic. The old wives' tales, the local legend… Like Lamorna had once told her – as Grandma Mary had before her – it was no good only half believing, or nothing would come of it.

With the shush of the incoming waves in her ears the only sound breaking the stillness of the night, and the prickle of gooseflesh along her forearms, Wenna has to admit it was easy to believe. Does she really want to find a sweetheart? Yes, she really does. But is there someone out there who is meant for her alone? She's always felt as if she was never good enough. Second best – or even third best after Tony. Why should anyone want her? Gazing out to where the moon is busy tipping a thin line of glittering light across the horizon, she slips an old lemonade bottle from her bag. Years ago, Lamorna gave her a copy of the words she and Grandma Mary said to the moon, and she pulls the bit of paper they're written on from her pocket.

Swallowing down a knot of emotion, as the hairs rise along the back of her neck, she draws herself up and says in a steady clear voice, '*I give my words to the grace of the moon, the power of the ocean, and the magic of nature. Please grant me the things I truly deserve.*'

For good measure, she holds the bottle up to the moonlight shimmering along its curves and kisses its flank. 'Safe journey, little bottle. I believe in you and the power of this sacred place. Let me have a bit of Lamorna's luck...' Sudden tears block her speech for a moment. 'I know I don't deserve it because I have jealous thoughts about her. And even though I won't answer her letters, I do miss her and love her deep down.' Unable to say more, as hope swells in her chest, she kisses the bottle again and tosses it into the waves. Wenna crosses her fingers and offers up a silent prayer as she watches the little dark shape bobbing along the path of moonlight towards the far horizon.

Chapter Ten

CORNWALL

Present day

I poke a finger through the hole in the knee of my jeans and wonder if it could be classed as fashionable. It's a hole after all, not a rip. People wear 'ripped' jeans, not 'holed' ones. And by people, I mean youngsters. I'll be knocking on the door of forty next year. Is that still young enough to wear ripped jeans? The thing is, right now, it's still a hole, not a rip. Hmm. Nothing ventured... Just as I pull open the cutlery drawer to grab some scissors to rectify the problem, the café door opens and in comes a pretty young woman with a dark, shiny ponytail swinging from side to side, and a confident demeanour. She's dressed in a black hoodie, red cropped top and faded ripped jeans. *Course she is.* Following in her wake (because she's left the door wide open) is a fresh ocean breeze and some *very* sandy footprints.

Why do some people never wipe their bloody feet? I shut the drawer, and force a smile, despite the annoying sand trail I'll have to sweep up. In my front-of-house voice I ask, 'Morning, what can I get you?'

The young woman wrinkles her delicate nose and huffs a sigh through crimson lips. 'I haven't decided yet.' Her accent is plummy, her tone bored and uninterested. 'Is that the complete list of food you've got, then?' She nods at the chalk boards behind me.

I take a breath while an imaginary response waits on my tongue. *Good God, no, those two chalk boards are just a tiny sample. Given that we are such a small café by the sea, we have an extensive list of gourmet food and drinks befitting the tables of The Savoy. We have a Michelin star chef ready and waiting to take any specific order for you, my beautiful, young, flat-stomached, ripped-jeaned, swingy-shiny-haired one.* If only I could say that. My smile feels like it's shrunk in the wash and my lips won't fit into it. Folding my arms I respond, with, 'Yes, but if there's something you can't see on there that you fancy, just say. Within reason, of course.'

Ripped Jeans' perfectly plucked brows raise slightly, and her big chocolate-brown eyes light up. 'Oh, okay, I'll take some smoked salmon on a slice of sourdough, lightly toasted with just a little low-fat cream cheese, and on the side, a couple of slices of grilled aubergine with an olive oil and garlic rub.' She taps her dimpled chin with long red fingernails while pondering the drinks menu. 'And a flat white.'

Maybe she'd like fresh yak's milk with that. Is this kid for real? 'I can do the flat white, but I'm sorry, the nearest thing we have to smoked salmon on sourdough is a prawn sandwich on white or granary. I can grill you a tomato on the side?'

Ripped Jeans' jaw drops, and she can barely conceal her disgust as she dismisses the suggestion with a wave of her hand. 'I'm not a prawn eater. Just give me a pot of Earl Grey and one of those toasted teacake things.'

I have to bite my tongue as I watch RJ grab a card from her expensive and minuscule handbag. She taps it impatiently on the card machine that isn't even ready yet. How bloody rude! No please, thank you, or even a smile. 'Hang on while I ring up the total.' My tone is short and certainly not sweet. A sigh is all I receive as I do so, and once the contactless card is approved, RJ strides over to a table by the window (trailing yet more sand), sits down and glues herself to her mobile phone.

It's been a slow morning in the Blue Horizon Café and the rude woman is the only customer at the moment, but then it is still only March. The tourist season in a few weeks will be manic, but right now, all I want to do is feign illness to my boss, put the 'closed' sign up and go home, not make a toasted teacake for some stuck-up prima donna. No chance of that, of course, I need the money. Lucy was only moaning to me at breakfast that she needs new trainers. They would have to be the ones that cost stupid money she saw in Truro last weekend, wouldn't they? Oh, and could she maybe have another phone for her birthday too? Marvellous. I can barely find enough for the mortgage each month as it is.

Cursing my ex for the hundredth time, I put two little pats of butter wrapped in silver paper on the plate with the teacake and walk back into the café. If Jacob hadn't left me and married his infant girlfriend, I wouldn't be in this mess, struggling to make ends meet as a single mum, would I? No. I'd be in the café part time like I used to be, and writing my novel the rest of the time. Once again, my dreams had been put on hold. The way life is progressing lately, I fear the 'on hold' will become the 'forever'.

'Oh! You scared the shit out of me … what the hell?' RJ glares up at me, open-mouthed, and spreads her hands as if to emphasise her last three words.

It takes a moment to realise my mood must have overtaken me and the 'setting down' of the tray on the table had been more like a banging down. The little metal jug of milk has spilled a puddle around the base, and the edge of one half of the teacake's soaking it up. 'Oh, sorry, my hand slipped,' I say, as I mop up the milk with a napkin.

'Right. Well, I can't eat that now.' RJ pushes the tray away in disgust and examines her phone, presumably for any splashes of milk.

Taking a deep breath, I pick up the tray and say, 'No, of course not. I'll get you another.'

'Nah, forget it.' A wave of the hand. 'I haven't time to wait for you to make another. I'll take a Danish and a flat white to go. I won't be paying extra, obvs.'

Shit. If I didn't need this job, I'd pour the remaining milk over this jumped-up little bitch's head. I can't be bothered to argue that the tea would be fine to drink if I got some more milk, either. I just want the woman gone. 'Yeah, obvs,' I snap, flounce back to the kitchen and slam the milk jug and plate into the sink. The plate gives a satisfying smash as it breaks into three pieces and I grasp the edge of the sink in a white-knuckle hold, while taking some deep breaths in an attempt to calm my raging temper. It doesn't work, just makes me light-headed.

A few minutes later I make the coffee to go, and put the Danish into a bag. I'm careful to choose the one with fewer almonds and icing sugar on it, and practically shove the two across the counter to where RJ is waiting, still glued to her phone.

She looks up at me and frowns as she puts her phone away. 'Bit rude, aren't you?'

This is it. The last fucking straw. The anger that I've been trying to keep a hold of for the last twenty minutes joins forces with the underlying cauldron of frustration that's been constantly bubbling away since Jacob left, and spreads like wildfire from my gut and into my mouth. 'I'm rude?' I fling my arms wide. '*I'm* fucking rude?! You need to have a long hard look at yourself, young lady!'

'Well, that's not helped you at all, has it?' The ponytail swings back and forth as RJ shakes her head and clicks her tongue against the roof of her mouth.

'What do you mean?'

'I write articles for *Lazy Days Travel Magazine* – mainly about the food and service I get in the restaurants and cafés I visit. I'm doing Cornwall at the moment, and so far, I'm not impressed. What's your name?'

I imagine the one she'll write about Blue Horizon Café and my heart sinks. Forcing my temper back in its box, I grab a yard brush and come out from behind the counter and start to sweep the sand from the floor. In what I hope is an unconcerned tone, I say, 'I see. My name's Merin Pascoe. And when you say unimpressed, do you mean Cornwall in general, or just this café?'

RJ sniffs and blinks at a strand of her long fringe, which has become stuck on her spider-leg eyelashes. 'In general. Cornwall is *so* backward – well, in these little places at least. I mean, no sourdough? And bloody prawn sandwiches. Really? So 1980s. If you don't want to get swallowed up by the big chains, I suggest you smarten up your act.' A sweep of the spider legs takes in the length of my attire and she adds, 'And your appearance. There's a hole in your jeans.'

Through gritted teeth I manage, 'There are several in yours.'

'Mine are supposed to be there, and they aren't holes, they're rips.'

I could cheerfully add a new rip to her hole. 'I think you should leave now. We backward Cornish folk don't take kindly to people who look down their noses at us.'

RJ grabs the coffee and Danish and stalks to the door. 'Don't worry, I'm going. You can be sure of a VERY honest write-up of this dump in next month's mag.'

'Oh, I can't wait,' I growl, as I sweep the brush along the sand trail.

At the door, RJ stops, turns her mouth down at the corners in a sneer of disgust and looks back at me. 'You really do yourself no favours, you know. I mean, look at this furniture. Pine tables do tend to stain, and again, very 1980s—'

That's it, and that's all. 'Aaargh!' I yell, and charge at her, thrusting the brush forward as if I'm jousting on an imaginary horse. 'Get the hell out of this café before I give *you* a few stains!'

RJ's eyes widen in fright as she flings the door open and makes a run for it.

I manage to get through the rest of the day without mishap, though my thoughts resemble the contents of a mixing bowl. A mixing bowl that's getting a brisk beating with a wooden spoon. Why the hell did I threaten RJ with physical violence? What if she tells the police? What will my boss Gillian say if she sees the scathing review about the café in next month's travel thingy? Why do I let Jacob get to me so much? It's been nearly two years since he left. I've had more than a sneaking suspicion that the fact his new wife is only eight years older than our eighteen-year-old daughter, and I'm nearly forty, might have something to do with it. Perhaps that's why I was so irritated by RJ. Actually, no. RJ was an obnoxious, entitled, thoroughly nasty piece of work. But the fact she was about the same age as the fragrant Carlie, whom Jacob dumped me for, after seventeen years of marriage, didn't help much either. Maybe I'm just someone who gets dumped though. My mind flits back to my first love, Pete – a boy I knew in school. We were going to be together for ever and live happily ever after. Yeah, that worked out well...

All this rehashing and worry are getting me nowhere apart from rock bottom. I grab a bottle and spray the countertop and wipe the surface clean of the blob of sticky jam that escaped from a donut earlier. If only it was as easy to wipe *my* surfaces clean. I could start again, unblemished, fresh, full of hope for the future with my writing dreams safe and secure in my unbroken heart. If I could do it all again, I wouldn't have agreed to go out with the handsome Jacob at university and get pregnant in the final year of my English Lit degree. I'd have stayed well clear of men until I was absolutely sure that I was emotionally strong, and a woman of independent means. Hell, I might even have realised my dream of becoming a successful author by now … but then there would be no Lucy, would there?

My little Lulu. I adore the girl, even though making sure Lucy is happy and wants for nothing is becoming harder because of her dickhead of a dad. Thoughts of Jacob's betrayal fire me up again as I spy another sticky blob of jam and scrub at it with the ferocity of a tornado. When it's been obliterated, I go back through to the kitchen and run the cloth under the tap. Lucy. There always seems to be tension between us nowadays. Perhaps it's a natural loosening of the ties between us as Lucy grows older? I'm not totally convinced by that though. The break-up of the marriage hit hard, even though Lucy, after the initial shock and upset had passed, said she was cool with it. How could she be? It must be a defence mechanism. Poor kid is probably pining for the old days.

Not for the first time, I dwell on the fact that it was somehow my own fault. Why had Jacob looked elsewhere? Was it too simple to say he was going through a mid-life crisis? Had I let myself go? Perhaps I'm a little thicker around the waist than I was when we'd met, but I'm still careful with my appearance, the holey jeans excepted. I remember with a smile that one lady customer had remarked how fresh-faced I looked the other week – commented on my 'sun-kissed' blonde, naturally curly hair and lovely green eyes. She was probably just being nice though; maybe she felt sorry for her plumpish over-worked waitress. Oh for God's sake, that thought can go straight in the bin where it belongs. Jacob is hardly God's gift with his little pot belly, is he? Why on earth is it always women who feel like they have to make the most effort to keep a partner? *Okay, enough! Stop all this rehashing, overthinking, and be positive!*

As I'm preparing to lock up for the day, the door opens and in comes Gillian. Well, in struggles Gillian, with a huge cardboard box, huddled up in a Paddington Bear blue duffle coat and yellow wellies. *She had better not walk across my newly mopped floor in those wellington boots…*

'Give us a hand, Merrin. I don't want to walk across your clean floor in these wellies.'

Mind reader. I laugh as I hurry over and take the box, which nearly pulls my arms out of their sockets. Gillian must be a very fit seventy-year-old to have walked from the carpark with this. 'Blimey, what the heck have you got in here?'

Gillian pushes her hood back, smooths her short grey bob and regards me with her studious green eyes. 'I decided to act on your idea and here is the result. Well, the first result – there's plenty more where that came from in the boot of my car.'

'My idea?' I reply, puzzled. Heaving the box onto a

table, I open the flaps to find tins of soup, beans, tomatoes and a bag or two of pasta.

'Yeah. You said we should start a community larder here one day a week with the left-over stuff we don't sell, plus collecting donations from supermarkets.' Gillian gives a broad smile and pats the box lid. 'I couldn't believe how much I was given from just one place. When I explained to the manager the dire situation of many people in the neighbouring areas, particularly Cambourne and Redruth, she organised a couple of lads to sort me out there and then! People are going to be fed. And it's all because of your brilliant idea!'

After a day of feeling like I've a boulder in my chest, my heart swells with happiness and a light feeling settles in my head. 'That's fantastic! I didn't realise that you had taken me seriously, as you didn't say much at the time.'

Gillian taps her temple and winks. 'I was thinking it through, my dear. Takes a while for stuff to sink in nowadays.'

The possibilities of this scheme rush through my blood in a stream of positivity. I'd been so sad hearing the local news a few weeks ago talking about how Cornwall was one of the poorest counties in the UK, and it was so hard for many families to make ends meet. This wasn't news as such – it had been known for a long time – but in these last few troubled years it was growing to be more of a problem. Brexit, Covid, God knew what else. A youth worker who came in the café only last week had mentioned that local youngsters were having to move out of Cornwall as they couldn't afford to buy the overpriced homes that were being snapped up by absentee landlords with an eye on the tourist season. Full-time, well-paid jobs were far and few between. Yes, I'm struggling, too, but at least I can put food on the table for Lucy, albeit with a monthly contribution from Jacob.

I can feel hope spreading inside me like sunshine through the darkest cloud. Maybe I'm not wasting my life after all, because I've a contribution to make. And even if I can't follow my writing dream right now, I can help others less fortunate than myself. Making a difference is the main thing after all, isn't it? 'We could start next week, on Friday,' I enthuse, hugging myself. 'I'll do some flyers to advertise it and I have a friend on local radio who could give us a shout too. We could distribute the food out the back door of the kitchen.'

'Great ideas!' Gillian smiles and then her dark eyebrows knit together as she nods at my knee. 'Oh. You've got a hole in your jeans, maid.'

'Yes.' I chuckle. 'I'm starting a new trend. Holes are in. Rips are out.'

Chapter Eleven

The trickle of people wating at the back door over the last three Fridays has become a bubbling stream today. I can't help but smile as I pack the last box of goodies. At last, the Blue Horizon Café Community Larder is getting known to a wider audience. This should never be necessary in the UK in this day and age, but it is, and so I'll do all I can to help. The radio announcement advertising us, and the leaflet drop around the village and wider community that Lucy and I organised last weekend, must have really worked well. I think of all the other people in the area who've piled in too. Vicar Lawrence at the chapel had spread the word at his coffee morning and Bible study group. Plus, Easter had been busy, and the tourists generous. Things are definitely looking better. Food collection boxes on the counter in the café have had to be emptied of spare change nightly, too, so we've been able to buy toiletries and a few more essentials not supplied free of charge by the local farmers and shops.

Gillian sticks her head around the back door, just as I go to open it. 'Are we ready?' She nods at the line of about twenty people chatting and milling about in the yard. 'Because we have quite a few takers.'

'We are indeed.' I signal to Sandra from the local bakery, who is lending a hand. 'Can you bring those few cauliflowers through? Just remembered Francis popped some over last minute from her allotment.'

'Already on it.' Sandra shoves her tortoiseshell glasses further up her nose and pulls on a red baseball cap over her close-cropped silver hair. 'Looks like rain out. Can't be getting my beautiful hair wet.'

I know as well as she does that Sandra's twinkly eyes and cheeky grin belie the pain and trauma she's been through over the past few years. The last – and hopefully final – round of chemo saw her long dark hair fall out and it grew back silver. At only forty-eight, this must have been an extra blow for her, but she's never heard complaining. I reply with a grin, 'I happen to think your hair is beautiful actually, very chic.'

Sandra shrugs and places the cauliflowers on a wooden tray. 'I'm getting used to it. And in the end, it's only hair. I have my wonderful hubby, my two lovely daughters, and as far as the doctors are concerned right now, my life back. Who could ask for more?'

As I pull the door wide and wedge it open with a rock I found on the beach, I decide to take a leaf out of Sandra's book instead of wallowing in the past as I'm wont to do. Mind you, since I've started organising the larder, there's not been time to do much wallowing, and I have to admit, there's more to be upbeat about lately. I tell myself I'm allowed to be proud of myself too. When Lucy went to Jacob's in Plymouth over Easter weekend, rather than mope about feeling lonely, I baked cakes and buns and made lasagne for the freezer. Some of the cakes and buns are now in these bags. Yup. Feeling useful and being part of my local community help put a new perspective on life.

I've been drifting through life since Jacob left – well … if I'm honest with myself, since Lucy started school. I've had one uninspiring job after the other: checkout assistant in Tesco, checkout assistant in the local shop, a brief stint in a hairdresser's, a shelf stacker, and, for the past four years, working in this café, which, I have to admit, tops all the others, even though it's not something I would have chosen as my dream job when as a kid I was asked what I wanted to do when I grew up. Organising this community larder might not seem like a lot to some people, but it is to me. I feel like I have a real purpose now, apart from being Lucy's mum. And the main thing is, it's all my idea, which is a real boost to my beleaguered self-esteem.

Gillian's putting the bags on the long trestle table outside in the little yard, and as Sandra and I carry over more bags, she asks, 'Did you put the last of the bread in from this morning's batch? Some of these bags look a bit empty.'

Damn it. 'I knew there was something. They're still sitting in the oven, I think. I put them in there to keep warm and they went completely out of my head.' On the way back inside the shop, I notice an older lady leaning against the wall, her walking-stick on the floor by the back gate. She looks to be a little out of breath and the fringe of her mop of white hair is clinging damply to her forehead. I hurry over. 'Are you okay?' I ask.

The lady looks up at me and blinks her pale blue eyes. 'I think so … just hurried a bit too much because I didn't want to miss collection time. My legs won't be rushed at my age, see.' A wan smile momentarily brightens her expression, then her lips sag, as if they suddenly have no energy.

My heart goes out to her. Poor woman, feeling under so much pressure to get food that she's worn herself out. Life shouldn't be like this for the elderly, or for anyone else, come to think. 'Here, take my arm and your stick. Let's go inside the back kitchen and get you sat down for a minute. You'll feel better once you've had a drink of water and a rest.'

'Oh, no dear, I don't want to put you to any trouble … you're being so kind as it is, handing out food and whatnot…' The lady's eyes shimmer and she looks down at her well-worn brown lace-ups.

I can almost see a blanket of shame weighing her down, slumping the woman's shoulders, rooting her to the ground … diminishing her spirit. There's no need for her to be ashamed, but I can understand why she might be. Like my grandparents, the old lady's generation grew up being told to never borrow anything, or ask for help, but she obviously has no choice now. The injustice of the whole situation sparks a flame of anger in my chest, but I can't let it burn out of control. The last thing this lady needs is to hear me ranting. 'It's honestly no trouble at all … er,' I glance at a thin gold band on her third finger, 'Mrs…?'

'Mrs Ryan.'

'Okay, Mrs Ryan, come with me,' I say, as I tuck Mrs Ryan's blue-veined paper-light hand into the crook of my arm, and lead her slowly inside. The old armchair in the corner is clearly a welcome relief for her as she sinks into the cosy red leather.

'Ooh, that's better for me old legs.' She rubs the thin material of her black cotton trousers. 'My knees have no spring in 'em nowadays. No idea how I got so old.' Mrs Ryan's eyes hold a spark of humour as she flicks her gaze to mine. 'It happens when you're not looking, this old age malarky. One day you're fifty-odd, the next you're eighty-odd.'

I laugh. 'I can believe that. I'll be forty soon, but I only feel twenty.'

Mrs Ryan taps her temple. 'Oh aye. Inside here I'm still in my teens, it's just my ancient body letting me down.'

'Okay, Mrs Ryan, I'm just going to take some more bread out to my friends and then I'll make us a nice cuppa.'

Mrs Ryan holds her hand up. 'No, I'll be right as rain in a few moments, dear. I don't want to hold you up.'

'You aren't. And my name's Merrin.' I rush out with the bread, hoping that it will be okay to leave everything to Gillian and Sandra. There look to be even more people now than when I went indoors. 'Gillian, can you manage without me for a while? There's a lady who's had a bit of a turn. She's okay, just needs a cuppa and a rest.'

Gillian flaps a hand in dismissal. 'No problemo. Me and Sandra are working like the well-oiled springs in clockwork here. Off you go.'

Back inside, I stick the kettle on, shake some chocolate biscuits onto a plate and put them on the kitchen table. 'Have one of these, Mrs Ryan, the sugar will give you some energy.'

Mrs Ryan's eyes light up and a splash of pink finds a home in her cheeks. 'You're spoiling me, Merrin. Thank you so much.'

'Nonsense.' I say over my shoulder and grab two mugs from the cupboard. 'It's just a biscuit, and do you prefer tea or coffee?'

'Um ... tea ... please.'

The tremor in Mrs Ryan's voice snaps my head round. To my dismay, I see tears swimming in her eyes. 'Hey, what's wrong?' I quickly make the tea and hurry over with the mugs and a box of tissues, and sit on a kitchen chair opposite.

Mrs Ryan takes a moment to blow her nose and take a few deep breaths, then her watery gaze moves from my face to the table top. 'Don't mind me, I'm just a silly old woman.' Her voice sounds empty, resigned.

'I know that isn't true. Come on, spill the beans.' I pat her hand gently and try a smile, but Mrs Ryan's face crumples again and a steady stream of tears etch a path through the creases and lines.

More nose-blowing and table-watching, then at last Mrs Ryan says, 'I think it's because you've been so kind to me. I'm a stranger to you, but you've taken me in and made me tea and biscuits. I can't remember the last time I had tea and biscuits with –' a sob hitches along a breath '– with anyone.'

A prickle of emotion starts behind my eyes too, as I

think about this poor woman all by herself in the world. 'Oh dear. How come?'

Mrs Ryan takes a sip of tea and sighs. 'I'm a widow, never had children, sadly, so there's no immediate family around. I have nieces and nephews who come and see me now and then, but they all have their own busy lives, don't they?'

I take a sip of tea to wash away the thickness in my throat. 'I suppose they do, yes. How about friends?'

Mrs Ryan sighs again. 'Mostly dead and gone. There're one or two of the old gang left, but they are all in ill health. Either they're with relatives or in care homes. That's my biggest worry.' Her sharp blue eyes radiate fear as they focus on the wall behind me as if it's an abyss.

'Care homes can be really good places...' I begin, and then shut up. What do I know about them, apart from what I've seen on the news?

'Oh, I don't doubt it, but I've been used to my independence. Finn, my husband, has been gone for near on five years, and I have been lonely ... but rather lonely than be stuck in a bed poorly, being fed and changed like a baby.'

Mrs Ryan is close to tears again so I think quickly and swap tack. 'How about joining a club or something? I hear they have interesting things going on at the chapel.'

'Do they?' Mrs Ryan looks vaguely interested. 'I didn't know that. I tend to just stay at home and watch telly. I pop out to the shops to get a few bits a couple of times a week, but that's it. As I said, my legs are buggered nowadays. Managing my finances is getting a bit tricky these days too, that's why I came here today, much as it pained me to do so … and I don't just mean because of my legs.' Shame is back and curves her lips into a sheepish grin. 'You or one of your friends must have put a leaflet through my door.'

Sandra bustles in at that moment and asks Mrs Ryan where she lives. Nodding at her reply, she says, 'Ah, that would have been me with the leaflets. I did the bottom lanes. My name's Sandra. How are you feeling, my lovely?'

Mrs Ryan manages a watery smile. 'Better for a sit down and cuppa, thank you.'

'I can pop you back home when you've finished, if you like. Save you walking and it's on my way home,' Sandra says, crunching into a chocolate biscuit. 'Best not forget your bag of goodies either, eh?'

Mrs Ryan sniffs and dabs at the corners of her eyes with a tissue. 'That's so kind of you, Sandra, if it's not too much bother.' Sandra says it is no problem at all and pats her hand. Mrs Ryan smiles. 'I think I might have seen you in the bakery, though I don't go in much.'

'Yes, I've worked there must be five years now. Had time off recently 'cos of cancer treatment.' Sandra takes her cap off and ruffles her fingers through her short crop. 'Getting back to normal now, though.'

The older woman's face falls. 'And here I am moaning on about my legs and getting old. So sorry, dear.'

Sandra flaps a hand at her and puts two bags of groceries on the table. 'Here's your stuff, and nothing to be sorry for. We all have our problems, and if we can't moan to our friends about them, who can we moan to, hmm?' Mrs Ryan's smile lights up the kitchen, but her eyes are brimming with tears. I can tell that Sandra's comment about 'friends' has really bowled her over. 'Right, you all set?'

Mrs Ryan nods and I take her arm to help her up from the chair. 'Here's your stick, lean on that, and slip your other arm through mine while Sandra carries your shopping to her car.'

Once settled in the front seat, Mrs Ryan smiles up at me. 'Thanks again for your kindness, Merrin. I can't tell you how much I've enjoyed the company under the circumstances.'

'I've loved meeting you too.' And I'm not just being polite. Mrs Ryan has a quiet dignity about her and I'm sure she has a few stories to tell too. I close the car door, lean my elbow on the roof of the car and look in through the window. 'I was thinking, maybe next week I could deliver some groceries to your house, instead of you having to struggle down here. What do you think?'

'Well, that would be asking too much … I couldn't—'

'You didn't ask, she offered,' Sandra says. 'And now you will accept, and that will be that. Simples.' She gives her a cheeky grin and starts the engine.

I raise my voice above the engine noise. 'Give Sandra your phone number and I'll call you in the week, Mrs Ryan.'

'Thank you so much.' Mrs Ryan's lively blue eyes crinkle at the corners and she pats my hand before beginning to wind up the window. When it's halfway up, she says, pink-faced, 'And please call me Morwenna. Wenna for short, my friends always do.'

I feel honoured, both to be counted as a friend and to be

invited to use her first name, as I know so many older people prefer formal terms. 'You are most welcome, Wenna. See you next week.'

As I watch the battered old red van trundle down the narrow lane, I can't help but smile. What a good day it's been. More takers for the community larder, more donations, and, to top it all, meeting Wenna. She seems quite a character, and I'm very much looking forward to getting to know her better.

Chapter Twelve

'**M**um, have you seen my phone?' Lucy shouts from the top of the stairs.

I've only been home ten bloody minutes and now I'm scurrying around trying to tidy up and sort dinner. 'Nope!' I shout back from the kitchen, not even bothering to look. If Lucy can't be arsed to even come downstairs, I can't be arsed to drop everything after a hard day to search for it. I'm surprised it's not surgically attached to Lucy's hand like normal, anyway. I release a long breath and look around the messy kitchen. Toast crumbs and jam puddles on the table, a pile of Lucy's dirty laundry on the floor next to the washing machine. Next to it? Why isn't it inside the damned thing? Did Lucy run out of energy at the last second, her poor little arms refusing to heave it those last few centimetres into the drum? And it wouldn't have hurt her to have stacked her breakfast and lunch dishes in the dishwasher either, would it? Okay, she's so exhausted after revising for her A level exams (as she reminds me every five seconds), but it would only have taken a few minutes, for God's sake.

I stack the dishwasher, shove the dirty laundry into the washing machine and wipe the table free of jam and toast crumbs. I always seem to be wiping jam from tables and surfaces. Other people's sticky messes are my speciality. Maybe I should put an ad on the socials. Another long sigh. Okay, try not to be a grump, it's been a hard day at work, that's all, now the tourists are here in greater numbers. It's good news for the café, but it does take a lot out of me. Is it too much to expect my eighteen-year-old daughter to lend a hand around the place? Lucy's always saying how she cooks for her dad and Carlie when she's there. Why does she never do it here, then? There're the endless gifts they shower her with too. Those trainers she wanted, a new phone, God knows what else. It's a wonder she hasn't gone to live with them.

I stomp over to the sink to rinse out the cloth, and a school photo on the windowsill of Lucy in Year Five catches my eye. Her dad's navy-blue eyes, curled chestnut bunches, gappy smile, freckles over her nose. I find myself blinking away sudden tears. It doesn't seem five minutes since those days. Jacob was still living here, we used to be a great little family, laughing, have fun ... or am I just sweeping the arguments and little niggles under the carpet, looking at the past through a rosy lens? Money was tight back then, as Jacob had just started a new job at the estate agent's before he worked himself up the ladder. If I'm honest, we did argue and disagree about the silliest things, though Mum had said that always happened when you worried about bills and stuff, and not to worry, because strong marriages always survived.

Seemingly ours hadn't been. It certainly wasn't strong enough to get round the Carlie obstacle, was it? The Carlie obstacle that just happened to be the daughter of the owner of an estate agent's in Plymouth. The estate agent's where Jacob was now a partner. He took the easy way out, started afresh. Trying to save our marriage was too much like hard work, obviously. Putting the cloth down, I pick up the photo frame and gaze into my daughter's nine-year-old eyes. It's no use wishing the clock could be turned back to those days. Things had moved on, and soon my little Lucy will be gone. In September she'd be at university and there'd be no messy kitchen to come home to, no laundry left by the washing machine … no jam puddles. I need to treasure every moment I have with her now, not moan and grump about things that don't really matter. The clatter of Lucy's feet on the stairs snaps me out of my ponderings, and I dab a bit of kitchen roll under my eyes.

'Mum, you clearly didn't look for my phone at all. There it is on the bread-bin.' Lucy's standing by the table dressed in fluffy pink PJs, pointing a finger of disbelief at the thing. Her chestnut hair, now with added blonde highlights, is a messy nest because of the constant raking it through with her fingers that she does when she's studying, her navy eyes look like the ocean under a raincloud, and her freckles … her freckles aren't there anymore. 'Mum? You okay?'

Aware I'm just staring trance-like, I muster a smile and swallow a knot of emotion. 'Yeah … yeah. Just thinking of when you were little.' I wave the photo at her and set it back on the windowsill. 'Sorry about not looking for your phone, I was busy tidying up.'

Lucy frowns, walks towards me and slips an arm around my shoulder. 'Don't worry about that – I should have dragged my lazy arse downstairs ... you've been crying. What's wrong?'

Gulping down tears, I consider saying it was a hard day and I was just a bit tired and emotional, but something stops me. These are the moments that matter, the important things in life. Closing my eyes to better remember the feel of Lucy's arm around me, the smell of her floral body spray mixed with cheese and onion crisps, the almost tangible concern and affection my daughter feels for her mum. 'I was just thinking of ... of the past and that soon you won't be here anymore... I'm really going to miss you, Lulu.' I look into Lucy's eyes and see the mirror of her tears.

'You haven't called me Lulu for years.' Lucy gives a watery smile and sits me down at the kitchen table.

'That's because you told me it was too babyish when you were twelve.'

'Did I?'

'Yep. But I can start calling you it again, if you'd really like?' I tip her an impish grin.

'Um, no. I think Lucy's just fine.' She laughs as she fills the kettle. 'Tea?'

'Please.' As I watch my daughter make the tea, a struggle starts in my mind between asking some blunt questions, or letting this new closeness we're sharing continue. Important moments need honesty though, don't they?

Lucy comes over with two mugs and a packet of chocolate digestives under her arm. 'I will be able to come and visit, you know. I'm only going to Bristol – if I get the grades of course – not Aberdeen.'

'I know. And I don't want you to be worried about coming home all the time, you're there to have fun, meet new people... I suppose it's just the end of an era, isn't it?'

Lucy's eyes glisten and she takes a drink. 'I ... I suppose it is, yes.'

She looks about the same age as she was in the photo, right now, and all I want to do is take her in my arms and tell her I love her so much. I won't though, because that will make us both cry, and no matter how much I would tell her the opposite, Lucy would think I don't want her to leave. There's no way I'm making her feel guilty for following her dreams. 'But you are going to have the best time.' Reaching across the table I take one of Lucy's hands in mine. 'THE best, are you listening?'

Lucy nods and wipes away tears. 'I know. I suppose I've been worried about leaving home too, from time to time. It's all a bit scary going out into the world.'

This is unexpected, but then Lucy never confides in me these days. 'Of course it is. You'll be okay though ... and you know you can always talk to me about things.'

'Yeah. I don't like worrying you though, now that...' She shrugs. 'You know.'

I frown. 'Not really...'

'Now you're on your own. I know you are still upset

about Dad and Carlie. I hate to think you'll be lonely.' Lucy blows her nose and stares out of the window at the wind moving through the branches of the old apple tree.

Blunt questions win the struggle and I ask, 'Is that why you don't say much about what you get up to when you're there? Well, apart from that you do the cooking...' Why did I say that? It sounded like a recrimination.

Lucy raises an eyebrow. 'I only cook because Carlie can't ... and to impress Dad, I suppose.' She pauses, folds her arms, and a few cheese and onion crisp crumbs drop from her lapel onto the table. 'Thing is, he doesn't take that much notice of me anymore, he's always too busy, and when he's not, I always play second fiddle when Carlie's around.'

Bloody hell! I try to lock down my utter surprise at this news. This is not what I imagined at all. How to respond? I don't want to put Lucy off her track by going over the top. Arranging my face into a thoughtful expression, I try, 'Oh right. I thought you liked going over there.'

'That's because I didn't want you to worry when I'm away. You've been through enough as it is.'

'Oh, love. You don't have to worry about me. Yes, I was devastated when your dad left, but I'm definitely over it now.' *Really? Yeah, right.*

'Hmm. Well, I'll be glad when I'm at uni, so I won't be expected to go over there so much.' She shrugs, bites into a chocolate digestive, and speaks out the corner of her mouth. 'That will be my excuse to Dad of course. I don't want to upset him ... mind you, he'll probably be relieved.'

My heart sinks. My poor baby has been keeping all this to herself. I suspected she hankered for the old days just as I do, but had no idea she was so unhappy. 'I'm sure that's not true, sweetheart. Your dad loves you. And I thought everything was great between you.' I swallow and decide to forge ahead along the truth-path I've started down. 'I honestly thought you'd rather live with them at one point. They give you lots of gifts, stuff I can't afford. Plus, I'm at work all hours, and we don't have much time together...'

Lucy holds a hand up. 'Stop right there, Mum. Yeah, he buys me stuff, but that's because he's guilty. Thinks he can buy me off with expensive trainers and shit ... but I can see through that. There's no amount of money or gifts in the world that can substitute for love, is there? For quality time spent?' Lucy's bottom lip trembles and she takes a gulp of tea. Then she gives a humourless bark. 'Living with them? God, I'd rather poke my eyes out with a rusty nail. I love being home here with you, eating proper home-cooked food, and having you run around after me like I'm still the little girl in that photo.' She nods at the windowsill and adds a wistful smile.

My throat is in danger of closing off completely now, but I blink back tears and laugh. 'Oh, I see. You love it here because I do your laundry, pick up after you and generally take care of you twenty-four-seven, eh?'

'Of course. Why else would I stay here?' Lucy answers, deadpan.

'Cheeky monkey.'

'That's me.' Lucy reaches her hand across the table and squeezes mine. 'Seriously, Mum. I know I can be a pain in the arse moaning about stuff, but I do appreciate everything you do for me. Now I'm off to uni I can't help but feel sorry that you never finished your course because you fell pregnant with me. I know how much you wanted to write…' Her cheeks flush pink and she can't hold my gaze. 'I'm not great at showing my feelings and talking about them either, but you know … that I love you, don't you?'

Truth be told, I wasn't completely sure until now. Relief at my daughter's revelations clash with sadness about Jacob's treatment of her. When did he become so self-centred, so cold? Yes, he had shown me what kind of guy he really was in no uncertain terms, but how dare he make Lucy feel so unwanted? Swallowing down anger, I look at my daughter's face. On the surface she's so grown up, but her downcast expression and pink cheeks reveal her youth and vulnerability. 'Of course I know you love me. And the uni thing – I never ever regretted my decision to have you, okay? Besides, if I organised myself more, I'm sure I could crack on with my novel. I'm just a lazy arse like you.' I laugh, because that's true in part, but mostly it's because I'm just knackered all the time. 'And you'll always be my little girl, no matter how old you get, and how far you go, do you hear me?' My voice breaks and I put a hand to my mouth to force back a sob.

'Aw, Mum,' Lucy whispers, two big tears cascading down her cheeks.

I stand up and open my arms. 'Come here right this minute and give me a big hug, Lulu.'

Lucy rolls her eyes. 'Great. We're actually going to do the big hugathon thing now, eh?'

'We bloody well are. Otherwise, there will be no lasagne and garlic bread for dinner, young lady.'

Laughing, Lucy steps round the table and into my arms. The hug feels like a safe cocoon, full of love, warmth and belonging. One day soon, Lucy will move on, but now I know my daughter's love is without question. Yes, it's the end of an era and that will take some time to come to terms with. Everything changes sooner or later, and we all have to deal with it in our own way. Some of us don't deal with it very well. Especially change that is foisted upon you. It's like having to get rid of an old but favourite winter coat that's worn out, and the replacement feels a bit uncomfortable. Maybe it pinches under the arms. It's certainly not as warm, and the pockets aren't deep enough for all your stuff, but you have to accept it, because change is all part of life, isn't it?

———————————

The Blue Horizon Café is at last a bit calmer. The breakfast rush is over and there's a little lull like a calm sea pool before the tide turns again and the lunch mayhem begins. I'm thankful that the scathing review written by the lovely RJ in *Lazy Days Travel Magazine* doesn't seem to have had an impact. It's not the kind of thing Gillian reads anyway, so I think I've swerved that particular bullet. Hmm, time to take a breather by the door. I wish I could take a coffee down to the beach, just a few hundred yards away. I can smell the seaweed and salt air on the breeze ... so close, yet so far. Two elderly ladies and a couple of young women with toddlers are the only customers, so I might get away with having a coffee outside on the bench, as long as I keep one eye on the tables.

At the door again a few moments later with my cappuccino, I'm just about to step outside, when a vaguely familiar-looking guy lopes up the sandy path. He's wearing a red Guns N' Roses T-shirt over faded jeans, a yellow beanie hat and a broad smile.

'Merrin Pascoe, as I live and breathe.' He stops in front of me and sweeps his beanie off to reveal bouncy brown curls – with a mind of their own under a wave of static – a shade darker than his twinkly eyes.

It takes a moment to register where I know him from, not least because the teenage boy I knew in school has grown into a man ... and a very nice-looking one indeed. I can't believe it. I was only thinking about him recently when I was feeling sorry for myself. 'My God, is it Pete Veryan?'

'It is indeed.' Pete takes my hand, kisses the back of it and gives a little bow.

He shows no sign of letting go of it, and suddenly I'm right back in the schoolyard again, complete with a couple of hot cheeks and a tied tongue. Clearing my throat and avoiding his intense stare, I manage, 'Bloody hell, it must be, what ... twenty years?'

'Nearly twenty-two.' Pete grins and frees my hand at last. 'I went off in my gap year, remember, and never came back.'

How could I forget? He was my first love, for God's sake, and he'd dumped me. There was a time when I thought my heart would never be whole again, but then I'd gone off to uni and met Jacob. Marvellous. Great choice, Merrin. Somehow, I affect nonchalance. 'Oh yeah. Backpacking, wasn't it? Where did you end up?' I smooth my green and white stripy apron (how fetching), take a sip of coffee, and sneak a glance back inside the café to make sure none of the customers want anything.

Pete takes my elbow and nods inside. 'Can we get a table, if you're not busy? I'd love a chance to catch up.'

Could we? Not sure I'm ready for a twenty-two-year catch-up along with the ins and outs of my marriage. 'Well, I'm not supposed to…'

I get the lopsided grin that used to set my seventeen-year-old heart racing. 'Ah, come on, Rin. If the customers get ugly, I'll sort 'em.'

A smile breaks through my reserves. Rin. He was the only one who'd ever called me that. What could it hurt? 'Okay, but only ten minutes.'

'Cool.' He points at the cake stand. 'And can I have a coffee and one of those scones?'

Pete grabs a corner table by the window, while I get his order and ask if the customers need anything else. They don't, which gives me no excuse not to go over and sit with my first love. This feels so surreal. I might wake up in a minute. I put his coffee and scone on a tray, and wish I'd washed my hair this morning, put more make-up on and smartened up a bit. What must he think of me in this apron, my hair scraped into a top knot, and holey jeans? Then I remind myself that holey jeans are the new ripped ones, and what the hell does it matter what Pete bloody Veryan thinks, anyway?

'Here we go,' I say, as I place the tray on the table. 'I baked that scone with my own fair hands this morning.'

'Wow.' Pete sticks his knife into a little pat of butter and winks. 'You always were good with your hands.'

A forest fire flames in my cheeks and I look into my coffee. That's a bit familiar, isn't it, after all this time? Disgruntled, I don't return his smile. 'Hmm. So, tell me all about your life.'

Pete has the good grace to shift his eyes from my pink face and takes a huge bite of scone. 'This is delicious,' he says, crumbs dropping on the table. *Nice.* 'Okay, I left Cornwall and headed to Portugal for the surfing and met up with Lenny Williams, you remember Lenny?' I nod. He was a year above us at school and always winning surfing competitions. 'We did well there and in the end, we decided to travel round Europe working in bars and stuff until we eventually ended up in Australia.' Pete pauses to sip some coffee.

I'd found out he ended up there, but I'm not letting him know I was bothered enough to ask around. 'Bet that was an adventure.' My voice is less than enthusiastic, but as he's talking, the hurt I felt all those years ago when he just upped and left comes flooding back. Upped and left, after promising we would be together for ever. More fool me. I was naïve enough to believe it. Probably just said it to get into my knickers.

'It was. We opened a bar on a beach in Queensland and worked it for nearly fifteen years. Made loads of money during the surfing season, and the tourists took care of the rest. We had a ball.' Pete gives me a big smile, his eyes sparkling with enthusiasm, and I can't help but smile in return.

'So, what went wrong?'

'Lenny wanted out.' He shrugs and shoves the last bit of scone into his mouth. 'He was married with a couple of sprogs by then, and the wife decided she wanted to move closer to her parents, which was five hundred kilometres away. Kids needed their grandparents, she said.' He chases some crumbs around his plate with a damp finger and licks it. 'He couldn't afford to buy me out, because he needed all his savings for the move, so we sold the place, and I worked as a surf instructor for the last seven years.'

'Right. So, you never married?'

'Nah.' He sits back in his chair and gives me a long look. 'Had plenty of relationships, but none ever came close to the woman sitting in front of me.'

Oh please. Surprised at how quickly the old resentment and anger at him is rising to the surface, I take a deep breath and muster a calm voice. 'So why did you leave me, just like that?'

A frown ripples across his brow, then a big smile lights up his face. 'Hey, we were kids. And from what I remember, we had started growing apart during our A levels...'

'Maybe. But that's because we were studying and didn't have the time for partying. Though you tended to have more time than I did.' I can't help adding the last bit. Pete had never been what you call disciplined where school work was concerned.

Looking a bit sheepish he says, 'Yeah. I guess. It's just that I felt I wanted to see a bit of the world before I knuckled down and had to grow up. I fully intended to come back.'

'Yes, I remember you saying, the day you left.' An unexpected lump of emotion forms in my throat. 'Something along the lines of you'd be back before I knew it, and you'd keep in touch. You didn't.'

Pete heaves a sigh and looks out of the window at the path to the sea. 'I really hurt you, didn't I?'

'You could say that. My first boyfriend, after two years of dating and telling me we'd be together for ever, just buggers off and never comes back.'

His gaze snaps back from the window and he shakes his head in apparent surprise. 'God, I didn't realise. I'm sorry, Rin. But I was a teenager. All teenagers say that kind of stuff, don't they? And I did love you, you know. In my unsophisticated teenage way.'

From the vantage point of the present, I feel a bit of understanding creeping back for the Pete in the past. When I'd gone over it all from time to time as I'd grown older, I did realise that teenage dreams and feelings, while real, didn't always stand the test of time. They certainly hadn't for Pete. We were sixteen when we first got together, so why should I be surprised at what had happened? Surprised or not, the hurt had been real. And what's that 'they' say about first loves? Oh yes, the first cut is the deepest. I check on the customers before taking a sip of coffee. 'Ah well, it's all water under a *very* old bridge.'

Pete shoves a hand through his mess of curls and brightens. 'I guess... Anyway, I decided it was time to come home. Australia lost its appeal somehow, or I'm getting too old for adventures.' He clears his throat and looks at me sidelong from under his lashes, suddenly shy. 'Are you married?'

And you want to know this because? 'I was. Divorced now. I have a daughter, Lucy, about the same age as we were when we were together last.' Almost to myself I add, 'Hardly seems possible.'

'Wow. You must have had her young.'

I nod and tell him the whole story about meeting Jacob at uni, and what came after. I breeze through it, as if reciting lines in a play, but without the emotion or modicum of realistic acting necessary for an encore. Then I quickly stand when I notice the elderly ladies getting ready to leave. 'Anyway, I must get on, Pete. Nice to see you again.'

Before he can reply, I hurry over to the ladies and ask if everything was okay. 'Lovely, thank you dear. Those eclairs were naughty, but we needed a boost, didn't we, Connie?' the taller of the two says, looking at her friend.

'We did. And if you can't eat eclairs at nearly eighty-three, when can you?' She waves at me as they leave, and I'm reminded of Wenna. I must pop her a bag of goodies over later.

The younger women get up to leave too, and as I chat to them about the delights of having toddlers, my heart sinks. I don't want to be alone in the café with Pete because there's nothing left to say to each other, really. Perhaps there'll be more people along in a few moments with any luck. As the last of them leave, I turn to the table in the corner, but I needn't have worried. Pete has gone. Must have slipped out when I was chatting. On the table is ten pounds and a piece of paper folded in half, my name scrawled across it.

Rin,

I'm so sorry I hurt you so much all those years ago, and if you let me, I'd like to try and make amends. It won't be easy, but can we start to mend our relationship with a meal and a drink soon? I'm in the process of buying a house just down the road in Perranporth, and working as a part-time chef in a bar, so whenever you can fit me in, give me a shout and I'll be there. I'd be stupid to think we could pick up where we left off, or even if you'd want to, so I'm happy to meet as friends, absolutely no strings. Maybe in the future we might be able to get back on track – providing you're not seeing someone – but I'd honestly be grateful for anything.

Love, Pete xx

Btw – my number's 07707349781

I sigh, put the paper and tenner in my apron pocket and clear his table. How do I feel about letting Pete Veryan back into my life? Okay, on the one hand, he's even more gorgeous than he was back then, and he seems genuinely sorry about dumping me. There's certainly a part of me that's flattered that he's still interested. God knows my confidence took a battering when Jacob went off with Carlie. Perhaps Pete might be just the guy to put a spring back in my step. But can I really risk it? It took me long enough to allow Jacob into my heart after being hurt so much by Pete, and look what happened in the end. Okay, it lasted seventeen years, but the end result was the same. I was dumped. Passed over. Found wanting.

Stacking the dishwasher, however, I find myself smiling as my memory presents an image of the two of us making out in the sand dunes one magical summer's night. Wrapped in each other's arms, time seemed to stand still. Nothing and nobody else mattered. Back then, Pete made me feel so beautiful, so special. So loved. We had all the time in the world, and we were going to walk life's path together towards a bright and happy future. Then the images screech to a halt, crash and burn, as I remember the shock of his departure. Sudden, unexpected, devastating. Do I want to end up like that again, twenty-odd years later, if Pete, on a whim, decides to take off once more? Can my heart take it?

Anger flares in my chest as I think yet again about how I was dumped by my lovely husband too. What the hell is wrong with me? Have I got some vibe going on that says to guys – *I'm a mug, use and abuse me*? Pete and I can't go back, can we? It's too late and besides, I need someone I can trust. I shake my head – if I need anyone at all. Perhaps it's all too much bloody trouble. Hearing customers come in, I leave the kitchen and put my front-of-house face on. What to do about Pete and his 'friendship' will have to wait until later. Right about now, I could do with some sensible advice from my oldest and best friend, Faye. Thank goodness she's due back from visiting her sister in California next week; she's been gone four weeks and I've missed a good heart-to-heart.

'Do you do proper Cornish pasties, luv?' a middle-aged

man with a bald head, wearing a Union Jack T-shirt and with a bulldog tattooed on his neck, shouts from a table. Five other similar-looking men sitting with him look at me expectantly. 'Cos we don't want any rubbish, do we ,lads?' Their rumble of agreement sounds like distant thunder. This is perfect. Just what I need. I take a deep breath and dredge up my best welcoming smile.

'Of course we do. Only the best served here.'

Chapter Thirteen

I stop the car outside a row of stone-built cottages, which overlook sheep-dotted farmland, and then over the rolling hills to where a blue smudge of Atlantic sleeps cradled between them. A beautiful spot, but certainly not the greatest location for a woman in her eighties who has to walk down into Porthtowan and back, carrying a bag or two from the foodbank. From the boot, I grab three bags and hurry along to the last cottage on the terrace. Each is a different colour and Wenna's is the light blue one – number 37.

As I lift my hand to knock, the door opens and standing in the hallway, wearing a smart red and yellow tartan skirt, crimson crew neck jumper, and a big smile, is Wenna. 'Merrin! How lovely to see you. I put my best jumper on because you said you'd be popping by.' She pats her tidy white curls and reddens. 'I was in a dreadful old thing last time you saw me, and I didn't want you to think I was a scruff.'

My heart squeezes. 'You didn't look like a scruff at all. Have you had your hair done?'

Wenna's smile stretches again. 'I have. A mobile hairdresser comes once every six weeks or so. I get pensioner's rates and put a bit by each week so I have enough.' The smile fades. 'Hope you don't think I'm taking advantage.' She nods at the bags in my hands. 'I go without so I can have my hair done, you see … makes me feel in the land of the living, and I hate it when my fringe is so long that I have to pull it back with a grip. Cut it myself once or twice, but it ended up looking like a dog's breakfast.' Wenna's bottom lip trembles and she looks at her hands. 'Bet you think I'm a right vain old madam.'

Indignant anger coils in my chest at the thought of Wenna having to apologise for having her hair cut and choosing between that and food. It is so demeaning for her and totally unnecessary. When I think of the enormous and obscene wealth some people have, while people like Wenna can't afford the basics, I want to rage and yell, march in the streets, shout it from the rooftops. Maybe I will one of these days. 'I certainly don't think you're vain, or taking advantage.' Putting the bags down, I take her hand. 'There's absolutely no reason for you to have to even worry about any of this. Makes me so angry that you do in this day and age. There's plenty of money swimming around, just not where it's needed. The people in charge need to bloody well sort it out.'

Wenna gives me a watery smile, which sends a bit of warmth into her pale-blue eyes. 'Thank you, Merrin. I reckon they should put you in that 10 Downing Street and I'll come and be your deputy.'

I laugh. 'Right you are. So am I invited in, or shall I stand on the doorstep a bit longer?'

Wenna flaps her hand and laughs too. 'Of course. I made some scones for you. Don't expect they will be up to your standard, but the family said they loved them years ago.'

I'm about to trot out the time-honoured British 'Oh you shouldn't have', then I think of the effort and expense that making them would have taken and notice the expression of pride on Wenna's face. Instead, I say, 'How lovely. You have hidden talents.' I receive a dismissive flap of a hand as I follow Wenna long the narrow hallway, noticing the peeling floral wallpaper and threadbare navy carpet. The hallway opens onto a little kitchen overlooking the fields, and a lounge through a side door. Everything is dated, or in need of replacement, but spotless nevertheless.

'Tea or coffee?'

'Tea, please.' I put the bags of food on the table and cast an eye across the brown 1970s fake-wood cupboards, with sliding doors and blue Formica kitchen table. On the countertop is an even older teapot placed on a crocheted white and blue doily, and a toaster in bold brown and yellow stripes sits next to it. The curtains at the window are yellow too, with frilly white piping, tied back at the wall with a yellow cord. Blimey. Loads of ceramic knick-knacks line the shelves, and a mug with the Queen's face and silver jubilee lettering stands proudly in a glass cabinet, with a selection of multicoloured egg cups. The whole place looks like a film set.

'Sit yourself down in there, maid.' Wenna nods towards the lounge. 'Take the best chair near the window. I'll bring the tea and scones through on my hostess trolley.'

What's a hostess trolley? I enter the lounge, which is a mash up of 1950s, 60s and 70s with an array of yet more ornaments in a glass corner unit, and on every surface available around the room. On the floor is a swirly blue, brown, and orange carpet, the window's framed by brown and white stripy curtains, magnolia woodchip on the walls, and a gas fire is mounted on the chimney breast. Against the back wall there's a long wooden sideboard, again with sliding doors, on top of which stands a tall ornamental clown made from intertwined brightly coloured glass. In his hand he holds a bunch of red balloons and next to him, a small ceramic child with a pink headscarf looks on, with wonder in her painted eyes. I notice that the medium-sized TV on a long low table looks more recent though, as it's a flat screen. A green well-worn leather armchair is placed with its back to the window, and a two-seater green and yellow leaf-patterned sofa is opposite the TV.

'Do you need any help?' I call over my shoulder, as a glint of sunlight on a glass bottle on the windowsill catches my eye.

'No, thank you. Almost done!'

I walk over to the window and look out at the neat garden and small patio, arrayed with tubs of bright summer flowers, and to the left, a line of rose bushes edge the lawn with a sprinkle of dropped petals like confetti at a wedding. There is a pair of gardening gloves and a trowel next to two hanging baskets on a plastic table. I expect that in the height of summer there'll be a riot of colour in both. I'm about to step away and sit in the armchair when my gaze falls on the bottle again. It's mounted on a wooden stand, and the raised lettering along its flank says 'Lemonade'. Inside, there's a curl of ancient paper, sun-bleached and as thin and delicate as a moth's wing. As the sun hits it again, through the paper, I can make out a few letters in faded ink.

A rattle of crockery heralds Wenna's entrance, as she pushes a wheeled contraption into the room (that's the hostess trolley then) bearing the big brown teapot, a tiny white milk jug, two floral cups and saucers, two plates and a larger plate of buttered cherry scones. 'Now then. Sit yourself down, Merrin, and we'll have a nice cuppa.'

'Wow, those scones look stunning.'

Wenna laughs. 'You haven't tried them yet.'

I sit down and bite into one. They're excellent. Much better than mine. 'They taste as stunning as they look,' I mumble with my mouth full of scone.

'That's so kind of you to say.' Wenna's proud smile is a joy to behold as she pours the tea and settles on the sofa.

I chew an idea around for a few moments along with the scone. 'I'm not just saying it to be kind, Wenna. These scones are so light, crumbly and just the right sweetness. Everything a good scone should be.' I pause, weigh up my words and ask, 'Would you be able to make a couple of batches a week – see how they went down in the café? I'd pay you, obviously.' I know Gillian will be okay with it as she was talking about giving me more say in ordering the other day. I think she'd seen my enthusiasm for organising the community larder.

Wenna nearly chokes on her own scone and takes a few moments to recover. Thumping her chest she says, 'Really? You'd really want *my* scones in the café?'

'Yes,' I say, with a smile. 'They're absolutely brilliant.'

'My goodness.' Wenna fans her face and dabs a tissue at the moisture forming in her eyes. 'I can hardly believe it … and yes, I'd be delighted to.'

Result. I take a sip of tea, feeling its warmth combine with that inside my heart. What a great idea. The café gets superb scones, Wenna gets some badly needed cash. 'Good. That's all settled then.' We talk about the practicalities of it, who would collect them and when etc., and then I remember the bottle on the windowsill. Curious, I ask, 'I couldn't help but notice the bottle with the curl of paper written on inside. What's that all about, if you don't mind me being nosy?' I have my suspicions but want them confirming.

'Not nosey at all. I'd be happy to tell you the story.' Wenna puts her cup down and goes over to the windowsill. 'This,' she says, coming back to the sofa with the bottle, 'is how I met my lovely husband.'

Intrigued , I say, 'Go on…'

Wenna chuckles and then her expression grows serious. 'Do you believe in magic, Merrin? You're a local girl, right?'

I wasn't expecting that. 'Er … yeah, I'm local. Not sure about magic.'

'Hmm. Well, magic brought my husband to me over the

Irish sea. Magic and the power of nature have brought many a girl in this village a husband over the years, too.' She chuckles again and takes a sip of tea. 'You must have heard the old message in a bottle tales, surely, even someone of your age.'

My suspicions are confirmed and I smile. 'I have. But I've never met anyone who was actually successful. My grandma first told me about it all, but my mum said it was all stuff and nonsense.' Wenna's face falls and I give her an encouraging smile. 'Will you tell me your story?'

A nod. 'I will. Many years ago, my grandmother told my elder sister to go to the beach when the midnight moon was full in June, to a particular beach round here – Magic Cove, or Chapel Porth, to give it its proper title. Then she was to either ask the moon and stars to send her a message from a sweetheart, or send a message in a bottle to a sweetheart. It was her choice. Just before the war, she decided to send one, and two years or so later, she received a letter in the post from a young man in America.' Wenna stops and looks away, misty-eyed.

Poor love's trying to hold back tears. 'Don't worry about telling me the rest, if it's upsetting you, Wenna.'

'No, I won't talk about my sister any more if you don't mind … it always upsets me when I do. But I will tell my story.' She picks up the plate of scones. 'Another?'

'No thanks. But I wouldn't mind more tea.'

I pour us both tea from the big brown pot, which was apparently Wenna's mother's, as Wenna clears her throat, sits back on the sofa and continues. 'Right, well, I went to the beach in June at midnight, the summer I was nineteen, not actually believing anything would come of it. I'd just taken a fit in my head to do it, have a bit of an adventure, you know?'

I nod. 'That's an old-fashioned phrase. But I think it means kind of on a whim?'

'Yes, it does. And there was something in the air that night. Everything felt ... right, I suppose. The only sound was the gentle breaking of the waves on the shore, and the moon was like a big silver penny floating amongst the stars. It was Mother Nature working her magic.' She pauses to smile. 'Anyhow, I asked the moon to send me a sweetheart, tossed that bottle into the ocean, and three months later I get a letter from Ireland. '

I shuffle in my seat. How the heck am I supposed to respond to that, without making Wenna feel like she'd just spun me a yarn? Coincidence is what must have happened, not magic. I should know because it sure as hell didn't work for me. I smile back across the room and say, 'What a wonderful story.'

'It was. He'd put his phone number in the letter, so I rang him and he visited from Cork a few months later. We were married on my twentieth birthday and we lived our life together here in Cornwall. We were never apart, not even for a night. Sadly, as you know, we weren't blessed with children, but we were very happy... I miss my Finn so much.' She gets up, takes a wedding photo from the glass cabinet and hands it to me. A young, blond-haired, blue-eyed Wenna is gazing up into the face of a tall, sandy-haired, handsome man, confetti in their hair, love in their eyes. 'That's my Finn.'

There's a tremor in Wenna's voice and my stomach clenches. How must it be to have met the love of your life in such a romantic way, be happy for the rest of it, until one day they are just snatched away? The heartbreak I felt after Jacob left must be nothing to the pain of losing your husband after sixty-odd years. Poor Wenna, it must have nearly killed her. 'I'm so sorry, Wenna. I can see how much you loved each other, and can't imagine how awful it must have been to have lost him.'

'It was awful. Still is.' She blows her nose and takes a drink. 'But we had the best time together. I wouldn't change a thing.' Wenna puts her head on one side, looks at me thoughtfully. 'You said you were divorced, on the phone the other day, when we chatted to arrange your visit ... is there anyone else on the horizon? Seems a shame that such a lovely lady is all on her own.'

All on her own. Those four little words makes me feel like an orphan, abandoned to the four winds like a child in some Dickensian novel. I'm not 'all on my own', I have Lucy, my friends, my job, and my parents, when they're not touring around Europe in their state-of-the-art campervan. I know what Wenna means though. There is no 'significant other', and, meeting Pete again, well, I'm not sure I want one. 'Yes, that's right.' I nod, setting the photo frame gently on the coffee table. 'But I have my daughter, Lucy, and lots of friends and family, so don't worry about me.' I shoot her a bright smile. Maybe it's time to change the subject.

Wenna's gaze is like a bright blue winter sky, swept of

cloud. 'Hmm. That's good, but I don't see why you can't try the magic. It couldn't hurt, could it? I'm guessing not many of you young ones believe it nowadays, but I'm sure it's still there. Many a maid has found her sweetheart over the years, as I said. Even before the phone was invented, the bottles would have an address and people wrote to each other. Nowadays you have emails and suchlike.' Wenna's smile lights up her face. 'These days you could be in touch as soon as the bottle lands on a foreign shore!'

Been there, done that, bought the T-shirt. 'I don't think so, Wenna. But thanks for thinking of me.'

'You imagine it's all nonsense, don't you?'

'Er … not exactly.' *A bit far-fetched to say the least, maybe. The old local legend takes a lot of swallowing.*

'Yes, I can see it in your face.' Wenna shrugs, lifts her hands and lets them fall on her thighs. 'Most people I've told think so, too. These days there's no room for magic. Just things. People seem to need more and more things to fill the gaps in their lives. Gadgets, cars, holidays, clothes, computers, anything so they don't feel they're missing out. *Things* make them feel successful, and the more expensive the thing is, the more successful they feel.' Wenna heaves a heavy sigh and holds my gaze. 'We need more simple things in our lives. Things to lift our spirits, like love, friendship, the sound of a child's laughter. The gentle kiss of a lover.'

To my surprise, I feel my throat thicken and I have to look away. Something moves inside my chest, slips into my heart, begs for release. It's the acknowledgement that I dread, the lonely nights, the too big bed. It's the yearning to be held in someone's loving arms, to share a private joke, to walk along the shore, hand in hand, hearts united, beating in time with the waves turning along the sand. No. No more of this. Jumping up, I mumble something incoherent, collect the plates and hurry into the kitchen with them. 'I'd best be getting off, Wenna!' I call over my shoulder. 'Lucy will be home soon, and I need to get a start on dinner.'

Wenna appears at my side as I place the crockery in the washing up bowl. 'I'm sorry if I upset you, Merrin, I can ramble on sometimes. I didn't mean to. I wasn't suggesting *you* fill your life with *things* either... I meant people in general—'

'Don't worry, you didn't. I'm absolutely fine.' I put my hand on Wenna's arm and give her a big smile I manage to find in the emergency reserves. 'It's just that I really do have to get going. But I've had a great time, and I'll be ringing you to talk about those scones in the next few days, okay?'

A bright smile. 'Okay. I'll show you out.'

At the door, I turn and give Wenna a quick hug. I'm struck by her frailty and lack of substance; a strong wind could probably blow her over. The image in the wedding photo pops into my mind's eye of the twenty-year-old Wenna. Beautiful, full of life, love and hope. How quickly we grow old. Oh God, I'm getting far too emotional about all of this. I step back and manage a wobbly smile. 'Thanks again, Wenna. I'll ring soon, bye now.'

'Bye now. And I'll just say one last thing and then I'll let it go ... it's June next week. Here's what I said on that magical night many years ago.' A mischievous smile plays over her lips as she thrusts a scrap of paper into my hand then she does a wiggly finger-wave and closes the door.

Unfolding the paper, I read, *I give my words to the grace of the moon, the power of the ocean, and the magic of nature. Please grant me the things I truly deserve.* Despite everything, I find myself smiling as I slip behind the wheel of my car. June moons, oceans and magic. Dear oh dear. As if…

Chapter Fourteen

I pull at the hem of my old blue and white checked dress. Why the heck didn't I put on trousers? These legs are too pale to be seen in public. Why didn't I listen to my inner voice, instead of throwing caution to the wind? Okay, it's a warm June evening, but as I watch my lovely friend Faye sashay along the beach boardwalk to the bar, wearing a tiny pair of white shorts, her long legs tanned by the Californian sun, I shuffle my chair closer to the table. For good measure, I unfold a napkin, and drape it over my two doughy uncooked baguettes ready for the oven, otherwise known as my legs.

Faye tosses her glossy dark hair and points at the fishbowl glass of G&T as she approaches the table. 'Ooh, you've got me my favourite!'

'Of course. I know my job.'

'The job of being my bestest friend and knowing everything about me, so you can pander to my every

177

whim?' Faye widens her emerald-green eyes and puts her head on one side.

'In your dreams, sweet cheeks.' I stand up and envelop my friend in a bear hug. 'It seems like forever since I saw you!'

Faye squeezes back. 'It does! You're looking great.'

Really? I don't feel it and the damned napkin's on the floor now. I step back and tug at my hem again. 'Think it's a bit too short for white legs.'

'Nonsense. Besides, summer's here and they'll soon tan up when you're jogging on the beach.' Faye sits down and closes her eyes as she savours her first sip.

'Jogging on the beach?' I lift my margarita and frown. When have I ever been jogging on a beach?

'You haven't. But you said last time we met that you were going to take me up on my new keep-fit regime and join me on a run a few times a week.'

The twinkle in Faye's eyes tells me I'd never said any such thing. 'Of course I did, yes. Must have said it just before I set off on that unicycle ride across a tightrope over the Grand Canyon.'

Faye laughs and puts her drink down. 'I'd love you to come with me though. I want to get really fit and toned before I go back out on my next manhunt.'

'Another one? Before you went off to America, you told me you were off men for ever, after the last disaster.'

'I've had time to think since then. The next one will be a keeper.' Faye thumps her chest. 'I feel it in here.'

If I'd a pound for every time she'd said that, I'd be able to give up work and write my damned book. Faye always jumped in too quickly with both feet, and she tended to pick the ones who never wanted the same things as she did. Thinking about it, since we'd left school, I'd dated a handful of men, and only ever been serious about two. Faye, on the other hand, must have found 'the one' at least twenty times. Though she'd got a devil-may-care attitude to life, and always seemed full of fun, now and then I'd been allowed to look through a crack in Faye's façade, and through it saw the vulnerable woman she really was. The crack was always quickly cemented over, however, and 'normal' service resumed. 'Well, I hope you're right,' I say, squeezing her hand. 'And you don't need to get fit, you look stunning as you are.'

Faye extends her arm and turns back the short sleeve of her yellow T-shirt. 'Look at that.' She pokes at her toned underarm with an expertly manicured fingernail. 'It wobbles and I'm only thirty-nine.' She leans in and lowers her voice. 'Can you believe it? Bingo wings at thirty-nine. I've also got a paunch developing after eating all those pizzas and burgers in California.'

I sweep my gaze over Faye's delicate bone structure, her cupid's bow mouth, stunning svelte figure and shake my head. 'Some women would kill to look like you.' *Me for one. And don't get me started about my stretchmarks.* 'You're imagining things.'

'That's lovely of you, but I will feel better if I take action, and you're coming with me jogging.' Faye grins and prods my hand resting on the table.

I sigh. 'If I get time, I might. Now tell me all about your trip. How's the lovely sister of yours and your nieces?'

Faye launches into an almost forty-minute exposition of all her adventures, which at times is very interesting, but mostly I find myself drifting off. The drifting off centres around Pete and whether to take him up on his offer of a date, and, of course, the past. The past is always the best place to live, because you can manipulate it, chop bits out that don't fit or are upsetting, maybe embroider sections to complete a prettier tapestry. The early years of my marriage when Lucy was little are an old favourite. The future was set, mapped out, safe. But there I go jamming on a pair of rose-tinted specs again. And now? What of the future, now? I doodle a series of hearts with a fingernail in the condensation on the side of my glass, watch the moisture around the edges distort their shape.

'And then a little green man came down in a rocket and asked me to marry him. Guess what? I considered it, because there hadn't been too many offers lately.'

'Eh? What are you on about?' I frown across the table at Faye's equally frowny face and folded arms.

'You haven't listened to a bloody word I said for the past five minutes, have you?'

'Erm…'

'And you're drawing little hearts on your glass…' Faye narrows her eyes and gives me a knowing smile. 'You're seeing someone, aren't you? Who is it? Come on, tell me.'

I destroy the hearts with my fingertips and put their cool pads against a flush of heat in my neck and cheeks. 'I'm not seeing anyone, but I did want to have a chat to you about the possibility of going on a date with an old boyfriend.'

'Oooh! Who is it?' Faye leans her elbows on the table, her eyes round with excitement.

'Pete.'

Faye leans back again as if seeking to distance herself from his name, a deep furrow knitting her eyebrows. 'Not *the* Pete?'

'Yeah.' My voice is no more than a whisper.

Unfortunately, Faye's is far louder, 'No. Not Pete Veryan from school, surely? The Pete Veryan who buggered off to Australia and left you heartbroken?'

'No, the Pete Veryan whom I settled down with, got married to and had three kids with.' I sigh, gulp my drink, grateful for the kick.

'But how can you even consider it after he hurt you so much?'

'That's a bit rich coming from the girl who went back to that Leon guy whenever he called you. Even after numerous dumpings. For God's sake, he treated you like a bloody yo-yo.' Faye's expression darkens as surprise and hurt flicker in her eyes. I'm surprised too. Why had I been so nasty? Probably because remembering the past is tearing me apart, and I'm not sure I can trust men ever again.

'Okay. Yes, you're right. But then I'm like that, aren't I? Let men walk all over me – pretend it doesn't matter...' She looks away across the beach and to the sparkling blue horizon beyond. 'You're the strong one. Always have been.'

Well done, Merrin. With a twist of shame in my gut, I reply, 'I'm so sorry for saying all that. I don't know where it came from. Must be all the rubbish Jacob kindly left me with. Feelings of insecurity, loneliness, lack of confidence.

Lots of crap like that – he was very generous. Now Pete comes back from the past and shows an interest, and you poured a bucket of water over the idea. Guess I was lashing out, and it shouldn't have been at you.'

'No need to apologise.' Faye's cheerful demeanour is back, thankfully. My lovely friend has never been one to sulk. 'I get it. Honestly. Now, let's have a look at Pete. Show me his photo – is he still muscular, got that sexy twinkle and just-got-out-of-bed look?'

'I don't have a photo.' Faye had hit the nail on the head with her description of Pete, except now he'd matured into even more of a hottie. Or 'well hench', as Lucy would say.

'No problem. I can look him up on socials.' She's already scrolling through her phone. 'Tell me all about how you met again while I find him.' I'm cut short in the story by Faye's excited shriek. 'Oh my God! Of course you should see him, Merrin. He's amazing. Always was, but he's even better now.' Faye thrusts her phone screen at me.

Seemingly, looks are more important than personality in Faye's world. What happened to the fact that he dumped me all those years ago? Pete grins at me from a sunny profile, the backdrop of blue sky and white sand adding to the overall handsome beach bum impression. 'Yes, nobody can deny he's good-looking, but as you *just* pointed out – he did a runner, left me in bits. My heart won't stand that again.'

Faye pulls a sympathetic face and nods. 'Especially not after Jacob.'

'Exactly.'

'Hmm.' She drums her red fingernails on the table. 'So

you were saying he left you a note on the table at the café. What did it say?'

'That he was sorry he hurt me, he's buying a house in Perranporth, and he'd love to mend our relationship … go out for a drink, just as friends, or whatever I felt comfortable with.' I shrug. 'He'd just be grateful to have me in his life again and added his number at the bottom.'

'Aw, bless him.' Faye sits back, folds her arms. 'You should definitely give him another chance.'

'Should I though? I need your honest opinion because I'm damned if I know.'

'Look. As he said, you can meet just as friends, see where it goes. It's only a drink, not a marriage proposal. Yeah?'

I smile. I have to admit I've been thinking along the same lines since I read his note, but wanted it confirming by my oldest friend. Talk of marriage puts me in mind of the conversation I had with Wenna the other day and I have to share it with Faye. 'You remember when I tried sending that message in a bottle from Chapel Porth after Pete buggered off all those years ago, to try and get him to come back?'

Faye raises a brow at the sudden change of subject. 'Oh my God yeah. I told you to try it 'cos my great aunt told me that's how she found her bloke. How gullible were we back then?' She laughs.

'I know, right. But I met an old lady, Wenna, who came to the community larder and she swears it's all true. She met her future husband in the same way, and so did her sister. She even keeps the original bottle with the message in it on the windowsill.'

This news is met with a thoughtful gaze. 'God, I wish it did work. I'd be down there like a shot.'

'My mum once said it was all nonsense and I tend to believe her, as it didn't work for me, did it?'

'Yeah, but my great aunt said the magic only worked if you truly believed. Maybe you didn't...' Faye drains her glass and stares at it. 'Or maybe we've just lost faith in the old ways now. The old wives' tales belong in the past. Wenna and my great aunt belonged to a different time. Superstition and magic have no place in our world really, do they? Modern women are more independent too – don't need a sweetheart to come and sweep them off their feet, eh?'

I hide a smile. 'Hmm.'

'What's the "hmm" for? Are you suggesting that I want a gorgeous man to come and do a bit of sweeping?'

'Hey, don't we all, honey?' I say in a silly American accent. I hold my hands up. 'Well, as long as he's not the same as Pete and Jacob. I've had my fill of being dropped from a great height and having my still beating heart ripped out and stamped on.'

'Very graphic.' Faye wrinkles her nose.

I swirl the remnants of my drink round my glass. 'And we can still be modern independent women, just with a great guy who's trustworthy, loving, fun and genuine by our side.'

'Not asking for much then?'

I grin. 'Nope.'

'Anyhow, are you going to give Pete a chance to redeem himself? Just meet up as friends, hey?'

I ponder this for a few moments and then look at Faye's encouraging expression. Oh, for Christ's sake. What could it hurt? It might also do some good. 'Yeah. Yeah, okay, you're right.' Draining my glass, I nod at Faye. 'I think it's your round.'

––––––––

The sound of laughter and the clink of glasses spills out of the beer garden; a warm welcome to passers-by. I look at the time on my phone and then back down the street. With a jolt, I see that the taxi's turning round in the car park, dependable, safe, ready to whisk me back home. Away. Away from the nerves in my gut, currently riding on the crest of a wave of nausea. Would it be okay if I decide to just pass on by, too? Come on, Merrin. It's just a drink, as Faye had said the other day, and as Lucy had also said earlier, when she'd put the finishing touches to my hair.

Moving my reluctant feet a few steps closer to the beer garden, I carefully finger the soft waves in my hair that my daughter so lovingly fashioned with straighteners. Have they fallen flat on the short journey to Perranporth? No, they appear to be in place. Maybe I shouldn't have let Lucy put so much eyeliner on though, along with the crimson lipstick. Lucy, bless her, had insisted I put on my matching red and white checked summer dress, but it was too low cut for a casual drink with a friend, wasn't it? I never listen to my cautious side, do I? But it had been hard to do it earlier when my cautious side had whispered that I was trying too hard as Lucy, a proud smile on her face, had stood back and admired her handiwork. The cautious side was shoved back in its box, because there was no way I could have changed and taken off some of the make-up, after all Lucy's hard work. *Bugger it. Get a move on.*

At the entrance to the beer garden, I scan the benched wooden tables for a sign of Pete. There he is looking relaxed and handsome as ever, sitting under a blue and yellow umbrella, dressed casually in a white open-necked shirt and light blue jeans. He's nursing a pint, and opposite him on the table is a glass of white wine. He remembered one of my tipples. Sweet of him. Bet he didn't remember my preference for spritzers in summer though. As I approach, he jumps up and gives me that big warm smile that used to make my heart turn to mush back in the day and flings his arms wide. Will it be more awkward to remain at a distance, or to step into them? Ah sod it. Friends hugged, didn't they? As his arms close about me, he says, 'Wow! You look absolutely stunning.'

Any awkwardness scurries away into the shadows at his words when I feel the warmth of his embrace and inhale the familiar scent of his skin. The cologne's new though, as are the breadth of his chest and his muscular upper arms. 'Thank you. You don't look so bad yourself.' Stepping back might be a good idea, however, before he can plant those kissable lips on mine. His warm brown eyes are staring at my mouth as if he's going to do just that, and I almost stumble in my haste to slide onto the bench. *You don't get to jump back where we left off that easy, matey, even if you are well hench.*

Pete smiles, sits opposite and indicates the glass in front

of me. 'I took the liberty of ordering you a drink. I remember what you liked back then, but just say if you'd like something else.'

Returning his smile, I take a sip. Bloody hell, it's a spritzer with soda, not lemonade. Just how I like it. 'Top marks for getting it right.' I lift my glass to his. 'Cheers. Here's to us meeting again.'

'Cheers. I'm so glad we have; I can't tell you how much.'

Pete's twinkle is switched on to full, as is his bright white smile. Damn, I'll need to put my shades on at this rate. 'Me too. So, how's the house move going? Has the sale gone through?'

'Next week. Can't wait! You can see the sea from the garden if you crane your neck and you can be on the beach in five minutes.'

'Sounds perfect. We were going to try for a house nearer the sea in a few years, but...' Why the hell have I started talking about me and Jacob? There is no more me and Jacob. 'But life took a different turn, as you know.'

A sympathetic smile lifts one side of his mouth. 'Must be hard still. What with having the worry of taking care of your daughter, all on your own.'

For some reason, this irks me. And it's more than hearing those words 'all on your own' again. It's probably because he knows nothing about me anymore. Okay, he's trying to be understanding, but Pete doesn't get to swan off to Australia for the past twenty-two years and then presume to know what's hard for me and how I look after my daughter. 'Actually, we're doing fine. Lucy's not a little kid – far from it. She'll be off to uni very soon. Jacob sees her every other weekend so…' I trail off, very much aware of awkwardness shimmying out of the shadows and boldly reclining on the table between us.

'Oh, I didn't mean you weren't handling the lone parent thing…' Pete draws his hand across his chin and shuffles about on the bench. 'I mean, what do I know about parenting?'

I take a swallow of wine and smile at him. He's embarrassed, and it's all my fault for bringing up the past and stupid Jacob anyway. Poor guy. 'I know you didn't. Anyway, tell me all about Australia!'

Happily, we get on really well for the rest of the evening – awkwardness has found other people to annoy – and we never run out of things to say … but… Why is there always a 'but' with me these days? Why can't I let myself go, enjoy Pete's company without analysing and second-guessing what might happen next? Live for now, each hour, each minute, for God's sake. Watching his eyes light up as he regales me with stories about his life in Australia, I'm conscious of the fact that he's still very attractive to me, and I'm really enjoying his company, 'but' … there's something missing. The old feelings have gone. My heart's not skipping a beat, is it? No anticipation or excitement wriggles like an eel in my belly as I think of what's to come. I laugh at something he's said, hopefully in the right place, and drain my glass… It's not working. Being with Pete again is an eagerly and long awaited Christmas present that turns out to be an empty box, once the wrapping's come off.

'I'm having such a great time. Fancy another?' Pete points at my glass and takes my hand across the table.

No. No I don't. I want to go home. It was nice to catch up, but that's it now. The past is the past, and there it must stay. No point in dragging it into the present and pretending it will slip right into its old shoes. The shoes are too old, worn, and certainly out of fashion. Then I imagine Faye's voice yelling in my ear. *For goodness' sake stop being so bloody dramatic! Give it a chance. Get to know him again. It's not going to feel exactly the same straightaway, is it? What do you expect?*

Torn between following my heart and Faye's sensible advice, I squeeze his hand and swallow a hard lump that's appeared from somewhere. No. No, I'm sure my heart has it right. I might be ready to trust someone again, be with someone again … but it certainly won't be with Pete. Sad, perhaps. But there we are.

'I don't think I do, thanks. I've got a busy day in the café and it's foodbank day tomorrow – so we'll be rushed off our feet. But I've loved catching up, too.'

'We'll do it again soon though, eh?' Pete strokes a finger up the inside of my forearm, a slow sexy smile curving his mouth.

I don't think so waits on my tongue, but I'm too much of a coward to let it out. A bright smile. 'Yeah, I'll call you when I have a minute.' I'm already standing up and shrugging my denim jacket on. 'You know what tourist season's like here.'

Pete looks like he's been slapped as he stares up at me, surprise in his eyes. And who could blame him? One minute we're laughing and squeezing each other's hands, the next I'm doing the Cinderella act. 'Oh right.' He gets to his feet and clears his throat. 'I … I thought we were having a good time … like we used to, Rin?'

'We were!' My voice sounds like it's been stretched and twisted. 'I'm just a bit tired, and as I said, it's going to be a busy day tomorrow.'

His smile is uncertain and he slips his own jacket on. 'No worries. I'll walk you to the taxi, yeah?'

'No, it's fine.' I look at my phone, my heart thumping in my chest at the lie I'm cooking up. 'I asked the taxi guy to pick me up at 10.30 outside. It's twenty-five past, so I'll be off.' I give him a quick peck on the cheek. 'Thanks again, Pete. It was lovely to see you again.' God, my voice is as wobbly as Pete's smile as I make my escape, hurrying into the pub and through the other side, like a scalded cat.

Creeping halfway up the stairs, I see that Lucy's bedroom light's on. Must still be studying. There's no way I want to give chapter and verse to her about the evening. All I want is to get under the duvet and slip into oblivion. Best use the downstairs loo and forget cleaning my teeth until the morning. Can't risk the bathroom, or Lucy will be there like an excited puppy, asking for the lowdown.

Mission accomplished, I lie in bed looking at the moon peeping through a gap in the curtain like an examining monocle. *Go away, moon. I have nothing to be guilty of.* Pete's a big boy and can cope with rejection. God knows *I* had to all those years ago. Closing my eyes against further scrutiny, I take a deep breath and release it slowly.

As I'm drifting off, Wenna's "old wives'" tale about the moon in June and the message in a bottle whines in my head like an annoying mosquito. My eyes fly open again and I stare at the moon. Ridiculous idea. Well, actually, it's lovely and romantic, but it's all coincidence, has to be, and certainly shouldn't be believed in, in this day and age. As Faye said, Wenna's era was one of make-believe, magic and superstition. The world's moved on a bit from then, to say the least. Since the 1960s, there've been moon landings, incredible scientific and medical breakthroughs, and the bloody internet for goodness' sake. Wenna and her sister's story can easily be explained away. Modern independent women don't entertain that sort of malarkey.

I turn over and close my eyes again … but the moon is persistent, shining its monocle in my face through the curtain. There's nothing for it but to drag my arse out of bed and close the damned thing. Through the window, everything in the garden looks so ethereal, bathed in a soft, shimmering silver moonshine. I expect there will be a few dancing pixies along in a minute, if I look close enough. Pushing the top window open a bit more, I take a breath of night air, and a whisper of the ocean, a mile away, drifts on the breeze. Suddenly a frisson of excitement appears in my chest and goosebumps run the length of my arms. This is crazy. Maybe I'm losing it, but there's a warm feeling spreading through me and a desperate need to believe something might actually come of this. *You have to really believe in the magic, Merrin,* an inner voice whispers.

I picture Wenna and all the others who've gone before, standing in the shallows one June night, the moon in their eyes, wishing for love, and I smile. My heart's racing and I can hardly believe I'm doing this. But I am. It feels … right somehow. Deadly serious and wishing with all my heart, I say, 'Okay, moon, floating above Chapel Porth or Magic Cove as all those women in the past believed, bring me a sweetheart.' Taking the scrap of paper that Wenna had given me from the nightstand I read, '*I give my words to the grace of the moon, the power of the ocean, and the magic of nature. Please grant me the things I truly deserve.* I'll come and find the message in a bottle soon,' I add, with a sigh, feeling suddenly foolish. If only old legends came true. I imagine Wenna chuntering, *They certainly don't come true for those who can't even be bothered to go down to the beach to do their wishing.*

Back once again under the duvet, I yawn and feel my eyelids grow heavy. The magic will either work or it won't. Knowing me, it won't. It didn't before, and this time I only did it on a whim really. And yet… Okay, enough is enough. Sleep is coming, and tomorrow's another day, all fresh and shiny. It's mine to do with what I will. Hell, I might even go for a jog down to the beach. That will give Faye something to smile about.

Chapter Fifteen

GOOD HARBOR BEACH, GLOUCESTER, MASSACHUSETTS

1993

Lamorna slips her arm through Harry's and pulls him a few steps nearer to the waves breaking on the wide windswept shore.

'Hey, that's close enough. My sneakers will get wet!' Harry laughs and looks down at his wife. His blue eyes, though nestling upon a mesh of crow's feet, are still as twinkly as they ever were and still make her stomach flip when he gives her that long lingering look.

Lamorna laughs and ruffles his white curly hair. 'This from a man who stormed the beaches at Normandy? A bit of salt water will do you good.'

'Normandy was long ago, my sweet. I'm used to the comforts of home at my age.'

'Seventy-two isn't old,' she responds, lowering herself to the sand and pulling off her socks. 'Neither is seventy. And to prove it, I'm going in for a paddle.'

'Well, if you are, then I am too.' Harry chuckles and rolls up his trouser legs. 'But if I fall in, you're coming with me.'

'Ha! We won't go far, just enough to feel refreshed.' Lamorna rolls up her jeans and adds, 'And there's no reason we can't start swimming again now that spring's here. You can wear a wetsuit if you like, just as long as we reconnect with our magic ocean.'

'Yeah, we will … when the water's warmed up a bit.' Harry winks and sets off at a fast walk, tossing over his shoulder, 'Come on then, slowcoach, I stormed the beaches at Normandy, don't you know!'

A shrill shriek of laughter escapes as a playful wave catches Lamorna unawares and soaks her legs through to the thigh, but she doesn't care. Just being here on this beach switches on all her lights, exhalation races with adrenaline in her veins, and joy lifts her heart as high as the cluster of fluffy white clouds sailing across the sun. 'Wow, this makes me feel alive! I adore this place.' Lamorna tugs the sleeve of Harry's light green shirt, and pretends to pull him in.

'Hey, I told you, if I'm going in, you're coming too!' He grabs a bunch of her long turquoise cotton blouse and wiggles it back and forth.

Helpless with laughter, Lamorna bends forwards, hand on her knees to get her breath back. 'Okay, you win.' She looks at Harry, whose lovely face is wreathed in sunlight and a warm smile. His tanned skin has more than a few creases nowadays, but he's still her blue-eyed American boy. Lamorna traces her fingertip across his lips and follows on with a gentle kiss. 'You're still as handsome as you were when I first laid eyes on you in that Cornish lane.' Harry shakes his head and starts to disagree, but she puts a finger to his lips. 'I'll be forever grateful to the grace of the moon, the power of this ocean and the magic of nature that brought you across the world to me. I couldn't have wished for a better life partner.'

Harry pulls her close and kisses the top of her head. 'Oh, my darling Morna. Me too.'

Lamorna feels melancholy swirling in her gut and she pulls her feet out of the sucking sand as the tide drags at her legs. 'I often look out at this beach from our window and try to reach out my thoughts to my little magic cove all those miles away. I know this beach is bigger and wider, but now and then when it's deserted, in the early morning, and the sun peeps over the dunes, it's so similar. I feel deep inside me that the two places are connected, somehow,' she says, wistful.

'You never know, stranger things have happened. If the magic can bring people sweethearts, who knows what else is possible?'

'That's what I think. It worked for Wenna too when she found Finn...' Lamorna's voice trails off, and a weight of sadness settles in her chest as it always does when she thinks about her sister. They're still estranged after all these years, despite Lamorna's attempts to bridge the rift between them.

'Hey, don't dwell on Morwenna. It always brings you down, and you can't do any more than you've done to try and make things right.' Harry slips his fingers through hers and leads the way out of the waves and onto the warm sand.

Lamorna knows he resents her sister, hence the refusal to call her Wenna. She's always Morwenna to him, and sometimes 'that damned woman'. Lamorna pushes a strand of her long grey hair from her eyes and turns to face the ocean again. Sunlight dances along the rolling blue like sparklers and the horizon line is a smudge of navy under the pale blue sky. Such beauty has no place for sad thoughts, but Wenna won't go away. 'Mum once told me the reason she doesn't write is because she's jealous to death of me and what we have out here. Always felt like she was playing second fiddle. The fact she can't have kids ate away at her like a cancer too. Mum's words, not mine. I asked her how she knew this, and she said, "A mother knows."'

Harry sighs and folds his arms as he watches the trajectory of a pelican heading for the water – white wings outstretched, braced for landing. 'I remember you telling me, yes. But it's not your fault. You never did anything to make her feel second best. I know you said that your mum might have. But parents were different back then, not as much time to coddle kids. They mostly did their best though.'

'They did … and they were built of strong stuff. I can't believe they're almost ninety-six now.' She heaves a sigh. 'I just wish it could be different for me and Wenna. One day I hope we meet again, or at least start to talk again. I feel that she sometimes goes down to the beach and thinks of me … of the times when we were happy, playing there as kids.'

'Perhaps she does, darling.' Harry tucks a stray strand of hair behind her ear.

'I miss my parents, Cornwall, you know … still.'

'It's only natural.' Harry's old twinkle turns his eyes into a mirror of the ocean. 'For what it's worth, I think your spirit might divide its time between Cornwall and here, once you're gone.'

Lamorna laughs. 'What a great thought. My spirit could keep an eye on Wenna and have a hand in any future bottle sending and receiving too.'

'Yeah, and mine could come and keep you company. Sing the old Police song "Message in a Bottle" to all the young hopefuls as they stand on the shore under the June moon.'

'Message in a bottle?' a young voice says behind them, making Lamorna jump.

'Ethan! Where did you pop up from?' Harry asks, giving his twelve-year-old great-nephew a bear hug.

Ethan rolls the sleeves of his red and yellow checked shirt and wipes his forehead with the back of his hand. 'I thought I'd run the two miles up from our house to see my favourite great-uncle and aunt. School's still out until next week.'

Lamorna hugs him too, and ruffles his mop of sandy blonde hair. 'So it is. You're growing into such a handsome chap. Your eyes are nearly as blue as my Harry's.'

'And it won't be long before you're as tall as me, either.' Harry lands him a play punch on the arm.

'Ow, that hurt,' Ethan says, with a chuckle, and puts his fists up in boxer stance. They dance round each other, kicking up sand and pretend to fight for a few moments.

Then Ethan asks, 'What was this message in a bottle thing you were talking about just now?'

Lamorna raises an eyebrow at Harry. He nods his assent, so she tells Ethan their story for the next ten minutes, with plenty of interjections from Harry and eye rolls from Lamorna because he keeps going off on a tangent. 'And that, my dear boy,' she finishes with a sigh, 'is the magical and wonderful story of how we met, married, and came to be still together after more years than I care to remember.'

'It's so awesome,' Ethan says, his eyes round as the pebbles he's creating a pattern in the sand with. Then he smirks and looks off over the ocean. 'Hard to believe that magic really does exist though.'

'Yeah. Especially for you youngsters nowadays,' Lamorna says with a sad little smile. 'You have all this new technology, computers and suchlike. Great inventions, but I do wonder if it's at the expense of some really important traditions and old ways.'

Ethan snaps his head back to her. 'Oh, don't misunderstand me. I'm not saying I don't believe your story, Aunt Lamorna. But that was a very long time ago, in an old country. It would be totally radical if it would work for me in my country and in these times.' A smile lit up his face, and Lamorna thinks what a lovely boy he is. His beautiful soul seemed to shine right out of him.

'Totally rad.' Harry nods solemnly, which causes Ethan to laugh out loud.

'There's nothing stopping you trying it in a few years … say, when you're sixteen?' Lamorna says. 'We still have the bottle I sent, and there's no finer person I'd like to give it to.'

Ethan's eyes light up. 'Really? Wow. Yeah, I'll try it.' He stands up and brushes sand from his jeans. 'And you know a while ago I was asking you all about teaching, Aunt Lamorna?' She nods. 'Well, I think I want to be one. A great and respected one – just like you were.'

Lamorna's heart swells and she has to blink away sudden tears. 'Oh, Ethan, what a lovely thing to say.'

Ethan grins, hugs them both and then touches two fingers to his brow in a quick salute. 'Okay, I'm gonna get home now. Mum says to come for dinner Sunday if you're not busy. See ya!'

Lamorna and Harry stand hand in hand as they watch him race off down the beach into the distance like a gold flash of sunlight. 'What a great kid he is,' Harry says.

'Yep. And what a great man he'll become. Kind, honest and true.' Lamorna doesn't know how she knows that, but she does.

As they climb the sandy steps to their house a while later, the phone rings out shrill and insistent in their living room. Harry hurries to answer it while Lamorna fills the kettle in the kitchen. She's about to shout and ask her husband if he wants a coffee, when he appears at the door, pinch-faced, his mouth a thin line.

Lamorna's heart leaps into her chest and she clutches the back of a kitchen chair. 'What is it, Harry?' she manages in a trembling voice.

He puts his arm around her and says quietly, 'Sit down,

my darling. It's Wenna … with some upsetting news about your mum…'

———————

Ethan races down the sandy slope to the moonlit beach, the weight in his backpack bouncing against his right shoulder blade. He stops upon reaching the gentle surf caressing the sand, and gazes awestruck at the enormous mercury moon breaking through the tatters of a thin black cloud, swept by an eastward breeze. The shush of the waves in his ears calms his racing pulse and the eeriness of the scene shifts into something else. Something magical. Excitement builds in his chest as he feels the hairs go up along the back of his neck, and chills travel the length of him. Great Aunt Lamorna was right. If you really believe in stuff outside of the ordinary, let yourself go, allow yourself to unite with a greater energy, then anything is possible.

Ethan hopes what he's about to do is possible, and smiles to himself as he pulls an old glass bottle from his backpack. He's so honoured that Lamorna and Harry gave such a sentimental and precious piece to him, and he's going to give it all the positive energy and hope he's got. It's his birthday too. Sixteen today … maybe that could throw in a bit of added power to the proceedings. As the moon tips a glittering moonbeam path along the ocean before him, Ethan reads the words his great aunt gave him.

I give my words to the grace of the moon, the power of the ocean, and the magic of nature. Please grant me the things I truly deserve.

Wow. His heart swells with pride when he thinks of all those who have gone before him, uttering the same words over the centuries, standing on a beach under a June moon, just like him, but at the other side of that big expanse of water right in front of him. He knows his friends would say he's a dumbass for doing something like this – and why didn't he ask a girl out like any normal kid? Ethan doesn't want to be a normal kid. He wants to be a bit different, to have the strength and determination of people like Lamorna and Harry. Hell, Harry stormed the beaches on D-Day. Ethan can't match that, but he will try his best to be a good man, a kind man … and one day he wants to be a teacher, like Lamorna.

The bottle sparkles silver along its flank as he lifts it up to the moon, and the message he's written shifts inside as he turns it around. 'Okay, little bottle. Have a good journey and don't get swallowed by a whale.' Ethan chuckles softly. 'I don't know where you'll end up, but I hope someone wonderful finds you.' Then he assumes his best shotput stance and hurls the bottle out and up into the star-spangled sky, only releasing a breath once he hears it land with a little splash. That's it then. Done. Ethan hugs himself and does a crazy little dance in the waves before turning and heading towards home.

Chapter Sixteen

CORNWALL

Present day

I've been awake since the crack of a sparrow's fart, so might as well stop gawking at a spider making an intricate web in the corner of my bedroom ceiling and get up. Thoughts of me upsetting Pete last night, Lucy going to uni, the community larder, Wenna's story, what will happen to me in the future, and if I'm doing my best for everyone have been making intricate webs in the corners of my brain too. Do brains have corners? They have tops, middles, bottoms and sides, but corners? I feel like mine does. Mine has dusty corners with old memories wedged tightly into them. Memories which are too painful to see the light of day, but leap out of the dust at you, when you least expect them. Other corners house annoying thoughts that won't leave you alone, at unearthly hours of the morning. Constantly weaving, spinning silken threads between each other, eventually becoming one seething mass of insurmountable problems.

One particular bit of thread isn't really a problem, it just dangles a thought now and then, but I blow it away, because enticing as it is, I'm not sure I have the energy. Throwing the curtains wide, I see the moon has gone off shift and the sun's taken over. Where last night the grass was moon-dappled with soft, shimmering silver, and a hint of dancing pixies, this morning fingers of sunlight are stroking away the dew from the grass and lifting a few handfuls of mist from the shadows. The thought dangles from its thread again and I pluck it free. Bugger it, why not? It's almost 06.00 – a jog on the beach will do me good, before the day comes rushing at me with a long list of jobs to tick off.

———————————

Chapel Porth Cove is empty of tourists, dog walkers and any other human, which is how I like my beaches. Selfish it might be, but there's something about a virgin stretch of sand washed of any footprints, apart from those of seagulls, and my own. The Atlantic is in a gentle mood, shushing a roll of turquoise waves up the beach, while the sunlight scatters a few sparkles across the deeper blue, like a shower of diamond confetti. I run down the slope to the sand and do a few stretches, as if I know what I'm doing, like a proper jogger. I'm wearing a vest top and shorts, so I must be, eh? I've decided to run barefoot on the hard wet sand, as I assume it's easier than wearing trainers. Given that the beach isn't the biggest, I'll do a few back and forths, and then see how I feel. No point in going mad the first time.

One final stretch of my legs, each foot in turn braced against a barnacled rock, and a huge breath of salt air to boost me, I set off at a slow jog. My ponytail swings from side to side in time with my footsteps, a pleasant breeze at my back whispers encouragement, and after a few minutes, my spirit stirs somewhere deep within, and starts to climb. Oh, the joy of being alive and alone on a deserted beach! Whenever I'm next to the ocean, my woes and worries are yanked out and blown away over the horizon. Nothing seems to matter, apart from filling my senses with the beauty and majesty of nature. Of course, the woes and worries will be waiting in the wings to take over afterwards, but for a time, they're gone. Banished. Obliterated. I should do this more often.

Twenty minutes later, I stand at the shoreline, bend forward, hands on thighs, and exhale with a whoosh. Wow. I feel so alive, ready for anything. I turn around to check I'm still alone. I am, apart from a few gulls and jackdaws, so I let out a 'Whoop!' I laugh to myself and walk into the breakers to cool my feet, an ear-to-ear grin stretching my mouth when I think of Wenna's story again. I bet she didn't come jogging here when she found her bottle all those years ago. I bet she walked serenely, her belief in the power of the ocean and the magic of nature floating under her footsteps. My half-hearted gabble at the moon last night was a bit disrespectful really, when I think of all the women down the ages who had supposedly found their sweethearts in the way Wenna and her sister had. But what does it matter? It's just a story anyway. A lovely one, but a story nevertheless. I tried the first time and nothing happened, did it? So why should this time be any different? A memory of the frisson of excitement and goosebumps I felt last night and the conviction I had that something would happen is nagging at me, as is the memory of a warm feeling spreading through me ... but in the light of day, the whole thing seems a bit imagined ... so I tell it to shush.

Much as I don't want to leave the beach, a day in the shop awaits. I'll make Lucy a cooked breakfast when I get back, before I go to work. It'll cheer her up after all that hard exam revision she's been putting in. With one final look at the waves, I turn and walk back along the beach, but a tapping noise by the rocks halts my progress. *Chink, chink, chink.* Turning to my right, I take a few steps towards the rocks to investigate. Leaning a hand against the damp uneven surface, I scan the few feet of beach between them and the waves. Nothing. There it comes again. *Chink, chink, chink.* It's coming from a seaweed-strewn rock pool, just beyond where I'm standing. There's a seagull dipping its beak now and then. Is it causing the tapping? But what's it pecking at? Muscle and crab shells don't make that noise... A giddy wiggly feeling shows up in my belly and I shake my head at the images it offers.

This is nuts. I turn to walk away once more, but curiosity has me anchored. Oh, for God's sake. I hurry over to the rock pool and the seagull flies off with an annoyed squawk. Nothing but seaweed and a few tiny crustaceans. Waste of time. I'm about to leave once more, but the sun chucks a handful of diamonds into the water, and a few bounce off the shoulder of ... of a partly submerged... My brain knows the word but won't let me acknowledge it for a nano second. Then it does. *Bottle*. Immediately, my logical reasoning elbows aside flights of fancy. It's just an old bottle chucked off a ship by some environmentally unfriendly person, that's all. My hand shoots into the seaweed, grabs the slippery neck and then I realise it's wedged under a crevice. I give it a wiggle and jerk, and it comes free. Then after a quick wipe with my fingers to clear a patch of what looks like green algae, I hold it up to the sun. It has raised lettering on the front. I can't make all of it out, as it's obviously an ancient bottle, but it looks like it says *Ginger er*. What's that? Then I trace the badly eroded letters of the second word with a fingertip, and realise it spells beer. Ginger beer.

The giddy wiggle comes dancing back and pulls me into the waves. I bend and give the bottle a good old wash, remembering that my grandma told me she used to have ginger beer in thick bottles when she was a child, so it must be pretty old. It feels old too. Not that I'm a bottle expert or anyth— My thoughts stop. Stop. STOP. Then they go into free fall as I hold the clean bottle up to the sun, because inside there's a scroll of paper. A scroll of paper with writing on it.

Really? I mean ... really? A garbled and frivolous chat to the moon through the window last night, and the very next day I find a message in a bottle? I couldn't even be arsed to come to the beach like Wenna and the others did. How is this *actually* possible? My heart rate is through the roof. This is beyond normal now. *Beyond* anything I've ever experienced. I have a logically ordered brain and assumed Wenna's experience was a coincidence. What about the other women who found a sweetheart? Okay, I have to concede there are maybe too many coincidences, and there's probably been some embroidering of the truth passed on over time, but the alternative to coincidence is too mind-boggling.

Excuses for last night's behaviour raise their objection to the alternative, like: I only talked to the moon for a laugh, because I was fed up, because it was a bit of fun, because… Oh for God's sake. I can't take back what I did now, and the evidence is real. It's solid, it's right here in my hands with the sun glinting off the edges. It feels otherworldly, as if it's a precious relic. Really? A precious relic? *Have a word with yourself, Merrin.* There are other words and thoughts spiralling in my mind right now though. Words that tell me this is the magic at work. The magic I so wanted to believe last night, if I'm absolutely honest, the magic that Wenna and her sister and Faye's great aunt experienced all those years ago. My hands tighten their grip around the bottle and I feel a series of tiny electric shocks travel along my wrists and up my arms. The sun chooses this moment to hide behind a bank of cloud and a shadow falls over the scene like a spooky cloak. I'm giddy, lightheaded and need to ground myself. I can't allow myself to be swept away by this. If I take a deep breath and pretend none of this is happening, I'll be fine. Get a grip. It's a bottle with a message inside. You're going to be late for work, just take it home and open it later.

I've had a busy day in the café, but all the time I've been taking orders, cooking food and wiping tables, my thoughts have been consumed by the bottle 'hidden' in my wardrobe. Thank goodness it's my morning off tomorrow, so I'll have time to ponder and come to terms with what's been a bit of a shock, to be honest – and that's before I've even read the damned message. Sandra comes in, just as I'm ready to lock up for the day.

'Hey, Merrin. I was wondering if you'd be able to pick up Wenna's scones tomorrow, because the hospital has changed my appointment at short notice.' She clocks my concerned expression and adds, 'Nothing's wrong. Just a check-up.'

Despite it being my day off, I have no option really, given that Sandra volunteered to collect the scones each time as it was near her home. 'Yes, no problem. How's it all going?'

Sandra pushes her glasses along her nose and smiles. 'It's going well. I've not felt this good in ages.'

We step outside and I lock up. 'Very glad to hear that, my friend.'

She scrubs a fist at her short spiky hair and frowns. 'Hope you don't mind me saying but you seem a bit sad, or at least not yourself.'

Apprehensive, shocked and a bit mystified, definitely not myself, but not sad. 'Really? No, just things on my mind, you know.'

Sandra squeezes my arm. 'Well, if you ever want someone to chat to, I'm your woman.'

As I watch her walking away, I think how lucky I am to have such good friends. And how lucky I am to live in this tight-knit little community too. We're tied together by the history of our land and ocean, by years of farming, fishing and mining. Yes, things have changed nowadays – the mines have gone, for one – but our Cornish heritage is alive and well and living in the hearts of those still with us, and of those yet to come. Thinking of community and friends, I wonder what Faye will make of the whole thing. I imagine her going into raptures, shrieking and demanding to see the bottle and read the letter. Hmm. Maybe I'll keep it to myself.

Dinner over, and Lucy at a friend's, the bottle will wait no longer. At the top of the stairs, I wonder if it's actually still there. Maybe the whole thing was an aberration. My hand closes around the handle of the wardrobe and I suck in a deep breath before pulling it open. No. No, there it is, just where I'd left it, nestled between my winter boots and an old shopping basket. Away from its windswept setting, and with the absence of diamond-chip sunlight, the bottle has lost quite a lot of its otherworldliness, but my stomach still turns a few cartwheels as I take it over to my bed and sit on the edge. On the edge. A good description of me at the moment.

The top is bound with tape, some kind of wire and what

looks like old fabric underneath that. Everything about it is old. And that's when it strikes me. Whoever sent this must be very old now, possibly dead. There's no way a contemporary of mine would have used an old bottle like this. Why didn't I think of this before? Well, I did, but didn't draw the relevant conclusion. My heart sinks a little. So, this is yet another coincidence, all the old wives' tales are just that. Tales. I unwind the wire and tackle the tape with scissors. This thing must have been floating on the ocean for years. By the look of it, maybe as many as seventy or more… So there's no chance of some magical sweetheart for me after all. A little voice from some dusty corner of my brain whispers, *It would have been quite nice to have had a bit of magic in your life, wouldn't it?* I shake my head. Magic doesn't exist, remember? The voice comes back stronger, bolder. *You know you don't believe that, Merrin. Remember how you felt last night? Just trust your instincts and go with it.*

At last, the bottle top is free and I unscrew it. It's a bit tricky getting hold of the scroll of paper, but I turn the bottle upside down, give it a shake and tease it out with my finger nails. The paper is unlined, a bit dry, but doesn't feel like it's really old. With mounting excitement, I unroll it, smooth it out, and weigh it down with two pebbles from a pebble jar I keep on my nightstand.

1997

    My name is Ethan Marshall and I'm sixteen years old. I live in Gloucester, Massachusetts with my parents and older sister Melissa. My great aunt Lamorna told me about the legend of Magic Cove in Cornwall, Great Britain, near where she's from.

She said she found her sweetheart (my great uncle) by sending this very same bottle all the way from there, one moonlit June evening, just before the Second World War. She asked the moon, the power of the ocean and the magic of nature to send her a true love, and it did!! So, I'm hoping that I might find my own sweetheart, or at least a pen pal! If you are someone who believes in magic, call or write me.

Yours truly,

Ethan

My heart is thumping like a jackhammer in my chest and my stomach flips over. Wow! So it's not a really old letter, just a really old bottle. Even so, it means the damn thing has been floating in the ocean for twenty-five years. Ethan must be, what … forty-one now? Amazing. I re-read it and the giddy wiggly feeling that has been with me on and off since I found it shows up in my belly again as I realise something. This bottle has been back and forth across the Atlantic twice! Not only that, it's come back to exactly the same place that it was first sent from, eighty-odd years ago. A shiver runs through me and all the hairs stand up along my forearms. I put the letter down and rub them briskly. The little voice starts to whisper about magic again, and this time I let it… And Great Aunt Lamorna, eh? I wonder…

I woke in the night a few times, my mind full of the message in a bottle. Now at breakfast, it's still floating

212

around the ocean of puzzles in my head and will be until I've seen Wenna. If my hunch is right, then it's too big to be a coincidence and I might have to concede there might be a bit of magic at play. Not where finding a sweetheart is concerned, but in all other respects.

'You actually on this planet this morning, Mum?' Lucy asks as she clears her breakfast dishes from the table.

'Hmm?'

'You've been pretty monosyllabic, and that's not like you.'

'Yeah. Just miles away.'

Lucy cocks her head to the side. 'So, what do you think?'

'About what?'

The dishes go back on the table, and she folds her arms, fixes me with the piqued glare she's perfected since being a new born. 'About toad in the hole or chicken cacciatore?'

Now would be a good time to tell her I have no clue as to what she is talking about, but the narrowing of those navy eyes tells me to wing it. 'Oh, I think the chicken might be nice, lovely.'

A nod. 'Yeah, I was thinking making toad in the hole might be a bit stodgy for this time of year. Okay, make sure you get us a nice bottle of wine to go with it.'

Lucy's cooking for us? I nearly choke on my tea. How the hell have I managed to tune such momentous news out of my consciousness? I beam at her. 'Can't wait. Should be back on time tonight, as Wednesdays aren't normally the busiest.'

'You really are on another planet, aren't you?' She

shakes her head and takes her dishes over to the sink. 'Sunday, Mum. Not tonight.'

'Sorry, Lulu. I'm dead chuffed, honest.' And I am. The only people she's ever cooked for are her dad and the madam. But then I remember the reason why and realise this meal will be cooked for one simple reason. Because she loves me.

At last, I pull up outside Wenna's house and look out over the fields to the sleepy blue ocean. So many secrets in its depths. If only it could speak. I know it does a lot of shushing and roaring, but the juiciest gossip is known only to itself.

'Merrin? How lovely to see you,' Wenna's voice says, from behind me.

I turn round and hurry over. 'You, too.' I plant a kiss on her cheek and catch the scent of roses and freshly baked scones. 'Sandra has a hospital appointment, so I said I'd collect the scones this time.' Wenna's expression clouds at the mention of 'hospital', just as mine had yesterday. 'Nothing to worry about. Just a check-up.'

'Oh good. Well, in you come, I'll pop the kettle on.'

Back in Wenna's comfy chair in the 1970s sitting room, my gaze falls on the bottle on the windowsill and excitement builds in my chest, when I think of the letter and what I'm going to ask her. The rattling of the hostess trolly heralds her arrival, and I help her take the tea things off it and put them on the little table between my chair and hers.

'Shall I pour the tea?' I ask, my hand already hovering. I notice that it's trembling so flex my fingers.

'Please, Merrin. And a biscuit? These ginger snaps are my grandma Mary's.' Wenna's eyes twinkle and she giggles. 'Well, they aren't hers, obviously, as they'd be very old now and not taste very nice at all. But it's her recipe.'

'Hmm. She was the one who started you both off on the message in a bottle thing, wasn't she? You and your sister?'

Wenna takes a bite of a ginger snap and nods. 'Hmm.'

'Was your sister's name Lamorna, by any chance?'

Wenna's eyes pop, her cheeks puff red as if she's blowing up an invisible balloon, and she puts a hand to her mouth to stop the biscuit spraying everywhere. Once she's swallowed, she takes a sip of tea and pats her chest. 'You nearly made me choke, maid. How on *earth* do you know that?'

As an answer, I hand her the letter, and while she reads it, I explain briefly what I've been up to. 'It was a hell of a shock when I laid eyes on it in the rockpool, I can tell you. I only wished on the moon on the spur of the moment, that's why I didn't go down to the cove … and then when Ethan said in the letter that his great aunt Lamorna had sent it from here, just before the war, I remembered that you—'

'That I'd told you my sister sent one before the war, and found an American sweetheart.' Wenna dabs at her eyes with a tissue. 'This is incredible.' She flaps the letter at me. 'Incredible!' She's laughing and crying all at once, and I don't know what to do, or say. I know how she feels though.

'It is. The most incredible thing is that the bottle has been back and forth across the ocean.'

'No, Merrin.' Wenna shakes her head and wipes more tears away. 'The most incredible thing is that you asked for a sweetheart, and the next day, there you are!' She laughs again. 'Not only that, it's my Lamorna's great nephew. And if that ain't magic, I'm a Dutchman.'

I wonder if she's not realised something. 'You *have* twigged that this letter is twenty-five years old?'

'Course, why?'

'Well, you sound like you're suggesting that Ethan is still going to be available. He'll be forty-one now.'

Wenna points an arthritic finger at me. 'Mark my words. He will be.' She looks at her wrist watch. 'Hmm. A bit early still.'

'For what?'

'A transatlantic telephone call.'

My heart clenches. 'I … no. I don't think I'll be calling. No … no. It's a very long time since he wrote this letter, he's probably married with kids by now. And he certainly won't be living at his family home, will he?'

'Stop babbling and do it.'

'No … I…'

Wenna leans across and puts her hand on my arm with a surprisingly strong grip. 'You must. You have to. Surely after finding the bottle, the letter, the link to my Lamorna, you're not going to just turn your back? It's unthinkable.' A pause. 'Disrespectful.'

The wobbly chin is diminished by the fire in her eyes and I know she's right. What will it hurt, anyway? I'll probably find the number's not recognised now, or if it is, I'll be speaking to the new owners or something. Wenna's right, to ignore it now would be disrespectful. To whom, or what, I have no idea. The wiggle in my belly tells me this isn't the end of the story either.

Chapter Seventeen

GLOUCESTER, MASSACHUSETTS

Present day

Ethan makes more coffee and takes it out onto the deck. The long expanse of Good Harbor Beach is fuller than he'd like, but then it always is at this time of year. Has been since he can remember, but he wouldn't change it. The family home holds so many memories for him, always full of light, laughter, the smell of hot sand, salt ocean and midnight bonfires. Hmm. S'mores. Now that would be a nice end to the day. S'mores toasted over a fire with a few beers and a good friend or two round to join him.

Ethan flops down on an old deckchair and with his toe pokes the peeling paint of the old handrail running around the wooden balcony. It needs painting, but that's a job for the fall. He stretches out his long legs, rests his feet on the rail, gently crossing them at the ankle. Then he prods his thigh muscles and pulls the legs of his shorts up. The tan needs work, but then wearing shorts on his walks for a few weeks should soon sort that out. A gaggle of young vacationers run past on the beach below, yelling and shrieking as they splash into the waves a few seconds later. He finds himself smiling. God, he loves this place, and he can hardly believe it belongs to him now. He heaves a contented sigh and closes his eyes.

The sound of the phone ringing behind him in the living room intrudes on his nap, and he quickly scrambles up. Must be Mom. Nobody else uses the home phone nowadays.

'Hi, Mom, how's everything in sunny Florida?' Ethan yawns and ruffles his tawny hair in the mirror above the fireplace. His good friend Jodie said he looked like a lion the other day. Must get his mane cut.

'Um. I'm not your mum,' says a British voice with a giggle. A throaty attractive giggle, it has to be said.

'Hey, sorry. I always figure it's her, as nobody else calls the home phone now. People reach me on my cell.'

'Ah, right. Yeah.'

Ethan waits, but nothing else is forthcoming through the awkward silence developing on the line. Nothing tangible that is, but he's getting a weird spooky feeling in his gut. 'Can I help you?'

'If you're Ethan Marshall. Possibly, yes.'

'That's me.' Ethan thinks there's something familiar about the accent. British, certainly, but…

'You're probably going to want to sit down to hear what I've got to tell you.'

Ethan looks through the mirror at his ruffled-up mane and surprised expression. 'I am?' He sidles over to the big red leather sofa and sits down.

'Years ago, when you were sixteen, you threw a message in a bottle that had once belonged to your great aunt Lamorna into the ocean...' The woman clears her throat as Ethan's heart slips into his own throat. 'I found that bottle and read your letter yesterday.'

For a few moments all Ethan can hear is his heart thumping in his ears and an answering pulse in his neck. He's placed the familiar accent – Cornish. The letter got there. It actually fucking got there! 'Oh my God! You did? That's incredible!'

'That's the exact word Wenna, Lamorna's sister, used when I told her yesterday.'

'Wenna's still alive? That's so cool. Aunt Lamorna talked of her often...' He finds he has to take a few deep breaths and loosen the tight grip he's got on the phone. 'Jeez. Sorry, this is all such a shock. An exciting one, though.'

'I bet. It was for me, yesterday. That bottle has been back and forth across the Atlantic from the exact same place *to* the exact same place. Can you believe it?'

'I'm starting to, unless I'm gonna wake up back on the deck in a minute, and it's all been a dream.' The woman laughs, and Ethan feels an eerie connection. 'You haven't told me your name.'

'Merrin Pascoe. I met Wenna recently and she told me all about the old tales of midnight June moons, the power of the ocean and the magic of nature. She told me about

Lamorna, and how Wenna herself found a husband in the same way.'

'Amazing.'

'Totally.'

'So you're looking for a sweetheart too?'

'Ha! God, no. It was just a silly whim, or so I thought ... the very last thing I imagined I'd find was your bottle the very next day. And after the twenty-five years it's been bobbing around out there too. I told Wenna that the number wouldn't be in use, or that the house would have new owners or something. One more miracle is that you're actually still at the same address, after all this time!'

'I'm not normally. This is our old family home, which I use in the summer. Lamorna and Harry lived just a few miles down the road. My parents moved to Florida and were gonna sell up, but I hated the thought of it going to someone else, so my parents are letting me buy it little by little. I'm a teacher inland and live in a rental outside the holidays. I'm hoping to find a teaching job close by though, so I can live here permanently.' Ethan shakes his head, as yet another incredible realisation dawns. 'Can you believe I only got here about three hours ago? I'm here for a few weeks and then—'

'Oh my God. So, If I'd have called earlier, you wouldn't have answered.'

'Exactly.'

'And I probably wouldn't have phoned again. A wild goose chase and all that.'

'Wow.'

'I know.'

Ethan's stomach flipped, as he galvanised himself to drop another bombshell on Merrin. 'And guess what else, Merrin?'

'What?'

'As I was about to say, in two weeks' time, I'm coming over to Cornwall on holiday. As you know, I have the Cornish connection with my great aunt Lamorna. Thought I'd look up her old haunts. See where my Grandad Bill's brother Harry was stationed during the war, you know?'

There's a silence on the line and then he hears a surprised giggle. 'This is, and I know this word's been overused in the last few days – incredible!'

'Can we meet when I come over?'

'Of course! Just try and stop me. Can't wait until I tell Wenna!'

Ethan laughs. 'She'll think it's incredible!'

'That's because it is. Bloody incredible!'

They end the call after swapping cell numbers, and for some time, Ethan sits staring at the wall in total bemusement. It's crazy but he felt a connection ... and instantly drawn to this Merrin. Madness. He needs something stronger than coffee, that's for sure.

'I've decided,' Jodie says as an opener as she walks up to him on the beach that evening. 'I'm coming with you.'

Ethan throws a stick of driftwood onto the fire and

indicates a beach chair next to him. 'You are?' He has no idea what she's talking about, but that's not unusual for Jodie. 'Want a beer?' He leans forward and flips the lid off the cooler.

'I could definitely use one after the day I've had. You'd think my boss is the King of England the way he talks to us all.' Jodie sits in the chair and tosses her baseball cap at him.

'Hey, what did I do?' Ethan laughs, noticing the way the retiring sunlight picks out the copper highlights in her chestnut curls.

'Nothing. Just felt like goofing off. Fed up of being an adult today.' Jodie's dark eyes dance in the firelight.

'S'mores?' he asks, holding up the marshmallows.

'Of course. And I want *all* the chocolate.' With her chin stuck out, arms folded and mouth twisted to the side, Jodie looks like a petulant teenager, not a woman approaching her fortieth birthday.

'You know, right now, you look exactly as you did when we were in college.' Ethan hands her a toasting fork, the crackers, chocolate and marshmallows.

'And you know all the right things to say, Ethan Marshall.' She shoots him a grin and gets busy building her s'mores. 'So, what do you think about me coming with you, huh?'

'With me where?'

He receives a withering look. 'To Cornwall, of course.'

Ethan nearly drops the s'mores into the fire. This was out of the blue to say the least. 'Um … I…'

Jodie tucks her hair behind her ears and Ethan can tell

she's trying to hide her disappointment. 'Hey, no pressure. Just an idea.'

What does he say now? Honesty is the best policy, his mom always says. 'Bit of a surprise, that's all. This trip was something I'd planned to do alone, you know?'

'Yeah. Of course. Thought you might like company, but I get it.'

The crackle of the fire and the whisper of the ocean are the only conversation to be heard in the still evening air, as an awkward silence lengthens between them, filling in the gaps where their words should be. There was a time when he'd have leapt at the chance of Jodie coming with him, back when she'd been his girlfriend when they were kids, but then she'd married his best friend Harvey, and that was that. The ruins of that marriage were still fresh, but the divorce had come through last month and now as Jodie kept telling him, she was as free as a bird. So, how does he feel about that? On a whim, before he can ponder it more, he says, 'You know what? I think it might be nice to have some company after all.'

Jodie looks up from her toasting, an ear-to-ear grin on her heart-shaped face. 'Really? You don't have to say that just to cheer me up, you know.'

'I know this. Yeah, I think it will be cool. And an even more cool thing happened this afternoon too. I got a phone call from Cornwall!' As he tells Jodie all about the message in a bottle, a bunch of butterflies show up in his gut. An exciting adventure awaits, just like his Great Aunt Lamorna said it would.

'You're as bad as Wenna,' I say to Faye, as she shrieks again and does a silly little dance on my patio.

'What do you expect? My best friend drops casually into conversation that she's found a twenty-five-year-old message in a bottle, from a hot guy in America, *and* he's coming next week to meet up?'

I hold a warning finger up. 'Er, one, I never said he was hot, as I have no clue what he looks like. And two, he was coming anyway, before I called. He's not coming to meet me.'

Lucy comes out into the garden with a tray of G&Ts and nibbles. 'Mum seems to think that we should all calm down about it. I mean, this kind of thing happens every day, yeah?' She shakes her head at me, sets the drinks on the wrought-iron table and sits in a garden chair.

'I know, right?' Faye grabs a glass and takes a big swig. 'I'd be a bag of nerves if I was her, but no, Mrs Cool As here thinks it's no biggie.' Faye shoves her sunglasses onto her head and looks at Lucy. 'You sure it's okay me gate-crashing your meal like this, Luce? Because I only popped over for a natter.'

'It's fine. I've made enough for an army, Auntie Faye.'

I wonder if Lucy's being polite, but I haven't had a chance to speak to her alone since Faye descended on our Sunday afternoon like a whirlwind half an hour ago.

'You're a treasure, but less of the Auntie Faye. Makes me feel like I'm a hundred years old.' Faye shoots her a smile and tosses a handful of peanuts into her mouth. 'Now,' she mumbles from the side of her mouth. 'Where are you going to meet this Ethan? Are you inviting him over for a meal?'

I shake my head. 'Wenna suggested we meet him on the beach at Chapel Porth, given that's where it all started.'

'On the beach? With Wenna?' Faye pulls a face. 'That's hardly the most romantic, is it?'

'No. And that's how I like it. I don't want romance. I found that out the other week when I met up with Pete again. I'm not ready.' I quickly swallow down my words with a swig of gin. Bugger. I'd forgotten Lucy didn't know about that, now I've let it slip. My daughter sits up straighter in her chair and puts her curious face on. Marvellous.

'Mum? You met a guy called Pete?'

Before I can answer, Faye says, 'Yeah. He was an old boyfriend from our school days. Your mum was smitten back then, but he buggered off to Australia for twenty-odd years. Now he's back and wants to take up where he left off.

'Thanks, Faye. I can speak for myself.'

'So you binned him off?' Lucy asks, her dark eyebrows knitted together over narrowed eyes.

'Such a nice turn of phrase.' I sigh. 'I decided it wouldn't work, yes. Too many years have passed and I wanted to find someone I could trust after your dad and everything.'

'Maybe this Ethan will be the trustworthy prince we all hanker after?' Faye says, taking another gulp of gin.

'No. As I've said, I'm not looking for romance. It will be nice to meet him and talk all about Lamorna with Wenna and him. Really looking forward to it.'

Lucy puts her head on one side. 'So why did you meet

Pete, if you're not looking for anyone?' She gives Faye a conspiratorial glance and Faye nods.

'Exactly. I think she's hedging her bets.'

I'm beginning to feel ganged up on. There's absolutely nothing going to happen between me and Ethan. It's ridiculous. 'You can both think what you like. I met Pete because I thought I'd give him a chance, as friends, as you suggested, Faye,' I say pointedly. 'I'm meeting Ethan with Wenna, just to talk about the past, and to discuss the whole message in a bottle thing. Pretty incredible when you think about it, isn't it?'

'Incredible.' Lucy nods.

'Totally incredible,' Faye says.

'That's the doorbell,' Lucy says, jumping up.

'You expecting anyone?' Faye asks.

'Nope.'

'Bet it's Ethan come early,' Faye says with a giggle.

My heart plumets as I hear a familiar voice. What the hell's he doing here? About to hurry to the front door, I'm hovering over my seat as Lucy, all smiles, comes through to the garden, followed by a sheepish-looking Pete.

He lifts a hand, and pushes the other through his unruly mop. 'Hi all, sorry to intrude. I was going to head off, but Lucy insisted I came through.'

'Talk of the devil and in he walks!' Faye says, standing up, tossing her hair and smoothing her short red summer dress over her hips. 'Pete Veryan, as I live and breathe!' she stands on her tiptoes and places a kiss on his cheek which makes his face even pinker.

'Faye?' Pete says. 'Wow, you haven't changed a bit.'

Faye gives a throaty laugh and a playful slap on his arm. 'Stop it! It's twenty years since I saw you.'

'Still as gorgeous.' Pete's twinkly brown eyes sweep the length of her, I note.

Faye tosses her hair again and looks at him sidelong from under her lashes. 'Why thank you. But you have changed, I must say.' She gives his large tattooed bicep a squeeze. 'Definitely filled out a bit.'

'Would you like to stay for dinner, Pete?' Lucy asks, much to my horror.

Pete looks at me, a question in his eyes. 'Um ... well, if your mum doesn't mind. I'd love to. Don't want to gate-crash.'

'You're not gate-crashing!' Faye says, pulling a chair up for him. 'We have a lot of catching up to do.'

I find a polite smile from somewhere and go with Lucy into the kitchen to help with the food. Lucy closes the kitchen door behind us and claps her hands like an excited child. 'Oooh, he's very good-looking, Mum. I invited him to stay, so you get another chance to make a good impression.'

Oh, for goodness' sake. 'I don't want to make a good impression. And you and Faye can't seem to see beyond his looks. He dumped me years ago, what's to stop him doing it again?'

'You were kids back then. He's probably regretting it now, and is desperate for another chance.'

My daughter's hit the nail on the head, but I need to make my feelings crystal clear, before we continue with the evening. 'Maybe. But Lucy, I'm really not interested. I was very hurt when he left me, and then it all happened again but even worse, when your dad did the same thing. Not sure I will ever trust a man again, to be honest. But Faye obviously is interested in Pete, and he's attracted to her too. Let's try and get them together instead, eh?'

Lucy's face falls. 'But I want you to be happy. To have someone when I'm gone.'

My heart swells with love. 'That's sweet of you to worry about me, but I can be happy without a man, you know. If it happens one day, then it happens. I'm not going looking for it though, okay?'

A little smile. 'Okay. Now can you stick the bread in the oven and make yourself useful?'

'Yes, chef.'

The getting together of Faye and Pete doesn't prove too difficult, though Pete gave me a questioning glance when Faye suggested we should 'all' meet up for a drink soon. I decide to take the bull by the horns and wait for Pete to come out of the bathroom, having given Faye the go-ahead when he went into it.

'Oh, hi. I haven't had chance to talk to you alone, so hope you weren't annoyed that I came over,' he says with an apologetic grin.

'No, of course not.' I smile and take a deep breath. 'But cards on the table, I don't think me and you are going to work. Too much time has passed and we're different people now.'

Pete doesn't look particularly surprised, but he frowns and looks away. 'Hm. I got that impression at the end of our date … just wanted to make sure, you know, by popping over for a chat?'

'Yeah, I'm sorry. I should have said something at the time. But I didn't want to hurt you.'

'Like I hurt you?' His kind brown eyes find mine.

'Yeah, but that's all water under the bridge. Let's be friends, hey?'

'If that's all we can be, then yes, always.' Pete leans forward and kisses my cheek.

Phew. Such a relief to have got that out of the way. As we walk down the hallway towards the kitchen and outside, I say over my shoulder, 'And if you're at all interested, Faye seems to be.'

'In what?'

'You, you dope.'

Pete smiles. 'We'll see.'

Later, after Pete has gone, Faye lowers her voice and says in my ear as we stand on the doorstep, 'Are you absolutely sure that you don't mind me meeting Pete for a drink? I'd hate it if there was a chance for you both, even though he's hot, lovely and a good laugh.'

'Yes, absolutely. No need to lower your voice, Lucy knows all about my feelings on the subject.' In the background we can hear the tinkle of glasses and crockery as Lucy clears away.

'You've got a good kid there, Merrin. A credit to you.'

'I certainly have. I'm gonna miss her when she goes to uni.'

'Yeah, but you'll have your American guy to snuggle up to by then.'

I laugh, despite wanting to strangle my friend. Why does she never take no for an answer? 'Will you stop? I don't need a man to make me happy, as I told Lucy earlier. My priorities are Lucy, work, and helping my community with the larder. And if I ever get any spare time – writing the damned novel! Men tend to bugger everything up.'

'You say that as if you've had a long line of them.'

'Jacob was enough. Now go, I'll ring you in the week to see how your date went.'

Faye wrinkles her nose and shrugs her denim jacket on. 'Okay, and keep me up to speed on Ethan. You're meeting him a week on Thursday, yes?'

'Yep. And of course I'll keep you posted. I'd never hear the end of it if I didn't.'

I wave her off down the path and giggle as Faye curses, stumbling in her high heels as she totters along the uneven country lane. She and Pete would make a good match. Both outgoing, slightly crazy, up for anything. Maybe this time Faye would find the one she's been looking for all these years with my old love.

Tonight, the June moon has slimmed down slightly, already losing the fullness it had on the night I wished on it. I wonder if Ethan is looking at the same moon? No, you daft bat. It will still be light over there, right now. A wiggle of excitement shows up in my chest when I think of meeting him on the beach soon. It will be so amazing for Wenna to chat with him, and swap stories about the message in a bottle and their shared relative. It's not every day something like that happens, and I for one am very much looking forward to it.

Chapter Eighteen

'Are you sure he said one and not two?' Wenna peers at her watch like an oystercatcher examining a whelk.

'Yes, Wenna. Stop worrying, it's only ten past.' I straighten the picnic blanket and hand Wenna a mug. 'Let's have some tea.'

Wenna shifts her bottom from side to side on the blanket and sighs. 'I hope I'll be able to get back up off this thing. My knees have no spring in them these days.'

'I'll help you. Now, do you want tea or not?'

'I suppose so. Do you think he'll like my scones?'

'Of course. Everyone loves your scones.'

'Ooh.' Wenna nudges a bony elbow into my side. 'Is that him up there? The one walking down the slope with the messy caramel hair, blue shirt and black shorts?' I shade my eyes against the sun and look to where Wenna's pointing. 'The tall one. Can you see him?'

'Yeah, I can. But we have no idea what he looks like so—'

'It's him, I can tell. He's so handsome. Walks like an American.'

I laugh at her excitement and place a hand on her arm. 'How do Americans walk?

'Like that man. Confident long strides. He's got broad shoulders too, means business. Got a look of Lamorna's Harry too.'

'Okay. Well, I'm sure we'll find out in a second. I told him we'd be sitting on a picnic blanket in the shade of the rocks.' We both watch the man approach. It does seem like he's making a bee-line for us.

A few feet away, he raises a hand, his broad smile lighting up his ocean blue eyes. Wenna was right. He's certainly handsome. 'Merrin and Wenna?'

'Wow, such a deep sexy voice. Sounds like a film star,' Wenna whispers to me.

I nudge her. 'Shh.' Then I get up and hold my hand out. 'Hi, Ethan. It's wonderful to meet you.'

'You, too. In fact, it's incredible.' We laugh at the in-joke and I note his large hand swallows mine up in its firm grip. Then he bends forward and shakes hands with Wenna. 'So great to meet you, Wenna.'

Wenna blushes. 'And you. Such a momentous day.'

I indicate the blanket. 'Please take a seat, Ethan. We have tea and scones.'

'Tea and scones? How very English.' He sits down cross-legged with his back to the ocean.

'It's more Cornish than English, because we have clotted

cream and jam to go with them,' Wenna says with a big smile.

'Wenna made the scones too. You're in for a treat.' I say, taking out the scones, cream and jam from the cool box.

'Wow, you're spoiling me.' Ethan takes a plate and gives me a big grin.

While he and Wenna talk about scones I can hardly take my eyes off him. It's as if they are pulled to his face by invisible strings. And what a face it is. Handsome, but not in a superficial way, he has depth and character, which is etched into the tanned skin and strong jawline, he has lovely crinkles around his eyes when he smiles ... and there's something else... I just know without a shadow of a doubt that he's a good guy. He has the kind of soul which shines from within, and I immediately trust him. My gaze drops to his broad chest under his light blue T-shirt, and the tail-end of a tattoo on his well-defined bicep is peeping out from under the sleeve on his right arm. Looks like a mermaid's tail. Lucky mermaid. I feel a flush of excitement in my belly and embarrassed at the way my body is reacting to him, I busy myself with the flask of tea. This is very unusual for me to be drawn so strongly to someone. In fact, it's never happened before. 'Do you take milk and sugar in your tea, Ethan?' I say to the sand.

'Just a dash of milk, please, Merrin. And do I put jam on the scone before the cream?'

Wenna laughs. 'Yes. That's the Cornish way, my boy. In Devon they do it the other way around.'

Ethan lifts the scone to his mouth and we both watch him take a bite. A bit of cream lands on his chin and it's all I can do not to lean forward and scoop it off with my finger. 'Hmm ... so delicious.' *You're not kidding.* 'Heaven on a plate.' Ethan closes his eyes and does more appreciative moaning, which doesn't help me at all.

'Thank you, Ethan. So glad you like them,' Wenna says, patting her hair and glancing at me, pride shining from her face.

We talk about mundane things, like what the flight over to London was like, where he's staying in Cornwall, the fact that he's jet-lagged, then he says, 'This is all very surreal. Us sitting on the very beach that my great aunt Lamorna sent that bottle from all those years ago, and me sending the same one too. I can hardly believe it.'

Wenna sits up a little straighter and puts her shoulders back. 'Well, I can. This beach is magic, I've always said so. And now all this has happened with you two, we have proof. Not that I needed any after our Lamorna met Harry and I met my Finn. Grandma Mary knew the truth and passed it on. It's your duty to do the same down the generations.' She looks at me and then at Ethan, her face serious, determined.

'You don't need to convince me, Wenna. Aunt Lamorna believed it all. She was a remarkable woman, came from here to America, knew nobody apart from Uncle Harry, but made a real success of life, nevertheless. She always wanted to be a teacher, she told me, but thought it wasn't for the likes of her. Uncle Harry encouraged her and she did a quick college course and ended up teaching in a school for almost thirty years. Managed to raise a family too at the same time.'

Wenna nods and quietly sips her tea. She looks like she's trying to hold back tears. Ethan's frowning and looks like he's about to ask her something, so I say, 'Sounds as if nothing would get her down for long, Ethan.'

'That's right. Nothing ever did. I became a teacher because of her. I wanted to follow in her footsteps, you know? I admired her guts and determination.' He pauses and looks over his shoulder at the ocean. 'That day when she told me about the message in a bottle that she threw into that water over there and later on showed me the original bottle and letter, I couldn't help but believe her.' He laughs and turns back to us. 'You might think it a little strange for a sixteen-year-old kid to believe in June moons and stuff, but Harry and Lamorna were such genuine people. If they believed it, then so did I. I guess I was a bit of a loner too, and thought it would be cool to get a reply. Of course, after a few years when nothing happened, I had to concede whatever magic was there for my aunt and uncle wasn't going to happen for me. Who would have thought it would actually work after all this time? Twenty-five-years late, but it did. It worked!'

'It hasn't worked yet. Not until you two darlings get together,' Wenna says with a chuckle.

I'm mortified and flap my hand in front of my face. 'I can't believe you just said that, Wenna,' I hiss.

Ethan laughs at my discomfort. 'Don't get embarrassed on my account. I know it was just a whim on your part, and that you're not looking for a husband, don't worry.'

It's Wenna's turn to be mortified and she glares at me, opened-mouthed. 'You told him it was just a bit of fun?'

'Well, yeah, I did.' But having met Ethan, I'm beginning to wish I hadn't.

'That's very disrespectful.' She twists her mouth to the side and folds her arms.

'How do you mean, Wenna?' Ethan asks.

She throws her hands up. 'Because the great magic of nature and the power of the ocean have guided your bottle to her.' She jabs a finger at me. 'After all those years floating out there.' She jabs a finger at the water. 'Just in time for her to find it. AND it was the same bottle that my sister –' she swallows and dabs at her eyes with a napkin '– that my sister sent from here. But Merrin knows best, obviously.' She spits the last five words out as if they have a bitter taste.

I look at Ethan's shocked face and know mine is reflecting his expression. Why on earth was Wenna being so nasty? 'I ... I'm sorry you're so upset—' I begin, but she cuts me off.

'Do you blame me?' Wenna turns her tear-stained face to me. 'It's Lamorna's doing, all this, trying to make you and Ethan happy from her spirit world. She wants you to be together, don't you see? She told me toward the end of her life that she'd look after me if she could, and she'd look after those who believed in the magic of her cove, and in Good Harbor too.' A watery smile. 'You so remind me of her now and then, Merrin. It's a message to me too, to tell me she's forgiven me. Though I don't deserve it,' she adds wistfully. Then a sob breaks free and Ethan and I look at each other, bewildered.

I hadn't realised Lamorna had passed, but I should have

expected it, her being quite a bit older than Wenna. 'Hey, Wenna. Come on, let me help you up and take…'

'No. I don't want to be helped up and taken home. I want to tell you why I don't deserve forgiveness. My lovely, lovely Lamorna never stopped loving me and hoping we'd be together again, but I ruined it all. Selfish, miserable me.'

Ethan leans forward and pats her hand. 'I'm sure you didn't, Wenna…'

'I did!' she wails and blows her nose trumpet-like. 'After she'd got married, it was time for her to go to America, and we all went to the train station to see her off. Except I marched off before she got on the train, because I was in a mood that she was going. I never said goodbye and how I felt about her. I worshipped the ground she walked on, but I never acted like I did. I acted like the spoilt brat and decided that Lamorna had abandoned me.'

Wenna shakes her head, sniffs and takes a sip of tea. I ask her if she wants to go home but she holds up a hand. 'I need to get this out… She wrote often, but I never wrote back, though I wanted to, and over the years she paid for Mum and Dad to go over to see her, our brother Tony too and his wife and children. I always made an excuse that I was too busy, or later, when I was married, that Finn needed me and couldn't get time off work. Not true of course. Finn begged me to reconnect with her but I refused. One excuse after the other. And why?' Wenna's desperately earnest eyes find mine. 'Because I couldn't admit that I was wrong. The whole charade had gone on too long, and I was too much of a bloody idiot to admit it.

'She came back to Cornwall once too – I went to

Scotland on holiday. A grown adult behaving like a toddler. God, I was such a stupid cow. As well as all that, I was jealous of her, pure and simple. I felt she was always the favourite, mostly my mum's fault, and as you say, she achieved so much. Off she went to America, made a new life in the land of the free ... and had her lovely children of course ... whereas I never could...'

Ethan sighs and touches her arm. 'I'm sure she knew that you cared for her. She always talked of you fondly. She told me once that she was looking after you on this very beach when you were little and you ran off after a seagull. She said you were always a feisty, strong and determined little girl.'

'Did she?' Wenna's lips wobble and fresh tears appear. 'Hmm. Lot of good it did me, eh? Too stubborn. And as I said, me and Finn had a happy life, it's just that sometimes I did wonder what else I could have done with mine, you know? Made something of myself like Lamorna did.'

This is all so terribly sad and I want to ask if they ever met again, but I don't want to open old wounds. Ethan says that stubbornness could be seen as strength too, but I keep quiet. I can tell she needs to get everything off her chest. 'Would you like another cup of tea, Wenna?'

'Could do with a strong gin.'

Ethan laughs. 'I'm sure we could find a pub somewhere?'

'Only joking.' Wenna smiles. 'I'd be asleep for the rest of the day if I had alcohol in the afternoon.' Then she heaves a sigh. 'Ah, Lamorna,' she says to the ocean. 'If only I'd come to you a little sooner.'

'You were going to America?' I ask.

A nod. 'Our mum had passed away and I'd phoned to tell her. Dad couldn't bring himself to ring her. Lamorna had been expecting it, but she was terribly upset of course. After that day, we wrote back and forth and spoke on the phone. It was so lovely to be back in touch. Then Dad died too. In a sad way, our parents' deaths had meant we started talking again. We grew closer, but I still never told her the truth about why I didn't say goodbye, or visit all those years. She never asked, and I think, on some inner level, she already knew. Then about ten years or so later, she called to tell me she'd got breast cancer. It was in the early stages and they thought she'd be okay with radiation treatment ... but it gave me a much-needed wake-up call. After the cancer letter, I told her I'd a few savings and would come over to see her on my own. Finn was actually working, so not an excuse for once. I was going to tell her how much I'd admired her when I was a girl, and how I always wanted to be like her ... but she died of a stroke the day after her eightieth birthday in 2003, a few days before I was due to go out to Massachusetts.' Wenna blows her nose again. 'All those wasted years, and all of it *my* fault.'

I don't know what to say, but luckily Ethan does. 'Hey, Wenna, please don't beat yourself up. Aunt Lamorna told me she was overjoyed that you were back in touch. She never blamed you for anything, and as I said, she always talked very fondly of you.' He spreads his arms wide and looks around. 'And about this place. I know she missed Cornwall very much. Once she looked out over the ocean from the deck of our house that now belongs to me, and said, "Far over the waves in that direction, Ethan, is my little beach. My little beach that I played on as a child and the one that I sent the bottle from, which changed my life. You should visit one day." And now I have.' He smiles and squeezes Wenna's hand.

'I'm so glad you did too.' Wenna says with a warm smile. 'As I said, it's Lamorna's way of telling me she forgives me, so I'll try to stop beating myself up like you said.' She wipes her eyes and takes a deep breath. 'Now, tell me, Ethan, you're single, I take it?'

Wenna's about as subtle as a brick, but I hold my breath, interested to hear the answer as much as she is. Ethan grins. 'I am, yes. I was married briefly, but it didn't work out. I've been divorced about seven years now.'

'No kids?'

'Sadly, no.'

'There we are then.' She nods at me. 'Merrin's the same, not long divorced, a lovely daughter Lucy who's off to university in September, so both no ties. Perfect.'

'I'm sure I don't figure in Merrin's plans.' Ethan shoots me an apologetic glance and then he lifts a finger. 'By the way, do you know what the name Merrin means in Cornish?'

Grateful for the change of subject I say, 'Not really. Though I think I remember my grandma mentioning something about a pearl.'

Ethan gives me a wide smile showing his own set of pearls. 'Your grandma was correct. It means pearl of the sea, isn't that cool?'

'Wow, yeah. I've always loved the sea. Makes me feel calm and uplifted when I'm next to it.'

'Maybe you're descended from mermaids,' Wenna says, with a stiff little smile that looks more like a grimace.

I know I've hurt her by 'disrespecting' the message in a bottle, and telling Ethan I'm not interested in romance, and I wish I could fix it. There's a churned-up feeling in my gut and my heart lifts every time he looks at me. It's ridiculous, but I'm captivated by him. Totally. Is there such a thing as love at first sight? Maybe. Could it be to do with the magic at work in the cove again? Before today I would have said absolutely not. Now? I have no clue. I shrug. 'Perhaps I am, Wenna. This place is certainly magical, as I will freely admit now. Too many things have happened for me to write it off as a coincidence anymore.' I hope me coming clean will help her mood.

Wenna's expression softens and I get a genuinely warm smile this time. She's about to say something when Ethan rolls up the cuff of his T-shirt and nods at his tattoo. 'Yet another magical happening.'

Wenna and I stare at the tattoo of a mermaid swimming around his bicep. She has long golden curls, like mine and is offering up a seashell with a pearl in the middle. I'm dumbstruck. 'Oh, my word,' Wenna says. 'How many more magical happenings can I cope with?'

'Amazing,' I say in a small voice. The mermaid's face really does have a look of me.

'Incredible, you could say?' Ethan smiles at me.

'I definitely could.' I find myself smiling back at him. A

stretchy smile, that if I kept it up would hurt my cheeks, but I can't help it. Ethan glances at his watch and my stomach turns over. I don't want to let him go. Before I can stop myself, I say in a rush, 'How about you both come over to mine for a barbecue this weekend? It will be a kind of early leaving do for Lucy, and my parents are back in the country so it would be nice for you to meet them, Wenna. And my friend Faye and friends from work will come too. It would be nice for you to meet everyone, Ethan. You could say you'd made proper Cornish connections when you get home.'

He does a big stretchy smile too, and the azure blue reflecting from the sea and sky find a home in his eyes. 'That would be great. Is it okay for me to bring my friend Jodie? She's over here with me, but didn't come today as she thought we'd have lots to catch up on.'

The words *my friend Jodie* wipe the smile right off my face and sets my stomach churning in an altogether different way. My thoughts pick up cudgels and rush at me all at once. Jodie is a woman's name. Is she pretty? Can men be just friends with women? But then if she was a girlfriend he would have said, wouldn't he? No reason not to. Somehow, I manage to squeeze a reply past all the questions, 'Oh, yes of course. The more the merrier.' I get side-eyes from Wenna, but luckily, she says nothing.

'That's great,' Ethan says. 'We're off to look at what remains of Harry's camp tomorrow and then after that, we're touring around Cornwall looking at all the historical stuff and the coastal villages, of course.'

With his friend Jodie, my mind supplies, so I tell it to shut up. 'Sounds great. So, shall we say about 5pm on Sunday at mine? I'll text you the address.'

'Sure thing. I'll look forward to it.' He extends a hand to Wenna. 'Can I help you up, young lady?'

Wenna hoots. 'Young lady! It's a long time since anyone has called me that.' She allows herself to be helped up and leans against him to get her breath. Shame he didn't help me up too. 'We'll so look forward to seeing you again, won't we, Merrin?'

'We will. It's been an absolute pleasure.'

Ethan shakes my hand and the mermaid wiggles her tail. 'Are you going my way?' He indicates towards the carpark.

'Yes, young man. Can I put my arm through yours while we walk? The sand can be a bit uneven for my old pins.' Wenna winks at me and I have to turn away to smile. She walked down onto the beach almost as quickly as I did earlier.

There's a couple of pigeons on our car when we get to the carpark. They're cooing at each other and watching us with their bright orange eyes as we approach. 'Ha!' Ethan says. 'British pigeons have the same old crooner tune as ours in the States.' We look at him, puzzled. 'They always stop short in the third verse. It goes coo, coo, coo, coocoo. Coo, coo, coo coocoo. Coo, coo, coo… Then it stops short and they start from the beginning again. It's as if they've for—'

'Forgotten the words!' I exclaim. 'I've always said the same thing!' I laugh and notice a knowing look pass across Wenna's face like a shadow.

'More magic.' She nods sagely at us both.

Heat flares in my cheeks and I rummage in my bags for my car keys. 'Okay, see you Sunday, Ethan.'

Ethan kisses Wenna on the cheek and I wonder if I'm going to get the same farewell. 'Yes, Sunday. Text me your address.' He steps back and raises a hand before walking away.

'No kiss for you, then,' Wenna says, when he's out of earshot.

Rub it in, why don't you? I'm disappointed, but then what do I expect? I told him I wasn't looking for romance. He's not remotely interested either. 'No,' I say with a little smile. 'But then that should tell you he's definitely not interested in me and that the magic has stopped working.'

'*Au contraire*, Merrin.' Wenna wiggles a forefinger back and forth at me as she gets in the car. 'It means he is interested in you but feels awkward around you. You told him you weren't looking for anyone, so he's trying to protect himself. It's obvious to anyone with eyes that he's very much attracted to you.'

My heart jumps. 'He is? I hadn't noticed.'

'You must be out of practice then. It's also very obvious that you're attracted to him too.'

Buoyed by the thought that he's attracted to me, I get in the driver's seat, buckle up and answer, 'I can't deny he's a very handsome man, but more than that, he has a genuine personality and kind nature. A man of integrity. I knew it from the first few seconds of meeting him.' I stare through the windscreen at a pigeon strutting along the wall and smile. How weird that we both thought about the forgotten words thing. Kindred spirits.

As if she'd read my mind, Wenna says, 'You're perfect for each other, and as I said before, if you ignore what's right there in front of you, you're being disrespectful to the magic that brought him here, and to my lovely sister too.'

I sigh and start the engine. Might as well tell her what my heart has come up with. 'Look, I'm not promising anything, but let's see what develops, hmm?'

Wenna beams across at me. 'Wonderful! I can't wait for Sunday now.'

Chapter Nineteen

Thankfully, Lucy was over the moon that the quiet family barbeque I'd planned with just my parents as guests had morphed into a party, because of my 'on a whim' invitations. Mum and Dad were thrilled too – they always love a shindig and Mum said she'd get here a bit earlier to help me with the food. Thinking of which, I grab the sausages from the freezer and put them on the side to defrost. I'm so looking forward to seeing Mum and Dad, as I worked out it's nearly six months since they went off in their campervan around Europe again. They seem to spend more time abroad than they do here now, but good luck to them. *Going on adventures in your retirement is better than sitting in front of the TV watching* Countdown, *taking root, feeling your bones crumble and waiting to die*, Dad so colourfully said, last time we'd spoken.

Lucy comes into the kitchen and selects a knife from the block. 'I'll get started on the salad, shall I?' She waves the knife about as if she's slicing an invisible cucumber in the air.

'Yeah, that would be good. Sandra's bringing the rolls from her bakery, Gillian is bringing some rice dish or other, Wenna's bringing some scones, and Faye is bringing herself, some booze and Pete.' I laugh.

'Auntie Faye's never been very good at cooking, has she? Finding new men is her speciality though.' Lucy grins at me and puts the knife on the chopping board. Suddenly serious, she says, 'Are you really okay about her and Pete getting together?'

'Totally. They make a great couple. I don't regret meeting up with Pete though, because he made me realise I deserve better. I could never trust him again.' *Unlike Ethan.* 'There was no spark either. Sad but true.' *Unlike with Ethan.* I slam the door shut on the conversation my brain's trying to provoke me into, and pass Lucy some tomatoes.

'You haven't said much about your meeting with the mysterious Ethan, apart from his relationship with Wenna's sister and the message in a bottle magic. You seem a bit shifty when I ask questions about what you think of him.'

My brain must have whispered to her as I handed over the tomatoes. Her saying I'm shifty makes me feel shifty and sends a crimson tide into my face. With my head in the fridge, I say over my shoulder, 'I told you he's handsome and really nice. Like me, he's not looking for a partner, and he's bringing his friend Jodie. Nothing much else to say.' There's no way I'm telling my daughter that I can't stop thinking about him morning, noon and night. I'll never hear the end of it if I do.

'Hmm. Well, I can't wait to meet him and suss him out... Wenna, too. She'll give me the truth of the matter.'

I laugh and put some corn on the cob in the sink to prepare. 'The truth of the matter? You sound like a high court judge.'

'I always get to the truth, Ma,' she says in an American accent and jabs the knife through the air at me.

Just then, we hear the rumble of an engine on the drive, and Lucy runs outside to greet my parents. 'Gran and Grampy!'

I dry my hands on a tea towel and hurry after her. They're in the middle of a group hug on the drive, and I'm catapulted right back to when Lucy was little and they used to visit. It doesn't seem so long ago, but now my dad's hair is thinning and grey and Mum's chocolate curls have more than a few white streaks. But they still both look full of energy and life and Dad even manages to swing Lucy round like he used to, albeit once, instead of three or four times.

'And here's my baby girl!' Mum cries and hurries forward to wrap me in the kind of hug only she can give. Love envelops me, along with the scent of patchouli oil she's worn since forever.

'Still wearing patchouli then, you old hippy.'

'Oi, less of the "old",' she says, and pinches my cheek. Then she puts her hands on my shoulders and steps back, her jade green eyes, twins of my own, scanning my face. 'How are you doing, sweetheart? You're looking good, I must say...' A cheeky wink. 'Who's put that sparkle in those lovely eyes?'

The gorgeous Ethan, of course. I squirm as the crimson tide starts to flow up my neck for the second time today and flap her away. 'Nobody. Still Sally Single!' *Sally Single? What am I on?* 'Dad! Give me a hug,' I say, in a too-high overstretched voice, and see Lucy and Mum share a questioning glance. My cheeks are on fire now and I spend a long time hugging Dad, until they have cooled to a more acceptable, used-BBQ-pit kind of glow.

'It's lovely to see you, sweetheart,' Dad says, and puts his arm around me as we walk up the path. 'Your mum's right. You do have a bit of a sparkle going on. It's been a while since you've looked so happy. That bloody Jacob has a lot to answer for.'

I glance up into his pale blue eyes full of sympathy and love and swallow a lump of emotion. Dad's always been there for me through thick and thin, doing his protective Dad act. It used to annoy me when I was younger, but now it feels more like a warming comfort blanket that I can pull out of a drawer, when things get a bit too cold out there. I smile to myself. On second thoughts, it's a good job they are often abroad, or that blanket might get a bit too claustrophobic. 'Thanks, Dad. What Jacob did really doesn't bother me now. I'm feeling stronger and more confident in myself. Maybe that's the sparkle you can see.'

'Nice to hear it,' Mum says behind me, as we walk through the kitchen door. 'But there's something else as well. A mother's intuition.' She puts her bag on the table and taps the side of her nose. 'I'll find out what – or who – it is before the end of the evening.'

I shake my head and busy myself with the kettle. My

heart's galloping as I think about what's to come. I stand no chance under the watchful eyes of Mum, Lucy, Wenna and Faye. I hope they don't go over the top and send poor Ethan running for the hills. Then my mind wanders to *my friend Jodie* again, so I shove her into a drawer with the teaspoons.

The first to arrive are Sandra and Wenna, as I'm putting the finishing touches to the cold food on a long trestle table on the lawn. 'What lovely decorations,' Wenna says, tapping a yellow balloon hanging from a string of fairy lights. 'They'll look gorgeous all lit up when the sun goes down. And doesn't that table look splendid?' She plants a kiss on my cheek.

'I'd never have thought to make pasties for a BBQ. They smell delicious,' Sandra says, handing me a big bag of fresh rolls.

'I wasn't going to, but Lucy insisted as they're her favourite. She said I had to, as it was her leaving do – well, almost. Still got a month to go.'

Lucy waves from the kitchen door. 'Yeah. If I get the results I need, don't forget. Still, it will be nice for our American guests to have a proper pasty.'

Sandra tilts her head and frowns. 'American guests?'

I'm saved from responding by the arrival of Gillian, Faye and Pete, and I hurry over to greet them.

A little while later, I'm feeling happier, and a bit more relaxed. The garden's full of the babble of conversation and laughter, and Dad's rigged up some speakers for some background music. Lucy and I do the rounds with the wine and beer, so just Ethan and Jodie to come now, and then I'll put Pete to work on the BBQ. He called me the other day to offer his cheffing services, and I gladly accepted. Dad will probably help too, as he loves to cook BBQ'd food. The rest of the time he's not fussed. Mum says it's a throwback to cavemen days. I look at her laughing at something Wenna's said, and wonder how long it will be before Ethan crops up in their conversation.

I'm taking a platter of burgers out to Pete when Faye slips in through the door like a wisp of smoke in her silver-grey jumpsuit and stops me in my tracks. 'So, where's this Ethan, then? Forty minutes late already.'

'He'll be here. Well, him and his friend Jodie.' I go to walk past again, but she puts her hand on my arm and fixes me with that steady gaze of hers, the one that misses nothing. Nothing at all. Not a stutter, a quiet half-truth hidden under a louder sentence, or even a rapid blink or blush.

'Give me those burgers, I'll pass them on to Pete, then I'm back in here and you're going to tell me exactly how you feel.' She points a lilac nail at me. 'Because I knew you were giving me the brush-off about him on the phone the other day, and it stops now, lady.' She flicks her sleek dark hair over her shoulder, grabs the platter and goes outside.

There's no escaping the inevitable, so I wipe the side down while I wait for her to come back. In a way, it will be a relief to get everything off my chest to my oldest friend. Untangle these feelings I have wrapped around incoherent words, because my thoughts are all over the place. All I can see when I close my eyes at night is Ethan, and he's there when I open them in the morning. I've met him once. It's not normal. But then neither is the reason I met him, is it? Magic brought his bottle here, so what else might it bring?

'Right, let's have it then.' Faye grabs my arm and marches me upstairs to my room like I'm an unruly child.

'Hey, what's the big idea?' I ask, unable to stop a giggle breaking free as she pushes me down on the bed.

'Spill.' She folds her arms and leans a hip against the dressing table.

'Right, I told you on the phone that Ethan's good-looking and a really nice guy. The thing is…' I take a deep breath and let it out. 'The thing is, I think I might be falling for him after only one meeting. It's madness.' I tell her about how a gut feeling told me he was a man I could trust, and the way I responded to him, was totally captivated by him. Then a tangled thought I've been carrying around unravels itself and I say, 'Truth is, Faye. I'm really freaked out by it all, and I don't know what to do.' Tears press against the back of my eyelids, which is both alarming and a bit of a surprise. How can I care so much about a man I don't know from Adam, as my mum says?

Faye sits beside me and holds my hand. 'I'm not surprised you're freaked out when you take into consideration the magic twenty-five-year-old message in a bottle thing, Lamorna's story and the fact that Wenna told you it was her sister's spirit trying to get you both together.'

Puzzled, I say, 'I didn't tell you about that bit?'

'No. Wenna did just now. I pounced on her, demanding to know exactly what went on when you met Ethan, and she obliged. Your mum is totally fascinated by the whole story too, and made me promise to keep her posted, because she says you're about as forthcoming as a clam.'

Great, Mum knows too … but then I knew it wouldn't take long for the gossip to get round. I heave a sigh. 'Is it any wonder after what Jacob put me through and, to a much lesser extent, Pete before him? Then Ethan appears, out of the blue from America, apparently because of some old legend I went along with on the spur of the moment. I wished on the June moon, and then because of the power of the ocean, the magic of nature, oh and perhaps with a bit of a shove from the spirit of Lamorna, I get all these strong feelings for him that I don't know what to do with. It's as if I've known him for ever after just one phone call and a picnic on the beach. I'm scared, Faye. I feel like I'm living in a bloody fairy-story right now and I need to wake up. I need to slow things down a bit.'

She squeezes my hand again. 'I can see it would be a bit unsettling, but sometimes there are things in this world that can't be explained away logically. You have to go with it and allow yourself to believe what's happened and trust your gut. And what's the point of trying to slow things down? The magic of the cove and maybe Lamorna brought his bottle to you, for goodness' sake. This whole bloody thing is extraordinary, so why pretend otherwise? Tell him how you feel tonight.' Faye's emerald eyes twinkle with excitement and she gives me an encouraging smile.

'Yeah, right. After I told him I wished on the moon on a whim? After I told him there's no way I'm looking for a partner?'

She shrugs and raises her brows. 'Well, yeah. Tell him you made a mistake and that you feel there could be something between you.'

'What if he says he's not remotely interested in me?'

'I don't think that will be the case, but what do you have to lose?'

'Pride, self-worth, confidence perhaps?'

'And if you chicken out, you'll always be wondering, won't you? What's worse, hurt pride or, years down the line, regretting that you never went with your gut, hmm?'

I consider this as the chatter from the garden filters through the window wrapped around the smell of charcoal. I'm glad I've unburdened myself to my best friend and many of the tangled and jumbled thoughts are now out in the open and easy to read. I know she's right too. But there's one more thing that's been nagging at me like a sore tooth. 'This friend of his, Jodie. My gut's telling me there's more to it. It's all a bit hazy, but...' I shake my head, unable to put it into words.

'We'll soon find out. And leave her to me. I'll keep her talking while you get to know what's really going on between her and Ethan. You know I'm an expert on body language and reading between the lines, Merrin. If there's anything going on, I'll know. I'm guessing you will too.'

A bit of relief creeps in and settles in my chest like a well-fed cat in an armchair. It's always better to have a plan, and to have someone as lovely and caring as Faye in your corner. 'Thanks, Faye.' I look at the bedside clock and I begin to wonder. 'Forty-five minutes late now. Maybe he's not coming.'

Faye moves over to the window and says over her shoulder, 'I just heard a sexy American accent...' She cranes her neck. 'And, oh my word, the man has landed.' She turns to me, fans her face and pretends to swoon. 'There's no wonder you're smitten, he is drop dead!' Then she scans me top to toe and shakes her head. Pulling open my wardrobe, she selects a slinky low-cut dress that I've not worn for years, and says, 'Get that shirt and jeans off, and this on. Next, redo your make-up. Then get down those stairs and do me proud. Say, "Yes, boss!"'

I laugh, despite my stomach tying itself in knots. 'Yes, boss!'

Chapter Twenty

E than laughs at something Wenna's just said, and scans the garden again. No Merrin. He brushes a hand through his hair and wishes he'd had it cut today, when he and Jodie went into Truro. Jodie had insisted it looked stylish and a bit 'bad boy', whatever that meant. He thought he looked more like a lion that had been in a fight. It was almost past the collar of his new green shirt that Jodie had also insisted he bought. Jodie is doing a lot of insisting nowadays, and seems to take an awful lot of notice of his appearance … and in him generally, if he's honest. He's begun to wonder if she wants to be more than friends. Unless he's so out of practice he's misreading her signs.

At lunch, she'd leaned forward and dropped a sweet kiss on his cheek and told him how much she was enjoying the trip and spending time with him. Her big dark eyes seemed to be asking for more than conversation, but he had smiled and said he was having a great time too. Then his gut had made him change the subject to more neutral ground – the architecture of Truro Cathedral. Since they'd left the States, Ethan had been very unsure of why he'd told Jodie she could come with him, just like that. The truth evaded his questions, slipping from his grasp and evaporating like mist on a hot day. Did he want something more? Were the old feelings he'd had for her since high school still lurking inside him somewhere, waiting for a chance to come out into the light? They'd been friends for years, but now with Harvey out of the picture ... then Merrin comes out of the house and kicks his ponderings over the Cornish hedge and into the stratosphere. My God, she looks absolutely stunning.

Jodie takes his arm. 'Is that Merrin, then?' she says, in a strained voice.

'Yes. Not sure who the dark-haired woman with her is. Might be her friend Faye. Wenna mentioned her before, when she was introducing us to everyone.' Jodie has an odd look on her face and seemingly can't take her eyes of Merrin. Neither can he. She looked very attractive on the beach the other day, and she's often been in his thoughts since, but now in that slinky black dress that clings to every curve, the subtle make-up that brings out the stunning green of her eyes, and her hair like a shaft of sunlight... Wow.

'You must be Ethan,' the dark-haired woman says, coming towards them with Merrin in tow. 'I'm Faye, pleased to meet you.'

He introduces Jodie and they all shake hands. He notices Merrin and Jodie's hands only join for seconds and then drop as if they're handling something unpleasant. What's the deal with that? 'Sorry we're late,' he says to Merrin. 'We went to Truro and then took a wrong turn on the way back.'

'That's okay. You didn't miss anything.' Ethan gets a huge smile which demands his mouth copy it.

'We brought some wine and chips,' Jodie says, pulling a bottle of Merlot out of her bag. 'We didn't know what else to bring, did we, hon?' Her arm goes through his again and she pushes her side tight against him. Hon? That's new.

Faye takes the bottle and slips her arm through Jodie's on the other side. 'Hey, Jodie, come with me, I'd love you to meet Pete.' Jodie looks a bit surprised and starts to pull him along too. 'No. Leave Ethan here, I think Merrin has something to ask him about Lamorna and Wenna? Weird message in a bottle stuff.' She rolls her eyes and laughs a bit too loud. Then she leads Jodie towards a guy who's cooking burgers at the far end of the garden, Pete, as far as Ethan remembers. Faye's boyfriend.

'Wanna go and sit on the bench over there?' Merrin asks, as she hands him a beer from a cooler.

He raises the bottle and takes a sip. 'Lead on.' As he follows her, he tries to avert his gaze from the gentle sway of her hips and ass, without much success. *This needs to stop. The woman has told you she's not looking for a relationship.* They sit down, and Wenna and Laura, Merrin's mum, wave at them and then continue with their conversation. Ethan has the feeling they might be talking about him, as they keep glancing over and away.

'Jodie seems nice.' Merrin takes a sip from her beer and nods over to where Jodie's chatting to Faye and Pete.

'Yeah, she's great. We've known each other since school.'

'Really? Same as me, Pete and Faye, then.' She crosses her legs revealing a shapely calf and clears her throat, looking suddenly unsure of herself. 'You say she's a friend?' He nods. 'Only I did wonder if there was more between you. She calls you hon and she's obviously very close with you.'

So, it's not just his imagination then, if Merrin's noticed already. Interesting. 'No. We dated a bit when we were kids, but nothing serious. We broke up when we went to different colleges. She started seeing my friend Harvey who was at the same college. Then they got married. Sadly, they got divorced recently.'

'Oh, I see. How come?' Merrin's still staring at the back of Jodie's head.

'Harvey cheated. I think coming on this trip with me has given her a boost. An escape from the same old, you know?'

'Nice. Yeah, it would be good to escape the mundane for a while.'

She looks up at him, her expression wistful, faraway, and suddenly he wants to know more about her. What makes her tick. 'Are you happy with your life, Merrin?'

Her eyes dance, reflecting the deep green foliage of a rose bush behind her. 'That's a big question, Ethan. Where do I start?'

'At the beginning?' His eyes fix on hers. It's as though they are pulling him in, reading his thoughts, and he has to look away.

'Not on an empty stomach. Let's get some food and then you can have my life story.' Her hand brushes his as she stands up and goosebumps form along his wrist. What the hell is happening here?

They fill their plates and chat to Lucy and Greg, Merrin's daughter and dad, who are both really interesting and so welcoming. Jodie keeps looking over and he waves. She starts to walk over, but Laura steps in and starts up a conversation with her. 'Great burgers,' he says to Merrin, who's just come back from speaking with Gillian and Sandra.

'Good. You should try a pasty next, made by my own fair hand,' she says, placing one of them on his plate. Once again, her hand brushes his and it's like a tiny electric shock.

'Mmm,' he says, with a mouthful of burger, and a bit of ketchup escapes right onto the sleeve of his new shirt. He goes to rub it with a napkin, but she taps his hand.

'Don't, it will make it worse. Come into the kitchen and we'll get some cold water on it straightaway.'

Ethan watches the concentration on Merrin's face as she dabs cold water on his shirt with a cloth. He's concentrating too, on the curve of her mouth, the warmth of her body as she's standing so close, and the heady notes of her perfume as she moves her hair back from her forehead. Her eyes flick up to his and then back to the shirt, and if he's not mistaken, she's got a little blush going on in those high cheekbones. Maybe she noticed the way he was appreciating her looks and it embarrassed her. *Or maybe she likes the look of you too, Ethan? You thought of that?* Nah, he's not that lucky. To break the silence he says, 'Looks like you got it all out, to me.'

'I think I did.' She gets a dry cloth and scrubs at the wet patch. 'Yep. All gone.'

'Thanks. It's new. Jodie insisted I got it, so I'd never hear the end of it if I'd ruined it on the first wearing.' He smiles, but noticed Merrin's expression has gone a bit frosty.

'Right. Yeah.' She puts the cloth into the washing machine and moves to the door. 'We'd better join the others.'

Ethan realises he doesn't want to join the others; he wants to stay here in the quiet of a homely kitchen, with a woman he's strongly attracted to. He nods at their plates of food and drinks on the kitchen table. 'Why don't we eat that first? You promised me your life story, too.'

A flash of a smile curves her lips. 'Not sure I should neglect my guests.'

'Aw, come on. It's nice and cosy in here, and we'd get interrupted if we tried to talk out there.' Ethan pulls out a chair and sits down, a nervous flutter in his chest causing him to take a big gulp or two of his beer.

Merrin shrugs and joins me. 'Okay, but there's not much to tell.'

While she tells him about growing up here in this tight-knit fishing and farming community, meeting and marrying Jacob, having Lucy, and her work in the shop and food larder, he can't take his eyes off her. Once or twice, he loses track of what she's saying, because his imagination is painting pictures of them running hand in hand along the magic beach, or having a romantic meal, or watching a movie, or more intimate situations, which he tries to shake from his head, and endeavours to concentrate on what she's saying. 'A writer? What, you mean novels?'

'Yeah,' Merrin says, dabbing her mouth with a bit of kitchen roll and pushing her plate to one side. 'I always loved to write since I was a kid. Poems, little stories, songs even. But when I was in my late teens, I had an idea for a great story and wrote the first few chapters.' The dancing spark of passion alight in her eyes for the last few minutes dims, and she sighs. 'But then life took over and there was never enough time to give to the book.' Merrin sips her beer. 'I've done a bit more over the years, but I really want to finish it and see what happens. At the moment, I'm working like a crazy person trying to make ends meet ... so.'

'I get that, but please don't give up. I can see how passionate you are about the book and writing. That's something you need to hang on to. Maybe once Lucy's gone to university you might have a few hours in the evening to devote to some writing?'

Merrin presses her lips together, a thoughtful expression on her face. 'Yeah, I had been thinking along the same lines. It's having the confidence, I suppose, after so long. What if it's a pile of hogwash?'

Ethan laughs. 'That's not an expression we use in the States, but I like it. Until you write it, how can anyone judge if it's hogwash or not? Has anyone read it?'

She looks horrified. 'No way!'

'Might help.'

'I couldn't let anyone see it yet. Anyway, friends and family would give me the thumbs-up, so I didn't get hurt. I need someone neutral.'

'Like me,' Ethan says, surprising himself.

Merrin's eyebrows shoot up. 'Oh, I don't think so. I'll just wait and see what happens after Lucy's gone.'

'You need to be more determined than that.' Ethan sits back and gives her the hard stare. 'I remember Great Aunt Lamorna sitting me down and telling me never to forget my dreams and to go for the teaching career I didn't think was in me. She was one of the most, no, *the* most determined person I have ever met. As I said on the beach, she influenced me the most, put me on the right path.'

Merrin looks into her beer bottle as if she's searching for a response, but says nothing. Ethan thinks he might have come across too bossy, and is about to say so, when she lifts her eyes to his. 'I suppose nothing ever worth having comes easy.'

'You got that right.'

'Okay, I'll definitely give it a go once Lucy's gone. It might help to take my mind off the fact that she's flown the nest too.' Merrin's eyes fill, and she dabs them with kitchen roll. 'Sorry, I've no idea what's up with me.'

Ethan fights a desire to take her in his arms. He feels as if they've known each other for ever and it would be the most natural thing in the world to comfort her. Instead, he reaches out a hand and squeezes one of hers. 'I get it. Must be a big change when a child leaves.'

'Not looking forward to it, I must admit. Did you ever want kids?'

'I did. But my ex said we should wait until we had the house, the secure life and so forth. I went along with her as it made sense. Trouble was, it didn't work out between us, and then it was all too late.'

'Oh, that's so sad.' It's Merrin's turn to squeeze his hand.

Their eyes lock, and so much unspoken understanding passes between them. Aware that they're still holding hands, and neither seems in a rush to stop, he plucks up courage to say, 'You know I really would be happy to read what you've written so far. After I have, we could meet up for a drink in a bar, or for dinner, and have a chat about it. What do you think?'

Merrin's face lights up and she's just about to say something when they hear the back door close. 'Ethan? Ethan, honey, are you in here?' Jodie calls.

The lights go out in Merrin's eyes, and she snatches her hand back and carries her plate to the sink. 'Yeah, in the kitchen!' Ethan replies, wondering where all this 'honey' stuff is coming from. He also wonders why Merrin reacted in the way she did. Does she think there's something more between him and Jodie? Dare he hope she's interested in him?

Jodie walks into the room, her frosty gaze sweeping the length of Merrin. Then she gives him a dazzling smile. 'I was beginning to think you'd gone back to the hotel without me.' She laughs, stooping to slip an arm around his shoulder and place a kiss at the corner of his mouth.

What the hell? Ethan stands up and looks over at Merrin in surprise, just in time to see a shadow of disappointment fall across her face. Then she smiles at them both. 'I'm off to check on my guests,' she says, and hurries out.

'You two looked cosy.' Jodie slides into the chair next to him. 'Are you planning to take the message in a bottle story to its fairy-tale conclusion?'

Ethan notes Jodie's sarcastic tone and cool glance. 'What? No, we were just talking. I told you, Merrin's made it clear from the off that she's not interested in a relationship.' He's annoyed that this sounds as if he's making excuses. There's nothing to apologise for, is there?

'Hmm. I think the way she looks at you says otherwise.' Jodie examines her nails and looks out of the kitchen window.

Ethan's both surprised and pleased. 'You think so?'

'Yeah. Do you like her, in that way?'

He swallows and sighs, hoping his answer won't upset Jodie. 'I think she's attractive, and well … yeah, I suppose I do.'

Jodie looks back at him, her big dark eyes holding his in an intense gaze. 'But if you got together, one of you would have to ship out. No way would a relationship survive *that* kind of long distance.' She raises her hands and looks around the room. 'Could you see yourself living in this place … in Cornwall? I know it's cute, but it's really not you, is it?'

She's beginning to irritate him now. 'Think you might be getting *way* ahead of yourself there, Jodie. And how do you know Cornwall isn't me? I think it's a stunning place.'

A shake of the head. 'It's not. You love your beach house too much. Trust me, I know.'

This time she's irritating him because she's right. The thought of leaving that house, his beach, doesn't bear thinking about. 'Anyway, this is a silly conversation because I doubt very much that Merrin and I will ever get together.'

Jodie puts her hand on his knee and gives him a look that even he can't misinterpret. 'What about us? Could *we* get together?' Ethan raises his eyebrows, but can't reply because Jodie leans forward and covers his mouth with hers in a passionate kiss. He's so shocked he does little to stop her, and part of him is wondering if they could go back twenty-odd years.

'Wow,' he says when he's able. 'I wasn't expecting that.'

Jodie laughs. 'Well, you must be deaf, dumb and blind, then. All the signals I've been sending you on this trip… Short of coming into your room naked and offering myself on a plate, I don't know what else I could have done.'

'Er, told me how you felt, perhaps?' Ethan shakes his head in disbelief.

'I'm not good with words. I'm much better with actions,' Jodie murmurs, staring intently at his mouth, taking his face between her hands and kissing him again.

Seconds into the kiss, Ethan's heart sinks. No. This doesn't feel right. There's nothing there … the old feelings have gone and it feels forced, awkward. He doesn't want this. As Ethan's pulling away, he hears someone come in.

'Oh, sorry. I just came to get my phone. There it is.' Merrin's voice sounds distracted, as if she's unconcerned, but her eyes tell a different story. She grabs her phone from the table and rushes out.

Ethan stands up and goes to follow her, but Jodie puts a hand on his arm. 'Hey, where are you going?'

What does he say now? Jodie is one of his oldest friends and he cares deeply about her ... but as a friend. The kiss they shared just now has confirmed it beyond doubt. But how can he tell her this? He looks at her hopeful face, her eyes full of something that looks a lot like love. God what a mess. Ethan can't tell her the truth, even though he knows he should. It would crush her and he can't be so brutal. 'Erm. I thought she looked upset.'

Jodie shrugs. 'Maybe, but it can't be helped. All's fair in love and war, don't they say?' She holds her hand out to him. 'Come on, let's go. We can go back to the hotel and spend some quiet time together.'

Ethan is in no doubt what Jodie's 'quiet time' means. He shoves his hand through his hair and tries to think on his feet. What the hell is he supposed to do? If he tells her how he feels, it would be unbearable spending the next few days together before travelling back home. The bottom line is that he wouldn't hurt her for the world. Maybe a half-truth would work for now, at least until they are back in the States. 'Hey...' He shakes his head and comes back over to the table. 'You've landed me with a surprise here. I didn't know you felt like that about me ... not sure how I feel about it all, if I'm honest.' Which is true.

Jodie puts her head on one side and gives him a sweet smile. 'Okay, I get that. So, are you saying there might be a chance for us...?'

'I'm saying I'll need to think about it, okay?' Which is not true.

'Okay. There's no rush ... let's enjoy the rest of the trip and see how things go, hey?' She stands up, puts her arms around him and rests her head on his chest. 'I'm happy to take things slowly. I've waited long enough. I don't think I ever stopped loving you.'

Ethan immediately tenses. What the hell? This is not what he calls slowly. 'You loved me when we were in school?'

'Yeah,' she says into his shirt. 'I was an idiot to marry Harvey when I still had feelings for you. I tried to tell myself what we had was just a teenage crush, and it worked mostly. But you were always there – the one who got away. When Harvey cheated, I was angry and upset, but not as much as I should have been ... because of you.'

Jodie looks up adoringly into his eyes and he feels such a coward keeping quiet, but if it means Jodie won't be hurt, he'll have to live with it for now. He knows that she's been through a hell of a time with Harvey. He cheated on her and she was so devastated that she was on anti-depressants for a while, so he isn't sure that she's telling the truth about not being as upset because she was still in love with him. Maybe she's having some kind of breakdown and imagines being with Ethan is the answer? One thing's for sure, he can't stay at Merrin's a moment longer, he can't trust himself around her. Jodie would see that, and then be hurt even more. What a mess. Stepping out of her embrace he says, 'Okay. I'll just go and say goodbye to Merrin, Wenna, and everyone and then we'll go. I'll say you have a headache and that's why we're leaving early.'

'Sounds good to me. I'll wait in the car.' She drops a quick kiss on his lips and hurries out.

———

Merrin's chatting to Wenna and Faye in a quiet corner of the garden. The coloured lights above Merrin's head have come on, giving her face and hair an ethereal effect. Could she look any more beautiful?

'There he is!' Wenna says, as Ethan walks towards them. 'I was just saying to these two, I was going to come and drag you out here, if you were a minute longer.'

Ethan thinks she's had one too many G&Ts, she's having a ball. He kisses her cheek. 'It's been so great to have met you, Wenna, I can't tell you how much.'

Wenna pats her cheek. 'I got a kiss from the most handsome man in the world.' She flaps a hand at Faye and Merrin and pretends to swoon. They laugh, but Ethan notices Merrin's is a little forced.

'You flatter me, young lady.'

'Young lady!' Wenna hoots. 'He always calls me that. If only it were true, my dear.' Then she points a finger to the sky as if she'd just remembered something. 'Talking of young ladies, I was about to say just as you came out, how much these two remind me of my sister and her friend Gladys.' She nods at Faye and Merrin.

Ethan couldn't see the resemblance to Lamorna of either woman. 'Really? I remember Gladys as she came to visit once. I wouldn't have said—'

'No. Not in looks, in spirit. Gladys, like Faye, was

always so gobby and overpowering, but she was vulnerable deep down and with a heart of gold.' Wenna looks at Faye. 'No offence, lovely.'

Faye's brows shoot up and she laughs. 'None taken, I'm sure.'

'And Merrin has all the strength, guts and determination of my Lamorna. She doesn't always believe in herself though, and needs a good talking to – that's where Gladys comes in. No, I mean Faye.' Wenna hoots again. 'It's as if Lamorna and Gladys have both left a bit of themselves behind for you two to pick up. Well, Lamorna for sure.' She shrugs her shoulders and raises her palms skywards. 'After this latest message in a bottle miracle, I believe anything's possible.'

'Miracle's a bit of a strong description,' Merrin mutters into her glass and takes a big gulp.

'There she goes again. Playing it all down. Anyone can see you two were meant for each other,' Wenna begins, but Merrin holds her hand up.

'I don't want to talk about it anymore, Wen. I'm sure Jodie would have something to say about Ethan and me getting together.' She glares at Ethan. 'Shame you neglected to tell us you and Jodie were more than friends.'

Faye and Wenna's mouths drop open, and they look at him expectantly. Shit. 'We aren't … I mean…'

'Really? Well, it certainly looked like you were, when I walked in on the pair of you kissing just now.'

'Kissing?' Faye and Wenna say at the same time, with identical aghast expressions.

Damn it all to hell. Why has he turned out to be the bad

guy, when all he's doing is trying to prevent a good friend getting terribly hurt? 'Look, she was kissing me, I was...' He stops and rakes his fingers through his hair. 'Please, can we talk about this in private tomorrow, Merrin? I'm just about to leave, as Jodie's got a headache and—'

'Not sure there's anything to talk about,' Merrin snaps.

Wenna and Faye are glaring at him as if he's the devil incarnate. Ethan looks to the soft navy sky, tinged with the last few strokes of sunset, and blows down his nostrils. This evening has been a fucking disaster. Before he can think of the right words, out of his mouth comes, 'Jeez, Merrin. I don't see why you're in such a mood about it all anyway. Right from the beginning when we first spoke on the phone, you always said you didn't want a relationship – so what's your problem?'

Quick as a flash she retorts, 'You, not being honest! When I met you on the beach, my gut told me you were someone I could trust, someone who wouldn't let anyone down. Ha! What a joke!' She bangs her drink down on the table and marches off inside the house.

Apart from the background music softly wafting on the breeze, there is a sudden pin-drop silence. All conversation has stopped and every face is turned to his. He's torn between following Merrin or making a swift exit. Head says exit, heart says find Merrin.

'Are you and Jodie really an item?' Faye asks quietly, as people go back to their conversations.

'No. Not at all, but it's an unholy mess, to say the least.' He looks to the house and takes a step towards it.

Faye puts a hand on his arm. 'No. Let her settle and call

her tomorrow, Ethan. There's no point in talking to her now because she's in no mood to listen.' Wenna nods in agreement and gives him a watery smile.

'Okay. I'll do that. Goodnight.' Ethan sighs, and with a heavy heart, walks down the path towards his car.

Chapter Twenty-One

I eye the gin bottle and then the clock. Noon is far too early to start drinking, isn't it? Besides, that would be totally out of character … but on second thoughts, might as well start as I mean to go on. I've already cried off work for the first time ever, pretending to Gillian that I must have eaten a dodgy sausage or something at yesterday's BBQ. My acting skills were hardly RADA standard though, as I stuttered and stumbled over my lines, when replying to her question about who else had been affected. She thought it odd that I was the only person who was ill, and I recovered enough to say, well as far as we knew, because I hadn't spoken to anyone apart from Lucy today. That was another lie, because I'd spoken to Wenna, Faye and my parents. I would have spoken to Ethan too, if I'd answered his texts and four missed calls. There's no way I want anything more to do with him. How wrong can you be about a person?

I pour a tiny measure of gin into one of my 'for best' cut-glass tumblers, add a slice of lemon, a dash of tonic and three ice cubes. Sitting outside in the shade, I listen to the ice crack as it melts and gently swirl the liquid round in the glass. That's how my thoughts have behaved all morning. Swirling round and round my head, but far from gently. More like a whirlpool, smashing my feelings, thoughts and reasoning into each other, while failing to arrive at any logical conclusion as to the way forward. I know that I should wash my hands of Ethan, but I can't find strong enough soap to make them totally clean. One moment I resolve never to have anything more to do with him, the next, I find little specks of dirt that I missed, each made of hopes, dreams and images of Ethan.

I look up at the big patches of cerulean sky pinned to the branches of the battered oak-tree like freshly washed linen. The patches remind me of the blue in Ethan's eyes, so I close mine and take a big gulp of my drink, relishing the piquant zest of lemon, the cold bubbles, and the lingering path of alcohol spreading warmth inside my chest. After a while, the gin does its trick, and I begin to relax into a more philosophical frame of mind. In a way, I should be pleased that I walked in on Ethan and Jodie. At least now I can stop all this teenage mooning about over him. Mooning. How appropriate. The whole message in a bottle June-moon thing has not helped my logical thought. Yes, it was all very extraordinary, and I can no longer dismiss it as just coincidence, well, not easily, but I've allowed events to cloud my judgement and lead me right up the garden path. I obviously wanted to believe it was magic, fate, and Lamorna's helping hand. Wanted to believe in the fairy-tale and happy ending. My Cinderella to his Prince Charming.

He's certainly got the looks, and the charm. Or he had, until I found him making out with one of the ugly sisters. I allow a wry smile. No point in getting bitter and twisted, is there? But after all the crap I've had to deal with over the last few years, is there any wonder? *Cut yourself some slack, Merrin.*

'Slack. Yeah, I need more of that.' Okay, now I'm talking to myself. I probably need something to soak up the gin, as I've not eaten today. An image of BBQ leftovers in the fridge comes to me, and I take myself indoors to pile my plate high. Comfort food and drink. The slippery slope. I wonder what Lucy and my parents are having for lunch? They wanted to take me out with them for posh nosh, but I couldn't face it. Made some excuse up about needing to get a few ideas down for my novel. Ha! More lies. I lied to Faye and Wenna too when they phoned, full of concern for me. Begged me to hear Ethan out. I said I'd washed my hands of him, and that it was a silly idea in the first place. Of all the swirly whirlpool thoughts I've had today, this is the one that sticks to the sides the most. We live an ocean apart, and I certainly wouldn't have been so quick to leave here like Lamorna did all those years ago, mainly because of Lucy – there's no way I could just up and leave her. And I have a feeling that Ethan wouldn't come here, so what would be the point? It's all best left well alone. Especially now Jodie is on the scene … even though Ethan says she isn't.

With a leaning tower of chicken leg, sausage, rice and garlic bread on my plate, complete with another G&T, I make my way back into the garden and the 'comfy cushion' bench as Lucy calls it. Ten minutes later, the leaning tower is reduced to its mere foundations, and my chin is smeared with grease and mayo. I let out a tremendous belch and undo my jeans ... just as Ethan walks through the gate. Nooo! What the bloody hell is he doing here? How embarrassing! But if he heard my belch, he's too polite to show it, thank the lord.

'Hey, Merrin. You didn't answer my calls, so I came over. I couldn't leave it like we did last night.' He pushes his fingers through his tawny mop and fixes me with a bright blue gaze.

Bollocks. Why does he always look so drop dead? Unlike me right now, who must look more like the living dead. I wipe my chin with the back of my hand and hastily try to button up my jeans without being too obvious. It doesn't work. I turn to the side, mumbling, 'Oh, hello. I erm...' Nice, Merrin. So articulate.

'Sorry to come round unannounced.' He sits on the bench next to me. 'You okay?'

I swear his eyes just lingered on my chin, so I rub it again. 'Yes. Though not sure we have anything to discuss, to be honest.' That's better. Start as you mean to go on. Oh dear. He looks disappointed now.

'Please hear me out. If you still feel the same at the end of what I have to say, then at least I can say I tried.'

Poor Ethan, he looks so awkward and humble ... my instinct is to offer him a drink, but that would look like I want him to stay. So I don't. Cruel to be kind. I rub my chin again and sigh. 'Okay. I'm listening.'

Relief lifts the corners of his lips and he makes himself comfortable. 'Thanks so much, Merrin. I can see how the whole Jodie and I thing must have looked to you.'

'When you were kissing each other's faces off in my kitchen last night, you mean?' Childish, but I can't help myself.

'Yup.' He looks at the floor between his feet. 'Thing is, she took me by surprise with that kiss and with everything else she had to say to me last night.' His eyes flick back up to mine. 'I promise you there is nothing between us.' Ethan lifts his hands and lets them fall with a slap to his knees. 'Okay, the last few days she's been a bit more tactile, looked at me in a "more than friends" way, but I wasn't really sure. Then she started calling me "hon" last night, and eventually told me how she felt, after you'd gone back to your guests. You could have knocked me down with a feather.' He snorts down his nose and looks up at the patches of blue, through the tree branches, just as I had earlier. I must concede his eyes are an exact match.

Remembering that I'm supposed to be angry with him, I snatch back my thoughts to safer ground. 'And how does she feel?' I fold my arms and take a big swallow of my drink.

'Apparently, she's never stopped loving me since we went out together as kids. Said she'd made a mistake marrying Harvey, and that now they are over, she hoped I could feel the same about her.' He gives me a bewildered stare. 'It was a hell of a shock. I care deeply about her, but as a friend. And I'm going to be completely honest with you, I did wonder if there could be something more between us, when I said she could join me on this trip. But the kiss you saw confirmed that there absolutely couldn't. I felt nothing for her at all. In fact, it felt wrong, like I was kissing my sister or something. It's been a while since my marriage broke down and I suppose I might have been lonely? The idea of me and Jodie back together was like leaning on the old familiar, a bit like a comfort blanket. Stupid of me, I know.'

My heart's thumping in my chest as I know it's the truth. Honesty is clear to see in his face, and I know that my gut feeling about him on the beach wasn't wrong after all. 'So did you tell her how you felt?'

'No. I couldn't. It would have broken her. Right now, she thinks I'm out looking for a present for Wenna.' He clocks my look of contempt and holds his hands up. 'Hey, I really couldn't tell her. It wouldn't be right to ruin her holiday and put an end to our friendship, because I'm sure it would have, if I'd have rejected her outright. She had a rough time after Harvey, her self-esteem hit rock bottom and she ended up on medication. The woman Harvey left her for was half his age… I want to let her down gently, preferably when we're back home.' He slides his eyes away from mine. 'And Merrin, be fair – you told me you weren't looking for a relationship from the get-go. We felt close last night, when we sat at your kitchen table, talking about your novel and our lives, but I wasn't sure if it was more than you being friendly. I'm not great at reading signs.'

He has a valid point. And the fact that he didn't want to hurt a good friend isn't lost on me. Neither is the fact that Jodie has suffered exactly the same fate as me. Being dumped is bad enough, but being dumped for somebody half your age is brutal. Ethan really cares about people, which makes him all the more attractive. He honestly is the decent man I thought he was – his soul shines from within, makes his face glow. Makes his face glow? What the hell? Do I imagine he's some kind of alien? My thoughts are so surreal today, but I know what I mean. I smile at him and take his hand. Time to put my cards on the table, if we're ever going to move on from this. Time for me to be honest and decent too.

I take a deep breath and say, 'Yeah. Yeah, I did, didn't I? Thing is, I changed my mind when I met you that first time. Kind of freaked me out, to be honest. I've never felt such a strong pull towards someone as I did to you. Yes, I found you very physically attractive, but it went deeper. It was as if I had known you for ages, as if you could see into my soul and I yours. There was an instant recognition that you were a good man, an honest man. As I said, it scared me because how can you feel so strongly about a person you only just met? Unless … unless it was all to do with forces outside our control showing me where my feelings truly lie.' I stop, look out down the path and over the fields. I feel vulnerable and out of my depth. I want to put up hurdles to stop my heart galloping ahead. I manage to find a few, but it clears them one after the other like a champion steeplechaser. Now the tears have started gathering, pooling, trickling down my cheeks like rain drops.

Ethan takes my chin gently between his forefinger and thumb, tilts my face up to his, and wipes my tears away. 'You don't know how happy it makes me to hear you say that. I couldn't have wished for better.' I see his eyes are trying to copy mine, so he blinks and gives me the sweetest smile. 'I feel exactly the same way about you. It took a little longer than the first meeting, but I did feel there was something between us, even then. When I first heard your voice on the phone I felt a connection, though I still tried to tell myself it was all imagined. But I couldn't get you out of my head in the days after ... and then last night it hit me right between the eyes. Or you did, when you walked out of the house in that dress ... then again when we talked in the kitchen, I felt more and more drawn to you.' He stops and his Adam's apple bobs as he swallows hard. 'It was as though we were meant to be together, you know?'

I did. 'I felt the same, but thought it was all too crazy. We only just met, so how can we possibly feel so strongly? Maybe it's because of the unorthodox way we were brought together and the Lamorna and Wenna influence of course...' I shake my head. 'It's all so much to take in.'

'I get it. Absolutely, I do. My thoughts were exactly the same as yours as I lay awake in the middle of the night last night, thinking about you. Then I thought, you know what? I'm gonna accept it without question. Some things are beyond our understanding, and I'm cool with that.'

We look into each other's eyes and he drops his gaze to my mouth. My heart gallops up the scale and there's a giddy feeling in my chest. I know what's coming, and I'm powerless to stop it as his lips find mine, and I'm swept away on a tide of joyful passion. We break apart and I laugh as relief floods through me. But then unexpectedly, the words, 'Can we really do this?' escape from some vulnerable, wary, scared place that's never too far away from my surface. A place that's been built up strong and tall by Jacob's betrayal and rejection.

He spreads his hands and shrugs. 'Hell yes! There's no way we can go back now, Merrin, my pearl of the sea.'

That's the most romantic thing anyone has ever said to me, I think. But can we really work? I stroke my hand over the mermaid on his bicep, and allow my fears free rein. There's no point in allowing myself to be carried along on a shimmering rainbow, only to find it heads into a thunderstorm a while down the road. 'So, supposing it works out between us … where would we live? I know it might seem very early to be asking these questions, but I can't move to America. Lucy still needs me, even though she might pretend otherwise … and Cornwall is my home.' I swallow a lump in my throat that feels the size of a golf ball.

Ethan's sky-blue eyes find a few clouds and he furrows his brow. 'Yeah, it is a little soon to be talking about that, but I don't know … my work is there. Not sure I'd get a well-paid teaching job here. I teach American History, so…' He shrugs and looks at his feet. Silence squeezes in between us on the bench and elbows me in the side. I'm about to elbow it back, when he continues, 'Lucy will be away at university, too. Is she likely to be coming home often? If she's anything like I was as a student, I would see my folks a handful of times a year. Too much having fun and finding out who I was.' Ethan gives me a cheerful grin but it doesn't work.

'I don't expect you to understand. Lucy still needs me, even if she might not realise it most of the time. I'm her mum. There's no way I could be there for her if I moved three thousand miles away.'

The clouds in his eyes darken. 'You mean I wouldn't understand because I have no children?'

The euphoria that has been wrapped around me like a joyful hug since we bared our souls to each other releases me into stark reality. I feel a cold chill seeping through my bones and a sense of gloom settle across my shoulders like a dead weight. 'Yeah, I suppose I do.' No point in dressing it up.

'Right.' He folds his arms and stares into the distance.

'And while we're being so honest, I have a job here too, you know.'

'It's café work, Merrin. We have cafés in Massachusetts.'

'Nice. My job isn't as worthy as yours, obviously.'

He frowns at me. 'That's not what I was saying.'

Without warning, all the hurt, mistrust, apprehension and downright fear that have been such frequent visitors since Jacob betrayed me all arrive at the same time and bring enough luggage for a month. I was kidding myself if I thought I could allow the magic to work. I have responsibilities. Lamorna and Wenna hadn't the baggage I have. They also had no children to worry about, did they? The only constants in my life are Lucy and the café. If they were taken away, what have I got? I'd be lost, anchorless, cast adrift. And so, so far away from everything I'd ever known. No. No. I was right the first time when I considered this. It wouldn't work, so what's the point starting anything? I don't blame Ethan for not wanting to move here either, because he has a life that he's happy with. We're from different worlds and oceans apart. Well, one ocean, and that's plenty. I might have some of Lamorna's spirit, but it's not enough.

I get to my feet, noting my legs are trembling. 'It would never work, Ethan.' I look down at him and fight to carry on, as I watch his face crumple. 'As much as we might want it to ... best not to start anything. I'm so sorry.'

He stands up and pulls me into his arms. 'It's already started. You can't deny how you feel, and neither can I.'

His lips find mine but I pull away. 'I can't deny it, no. And believe me, this is breaking me...' A sob escapes and I put a shaking hand to my mouth. 'There's nothing I wouldn't give for us to be together ... except abandon my daughter. And that is what it appears I'd have to do.' Turning from his pained expression, I hurry towards the house, sobbing. The beautiful few moments when we'd shared our hearts were now lost for ever.

I hear him come after me and feel his hand on my arm. 'Please don't go, Merrin.' He spins me round to face him. 'We'll work something out, let's see how it goes and—'

'No!' I hold my hand up. 'No.' I say again, softly. 'Better to leave it here, than put us both through loads of pain and upset. I've had enough of that for a lifetime lately, I can tell you.' I swallow my tears and kiss his cheek. 'Let Jodie love you ... give her a chance.'

Then despite his protests, I turn, go into the house, and close the door behind me.

Chapter Twenty-Two

Ethan's trying his hardest to look happy, as Jodie makes him stand under the Land's End signpost for a photo. His smile feels like an overstretched piece of elastic that's ready to snap. Behind them the Atlantic roars as the wind taunts it, and he wants to roar back. Let out his frustration, tell Jodie he can't carry on. He wants to get in the car and drive back up to Merrin's, batter the door down, take her in his arms, make her see sense ... tell her he loves her. When he first realised that he did, in the early hours of the morning, it scared the shit out of him. But now he's resigned to it. There's no way he can dismiss it, but it seems there's every chance it will remain unrequited. There it will be, stuck like a lump in his heart – cholesterol clogging his arteries, a time bomb slowly ticking away, until one day it will stop. He sighs. At least then his misery will be over. Ethan can't believe how dramatic that thought sounds, but what's the point in life without Merrin?

'Ethan, smile, for Pete's sake! Point at the New York sign and give me a big cheesy grin!' Jodie says, pointing her cell phone at him and flicking her hair out of her eyes.

He looks up at the sign pointing out over the ocean – *New York, 3147 miles*. It's as if it's mocking him, rubbing it in just how far away from Merrin he lives, how hopeless their relationship would be if it was allowed to exist. He thinks again about the twenty-odd messages and missed calls he's sent her over the last few days. And the last-ditch attempt to see her last night around 7pm when he'd turned up at her house, and Lucy, pink-faced and shifty-eyed, had told him Merrin was out with Faye. He suspected it was a lie; all the signs were there. But what could he have done? Barge past her and make an even bigger fool of himself when Merrin threw him out again?

Focusing on Jodie's disgruntled expression, he manages, 'Okay, sorry.' Then he points at the sign and forces his mouth into a smile.

'Hell, Ethan, your face looks like a Halloween mask. What's wrong, honey?'

How long has she got? 'Nothing. Just feel a bit foolish.'

Jodie laughs and clicks the camera button on her phone a few times. 'Okay. That will have to do now. Let's get a cup of coffee from the café over there.'

Late afternoon and Ethan is parked outside Wenna's. He looks at the present he got for her, a ship in a bottle, and wonders if it falls a bit short. It's not a message in a bottle, but it was the best he could do, and at least when she looks at it, she will think of him.

'Come in, young man!' Wenna says, as she opens the door. Her keen blue eyes sparkle with warmth and a twist of his gut makes him suddenly realise he's going to miss her.

'That depends if you've made some scones, young lady.' Ethan raises an eyebrow and grins.

'You know I have, boy. In you come.'

He eyes the yellow and orange décor of the hallway, as he follows Wenna into the kitchen. Wow, it seems as if he's stepped back in time to the 1970s. Ditto in the kitchen. Ethan's ushered into a cosy sitting room packed to the gunnels with ornaments in cabinets and corners, under his feet is a typical swirly blue, brown and orange 1970s carpet, and he's invited to sit on a green and yellow leaf-patterned sofa. Despite needing an update, the place is neat, tidy and comfortable. All very Wenna.

'Tea or coffee with your scone?' Wenna asks, from the doorway.

'Has to be tea. How could it be anything else with your scones?'

She gives him a twinkly smile and flaps a hand at the window. 'While you're waiting, have a look at my own very special message in a bottle on the windowsill. That's the one my Finn sent me all those years past.'

Ethan goes over to an old bottle mounted on a wooden stand, then looks at the raised lettering along its flank that reads 'Lemonade'. Inside, there's a scroll of paper, sun-bleached and fragile. He can just make out a few letters as the sunlight finds it. Unexpectedly, he feels a rush of emotion and puts a hand to his mouth. Both Wenna and Great Aunt Lamorna found their sweetheart and true love in this wonderful way, and so had he. Sadly, the difference between him and them is that his true love would never be realised. He picks up the paper bag with the gift for Wenna in it, and places it on the armchair opposite the sofa before retaking his seat. *Hope she likes it.*

'Can I help, Wenna?' he calls.

He's answered by a rattling of crockery and the appearance of a little table on wheels followed by Wenna. 'No, all done,' she says, as she puts a plate of scones on the coffee table between them and busies herself with an old brown teapot and floral teacups. 'Do you take milk and sugar?'

'Just a dash of milk, please.'

'Oh, yes. I remember now. I don't have clotted cream today, just jam.'

'Perfect.' Ethan takes the cup and saucer from Wenna and nods to the seat behind her. 'I got you a little parting gift. Hope you'll find room for it in one of your cabinets.' He looks doubtfully at the ones around the room.

'Really? Oh, you shouldn't have. I have nothing to give you.'

'Nonsense. You have given me the pleasure of your company and that's more than enough.'

'Well, what a lovely thing to say.' Wenna's cheeks find some warmth and she picks up the bag, before sitting down in the chair. Carefully she pulls the ship in a bottle out of it and exclaims, 'How marvellous!' Her eyes are bright with tears. 'It can go next to the other one. Did you have a look at it?'

'I did. It must mean the world to you.'

'Yes, it does. And now it has a companion.' She holds the bottle aloft and gazes at the gaily red and yellow painted hull of the tiny ship. 'I shall remember you every time I look at it.'

A rush of warmth floods his chest. 'That's what I hoped. I know it's not quite a message in a bottle, but it's similar, I guess. It's a message from me to you, thanking you for your kindness and caring nature.'

Wenna pulls a big white cotton handkerchief from the pocket of her trousers and flaps it at him. 'Stop it, you'll have me in bits.'

Ethan grins. 'Sorry. I'll take one of these scones to hush my mouth, if you don't mind.'

'Take two!' Wenna jokes, and puts the bottle next to the other on the windowsill. Returning to her seat, she sips her tea and looks into the middle distance as if she's watching a scene only she can see.

Through a mouthful of scone, Ethan says, 'Penny for them?'

Her eyes flit to his. 'I was just wondering if you could write Merrin a message in a bottle. You know, as a last-ditch attempt.'

He chews this over with the scone and swallows. 'I don't know, Wenna... I told you on the phone that I went round there last night, and Merrin got Lucy to cover for her. How would I give her the bottle if she won't even answer the door to me?'

He gets a finger jab. 'You don't know Lucy was covering for her, it was just a hunch.' Ethan's about to argue against that but keeps quiet as Wenna's flapping a hand at him. 'You'd give it to her by calling at her house again and handing it to Lucy. Or failing that, go to the shop and give it to Merrin while she's at work.'

This idea isn't working. It's too contrived, false. And anyway, what would he say in the message that he's not said already in person? He says as much to Wenna and adds, 'It all seems so hopeless, Wen.'

She puts her cup down and folds her arms. 'Earlier, I said I had nothing to give you as a parting gift. Well, it turns out I do.' Her eyes become two blue chips. 'I have some advice. Never give up on your dreams. Always run towards love. And on your deathbed, don't have regrets about the important things you never had the guts to do. I will only have one – that I never saw Lamorna again and told her why I never said goodbye, or kept in touch. Though she did send you to us to show me she understands. She said she'd look after me long after she'd gone.' Wenna dabs a tear away. 'So, write Merrin a letter, bash her door down and carry her off, sit on a donkey and serenade her underneath her bedroom window at midnight.' She throws her hands up. 'Do anything! But whatever you do, don't do nothing.' A nod. 'There. I've said my piece.'

Ethan has to smile. 'What would Great Aunt Lamorna do, eh?'

'She'd probably do all those things I suggested, and

more.' Wenna throws back her head and cackles. Then she grows serious and pats his hand. 'Do something, Ethan, before it's too late. Merrin's as stubborn as an old mule, so I know it won't be easy. But let her know how you feel. You can do no more. And Ethan, if you are sincere about wanting to be with her, you might have to bite the bullet and move here. There are worse places to live.'

This is something he's begun to realise. 'Because of her not wanting to leave Lucy?'

'Yes,' she replies, simply. 'If I'd have been blessed with a child, there is nothing in the world that would part us. Not even a handsome devil like you.'

On the doorstep, Ethan can hardly form the words to say goodbye as he looks down into Wenna's face. She's crying again, but valiantly trying to find a smile. It keeps settling there for a second and then it wobbles off again. 'Look at the state of me,' she says with a shake of her head.

'I know how you feel, Wenna. It's been wonderful spending time with you.' Ethan has to take a deep breath to prevent his own smile wobbling off. 'And you have my address, so you can drop me a line.'

'Yes. And never mind. This isn't goodbye – just farewell.'

'You never know.'

'I do, actually. I'll be seeing you; I feel it in here.' Wenna lightly taps the left side of her chest.' Then she gives him a bright smile. 'I'll be seeing you, I said. Reminds me of an old wartime song that Lamorna and me used to sing. Lots recorded it, but Vera Lynn did it best.'

'I think I know the one. Something about, I'll be looking at the moon … but I'll be seeing you?'

She claps her hands together. 'Yes! Fancy you knowing that oldie. One of the last things Lamorna ever said to me was, "We'll meet again, as Vera Lyn says." We never did though…' Then she hums the tune and sings a few lines, but her lips tremble, and she has to stop. Wenna clears her throat and claps her hands again. 'Right, be off now and sort out how you're going to get through to that stubborn mule, otherwise known as Merrin.'

Ethan gives her a hug. 'I'll be seeing you, Wenna.'

'Count on it, Ethan.'

Back at the hotel, he finds that Jodie has gone for a walk. She sent him a text saying they could go to the lovely seafood restaurant they found a few nights ago for dinner later. They'll be home in a few days, so it won't be long before he can drop this pretence and tell her the truth. The strain it's putting him under is immense, but it has to be done. When he tells her, will it mean the end of their friendship? He hopes not, but he fears it will be. Best make the most of this dinner tonight, as it could be one of the last they share. The weight of that thought pulls his mood down to basement level. Nevertheless, he takes out the notepad he's just bought from the general store, and places it on the desk in front of the window that overlooks the rocky cove the hotel's perched upon.

'What would Lamorna say?' he murmurs, as he watches a gull spread its wings and take off from the rocks, and glide effortlessly over the Atlantic, the sun on its wings. A few moments later, he takes a deep breath, takes the top off his favourite pen, and begins to write.

Chapter Twenty-Three

Rivulets of perspiration are trickling down my back and underarms. Lovely. The words 'Hotter than July' pop into my head as I hurry to the carpark from the café, slide into the baking oven masquerading as my car, and rootle in my bag for sunglasses. Was that a film … or was it an old album Dad used to have? *Does it bloody matter?* asks my frustrated and overheated brain. *This July is hotter than a damned furnace, just start the car and get yourself home.* I picture myself in a refreshing shower, changing into a floaty sundress and then sitting in the shady garden with a cool drink. Maybe I'll ring Faye to see if she wants to go out for a quick bite later, I'm too tired to make food after cooking for, and waiting on, the eleventy-billion tourists who came into the café today.

The shower does the trick. I feel more human and less like a melting candle as I wrap my wet hair in a towel turban before going downstairs to call Faye. There's a bit of mail under the 'post cat' as I call it on the hall table, but it can wait. It's probably all junk anyway. On the comfy cushion bench, I put my feet up on a little footstool, sip a Coke and call Faye.

'Dinner tonight? Bit short notice, isn't it?' Faye says with a sigh.

'Hey, there's no obligation, just thought you might fancy it,' I reply, my mind already going through what I can make to eat from what's in the fridge.

'I'm a bit knackered, to be honest. Had a busy day in the baking heat showing tourists around houses that they have no real intention of buying, while Derek sits on his arse in the office stuffing his face as usual.'

'God, is he still being so lazy, even after you threatened to leave?'

'Yeah. He just said he was the boss, so he had to delegate. Also had the cheek to say people trust female estate agents more than male – especially pretty ones.'

I'm furious on her behalf. 'Sexist pig!'

'Yep. But I worry I wouldn't get another job so easily, and it's not so bad most of the time. Actually, I'm sure Jacob would take me on at his swish Plymouth office.' She laughs.

'Oh yeah, he so would. Not. Hmm. Well, okay. Maybe we'll catch up later in the week.'

'Yes. Have you heard from Ethan?'

'He's texted and called umpteen times, but I didn't respond.' I sigh as I divulge the next bit. 'And the other night he came round to the house, but I got Lucy to say I was out with you.'

'Merrin! That's so wrong, on so many levels.'

'Yeah, that's what Lucy said.'

'Poor kid. Bet she felt awful.'

'That's right, rub it in.'

'I will. It's not like you to run away from your problems.'

'Look, I didn't want to see him. I couldn't. I was worried I'd give in.'

'Would that be so bad?'

'Yeah, it would. Don't you get that I can't leave Lucy?'

'Yes, but have you even talked to her about it?'

'Kind of, but I don't want to put it all on her. It wouldn't be fair. I did say I'd miss her too much though.'

'What did she say?'

'She said she'd miss me too, but that I should follow my heart, obviously.'

'She probably meant it.'

'I don't know if she did or didn't, Faye. But what I do know is I'm not even going there. It's over before it's begun and that's the way it has to stay.' I heave a sigh and wonder if I'm making the biggest mistake of my life, but then I shove that thought aside with the strength of a Titan.

'I can see you're in no mood to see sense, but there's no way this thing between you is over. If you believe that, you're deluded, missy. Okay, speak soon.'

I stare at the phone after we end the call, wondering if I should at least answer one of Ethan's messages. He's going back to the States the day after tomorrow, and despite knowing it's best to leave well alone, I'd hate not to say goodbye. An upwelling of tears makes the words on his last text unreadable, so I wipe them away with the back of my hand.

Merrin, please get back to me. We can make this work, if we really want it to. I know I do, and I think you feel the same. Xxx

That was sent at 5am. Maybe he's given up at last. A tiny part of me hopes he has, but the rest of me is wondering if he's right. Could we make it work somehow? My ponderings are interrupted by the rumbling of my parents' campervan as it pulls onto the drive. Lucy jumps out, followed by Mum and Dad, and they all make their way over to me. I thought Lucy was staying at Nicola's for dinner?

'You eaten yet?' Mum asks.

'Just about to make something,' I say, hoping my nose isn't deceiving me as the prickle of vinegar fills my nostrils.

'Voila!' Dad exclaims as he holds aloft a paper bag full of fish and chips from the best fish and chip shop for miles around. 'Fish, chips and curry sauce, with plenty of salt and vinegar, okay for you?'

My stomach answers for me with a long loud grumble. 'You're a godsend, Dad.'

'Oi, it was my idea,' Mum says, hands on hips, pretending to be disgruntled.

'But it was me who told you where the best chip shop was.' Lucy narrows her eyes and pokes Mum in the belly before running into the house chortling. 'I'll get the plates in the oven!' she calls back over her shoulder.

'You've trained that one well,' Dad says with a laugh, as he follows Lucy with the bag of food.

Mum sits next to me, fixes me with a knowing look, and brushes a stray curl away from the corner of her mouth that the breeze is insisting on keeping there. 'Okay, let's be having the real story about Merrin and Ethan.'

I frown. 'Real story?'

'Yeah. Lucy came round, especially to catch me up on what's happened. She was really upset, to be honest.'

My heart plummets. Great. That's why Lucy didn't go to Nicola's. 'Marvellous. That's exactly what I need to hear right now. What did she say?'

Mum slips her arm through mine and kisses my cheek. 'That she feels you aren't going to see Ethan again, because you might have to move to America, and you can't do that because you won't leave her in England. Lucy says that Ethan is the love of your life, but you'll throw it all away and be unhappy and alone, all because of her.'

'No. Did she?' Mum nods and squeezes my arm. 'And I thought I'd done such a good job of pretending me and Ethan were a long shot, and it was too big a step. I said I'd miss her if I left, but nothing about the love of my life and the rest of it.'

'Lucy has eyes and ears, just like I do. We can read between the lines. She's right, isn't she?'

I heave a sigh that wants to go on for ever, up into the breeze and far away, taking all my sadness with it. It can't though, there's too much of it. 'Yes. I couldn't leave her, and Ethan says he couldn't move here because of his job. But I think, like me, he's very happy where he comes from.'

'Has he said outright that he wouldn't move here?'

I think about that one. 'More or less. He said it would be difficult for him to get a job here, as he teaches American history. He doesn't get that I won't leave Lucy either, as she's off to uni. But then Ethan's got no kids, so he can't understand.'

Mum's quiet for a few moments, then she turns to me and gives me one of her intense, miss-nothing stares. 'Look, love. Me and your dad don't interfere in your personal life, as you know. When you said you were going to marry Jacob, we knew he wasn't right for you, but it wasn't our place to try and dissuade you. You wouldn't have listened anyway.' Mum chuckles and I have to smile. 'But this time we can't just keep quiet and let it go. We only met Ethan briefly at the BBQ, but we both said afterwards that he is perfect for you. There's something going on here bigger than the both of you, and it won't be shoved in a box and nailed down.'

I roll my eyes. 'You've been talking to Wenna about magic and the spirit of Lamorna, haven't you?'

Mum shrugs. 'Yes, and I know I told you years ago that I thought the local legend was nonsense. But I can see it for myself now. How else can you explain what happened? And Ethan's perfect for you. Me and Wen watched you and him chatting on this bench the other night, and we thought it was as if we were watching the end of some romantic movie, where the two star-crossed lovers eventually get together. Don't disappoint the audience, Merrin. But most of all, don't disappoint yourself.'

A tsunami of opposing feelings whip up in my gut and thrash about for dominance. Anger and bewilderment break free first. 'Don't you get it, Mum? I can't leave Lucy. Would you have left me?'

Mum holds up a cautionary finger. 'No. But for one,

Ethan hasn't categorically said he wouldn't live here, and two, there might be a way you could both live here part of the time and live there the rest. Ethan would have to find some temporary teaching work or something else for six months of the year, when you lived here. It can be done if you want it badly enough.'

Really? I'm incredulous. 'Er, hello? How the hell am I supposed to do that? I need a job, and I very much doubt Gillian would hold my place at the café while I go swanning off to America for half the year.' I wave my hand at the house. 'This mortgage needs paying too.' I shake my head at her. 'Quite frankly, Mum, you must be living in cloud cuckoo land dreaming up an idea like that.'

'Not at all. Me and your dad had a long chat about it the other day, and made a decision. Lucy coming round today to tell us how she felt made us realise that we'd made the right one.'

Now she's lost me. 'What decision?'

'To give you your dosh now, rather than make you wait until we pop our clogs,' Dad says, coming up behind me with a tray of fish and chips. Lucy comes along with another, and they set them down on the table nearby. 'Come on, grub's up.'

———————

In a trance, I pick at my food. I might as well be eating cotton wool for all the enjoyment I'm getting. My parents have quickly explained their plan and totally stunned is an understatement. 'This is crazy. I can't let you do it,' I say, looking from Mum to Dad and back again.

Lucy mumbles through a mouthful of food. 'Yeah, but they want to do it. I think it makes perfect sense.'

'You're in on it too?'

She grins and a chewed chip makes a bid for freedom. 'Yeah, they told me their plan on the drive here.'

I hand her some kitchen roll, put down my fork, and take a huge swallow of the lager that Dad put in front of me. 'So let me get this straight. You're going to give me a big chunk of the proceeds of your house sale, and some savings, if I need them?'

Mum nods and squirts a big puddle of ketchup onto the side of her plate. 'Yeah. As you know, we sold the house and bought the camper. We have the rest of the money from that, and the sale of both your grandparents' houses too, after they died. They had a few savings too, and so do we. Your dad has his private pension from work as well. So really, we don't have any money worries at all!'

I shake my head. 'But if you give a big dollop to me, you will. How could you carry on doing all the swanning about Europe that you love then?'

'Like your mum's just said, we have pots of dosh,' Dad says, dabbing the corner of his mouth with kitchen roll. 'But to be honest, we don't want to. We'll do some, but not as much. Truth is, all this driving – well, it's getting a bit much for us nowadays. We'll go off to the sunshine in the winter months, but stay here in our beloved Cornwall in the summer.'

'Oh, and I know you'll miss working in the café, when

you're not here,' Lucy says, stabbing a chip and running it through some sauce. 'But when you are here, you will still be able to do your bit. Gillian will deffo keep you part-time.'

'I don't know about that,' I say, taking another drink. My head is swimming with possibilities, and my heart's so full of love for my parents I can hardly breathe.

'I do, 'cos I phoned her when I went inside to put the plates to warm and she said no probs. There's no shortage of people always asking her if she's taking on.'

Blimey. 'What about the community larder?'

Lucy shrugs. 'That's easily sorted. Gillian, Sandra and maybe Wenna might lend a hand. Me too when I'm around, and you when you're home.'

'So, you have no more obstacles in your way, now. Phone Ethan and tell him,' Mum says, with a huge smile.

'Hold on a bit. I'm not sure you both would like to live in that campervan indefinitely, as luxurious as it might be. Won't you need the comforts of home in a few years?'

'Yep. We'll sell the camper and get a little bungalow when we hang up our travelling boots.' Mum pats my arm. 'I told you, we are well off, so stop trying to think of obstacles that don't exist.'

I swallow a lump in my throat but it's no good. The tears come. 'Oh, Mum … Dad. I don't know what to say, doing all that for me … it's all a bit overwhelming.'

Mum's eyes swim too and she grabs my hand across the table. 'We're doing it for us as well, because we want to see you happy and actually enjoy the money. We couldn't do that six feet under, could we?'

'Hey. Stop talking about death now. You're both living for ever,' Lucy says, with a wobble in her voice.

'Yes, and ever and ever and ever,' I say, and smile at Dad, who's doing the rapid eye-blink thingy that he does, when he's in danger of shedding a few tears.

'Lucy will get a lump sum too, to help with her studies and live the wild life in big bad Bristol,' Mum says.

Lucy's mouth drops open. 'Me?'

'Yes. Don't get carried away though, it won't be as much as your mum gets, but it will be enough to have fun with.' Dad pats her hands and takes a swallow from his lager bottle.

I cup my face with both hands and shake my head trying to take it all in. 'It's all unbelievable. Completely.'

'Nah. Just doing it because we love you, and because we can. And make sure you sort out things with Ethan before we go off to Portugal at the end of this week. I want to go with peace of mind.'

'Off again already?' I laugh. 'You two are unstoppable.'

'We are,' Mum says, putting the last chip in her mouth. 'When's Ethan going home?'

I sigh. 'The day after tomorrow.'

'Then tomorrow is D-Day,' Dad says, and does a silly salute.

Everyone looks at me expectantly for a few moments, while I toss a few ideas over in my mind. I turn to my daughter. 'Look, I'm tempted to go for it now, but six months away is too much. Maybe two or three months at a time? It is only early days with me and Ethan, and besides, I really wouldn't want to be away from you longer, Lulu.

Even though you keep telling me you're an adult and independent. You might still need me.'

Lucy shakes her head, but I think I detect a little flash of relief in her eyes too. She holds her hands up. 'Okay. Whatever makes you happy, Mum.'

'Right, is it all sorted now?' Dad asks with a sigh.

'I suppose it is,' I say, as my head and heart go tumbling hand in hand into free fall. Wow. This thing might just work out after all.

Chapter Twenty-Four

E than watches the sun climb higher in the sky, the bold rays sharpening the fuzzy edges of the cliffs and drawing a clear navy line across the horizon. A dog walker hurries down the slope to the beach, the dog bounding towards the ocean like a speeding bullet. The walker raises a hand and Ethan raises one back. The guy's the first human he's seen in two hours since he arrived at Chapel Porth, known by some as Magic Cove. As Ethan unzips his dark-green hoodie, closes his eyes and turns his face to the sun, a long-ago memory uncurls and stretches itself. On the other side of the Atlantic when he was about fourteen, he sat on a rock staring moodily out at the horizon. His Great Uncle Harry had taken him fishing at dawn, but the one he'd hooked had escaped, and since then, they'd nothing to show for it. Harry nudged him and said he should cheer up, because there were plenty more fish in the sea. Then he'd said, 'Years ago, when I was a young man, I sat on this beach on Christmas Day 1941. I'd arranged by letter, with my Lamorna, that we should be on our respective beaches at the same time and wish each other Merry Christmas. We sent our love across the ocean.' Harry had stopped then and swallowed hard. 'And do you know something? I actually felt her love ride in on the breeze and sock me between the eyes!' He laughed and looked down at Ethan. 'The love of a good woman is a gift, boy. A beautiful gift that I'm sure you'll be lucky enough to receive, one day. Treasure it. Look after it, and never take it for granted.'

Ethan wasn't surprised to find his eyes were wet, and he wiped them on the back of his sleeve. He missed Harry and Lamorna and hoped they were jitterbugging somewhere, having fun and laughing. Ethan smiles. That they were having fun wasn't really in doubt, because his abiding memory was of them always laughing together. He heaves a sigh and a glance at his watch tells him that Merrin is two hours and ten minutes late. Unfortunately, he's not lucky enough to receive the gift of love of a good woman, it seems. 'She's not coming, you jerk.' Digging his hands into his pockets, he wonders, should he ring her one last time? The waves shush that idea, as they roll up the beach and wet his toes. *No. I have to let her go. I have her answer, and I'll have to learn to accept it.* Ethan picks his sneakers up and walks along the beach.

Back at the hotel, Jodie's outside his room. 'There you are! Where the Sam Hill have you been at this early hour? The car was gone too.'

'Drove down the coast, then went for a walk on the beach.'

'At dawn?'

314

'Yeah, as it happens.'

'I could have come, if you'd have told me.'

'I just got up and went. Spur of the moment, you know?' *How easily you lie, Ethan*. Needs must, he tells the nagging voice. It's only until we get home.

'Okay. So, breakfast?' Jodie slips her arm through his and kisses his cheek.

'Uh-huh.'

They walk down the hallway to the elevator. 'We fly home tomorrow evening,' Jodie says, looking up at him with those big soulful eyes. 'A shame we never got time to see the sights of London.'

'Uh-huh.' Ethan presses the call button.

'Can you say anything else but, uh-huh?'

He gives her a little smile, though inside he's in turmoil. 'Uh-huh.'

She gives him a playful push into the elevator. 'Ethan Marshall, I swear you could try the patience of a saint.'

'Uh-huh.'

Jodie laughs and rests her head on his shoulder. He quickly steps to the side and presses the button for the ground floor. Over breakfast, they talk about London, the trip, and how beautiful Cornwall was. He even manages to laugh and smile in the right places. It's quite the performance. Because inside he feels numb, but none of it is Jodie's fault.

Merrin. His mind, heart and soul are full of Merrin, and all he wants to do is cry.

'Lucy, tell me honestly, does this dress look okay with these shoes?' I look backwards at myself through my bedroom mirror, and frown at the yellow sundress patterned with daisies, and the red strappy sandals I've paired it with. When I turn up outside Ethan's hotel, I need to look perfect. Or as perfect as I can for me. Jodie's frowny face appears in my mind's eye. I'll cross her bridge when I come to it, and any other that might get built. What if he's out somewhere, for example? I'll wait until he's back, no matter how long it takes. Right now, all that matters is seeing Ethan again.

Smoothing my hands over the material across my bottom, I turn to the side and back again. Maybe the question I should be asking is the usual: does my bum look big in this? I turn back to face the mirror and carefully run my fingers through my hair. Lucy's made a fantastic job of smoothing my messy curls into sleek waves, bless her boots. I lock eyes with her through the mirror. She's not answered my question about the dress, and she's leaning in the doorway wearing a guilty expression.

'What's up?'

She walks into the bedroom, flops down on the bed and chucks a pile of junk mail on my bedside table. 'So sorry, Mum. These came yesterday and I was in a rush to get out … so I shoved them under the ceramic cat on the hall table that you call the post cat, and didn't really pay attention. The post came again just now, and that's when I found it … when I picked up the cat again.'

'Found what?' Lucy's bottom lip's wobbling and I'm starting to get a very bad feeling.

From her pocket, she pulls a light blue envelope and

hands it to me. It has no stamp and is addressed to 'Merrin, Pearl of the Sea'. There's a little drawing of a mermaid holding up a shell with a pearl in the middle. On the back, in black fountain pen, is written – URGENT. OPEN ME NOW! 😊 I stare at the little smiley face next to the words, and then back at Lucy's unsmiling one.

'You say this came yesterday?'

I get a nod in response. Then she takes a deep breath. 'It's obviously from Ethan and it's urgent. He must have hand-delivered it and the junk mail landed on top of it. So sorry, Mum. I hope it isn't too important.'

So do I.

'Hey, don't worry. I saw the pile of mail under the post cat too, and ignored it. It's not your fault, okay?'

'Yeah, but it's urgent.'

'It can't have been that urgent, or he'd have phoned, or called round again.'

Lucy brightens. 'Yeah, I suppose. And you look awesome in that dress and shoes.' She gets up and walks to the door. 'I'll leave you to read your letter in peace.'

My fingers shake as I open the envelope and read:

Merrin,

I was going to give you this message in a bottle, but thought it was too fake. You've already found the one that was meant for you, even though it arrived 25 years too late! So, I put it through your door instead – least I know it will find you quicker.

Wenna is a wise old gal, you know. I had a good chat to her and she made me see that I couldn't live a happy life without you. I kind of knew it deep down, but like you, I've been hurt before, and have a failed marriage behind me. That kind of thing tends to make a person a little wary. I could say things to you like: you complete me, I'm only half a man without you, you're my soulmate, you give meaning to my life ... stuff like that, but you might think it's too clichéd. It's all been said before in countless movies and books, after all. But you know what? All of it is true.

Of course, the way we met is unorthodox to say the least, and, as I said before, we should go with it, despite only having met three times. People will say we are mad, as we don't really know each other. But we do. I know your soul is at one with mine. Okay, true, I don't know what your favorite color is, or what your politics and musical tastes are, but so what? I adore you, Merrin. I love you like I've never loved anyone before...

A sob breaks free, and I have to stop reading for a moment. He loves me. It's here written down in black fountain pen. Joy bursts in my heart like a thousand fireworks, and I'm laughing and crying at the same time. Taking a huge breath, I dab away tears and carry on.

... and I have to have you in my life. If that means coming to live here, then I will. I'll find some kind of work, maybe not teaching, but hey, never mind. As much as I love my job and my home, I love you more. Lamorna wouldn't have brought us together – yes, I can see you rolling your eyes – if she thought we couldn't make a go of it. 😊

I'm not rolling my eyes. I totally believe in magic now, and if the spirit of Lamorna's helping it along, then yes, I believe in that too.

Okay, this is what I thought we'd do. Meet me tomorrow on our magic beach at dawn … which is 05.45, I checked. Yes, it's early, but think how fitting it would be for us to meet there alone on the beach where Lamorna, Wenna, and now we, have found our true love.

If you honestly don't feel the same, I will try to understand … I'm not a religious guy, but I pray that you'll come. I'll be waiting…

All my love,

Ethan xxx

I look at the bedside clock. 11.05. No! He won't be there now. The poor love will think I've stood him up, that I don't want him. My heart leaps into my mouth and I feel sick, desperate and panicky all at the same time. 'Lucy! Lucy!!'

The thump of her feet running up the stairs competes with that of my thundering heart. 'What's up? Is it bad news?' she gestures to the letter fluttering in my hand like a captive bird.

'Yeah. Until I make it right. Can you drive me to Ethan's hotel? I'm in too much of a mess to trust myself behind the wheel.'

On the way, I tell Lucy what the letter says. 'Why don't you ring him, tell him what happened and that you're on your way?' she says, breaking the speed limit on the A30 heading for Pentire, Newquay.

'Slow down, we don't want to get pulled over.' I blow a

snort of frustration down my nostrils. 'No. I want to see him face to face.'

It's almost midday as we swing into the car park at Lewinnick Lodge, a beautiful hotel standing on a windswept headland against the backdrop of the Atlantic Ocean. I remember coming here years ago, to meet an old schoolfriend for lunch in the restaurant with panoramic views from the deck. If only I was doing that today instead of coming on this heart-stopping mission. It's busy today in the height of the tourist season, and we thread our way through the packed tables on the way to reception. Lucy wanted to stay in the car, but I need her by my side.

'Hi, I wonder if you could ring Ethan Marshall's room for me, please?' I ask the young receptionist.

Her smile falters and a puzzle forms in her cool grey eyes as she looks at her computer screen. 'No Marshall staying here.' Then she peers at the screen again and nods. 'Oh yes, I remember now. Mr Marshall checked out after breakfast.'

She might as well have punched me in the stomach. My breath is snatched away, and I rest a hand on the counter while I try to snatch it back. *No. No, he can't have gone.*

Lucy slips her arm through mine and I lean into her for support. 'Are you sure he's checked out?' she asks, in her best calm and 'in charge' voice. 'Because he and Jodie weren't due to leave until tomorrow.'

'Yes, that's right. They had one more night booked according to this. But they went this morning.'

'Oh no. I don't believe it,' I hear myself say, though

everything is slowing down, becoming surreal, magnified, as if I'm in a dream. Or a nightmare. The scrape of cutlery on plates, laughter of people at the nearby bar, Lucy's questions to the receptionist, all sound too loud, yet far away.

'I'm sorry, no. I can't give away personal information. It's against data protection,' the receptionist informs Lucy.

'I'm only asking if you knew where they went, not what their credit card details are,' Lucy huffs.

The receptionist shrugs and folds her arms. 'Sorry, I can't say more.'

'Look, my mum here needs to see Ethan before he goes back to America tomorrow. It's vital that she tells him how she feels, because he thinks she doesn't want him, but she does. He loves her and she loves him.'

'Lucy, shush,' I say. 'It won't do any good. I need to sit down and do some deep breathing.' I look towards the open door to the seating on the deck and ocean beyond. My head's swimming, and there's not enough air inside. When I'm calm, I'll ring him.

The receptionist's eyes grow round and her eyebrows shoot up to her hairline. 'Hmm. Think you have *that* all wrong.' She glances around and then leans in, a gleeful gleam in her eye. 'His fiancée told me they were off to London to get her a ring. He proposed to her after breakfast this morning, and she was over the moon.' Then she turns, and hurries away.

I stare at Lucy's face, slack with shock, while my stomach turns over and over. I gulp in air. 'His fiancée? His fucking fiancée??'

'Come on, Mum.' She grabs my arm and steers me outside.

We have to perch on a wall, as all the tables are taken. I look down at the ocean forcefully crashing against the rocks, as panic and despair crash into my chest. Lucy takes my hand while I do some deep breathing and murmurs soothing words. Eventually I feel less lightheaded. 'I can't believe it. I really can't believe it. How could he say all those things in the letter, and then the next day ask Jodie to marry him?'

'I don't know, Mum.' Lucy's voice is flat, bewildered.

'I don't know what to do...'

She squeezes my hand and we both stare at the waves, silent, defeated. I bite my bottom lip as the sharp claws of misery hollow out my insides. 'Let's go home.' I stand and walk out.

In the car, Lucy says, 'You have to ring him at least. Find out what the hell is going on ... it's not like Ethan.'

A snort of derision shoots down my nostrils. 'How do any of us know what Ethan is really like? We've known him five seconds. The whole thing is total madness and I should have known better. I'm almost forty, not fourteen.'

'That's the woman who was cheated on, had her heart trampled on, and then dumped by Dad talking.' Lucy turns to me with tears in her eyes. 'Since all this message in a bottle stuff, you've become more like the confident, outgoing Mum I used to know. Don't let this set you back. The receptionist might be wrong. Ring him!'

A spark of hope flickers in my heart, and I don't know whether I'm strong enough to fan the flame. But I realise I

Wish Upon a Cornish Moon

won't rest until I know one way or the other. I close my eyes and exhale. 'Okay. I'll do it when I get home.'

'Mum, you can't just sit there staring at the wall. Look, I'll make some more tea and then try again.'

'No. We've been home four hours. I've called him once and texted three times. Nothing. No reply. That's it now. I have my answer.'

'He could have his phone off if he's driving to London or … or anything.' She throws her hands up in despair.

Bless her. She's been wonderful today and I don't know what I would have done without her. 'Yeah. Or aliens could have come down and abducted him.' I try a smile, but my lips give up halfway through.

'Just saying, there could be a simple explanation.'

'Leave it now, love.' I get up and walk to the door of the living room. 'I'm going for a lie down. My brain is frazzled.' And the rest of me, I think, as I climb the stairs with leaden feet. I want oblivion – a dark, calm place, where I don't have to think about Ethan ever again.

Chapter Twenty-Five

E than parks the hire car in the hotel lot and stretches. 'Wow, driving in central London is not a walk in the park,' he says to Jodie, who's checking her make-up in her compact mirror.

She snaps it shut and jabs a finger at him. 'What a good idea. We could take a walk in Hyde Park. I don't think it's far from here.' She takes her phone from her bag and brings up a map on the screen.

'Yeah.' He yawns and stretches again and an image of Merrin laughing on the beach comes to him, so he bats it away.

'About fifteen minutes' walk away.' Jodie looks at him, excitement shining in her dark eyes. 'Let's get checked in then go and explore. I can't wait until tomorrow. We'll go to Madame Tussauds, the London Eye, Buckingham Palace, St Pauls Cathedral—'

'Er, we'll have about five hours before we have to head to Heathrow. We won't be able to do all that.' He looks for his phone to check the exact flight time. It's not in his jacket or the side of the door. Odd. 'Have you seen my phone anywhere?'

'Must be in your carry-on bag in the trunk.' Jodie hops out of the car. 'Come on, we need to get moving if we're to make the most of the evening.'

Ethan follows her through the hotel with his carry-on over his shoulder, pulling his wheeled suitcase behind. Everything has been such a mad rush today, he's barely had time to draw breath. Jodie's idea about coming to London a day early to see the sights had seemed like a good one this morning. Right then, he'd wanted to put as much distance as possible between himself and Merrin. He'd felt a total clown for putting his heart on paper and dreaming up a dawn tryst like that. Pride had pushed him to the car and into the driver's seat, heading for London. Merrin had no place in his head, because he'd had to concentrate on the route, and there was no time to be lost, so they could make the most of their scant time before leaving for home. But now as they check in, and he follows Jodie into the elevator, a wall of doubt squeezes in behind them and blocks his mind to anything other than Merrin.

Jodie nudges him as they exit and walk down the corridor. 'Penny for your thoughts, hon?'

Ethan sighs, both at the use of "hon" and at the fact that he can't tell her he's wishing he was back in Cornwall with Merrin. 'Just tired after a tricky drive. I'll be okay after I've had a shower.'

'No. We're going to Hyde Park, remember? You can have a shower after that, before dinner.'

Had Jodie always been this bossy? Probably. A walk, and then dinner with her, is the last thing on his mind. 'Uh-huh.'

'Okay, this is my room and yours is opposite.' Jodie moves closer to him in the corridor, strokes a long fingernail along his jawline and says in a husky voice, 'You know, we could share a room later, if you like.'

Now what? How does he let her down gently without upsetting her? Ethan looks at his room key and swallows hard. 'We said we'd take it slow.'

A blush flares in her cheeks and he sees a flash of irritation pass through her eyes. Then she smiles a bit too brightly. 'So we did. Let's wait until we're home, we'll both be more relaxed. See you in a few minutes. Just going to freshen up.'

Ethan watches her go into her room, then he turns and goes into his own. This is unbearable. His ex-wife used to tell him he was too nice – a pushover. Maybe she was right, but he hates hurting people. Hurling his bag on the bed, he flops down beside it and exhales. Damn it. He's going to phone Merrin. Get it from her own lips why she didn't come this morning, instead of relying on the various scenarios his pride-addled stupid brain has cooked up. He unzips his bag and searches through for his phone. Where the hell is it? In the end, he takes everything out and goes through it meticulously. It's not there. He wouldn't have put it in his suitcase, would he? Mind you, he'd been beside himself when he'd packed it, so he might have.

Ten minutes later, he's sitting next to a pile of clothes and shoes on his bed, but still no phone. Panic grips his gut and twists it. Shit. Has he left it in Cornwall? His fucking life is on his cell. Merrin's number is on his cell... Putting his head in his hands, he curses his luck and then comes a knock on the door. 'Jodie, is there any way you could have picked up my phone somehow? I've been through everything and it's not there.'

Jodie frowns as she leans against the door jamb. 'I know what men are like when they say they've been through everything.' She laughs and pushes past him into his room. 'Right, let me look in this mess on the bed.' As he watches her searching, his irritation climbs up the temperature scale.

'It's not there. I checked.' He snatches her key card from the table where she placed it and marches to her room.

'Hey, where are you going?' she calls and hurries after him as he opens the door. 'I haven't got it. You must have left it in Cornwall.'

'But let's just check in your things, yeah? Before I call the hotel in Cornwall and get them searching too. I was a bit distracted this morning, rushing around packing. I might have shoved it in your bag when I put it in the trunk instead of mine. It's easily done.' Ethan picks up her carry on and unzips it.

'Hey, there's personal things in there.' Jodie strides forward red-faced and grabs the bag.

Something about the way she can't meet his eyes, and the protective way she pulls the bag to her chest, sounds an alarm bell in his head. 'Please check for me, then. Try the side zip.'

She slips her hand in and out of the pocket. 'Nothing.' Then she unzips the main part and does a perfunctory rummage. 'Nothing.' Tossing the bag down next to her suitcase and purse, she tries a bright smile, which looks false, and fails to cover the guilt written all over her face, or the awkward silence between them.

'Try your purse and suitcase.'

A squeaky giggle. 'Don't be silly. How the hell could you have put it in my suitcase or purse without realising? It's obviously at the hotel in Cornwall, Ethan. I'll ring them for you. Just sit down and be calm.'

He sits, but is anything but calm. Jodie's hiding something, and he's afraid he knows what it is. But why? Ethan watches as she pulls her cell from her purse and scrolls through her contacts. Then his eyes flit to the carry-on, which has fallen open, as it lay on its side by the suitcase … and he thinks he can make out a sliver of red under a pack of Kleenex. Ethan's temper is in danger of exploding as he jumps up and strides over to the bag. He moves the Kleenex, and the 'something red' is revealed. It's his red cell-phone cover. Snatching it up, he whirls round, thrusting the cell towards her. 'What's this then, huh? Funny that you missed it!'

Jodie's pink face drains to ashen, and she puts her own phone down beside her on the bed. 'Yeah, sorry. You must have put it in by mistake, like you said.' She can't look him in the face.

'You're lying. You took it and put it in your bag. Why?' Ethan's not yelling now, but his quiet tone is ice cold.

'I…' Jodie stops and shakes her head, looks at the grey speckled carpet between her feet.

Ethan looks at his phone and sees that it's switched off.

He never switches it off. Once he's reactivated it, he checks the missed calls and messages, in the vain hope there's something from Merrin. His eyes can hardly believe what they're seeing. Messages and a voicemail from Merrin. His heart raises a fist and punches the air. Merrin's contacted him. Then his gut clenches. Odd … they seem to have already been read… The first one was early afternoon. *I didn't get your beautiful letter until it was too late! I feel the same. Please call me!* Then the second an hour later. *Can we talk? I'm so sorry, Ethan, I really want you in my life. Please get in touch!* Next. *Is it true that you and Jodie are engaged?* What the hell? He stops reading and stares in disbelief at Jodie, then back at the message. Then he listens to the voicemail. *Call me, Ethan. I need to know the truth. I'm going out of my mind here … I love you.*

Jodie looks at him through her tears, until they spill over and trickle down her cheeks. 'I'm sorry. I picked up your phone when you went to the restroom at the motorway on the way here. I read the messages from … her … and couldn't let you see them. I was going to delete them all, but it was too late as you came back. So…' Her breath hitched on a sob but, Ethan has no sympathy. 'So I switched the phone off and quickly hid it in my bag.'

Processing her words is like wading through a swamp. A swamp that is littered with alligators, ready to wound, rip him apart. 'Let me get this straight. You read my messages, decided you didn't like what you saw, then stole my phone… How the hell did you know my pin?'

A shrug. 'I watched you type it in often enough. It's your birthdate.'

The devious little... 'And what's this about us being engaged?'

Jodie blows her nose and sighs. 'I'm not sure how she knew about that. I guess she must have gone to our hotel looking for you. I might have made up a story and bragged to the receptionist that we'd just got engaged and were going to London to buy the ring. Merrin must have found out from her.'

He's incredulous. Jodie's sitting on the bed in jeans and a floral top, cross-legged. Her long shiny hair swept from the familiar pretty face, which at the moment is pensive and tear-stained. Yes, it's definitely the Jodie he knows. Looks like her, has the same mannerisms, the same perfume. But that woman, the good friend whom he's known since he was a kid, whom he's loved and trusted with his hopes and fears, has apparently morphed into some evil monster. How could she do this to him? How? 'How could you be so cruel?'

Jodie looks down at the carpet again. 'I love you. Simple as that ... the old saying, all's fair in love and—'

'Don't!' He holds up a hand. 'If you love me, how could you hurt me like this?' Bewildered, Ethan leans his back against the wall and slides down it. He hugs his knees, glares at Jodie.

She waits a few moments and then the tears come again as she replies. 'I read your letter. If you remember, we were going out to dinner at the seafood place, but you weren't ready when I came round to your room? I waited for you while you were in the bathroom... You'd put the letter in the desk drawer, but not closed it properly. I went to look out the window at the view, and there it was. However I got through that dinner without breaking down, I don't know. All the time I hoped I could somehow make you love me, instead.' A watery smile. 'I was ecstatic this morning when you came back from your dawn walk and she'd not come to meet you. I couldn't believe my luck... Then to make absolutely sure, I suggested we left early. I'm sorry I hurt you, Ethan. But I had to fight dirty.' She's crying now, sobbing, snot and tears dripping from her chin, wailing like a banshee.

Ethan has nothing for her, not even rage. He's numb, as if all his nerves and senses have been stripped bare. 'And to think I didn't tell you the truth about Merrin to save your feelings. You mean so much to me, Jodie.' He shakes his head. 'Or you did.'

'Noooo! Please don't say that. We can make it right again, Ethan, I—'

Her words run out as he hauls his ass up and walks to the door. 'Goodbye, Jodie. I'll try and get a different flight tomorrow. There's no way we're travelling home together.'

'Ethan!' she cries, grabbing his arm, but he shakes her hand off and slams the door behind him as he leaves.

Chapter Twenty-Six

Incredibly, I must have fallen asleep, despite everything. I stare at the bedside clock, which tells me I have been out for almost an hour and a half. Emotionally exhausted, I suppose. The day so far plays back in my head, me in my daisy dress, the mermaid drawing on the letter, the receptionist telling me Ethan had left and he was engaged to Jodie – colourful snapshots of disaster. And now the bone-crushing sadness that took the ride home with me is back, and seems in no hurry to leave. Come on, Merrin, get your arse out of bed. I run my fingers through my hair, use the loo, and trudge downstairs to see what Lucy's up to. I find her in the garden drinking coffee with my parents and Wenna. What the heck are they all doing here?

'Here's my sleeping beauty,' Dad says, with a big smile.

'Hardly a beauty, unless fairy-tale princesses have bed hair and smudged mascara.'

Mum stands and envelops me in the warmth of a Mum

hug. I only just hold it together. 'How are you, sweetheart? Lucy's told us everything.'

'That's why we came over,' Wenna offers. 'Your mum and dad came and collected me.'

'I thought you'd like a bit of support,' Lucy says, handing me a coffee.

Smiling, I sit down at the table with them. 'You're all lovely, thank you.'

'What will you do, Merrin?' Wenna asks, her head cocked to the side, birdlike.

'I can't see what else I *can* do. I've messaged and phoned, but he's ignored me. And it appears –' I can hardly say the words '– he's engaged to Jodie.'

Wenna harumphs and folds her arms. 'I can't see that being true. The receptionist girl will have got it muddled.'

'So why hasn't he answered? Why ignore my attempts to contact him?'

'There could be lots of reasons,' Dad says. 'His phone might have run out of juice because he left his charger in Cornwall by mistake and can't find another, or he might have lost it.'

'Hmm, maybe. But unlikely.'

'Why so negative, Mum?' Lucy asks, putting her hand on my arm.

'Just realistic, Lulu. It's fate, I suppose, what with me not reading the letter in time and then missing him at the hotel. We weren't meant to be together.'

'Poppycock!' Wenna exclaims. 'If you have an ounce of Lamorna's spirit –' she narrows her eyes to blue chips '– and I think you do, you'd fight for him. Fight for the truth.'

Where do I find the words to answer that one? I'm gathering a few, when my phone startles us all as it rings out into the awkward silence. I pull it from my pocket and my heart leaps into my throat. 'It's him. It's Ethan!' I stare at the screen, open-mouthed.

'Well answer it, then!' Mum and Lucy yell at the same time.

'Ethan?'

'Merrin, thank God! It's so good to hear your voice.'

My heart's galloping in my chest and I can hardly breathe. Everyone leaves the table, and Mum gives me the thumbs-up before following the others inside. 'It's good to hear yours too. You got my messages?'

'Eventually. What a goddamned fiasco it's been. You not getting the letter, me being betrayed by Jodie... I can hardly believe it still.'

'Betrayed?'

'Yes. She took my phone and hid it in her bag, after reading your messages. Jodie also read my letter to you, and convinced me to leave Cornwall early, once you didn't turn up. I went along with her, because I thought you'd read the letter and decided to reject me without a word. What a mess.'

My God, this is a huge curve ball. It wasn't a forgotten charger or a lost phone after all, but a deliberate act of sabotage. My heart's still galloping, but it's also swelling with joy, and a rainforest of butterflies show up in my belly. Then the receptionist's bombshell pops into my head. 'So you're not engaged to Jodie?'

A hollow laugh. 'No way. That was some weird fantasy

of hers, which she inexplicably had to share with the receptionist. How could she do all this to me, Merrin? We've been friends for a very long time. Hell, she was my girlfriend for a while when we were teenagers.'

The answer is obvious to me. 'Okay, I know what she did was extreme, but it's probably because she loves you? Because she'd do anything to keep you?'

There's a pause and a sigh. 'That's what she said too, more or less. But if you love someone, don't you want them to be happy? I wish I'd told her the way I felt about you from the start. But because she was one of my oldest friends, and we were more than that once, I couldn't let her down. More fool me. So I am partly to blame. I should have been Mr Nasty instead of Mr Nice, as my ex used to say.'

'I like Mr Nice ... but yes, you should have told her. Did you let her think there could be something between you?'

Another pause. Longer this time. 'I kind of hinted that there could. I said we could take things slow.' I let out a sigh of frustration but he hurries on. 'Yeah, but I only said this to keep her happy until we got home. I was worried it might lead to her going back on meds or worse.'

Poor Jodie. I can't believe I'm feeling sympathetic towards a woman who almost ruined any chance of us getting together, but I reply, 'I'm not condoning what she did, Ethan. But you have been a little unfair to her. She would have been very hurt when she read your letter to me ... and believed you were leading her on. Jodie must be desperately in love to try to hang on to you after all that.'

Ethan groans. 'I've been an idiot, haven't I? I'm totally hopeless with relationships ... my ex-wife was right.'

My heart goes out to him. 'That's rubbish. I think you're pretty special.'

'You do?'

'Yes. And I think I know a way we can make this work.' I tell him about my parents giving me some money and the possibility of us living in two places, if things work out between us.

'That's perfect! Jeez, I'm desperate to see you, but once again fate keeps us apart.' *Wenna would have a choice word or two to say about that.* 'I can't extend my stay here because school starts soon, and I have to sort everything out. Also, Granddad Bill is coming to stay in two weeks' time. I could put him off, but school won't wait.'

My heart sinks a little, but I can't expect that he would be able to just cancel his flight and put his life on hold, as much as I'd like him to. I'm just glad we're back on track after such an horrendous roller-coaster ride. 'I get it. And I never knew your granddad was still alive.'

'Yeah, he was Harry's youngest brother. Must be about eighty-three or four. My grandma died a few years ago, as did my other set of grandparents.'

'Maybe I'll meet him one day. And until I see you again, we can FaceTime and call and text. It will work out, I promise.' And I know without doubt it will. I can feel that the strength of conviction in my voice was born of the kind of certainty that I felt when I first met him on the beach. Something deep inside my gut told me Ethan was a good man, with a good soul, someone I could trust, and it's telling me now that we could have a real future together. I'd better not tell Wenna, or she'll say it's Lamorna's doing from beyond the grave.

'You seem pretty sure about that.'

'I am.'

'So am I. I have this overwhelming calm feeling inside, you know? Like I'm certain everything will be okay now.'

Wow. He's just put my exact feelings into words … maybe Lamorna's spirit is lending a hand after all. 'Same here.' Then the frustration of having him so close yet so far pushes tears into my eyes. 'I really wish I could see you before you leave. Wish I could hold you –' my voice hitches '– and kiss you goodbye.'

Ethan sighs, and when he speaks, his voice is thick with emotion. 'Me too. I love you so much, Merrin.'

'I love you so much too, Ethan.'

There's a long pause, broken only by our sniffing and sighing. 'Okay, I'll be in touch as soon as I get home, and we can FaceTime, arrange to meet up. And email me your damned novel, yeah?'

I laugh. 'Yeah okay,' I manage, as I cover my mouth to stop a sob breaking free. 'Can't wait to see you again.' My throat closes over and I have to get off the line before I lose it big time. 'Bye, Ethan. Love and miss you.'

'Ditto. Bye, my pearl of the sea.'

I'm a blubbering heap a few moments later when my family come out to see me. Mum brings a box of tissues and a glass of chilled wine, and they all make soothing comments as I tell them what's happened, between bouts of wailing and weeping.

Mum takes my hand across the table. 'I can see why you're emotional, love. But overall, it's all good, isn't it?'

'Yeah, you and he are going to make it work, Mum,' Lucy says brightly.

'He's a good man, that Ethan. Knew it right off,' Dad says, and raises his coffee cup.

'Your dad's a wise man,' Wenna says. 'So, stop all this sniffling and put a smile on that lovely face.'

'But he's going home tomorrow, and I don't know when I'll see him again. It could be months until he can come back over, what with his job and his granddad.'

'Bill's still alive?' Wenna asks.

'Yeah. Did you know him?'

'No. I only remember him from family photos Lamorna sent. Nice-looking man.' Wenna looks into the distance, a little smile on her face.

Mum nudges her. 'Wonder if he wants a pen pal, Wen?' she says with an impish smile.

'Eh? No.' Wen's cheeks pinken. 'Too long in the tooth for all that malarkey.'

'What malarkey?' Dad asks, frowning. 'It's only letter writing. And this Bill will have memories of the old days with your sister that you can share.'

With a thoughtful expression on her face she replies, 'Hmm. That might be nice…'

'Let's sort Mum out first,' Lucy says, with a little shake of her head. 'I reckon it's obvious what should happen.'

'It is?' I ask.

Lucy nods. 'Yeah. You sort a few things out here, pack a bag and go off to America for two weeks.'

My jaw drops. 'Eh? I can't do that… You're going to uni. I want to go with you, make sure you settle in.'

'No need, Mum. I'm a big girl now. But if you must, just be back for the third of September.'

'She is a big girl.' Mum says. 'But if it makes you feel better, we'll be keeping an eye on her.' At this, Lucy rolls her own eyes heavenward. 'But there's no excuse for you to delay a moment longer. The money went into your bank this morning. Why not go and surprise him?'

Wenna claps her hands in excitement. 'Ooh yes, how romantic.'

It's me who's surprised. 'So soon?' They all nod. I let that sink in and a shiver of excitement turns my stomach over. 'Well, how can I surprise him when I don't even have his address?'

'I know a woman who does. And she could be persuaded to give it to you,' Wenna says, with a chortle.

I shake my head at her in bewilderment. 'You have it?'

'I do indeed. Well, the beach house one at least.'

'So your job at the café,' Lucy says in her business-like manner. 'I can cover your shifts until Gillian finds a replacement. I can start the day after tomorrow. Just as soon as you stop looking like a goldfish gasping for air, get your shit together and book a flight, really.'

Everyone laughs, apart from me. Once again, tears are threatening. Happy tears because my family are just so lovely. Wenna too. And the idea of being with Ethan in the next few days is exhilarating, if a little daunting. 'I … I suppose I could. But wouldn't it be presumptuous to just rock up and assume Ethan will want me to stay at his?'

'Oh, for goodness' sake,' Mum mutters. 'The man is in love with you. Is he really going to expect you to stay anywhere else?'

'Um ... I suppose not. It just feels like a big step to take – flying off without telling him I'm coming, and then doing jazz hands when he opens the door, yelling "Surprise!" He has school work to prepare...'

'Right, that's it and that's all,' Mum says, jumping up and slipping her hand under my elbow. 'Come on. We're going to Google what flights are available. Bristol should be your best bet.'

I allow myself to be steered inside, while Lucy gets her laptop, Wenna puts the kettle on and everyone discusses the flights and where they think the nearest big airport is to Gloucester, Massachusetts. Apparently, it's Logan International in Boston. Lucy soon finds that I will have to change in Dublin, so a ten-hour flight total and then a fifty-minute taxi ride to Harbor Beach. Or I could hire a car. There's no way I'm driving in a strange city, especially after a long-haul, so I shake my head. Dad says he's going to drive me to Bristol, and then they start looking for taxis from the airport in Boston. I'm happy to sink into their comfort cushion of support, listen to the buzz of conversation and let the activity go on around me.

Flopping down on the sofa, I close my eyes and clear my mind of everything but being in Ethan's arms. I remember the kiss we shared, the way it made me feel, and I ache to feel his lips on mine once more. And thanks to these wonderful people gathered here in this room, it won't be very long before I will. The old me is waiting close by, and I can feel her strength and spirit edging back into the heart of me. I can do this. I will do this. I open my eyes and see Wenna watching me with a sweet smile on her face. I smile back, and wonder if Lamorna's smiling somewhere too.

Chapter Twenty-Seven

y stomach is making peculiar growling noises as I sit in the back of a cab whizzing down the Yankee Division Highway. Maybe it's because of the ridiculous amount of traffic and the motion of the stupidly bouncy suspension. Maybe it's because of the food on the plane and the far too many glasses of wine. Maybe it's because of the jet lag. Or maybe it's the nervous energy that's being doing award-winning gymnastics inside me since I left Cornwall. I have a sneaking suspicion that it's a combination of all those things. The nervous energy does a forward roll and a back flip. What will happen if Ethan's not home? Will I just have to wander up and down the beach with a suitcase balanced on my head until he is? What will happen if, as Faye said yesterday, he's already gone to his rented house inland to prepare for his classes? She's not normally the negative one, but she had a point. I suppose I'll have to find a motel or something...

As the taxi speeds on, I respond to the driver's chatty conversation with one- or two-word answers, so he eventually gives up. I'm sorry about that, but my stomach won't let me be my normal gregarious self until I see Ethan's face at his front door. If I think about how fast it's all happened it makes my head spin. Gillian was lovely about it all and said that it would be great to have Lucy in the café. At such short notice, I thought she might have been a bit huffy, but no. No problem. Sandra said she'd be happy to do more of a hands-on job with the community larder too. She'd even managed to find donations of pet-food, as she remembered I'd mentioned an old gentleman I'd met in the line a few weeks ago, who could barely afford to feed his two cats now that it was becoming harder to make ends meet. Last winter he often had to choose between heating and eating, and now the electric bills were climbing ever higher. If the food donations could take care of two more little mouths to feed, it would take a huge weight off his shoulders.

And to top it all, my clever, clever girl had exceeded expectations in all her exams. The results came out yesterday, and she was beyond thrilled! So was I. My little Lulu had achieved two A* and an A. I'd told her she was clever enough to go to Oxford, never mind Bristol, and we'd had an impromptu celebration last night, which might have involved a bit too much champagne, and was certainly not a good idea for my poor head. It was worth it though. I close my eyes and wonder what she's doing now. Then I push all thoughts of home out of my head, as I don't want to arrive tearstained and puffy.

The taxi soon leaves the busy road behind and takes a more sedate pace through the streets of Gloucester, lined with historic buildings and affluent residential homes, and I buzz my window down to take some air. Next is a more familiar shopping outlet and the delicious smell of the Dunkin' Donuts cooking makes my stomach grumble even more, and then we're on a beach road right next to the ocean. A huge smile stretches my lips as I look at the beautiful beach-houses pinned above the rocky shoreline, the bobbing boats on the horizon, and the sunlight dappling the sapphire blue ocean. Everything is unfamiliar to me, except for the ocean. Because it's *my* ocean ... I'm just looking at it from the other side.

The taxi pulls to a halt on the aptly named Salty Lane, outside a large, wood-built white and grey beach house, which is staring straight out over the sand and ocean. Wow. I never expected anything so grand. I pay the driver and he gets my bags out of the boot. Thanking him, I mumble an apology for not being very responsive, but he just shrugs and drives off, leaving me standing in the lane, feeling suddenly very small and out of place. A glance at my watch tells me it's almost 10pm at home, but only 5pm here. I sigh. Let Ethan be home, please. Grabbing a handful of confidence with my suitcase and my bags, I trundle up the driveway, climb the wooden white steps to the front door, and knock.

Ethan's putting some finishing touches to a lesson plan and wondering whether to have a sandwich, when he hears a knock on the front door. His heart sinks. It's been a long day of prep and he's tired. He just wants to eat something, have a walk on the beach and a few bottles of Bud. Please don't let it be Jodie, coming to try and talk him round again. His mind gives him an unwelcome re-run of the journey home on the plane. Taking on board what Merrin had said to him about being unfair to Jodie, he'd called her and apologised. She was still very upset, of course, and agreed that he had been a 'prize dick' but said she forgave him and there was no reason why they couldn't travel home together like civilised human beings. Two people who had been friends since forever. So he'd agreed.

Trouble was, the whole way home, she'd tried to convince him that he and Merrin were doomed from the start. They were apparently an ocean apart figuratively and literally, unlike Jodie and him. They had grown up together, shared the same culture, knew what made each other tick, and what did he actually know about this stand-offish Englishwoman anyway? In the end, he'd had to be quite blunt for a change. Told her he was in love with Merrin and there was no way that would change.

Ethan thinks about the way her eyes had filled with tears, the way her bottom lip had trembled and her hopeful expression crumpled, as he walks along the corridor to the front door. Please don't let him see Jodie's face on the other side of it. Sucking in a deep breath he opens the door. He cannot believe his eyes. Can. Not.

'So, have you read the first few chapters of my novel, then? Thought I'd pop over to check,' Merrin says, with a huge grin.

He stares at her in disbelief, unable to move, act, speak. There she is, a vision in red shorts, blue vest top, her golden curls swept into a messy top knot, bright beautiful eyes twinkling at him like two bits of jade sea glass. Is she actually a vision? Ethan's imagined her often so perhaps he's conjured her out of thin air. Is he losing his mind? Then he sees her suitcase and bags, and suddenly his faculties return and he sweeps her off her feet, looks into her eyes and kisses her. 'Merrin...' he says, bewildered, as he sets her back down and holds her tight. 'Merrin ... what? How...?'

'I decided if you couldn't come to me, I'd come to you. I'm here for two weeks, if you'll have me?' Mischief dances around the edges of her smile.

'If I'll have you, she says? Are you crazy!' Ethan picks her up again and spins her around in the hallway.

'Hey, put me down,' she says, laughing. 'I'm exhausted and travel weary, don't give me a dizzy spell too!'

Ethan puts her down and grabs her luggage. Then looks down at her and shakes his head again, hoping she won't disappear in a puff of smoke when he looks away. 'Follow me, I'll get us a couple of cold ones, then we can sit on the deck and you can tell me all about it.' As they walk through the open-plan living area and kitchen, he keeps turning to make sure she's still there and mutters, 'I don't believe it. I really don't believe it.'

Merrin giggles. 'I was going to yell "Surprise!" at you

and do jazz hands, but thought I might have given you a stroke.'

'It's certainly a surprise!' he says over his shoulder as he walks onto the deck and waves at a chair. 'Okay, sit there and don't disappear while I get us a drink.'

Merrin furrows her brow. 'I'm not going anywhere, my 'andsome.' Then her mouth drops open. 'My God, look at the view!'

Ethan leaves her leaning on the handrail, marvelling at the vista, while he hurries off to get them a beer and some snacks. When he comes back, he sets the tray on the table between them and just stares at her, drinking in every little detail. 'So what the hell made you decide to just up and fly over here?'

'My family and Wenna ganged up on me and convinced me to. And I'm so glad they did.'

For the next while, she tells him about how her daughter had agreed to cover the job in the café and the fact that Lucy and her parents orchestrated the whole trip between them and put her on the plane.

'That's fantastic. I can't tell you how thrilled I am to see you.'

'Ditto.' Merrin puts the bottle to her lips and takes a swig of beer. Then she flings an arm out over the ocean. 'And this place. Wow! I never realised it would be so grand.'

This makes him smile. 'It's awesome. Back in the day when my grandparents built it, it was worth a fraction of the eye-watering deal my parents could have got for it now.

I'm so lucky they let me take it on. The whole place needs some TLC…' Ethan pokes the peeling paint on the handrail with his toe. 'As you can see. But I'll do it little by little.'

'Yeah.' Merrin stretches out a hand and he takes it. 'I can see how much you love this place, and I bet your parents are glad it's being kept in the family.'

A warmth fills his chest. Merrin immediately understands, she can read him – feel him. 'I'll give you the tour in a while. There are four bedrooms, I have the master overlooking the beach, but the others are yours to pick from … unless…' He stops as a worm of awkwardness wriggles through his thoughts. Clearing his throat he says, 'I don't know if you think it's too soon for us…'

Merrin leans across and answers him with a kiss. Then she holds his gaze. 'I think twenty-five-years is long enough, don't you?' she says, with a giggle.

This woman. 'Hell yeah.' He laughs and they clink their beer bottles together. A stomach growl reminds him he never did get that sandwich and he has an idea. 'What do you say to building a fire, having a BBQ on the beach and possibly some s'mores?'

Merrin smiles. 'Yes, please. I'm starving, even though it's normally my bedtime at home!'

'Oh yes, I'd forgotten about the time difference. You sure you're good with that? I can make you a sandwich and we can have an early night?' He gives her a cheeky wink.

'It's fine. In fact, more than fine. I've never had s'mores, though I've seen people have them often enough on my Netflix shows.' She stands up. 'Can't wait. Come on!'

This evening is perfect. Everything is perfect. The food, the fire, the gentle breeze, the conversation, the shush of the waves, the silver moon floating like an ethereal balloon in a star-spangled sky, and Merrin. This woman is perfect, and Ethan can't believe how lucky he is to have her by his side. He watches her while she's toasting s'mores and chatting to him, but he's only half-listening, because he's taking in every inch of her beauty. The way her mouth curves at the edges, as if she's always on the cusp of a smile, the tumble of golden curls escaping from her top-knot, the shade of her eyes, emerald now in the firelight, but ever changing like the swirling greens in the depths of the ocean. Perfect. He gives a contented sigh. He's mooning over her like a love-sick teenager, and he doesn't care. In fact, it's wonderful.

'Earth calling Ethan?' Merrin points her toasting fork at him and he grabs the marshmallow from it before she has time to react. 'Hey, that was mine!' She pouts and pretends to look annoyed. Not for the first time tonight, he gets a stirring in his groin and wants to kiss her and take her right to bed. She gives him a slow smile as if she can read his thoughts. Forget the bed. Ethan wants her right now, on this blanket on the sand. He smiles to himself. Not sure the neighbours would approve.

Ethan moves closer and gives her a long, passionate kiss. When he looks into her eyes, he sees they've become a dark smouldering olive green. 'It's way past your bedtime, Merrin,' Ethan whispers in her ear as he runs his fingers along the inside of her bare thigh and under the edge of her shorts.

'It is. But you know what? I'm not a bit sleepy,' she whispers back, and pulls him to his feet. 'Race you!' She takes off like a hare up the beach towards the house.

He doesn't need telling twice. Ethan grabs the blanket and gives chase.

Chapter Twenty-Eight

I wake to the sound of the ocean and the deep breathing of the man I'm in love with. What an amazing night. I stretch languidly as I relive vivid and delicious memories of our lovemaking, Ethan's smell is on my skin, his taste on my lips, his touch imprinted on my most intimate parts. I watch him sleeping. His mouth forms a loose pout as if in the middle of a kiss, one arm thrown behind his head, the mermaid wiggling as his bicep flexes. His hair flops over one eye and he stirs slightly, sighs, then carries on sleeping. Perfect. I could watch him for ever. But it's time to rise and shine. I've slept until 2pm. My sleep patterns will be all over the place for a while. I'll get used to it.

Slipping out of bed, I tiptoe across the cool floor tiles and peep through the yellow painted wooden shutters of the huge window. The beach is already peopled with a few walkers and some are swimming in the twinkling blue ocean. A sense of wonder envelops me and I think of Ethan telling me last night that he remembered Lamorna mentioning she believed our little beach back home and this place were connected. Even though they are very different, the ocean is the same, and I'm sure on moonlit June nights magic still happens as it did for Ethan all those years ago. As the ocean drives a few white horses to shore, I wonder what my family are up to on the other side of it. I sent a brief message to my parents, Lucy, Wenna and Faye to say I'm here, and all is well, but I'll ring soon. They are all so very far away … but I'm going to have to get used to that if things work out. If? No. When. There is no 'if' any more.

I'm cut short in my ponderings by the feel of Ethan's hard, naked body behind me, and his hands cupping my breasts. I turn to kiss him, and all thoughts of Cornwall disappear.

The days fly by so quickly, I can hardly believe it when I realise I only have two left before I go home. Being here in this place with Ethan has been amazing. We've done some fantastic things together, two standing out as my favourites. We visited the fascinating Witch Museum at Salem down the coast, which was all about the seventeenth-century witch hunt that took place there, and my very favourite – we went whale watching! I sit on the deck and look out over the ocean, picturing again the three huge humpback whales we'd seen breaching and landing with a colossal splash, drenching Ethan and me. It was exhilarating to see the power of the creatures, cutting through the choppy waves as if they were ripples in a paddling pool, chasing after small fish and gulping down plankton. Then on the return trip, we saw a pod of bottlenose dolphins and a right whale. On the evening of the same day, I had my first taste of lobster in a sea-food restaurant in the harbour, and Ethan splashed out on champagne to go with it. What memories. They will live with me for ever.

My phone rings out in the living room, and I hurry in to get it. Might be Ethan asking if I want anything picking up from the store on his way back from his school meeting. Picking up from the store? I have to smile; I'm sounding like I live here already.

'Faye! It's lovely to hear your voice.'

'Yours too. It seems like months since you've been gone.' I don't tell her it seems like minutes to me. 'How's Ethan? You all loved up?'

'We are! Ethan's had to go into school a few times for meetings and planning, but it's only a few hours away, so I've busied myself with… You'll never guess.'

'Making yourself beautiful and thinking of different ways to seduce him when he gets home?'

'No. Well, yes … but…'

'So what's it like, then? Did the earth move for you?' Faye's dirty laugh makes me giggle. I will miss her when I'm living here for a few months at a time.

'It's incredible. It's like we're meant for each other in every way, you know?'

'Wow, yeah. Me and Pete are at it like rabbits every chance we get.'

I laugh. 'I don't mean just in bed, but in general.'

'Yeah. I get you. I think I've fallen for Pete already ... and I know what you're thinking.'

'What am I thinking?'

'That I always fall for every man I meet, until he treats me like rubbish.'

'I wasn't, actually.' Which is true. 'I remember thinking you had a real good vibe going on last time I saw you together.'

Her squeal nearly splits my eardrum. 'For real! I'm glad you saw it too. Pete might be the one. The real one, this time!' I do hope so. 'Anyway, what have you been busying yourself with?'

'Writing!' I put my feet up on Ethan's big red sofa and grin at the ceiling. 'Ethan read the first few chapters and said, and I quote, "Your writing has depth – a real heart and soul, you know, babe." So that gave me both the confidence I needed and the kick up the arse to get on with it again. I'm using Ethan's laptop to write, sitting on the deck looking out over the ocean.'

'Wow! Get you! How your life has changed in a few short weeks.'

'I know. It's nuts. This house is awesome – I'll send some photos later.'

'Good. So, what's the book about?'

'A woman who doesn't know who she is ... pleases everyone else, and goes through the motions of life, until she finds her true passion. Not sure what it will be yet, as I'm only a few chapters in.'

'Sounds autobiographical to me.'

This pulls me up short. 'Bloody hell, is it?'

'Yeah. That's you, or it *was* you. Now you've found your passion – which is writing, and Ethan too. Why not add in the message in a bottle story, too?'

'Oh, I don't know…' But I think I do. That story is Lamorna's, Wenna's and mine. It's to be passed down by word of mouth, by the women of Porthtowan and Chapel Porth, just like it always has been. Otherwise, it might lose some of its magic. Hmm, but then again…

'Okay, I'll be off then. See you soon and send me those photos! Love ya!'

'Will do. You too!'

The house is silent, save the creaking of the wooden deck as a playful wind finds it. Lucy would love it here, and Mum and Dad. I can't wait for them to visit. I should hold my horses though, Ethan and I haven't finalised our future plans yet, and I've been thinking carefully about all that over the past few days. *You will sort it all soon.* I smile at the little voice of encouragement whispering in my mind, and go off to make coffee.

'Hi, honey, I'm home!' Ethan calls a few hours later.

'On the deck!'

'Been writing?' He drops a kiss on my shoulder, hands me a coffee and flops down in a chair.

'Yeah, a bit. Been gazing at the view too … I love it here.' I sigh and stretch out my hand to hold his.

'Good, because you'll be living here soon for a few months, won't you?'

I gulp. 'I hope so.'

'No hope so about it. There's no way you're getting away from me now, Merrin.'

'There's no way I want to.' I swallow some nerves down with my coffee as I know it's time to share my thoughts with him now. 'Thing is, we have to play it by ear for a while, Ethan. It's early days, and so we should stick to a few months here and there, while Lucy's more settled. And thinking about it, it's easier for me to be flexible than you. I know we argued when we first discussed it, and I said my café job was important too – which it is. But we have to be practical, so I'll keep popping over here while you hold onto your teaching job.'

'Hmm.' Ethan twists his mouth to the side. 'But that would mean we'd be apart for two or three months at a time, wouldn't it?'

'Yes, but as I said it wouldn't be for ever, and we can Zoom all the time – the weeks will fly by. Our love is strong enough to stand the test, I'm absolutely sure of it.'

He gives me an intense stare while he considers this. Eventually he says, 'Good to hear. I guess it makes sense, but I will miss you like hell.'

I squeeze his hand. 'Ditto. But just think how exciting it will be when we meet up again.'

I get a cheeky wink. 'Oh don't worry, I'm thinking about that already.' We laugh and gaze out at the ocean lost in our own thoughts. Then Ethan turns to me. 'I almost forgot, is it okay if Granddad Bill comes over to meet you before you go? I've told him all about you.'

'Of course, it will be my pleasure.'

'He's bringing a photo album of Lamorna and Harry to show you. Hope he doesn't bore you to death.'

'No way! How could I be bored? I'd love to see Lamorna. Wenna was going to show me some photos of her, but we never got round to it with everything going on.'

Ethan raises his eyebrows. 'You've not seen a photo of her yet?' I shake my head. 'I'll get one, and a coffee, yeah?'

'Yes please!'

Over coffee we talk about Lamorna, while I gaze at a large framed photo of her and Harry on their wedding day. Originally black and white, in later years Lamorna had it colourised, which brought them both to life. Lamorna was certainly a looker, very much like a 1940s film star that I'd seen once but never knew the name of. Her dark hair is rolled back at the fringe and covered by a lacy veil, while the cream and white wedding dress looks more 1920s than 1940s. I remark on this to Ethan, and he says that's because it had been Lamorna's mum's. She's got dark pencilled eyebrows over pretty hazel eyes and she's staring up at a tall, blue-eyed, fair-haired Harry wearing a half smile and a GI uniform. My heart squeezes as I catch a glimpse of Wenna in the tilt of her chin, and the curve of her smile. It's such a shame that they never met again. I wish I could have met her too.

Bill comes round the morning of the day I leave for home. My flight's in the evening, so we spend a good few hours with him. He's a lovely man and still handsome, with grey curly hair and grey-blue eyes. I bet Wenna would like him very much. We eat lunch on the deck and are never stuck for something to say. Bill tells me all about what the area was like when he built this house from scratch. He was a carpenter and owned his own construction business, and the pride shines from his eyes when he describes how he felt when he and his wife first moved in after they had Shaun, Ethan's dad.

'Sounds like you miss your working life, Bill,' I say, with a smile.

'I do, Merrin. And sometimes it all seems like yesterday, you know. I'm glad it worked out, as my pop wanted me to become a fisherman like Harry, and our middle brother John.' He lifts a finger to me. 'Talking of the old days, I have something that might interest you.' From his bag, he pulls out a small album, with mostly black and white photos inserted into yellowing card pages.

Images of Bill, his wife Grace, Harry and Lamorna as young people in this house, on the beach and on a boat, fill the first few pages, and Bill tells me that they all spent time together every summer through the years as they all lived close by. Then there's more of them all, and their sister Martha, with her family too, then all of them slightly older with children on the beach, and one on the deck exactly where I'm sitting now. Lamorna's there with her feet up on the deck rail, wearing a big, floppy straw hat, raising a tall glass of champagne to the camera, a happy smile playing over her lips. A little lump of emotion forms in my throat and I'm not sure why. Old photos can do that, I suppose, especially when you know the subject is no longer here. At the end, there's photos of the four of them when they're older, with a gaggle of grandchildren at play.

The last one of Lamorna makes the lump of emotion harder to swallow. She's probably in her seventies, sitting at the table in the dining room here, her chin resting on her fist, looking straight at the camera. That look tells me she's content, she's happy, she's proud of what she's achieved. Lamorna realised her dream of becoming a teacher through hard work and determination, which she passed down the line to my Ethan, and she's come a long way from her little Cornish village. Something inside tells me that she missed it all, and her Cornish family and friends like crazy, but she never forgot her roots. A fisherman's daughter who sent a message over the ocean one June night, many years ago.

'Here you are,' Ethan says, passing me a tissue. It's only then that I realise tears are rolling down my face. I laugh and dab them dry. 'Don't know why I'm so emotional.'

'I do,' Bill says, crossing his arms. 'Lamorna's story is the same as yours.' He shakes his head when I frown. 'I don't mean exactly the same, but it's a hell of a close one.' I realise he's right and take a deep breath to stop more tears. 'Do you believe in the magic now, honey?'

I look for humour in his eyes but find none. 'Yes, Bill,' I say simply. 'How could I not?'

Chapter Twenty-Nine

Wenna hugs Lucy and pushes something into her hand. 'It's not much, just a little something to remind you of home.'

Lucy opens the paper bag and inside is a piece of sea-glass the colour of her eyes, a shell, and a tiny bottle with a minuscule scroll inside. 'Oh, they are gorgeous,' she says and dabs her eyes. She's been crying all morning on and off, as have I.

'The bottle is a charm from a bracelet I had years ago, but I know it belongs with you.'

Wenna's got that mysterious, knowing look about her, and I ask, 'How come?'

'Well, when the maid's finished her studies and found out who she is, she can send a message one June when the moon's full, just like her mother before her, and a few others I know.' Wenna laughs and dabs at her own eyes.

Lucy laughs too. 'You know what, Wen, I might just do that.'

Mum rolls her eyes. 'Dear lord. Here we go again. Right, come on, we need to get a shift on if we're going to beat the traffic.'

On the way back from Bristol in my parents' campervan, I try to stop crying by thinking of Ethan, and our incredible journey, and my heart swells with love for him. How I wish he was here now to hold me, now I've said goodbye to my little girl and left her behind to start her own journey. A memory of our last day at the beach house comes to me, and I smile to myself. I wore the jeans with a hole in to the airport and told him about the pompous and rude young woman who'd said they should be ripped. I'd also told him about chasing her out of the café with a yard brush. He'd laughed and said they showed off my individual style and panache. Ethan always knows the right thing to say. Although it will be a few months before we're together again, I know it will soon pass, because we love each other and our souls are one. Soppy, I know, but I don't care.

Mum takes my hand and I squeeze hers. Thank God they took us up to Bristol, because there's no way I could have driven home in this state. Mind you, Mum's not much better. Her eyes are red-rimmed and puffy. I smile and she looks at me. I expect it's like looking in a mirror. Dad's holding it together pretty well, but then he always does. On the outside at least.

'Do you think Wenna will end up going to America too, to be with Bill?'

'Eh? I think you might be getting ahead of yourself a bit there, Mum.' I shake my head.

'I'm not so sure. She told me they speak on the phone a couple of times a week.'

'Really? Hmm. Well, you never know, do you?'

As we cross the border into Cornwall, my thoughts go to Lamorna. If Wenna does get together with Bill, she will certainly have had a hand in it. Gosh, listen to me. I've come a long way from the sceptic I used to be, before I decided to believe the old legend and wished for a message in a bottle one magical night under a June moon. I smile. Yes, I've come a long way, and like Lamorna, I also have a long way to go.

Wenna's on the beach perched on a rock. She's looking out at the hazy blue horizon and thinking of Bill at the other side of the ocean. How funny that they have so much in common, and how grateful she is that Merrin had given him her number. When Merrin had told her on her return from America that Bill had asked if he could call Wenna, she'd said it was a silly idea. But after thinking about it, she'd given Merrin the go-ahead to message Bill and say he had permission to call if he wanted. Thank goodness he had – because of him, these days her footsteps were lighter, her heart hopeful, and for the first time since her darling Finn had left, she could see the possibility of a happy future. Her future wouldn't be a very long one, but she'd certainly make the most of it. She might even go to visit them all in America. After all, it was long overdue, and she'd promised young Ethan that they'd meet again.

Wenna knows every extraordinary event that had happened recently was Lamorna's doing. Nobody would understand that, except for Merrin, Ethan, and perhaps Bill. In fact, if she closes her eyes slightly and looks with her heart, in the distance as the waves wash ashore, she can see the shadow of a little blonde-haired girl chasing a seagull, and that of an older girl walking by her side. The breeze picks up and ruffles Wenna's curls and she takes a deep breath of salt air, feeling suddenly alive, strong and ready for anything.

To the older girl who's slowly disappearing in the sea mist, she whispers, *Thank you, Lamorna. I'll be looking at the moon, but I'll be seeing you.*

Epilogue

MAGIC COVE

Five years later

The scene is set. The ocean powers in to shore, the moonlight rides the waves, casting chips of silver before it like ethereal confetti – a celebration of the night, the moment, and the wonder of nature. On a dark headland above the sand, a lone figure stands uncertain. A night breeze is sent to lift her silken tresses with gentle fingers and whisper encouragement. The cove holds its breath. Waiting…

Adrenaline coursing with anticipation through her veins, Lucy chuckles to herself as she splashes through a shallow rockpool and hurries across the dark sand to the water's edge. Mum will be overjoyed when she tells her what she's done, and her heart sends a silent plea to Lamorna. Ankle-deep in the frothy surf, Lucy tilts her face to the huge silver moon sailing across the star-pinned heavens, and whispers, 'I know you're here, Lamorna, and I thank you for watching over me. I can feel it with every ounce of my being on this magical night. Please guide my hand and make my wishes come true.'

As she takes Lamorna's bottle from an old red velvet bag, and holds it up to the moon, Lucy feels honoured that Ethan gifted it to her. It is their secret, as he knew Lucy wanted to carry on the old tradition to surprise her mum. A giddy swirl stirs in her belly and she clasps the bottle to her chest with an excited squeal. The fact that Lucy is studying to be a doctor and her day-to-day life is science-based has no bearing on what she's about to do. In Lucy's very open mind, there's room for magic too. In her time as a medical student, more than once she's known patients recover from a terminal diagnosis, where no medical explanation for it had been forthcoming. We don't always have all the answers, and she thinks that's so refreshing.

With every hair standing to attention on the back of her neck and goosepimples prickling her forearms, Lucy bows her head as a show of respect to the ocean, exhales slowly and says to the moon, *'I give my words to the grace of the moon, the power of the ocean, and the magic of nature. Please grant me the things I truly deserve.'*

Then, like so many others through the ages, she takes aim and launches the bottle up and into the ocean. Lucy hugs herself in delight as it lands with a little splash, and carefully follows the bottle's progress as it's pulled along the silver path of moonlight, dancing over the waves, until at last, it disappears from view.

———

Nearby, once more reunited, Lamorna and Wenna watch the scene, content in the knowledge that with the next generation, the old legend will live on. When Lucy heads for home, they link arms and follow the path of the moon across the waves, the ancient whisper of magic in their ears, and an ocean of love in their hearts.

Acknowledgments

There are so many people I would like to thank that have cheered me along on this writing journey, but I'd need another book to do it!

So, firstly I'd like to thank the whole team at One More Chapter, Harper Collins, especially my wonderful editor Charlotte (legend) Ledger. She has such a brilliant instinct for what will work and what won't, and is an expert at turning a good manuscript into a great one, with just a few tweaks. Charlotte is a champion title chooser too! Thanks a million for everything, Charlotte.

Thanks so much to my lovely writer friends who lend an ear, and share the highs and lows of this rollercoaster ride we call writing books. Linda Huber, Melanie Hudson/Brown, Lynda Stacey, Anita Waller, Celia Anderson, Christine Stovell and Kelly Florentia. Many more too — you know who you are.

A big cheer to all you lovely readers and reviewers. It makes such a different to know that my stories are being enjoyed! If you are thinking of leaving a review, just a one liner would be great. It really does help people notice the book. Thank you.

A huge thanks to the fantastic people who run our local community larder. This is where I got the idea for Merrin's.

Thanks for all hard work, Lynne, Denise, Jenny, Claire, Jean and Julie and Brian. Just some of the lovely people who help who run my local foodbank. One time I was there, Jenny told me about an old gentleman with two cats who was so grateful for the support at the larder. It's sad that people have to worry about feeding their companions as well as themselves. Thank goodness we have dedicated community members, who do all they can to make the lives of others a little easier.

Last, but certainly not least, big thanks of course go to my wonderful husband and family, without whom I would be sunk!

ONE MORE CHAPTER

The author and One More Chapter would like to thank everyone
who contributed to the publication of this story...

Analytics
Emma Harvey
Maria Osa

Audio
Fionnuala Barrett
Ciara Briggs

Contracts
Georgina Hoffman
Florence Shepherd

Design
Lucy Bennett
Fiona Greenway
Holly Macdonald
Liane Payne
Dean Russell

Digital Sales
Laura Daley
Michael Davies
Georgina Ugen

Editorial
Arsalan Isa
Charlotte Ledger
Jennie Rothwell
Tony Russell
Caroline Scott-
Bowden
Kimberley Young

Marketing & Publicity
Chloe Cummings
Emma Petfield

Operations
Melissa Okusanya
Hannah Stamp

Production
Emily Chan
Denis Manson
Francesca Tuzzeo

Rights
Lana Beckwith
Rachel McCarron
Agnes Rigou
Hany Sheikh
Mohamed
Zoe Shine
Aisling Smyth

**The HarperCollins
Distribution Team**

**The HarperCollins
Finance & Royalties
Team**

**The HarperCollins
Legal Team**

**The HarperCollins
Technology Team**

Trade Marketing
Ben Hurd

UK Sales
Yazmeen Akhtar
Laura Carpenter
Isabel Coburn
Jay Cochrane
Alice Gomer
Gemma Rayner
Erin White
Harriet Williams
Leah Woods

**And every other
essential link in the
chain from delivery
drivers to booksellers
to librarians and
beyond!**

Three years ago, Joy Pentire lost her firefighter husband and she still hasn't returned to the woman she once was. But then she meets Hope, one of the residents at the nursing home where she's a carer.

Hope has a secret gift that she wants to pass on. And Joy's life is forever changed.

Surrounded by the community in her Cornish hometown, Joy's unexpected inheritance soon leads to new opportunities, new friends, new love, and the part of herself she'd thought forever lost … her joy.

Available in paperback and ebook!

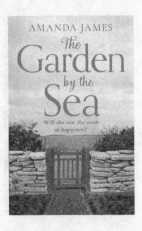

A precious heirloom passed down from mother to daughter…

Lowena Rowe's beloved mum always claimed her family seed box was special. Said to contain soil from Tintagel, the mysterious seat of the legendary King Arthur, whomever made a wish upon the box would have 'a beautiful garden, bountiful crops and love of their fellow man'. Lowena isn't inclined to believe the myth but can't part with the box, knowing how much it meant to her mum.

Starting over with a new home and a new job in the Cornish village of St Merryn, Lowena can't help feeling lost and alone… but she isn't the only one. Now, as a community of misfits finds solace and friendship in the shade of her growing garden, she realises there might have been truth to the mythical box after all, and she may just be growing the life and love she's always wanted…

Available in paperback and ebook!

When journalist Rosa Fernley's ailing gran, Jocelyn, passes on a long-held secret of her past in her dying days, Rosa embarks on a quest to Cornwall to find answers and resolution to free her grandmother from guilt and pain as she leaves this earth.

But in the wild, beautiful landscape of Tintagel, Rosa encounters something she could never imagine as the past comes to life and walks the beaches once more. Unravelling the truth of what happened to the man her grandmother once loved and left leads Rosa on an unexpected journey, one which unlocks not only her gran's secrets, but the secrets of who – and what – Rosa truly is…

Available in paperback and ebook!

YOUR NUMBER ONE STOP

ONE MORE CHAPTER

FOR PAGETURNING BOOKS

One More Chapter is an
award-winning global
division of HarperCollins.

Sign up to our newsletter to get our
latest eBook deals and stay up to date
with our weekly Book Club!
<u>Subscribe here.</u>

Meet the team at
<u>www.onemorechapter.com</u>

Follow us!
🐦 <u>@OneMoreChapter_</u>
❦ <u>@OneMoreChapter</u>
📷 <u>@onemorechapterhc</u>

Do you write unputdownable fiction?
We love to hear from new voices.
Find out how to submit your novel at
<u>www.onemorechapter.com/submissions</u>